NOWHERE MAN

Bruce G. Crawford   June, 2014

NOWHERE MAN
A Novel
Doug Williams

BREAKTHROUGH
BOOKS

Breakthrough Books
Houston, Texas

Bruce —
Thanks so much —
hope you enjoy

Breakthrough Books LLC
PO Box 131503
Houston, TX 77219

First Edition: June 2014
10 9 8 7 6 5 4 3 2 1

Library of Congress Control Number: 2013920440

Williams, Doug
Nowhere Man: a novel / Doug Williams—1st ed.

Printed in the United States of America
ISBN 978-0-9898884-1-7

Cover by Limb Design

For Mom today, Dad yesterday, and The Muse forever

NOWHERE MAN

PROLOGUE: From Whence Cometh Evil

ARLO DASH SLID his gym bag under the square metal table, recalling again what the guy—assuming it was a guy, he couldn't really tell—had said:

There are roads out of secret places that we all must travel, regardless of where they lead.

Well, he thought, it was time to take the first step.

He didn't have the faintest idea of where any of this would go, or whether or it would go anywhere at all. Would a nation that had been so thoroughly deceived for so long just naturally suspect deceit in the truth?

He'd find out soon enough.

He pulled the laptop from his backpack, turned it on, and looked around, checking the place out while the MacBook Air powered up.

A smattering of students, insomniacs, and self-styled hipsters, all half-hidden in low, after-midnight lighting, heads moving almost imperceptibly to the piped-in sounds of Dave Brubeck. His eyes regarded them with a kind of distant wariness, as if each held a clue to some unseen mystery.

After the momentary surveillance, he decided he'd made the right choice, and that in his Nike track pants and American University sweatshirt, he blended in perfectly, as invisible as mountain air.

That was good.

This particular all-night venue wasn't his usual place of business. He preferred an Internet cafe on Massachusetts Avenue, 10 or so blocks up from the White House toward Georgetown. But they knew him there, and tonight he needed a hide-in-plain-sight kind of place, a place where he was a stranger, where men in dark suits were not likely to come by and ask difficult questions that had dangerous answers.

Which explained why Arlo had opted for the little locally owned coffee bar near his 24-hour gym on Wisconsin, over by the Naval Observatory. It preserved his anonymity. In his game, anonymity was everything. It was security.

The Mac's 13-inch monitor came to life, the wi-fi connection engaging instantly.

He called up the browser program and typed a personal URL into the window.

Waited.

A man dressed in loose-fitting scrubs walked in and ordered a triple espresso, scanning the coffee bar like he was reading a teleprompter, looking at everything but seeing nothing. He smiled at the tattooed barista chick, dropped a bill in the plastic tip cube, and left, Arlo figuring he was probably heading back to the ER for a few more hours of mayhem and madness.

The web access page popped up on the laptop screen.

Arlo typed in his password, followed by some rapid-fire coding keystrokes.

He waited some more, thinking the wireless here was really slow.

Almost as if they'd choreographed it, four customers got up to go at once, leaving Arlo alone with a rumpled 40-something character reading James Joyce who looked like he'd spent the night in a bus station.

The Add Content box opened on the laptop screen.

He began to type, paused, thought for a few seconds, then

deleted what he'd written and thought some more, because the top—both the first sentence and the lead paragraph—had to be perfect. The bomb he was about to drop on the American war on terror demanded nothing less.

The front door opened.

A couple of girls, high end of their teens, pushed through. College kids apparently, talking about a professor one of them had a crush on, interrupting the giggles and shrieks and Oh My Gods with an order for two coffees heavy on syrups from bottles that were arrayed like fine scotches on shelves behind the register.

They paid without tipping. The barista chick watched their gabby exit with noticeable disdain.

Arlo stared at the glowing screen, still trying to nail that perfect opener, the one that everybody would be talking about when all hell broke loose, the one they *had* to be talking about if he was going to get the follow-up, the second-day story, the one the guy— yeah, he was pretty certain it was a guy—promised would *really* knock D.C. off the rails. The source, whoever it was, hadn't given him so much as a hint about that blockbuster, though, just telling him to be patient and if everything went according to plan, he'd learn—

From whence cometh evil.

Whatever that meant.

James Joyce rose to what resembled an upright position and pushed through the door in what resembled a purposeful shuffle.

Eyeing him with amusement on the sidewalk: the Scrub Doc, smiling easily as the disheveled guy passed, watching him go before coming back inside.

He approached the counter. The barista chick recognized him, and kind of melted under his gaze, flashing a goofy grin that transformed her into a punk-rock version of the two schoolgirls she'd silently dissed.

Arlo rubbed the back of his neck. That great top, the killer first sentence, the perfect lead—it just wasn't coming.

He squinted at the laptop screen as if it had the power to deliver a Eureka moment. No chance. Making a snap decision, he went straight to the middle of the story, the meat of the piece, and started detailing the facts, reasonably confident the lead would reveal itself once he hit his groove.

He wrote fast and furiously, so focused he didn't hear the short airy "swoosh" behind him or the soft thump that followed, just writing like a madman, lost in the moment—

"Stop typing."

Not hearing that, either, his brain hitting on eight cylinders—

"Stop typing now."

This time he heard it and looked up, the sight of the barista chick starting to register—

Sprawled over the counter, unmoving, something dark and sticky dripping from her head, pooling on the floor—

Scrub Doc walking toward him—

Arlo suddenly drowning in pure panic, heart racing like an Indy pole-sitter, not even thinking about finishing or editing or polishing what he'd written, just about posting it, getting it out there—

Trying to buy some time, pleading, "No, wait wait wait wait wait," aiming the cursor at the Publish button, the screen suddenly freezing, a message saying he'd lost the connection—

Scrub Doc closing in, holding a pistol that looked bigger than a bazooka—

Arlo standing, hands up like he was under arrest, starting to say, "Please don't, I won't tell anyone—"

Only getting to *Please*, the rest choked off from the blood in his throat, where the precise first shot entered—

Feeling himself fall backward, like in slow motion, watching Scrub Doc grab the laptop, thinking, God, I would have given it to you, you didn't have to—

The thought extinguished by a second shot that went through his forehead and a third through his heart, and as the darkness settled over him, Arlo Dash had no way of knowing that he had just witnessed *from whence cometh evil*, that he'd been its victim, and that his murder was supposed to be the end of everything, a final act that would keep the deceits of the past and the deaths yet to come hidden away in their secret place.

But it wasn't the end of anything.

It was only the beginning.

PART ONE: **THE NEW FACE OF PATRIOTISM**

ONE

IT HAD BEEN over a dozen years. Tom Fargo wanted to know if he really was free.

He scanned the sea of protesters in Washington's Freedom Plaza—not a sea, really, more of a big pond, a hundred or so people—and waited for the old feelings to return, to gnaw at him like the memory of something that didn't completely happen, a reminder of the rage and blind passion and zeal that would later be replaced by the insecurity and unease and anxiety.

But they didn't return, the old feelings. He felt safe, and knew deep down into his bones that it was no illusion, that he'd finally parted company with his past and was liberated from its fury and torments.

He'd won, his victory coming over the toughest imaginable adversary: himself.

Still watching the mini-mass of humanity without expression, Tom couldn't help but recall the days when his image had graced the signs and posters of the angry, the powerless, the disgusted. The days when he'd been the cover boy, literally, for everything they hated, a graphic piñata they'd beaten, whose candy they'd spit out. The days when terrorism was as real as the night.

But that was then. Terrorism was stale. Global corporate greed was now the scourge du jour.

He recalled the day, the *moment*, when terrorism wasn't so stale, the day he'd made his choice. He wanted peace, to feel secure again, and he often looked back and marveled at how that one choice seemed to have set into motion some vast plan, with the universe conspiring to make it pay off.

It did pay off, too. Took some time, but peace finally broke out in his head, and a sense of security followed, and eventually the feeling just stayed with him naturally—*organically*, his former friends would say—without the drugs.

Free at last, free at last.

Consequences? Sure. But like his Old Man always said, You pays your money, you takes your chances.

The Old Man. Tom smiled because he could, now that the nightmares had stopped.

On a whim, he decided to wander through the crowd, aware that his navy blue power suit, white shirt, red-striped tie, and twice-monthly haircut wouldn't have anyone confusing him with a member of the tribe.

Walking among them, he saw:

A man and his wife, 40s, with their teenaged daughter, the dad chanting, "Lost my job, found my calling."

Tom had chanted, too, once: "No war in the Gulf! No war in the Gulf!"

A half-dozen women, dressed in green T-shirts that read "Social Justice Now!," each with one fist pumping angrily in the air, the other fist gripping a huge bed sheet that carried a decently rendered drawing of the Constitution, except it began, "We the Corporations," and instead of signatures there were logos of the world's largest companies.

He'd carried a banner, too: "There's always U.S. money in weapons when there's any slaughter in the world."

A line of anti-poverty activists out on Pennsylvania Avenue, singing to the tune of "Happy Days Are Here Again": "The sun shines bright on the Wall Street crooks, more loopholes are coming soon."

He'd sung, too, to the tune of Pink Floyd's "Money": "Oil, it's a crime. We don't wanna be die-die-dyin' for it."

A gray-haired man with a bullhorn, screaming, "Power belongs to the people!"

He'd screamed through a bullhorn, too: "Power belongs to the people!"

At one end of the plaza, on a raised stage, a balding, paunchy folk-rocker with an acoustic guitar sat on a stool, his voice and message a galaxy away from Dylan or Seeger. Across the way a soccer mom railed against the military-industrial-corporate complex. To the right of the stage, a slender Denzel Washington look-alike, Black Panthers beret and shades, pounded on an upside-down iron skillet and chanted "Silence! Silence! Silence is for suckers," exhorting the crowd to join in.

Tom recognized him. Bobby Washington. Called himself Amadi, which Bobby had explained was African for "destined to die at birth."

A girl, maybe 15, dressed like an extra in *Hair*, paraded around with a charred American flag upside down on a pole, peace-sign patches sewn onto strategically frayed $200 jeans, trying not to spill her latte, screaming something about the International Monetary Fund.

Tom couldn't resist. He stepped into her path. "Excuse me, but what's the problem with the IMF?"

Her eyes went glassy, as if he'd just asked her the secret of life. They quickly sparked back up, accompanied by "Tax the rich, dude, tax the rich!" She flashed him a twisted smile, like they were both privy to some inside joke, before waltzing off and half-plaintively asking if anyone knew where she could score some pot.

Tom watched her, thinking back to that day a lifetime ago, right after U.S. forces had gone into Kuwait, when he didn't carry a flag or a cup of coffee, just a bucket of blood and a bucket of oil—which he poured on the front steps of a federal building in Los Angeles—and a backpack full of bricks, which he tossed through a bank window.

The past. He'd escaped it the only way you could: by doing something better.

Bobby Washington had changed tunes, was now going with "Class War, Not Oil War," head swaying, living in the moment, oblivious to the guy coming toward him—

A big guy, big and angry, with shoulders that needed a building permit, hate in his eyes—

And something in his hand.

Tom didn't hesitate.

He walked quickly toward Bobby, at an angle that would cut the beefy guy off, not running or trotting but still moving fast and trying not to ram into any of the protesters, his eyes cutting from the skinny black man, who was lost in Demonstration World, to the big guy, who was laser-focused on Bobby, red-faced and sweaty, thrusting out his hand, pointing—

Tom reached the guy maybe five feet before the guy reached Bobby. "Whoa, let's be cool."

The response was as mean as it was automatic: "Love it or leave it, faggot."

Despite himself, Tom smiled. "Heard that before."

The guy studied him, the suit and tie and short hair, weekend workout build, six-foot frame. Tom could see a hundred familiar questions running through his head, because he'd seen that same look before, a lot. Sure enough, one of them followed.

"You're somebody, aren't you?"

From behind them:

"Why that be Tom Tom the Traitor Mon." Bobby Washington was now standing and holding the skillet in a way that didn't suggest food preparation.

Tom turned. "Been a long time, Amadi."

"Thought you was outta the game."

"Just this one."

The big guy squinted suspiciously at Tom, then Bobby, then Tom again. "You don't look like one of them."

Bobby Washington laughed. "He ain't. Used to be, though. Was on the side of angels once. Now the boy nothin' but Satan's sideman."

"Satan's sideman," Tom said easily. "Haven't heard that before. I kind of like it." Bobby shrugged.

The big guy looked at the skillet dangling from Bobby's veiny, rope-thin arm. "Whatcha got there?"

Bobby, in turn, looked at the man's clenched fist. "Whatcha got there?"

In that instant, the big guy seemed to sag. Slowly he opened his hand to reveal a photo, high school yearbook type, of a blond, good-looking boy. The kid had his father's eyes, but none of the rage. An advantage of youth. "My son."

Tom and Bobby said nothing.

"He died over there, '91, the war in Kuwait. Friendly fire." A deep breath. "Nineteen. He was 19. He died serving this country, and you"—glaring at Bobby—"you stain his memory with your goddamned protests and anti-American songs and all."

"Nobody's staining his memory," Tom said softly. "Your boy's still a hero."

The man's eyes moved from the photo to Tom's face, his gaze deep and probing. "Wait a second," he half-growled after a moment. "Wait a second, wait a second, wait a second. I do know you."

As if all this were scripted, two women in their mid-50s approached, wearing Boycott Citibank T-shirts. They traded whispers, then one of them gestured toward Tom. There was a flash of recognition in the other's eyes. "You sonofabitch!" she shrieked. "You son of a bitch!"

Her realization spread to the big guy. "You slick bastard."

The woman: "You turned your back on the movement."

The man: "My boy dies while you're rioting in the streets."

The woman: "Threw away everything you stood for, and now you don't stand for anything good."

The man: "Then you wrap yourself in the flag and want us to believe you're one of us."

The woman: "I carried a sign with that cover of *Time* magazine on it, but mine didn't say 'The New Face of Patriotism,' it said 'The Death of Patriotism.'"

The man: "If you're the new face of patriotism, we might just as well live in Iraq!"

Bobby Washington: "What is it like, brother, to go through life with nobody on your side?"

Before Tom could answer, his cell phone vibrated. He listened briefly, nodded his head before killing the connection, and smiled at Bobby, the two women, the big guy. "Would love to continue this discussion, but I gotta go." He winked at Bobby. "Satan calls."

TWO

PENN MALLORY, THE senior U.S. senator from Florida, leaned his 6-4 frame back into the leather chair and planted a pair of size 13 handmade ostrich cowboy boots onto a mahogany desk that at its most charitable could be called chaotic. "Seriously? They called me that? Satan?"

He sounded almost wounded. Tom knew better. "They could've said you were a liberal."

"Yeah, but still." Mallory shook his head. "Jesus, what'd I ever do to them?"

"You made us safe again."

Mallory's expression slipped into a wry smile. "Call a man a devil, you're gonna see his horns."

Tom nodded. "Just ask bin Laden."

"Damned straight." Mallory appeared to drift off into thought for a moment before sliding the morning's *Washington Post* toward Tom, its Page 1 art a four-column picture of the previous day's protest at Freedom Plaza. Tom picked it up, and noticed that Bobby Washington was at the far left with one of his arms cropped off. "So is this gonna cost Satan any votes in 18 months?"

Tom thought it was interesting how Mallory just skipped right over the details—the presidential primary process, the fight for the nomination, the convention—and went straight to Election Day. "I doubt it. They're not organized."

"Neither's the Tea Party. But I'd be crazier than a lizard with sunstroke to ignore them."

"I was down there today. I think it's more fashion than passion."

Mallory cocked an eyebrow. "What, all these years you've been with me, and you're suddenly pining for your bomb-throwing anarchist days?"

Tom laughed easily. "I haven't been out there on the streets since, well, you know . . . "

"I do."

"And I got to tell you, boss, looking at them, sipping $5 coffee and tapping on laptops, I knew in a second my wild-in-the-streets life was in the rear-view mirror."

"It better be. Can't be having a commie as my administrative assistant. Christ, what would Limbaugh say?"

"Nothing he hasn't already said."

"Screw him, the fat gasbag." He got up and walked around the desk, past the fireplace and American flag, to a side table under a wall-sized map of the Sunshine State, still moving with the unexpected grace that had made him an All Southeastern Conference defensive end at the University of Florida. He poured himself a glass of water. "I told that son of a bitch your paw prints were on damn near every piece of major homeland security legislation since 9/11." He took a noisy gulp. "Know what he did? He looked me straight in the eye, poked me in the chest with one of those sausage fingers of his, and said, 'Penn, the worst thing that can happen to a man of conscience is to let himself be surrounded by traitorous souls.'"

"What'd you say?"

"What do you think I said? He's Rush Limbaugh, for Chrissakes. I promised him I'd watch you like the hawk I am!" They both laughed. Tom understood that the public Mallory was often in conflict with the private Mallory. It was a necessity, an occupational hazard in a trade where getting as many votes from as many people as possible was the end game. If his boss had to throw some red-meat rhetoric to the ravenous right, Tom could live with the noise, because he knew what was said behind these closed doors was, at its core, what his boss really believed. That's what mattered.

Mallory returned to his desk with the glass of water, ran his hand over a head that had gone bald in the mid-'90s, halfway through his second term. "But seriously, you think this protest thing'll hurt me?"

"I don't, no. They don't want to be a political party, and even if they did, you probably wouldn't get their votes anyway."

"So the hell with them, right?"

"Stay the course, just keep raising money, spread it around, buy whatever—"

Mallory interrupted him with an extended hand, palm out. "Hold it. You know the rules. No talk of fundraising in the Senate office. That's what Warrenton and New York Avenue are for." Warrenton being the Virginia location of Mallory's political action committee; New York Avenue being home to the offices of Patriot's Blood, the tax-exempt "social welfare" organization that, while technically independent, conducted public communication and built grassroots support on behalf of issues designed to support Mallory, his allies, and his campaigns. Its name was taken from a quote by the Scottish poet Thomas Campbell: "The patriot's blood is the seed of freedom's tree."

"Sorry," Tom said.

"I know you think I'm over-sensitive on this, but there's a place for doing what we have to do, and that's here, and there's a place for doing what we have to do to win, and that's there. I don't want one getting in the way of the other. Blur those lines, a man gets corrupted."

"Understood."

Mallory sat forward, elbows on the desk, and stabbed his left index finger into the air toward Tom. "But let me be clear: We will do what we have to do to win. There is nothing, not one damned thing, that's gonna get in the way of me moving into the White House. Nothing."

Tom nodded and started to reply. But before he could get a word out, they heard the screaming.

THREE

THE MAN WAS barely taller than a garden gnome, dark hair lacquered to a full midnight-blue shine, a charcoal suit that was a little too fitted, silk tie, chunky gold bracelet on one wrist. The woman was an Amazonian blonde, 6-feet-plus in heels, at 28 about half his age, the body of a world-class athlete, the voice of Minnie Mouse on helium.

"I told you, there are no other women!" he shouted just north of her navel.

"Oh, I am so sure."

"Baby, what do you want from me?"

"I want you to quit seeing all those whores!"

The man cut his eyes up and down the wide corridors of the Hart Senate Office Building, then refastened them on her, hard. "Nice talk." Deftly avoiding the question.

"And you call yourself a leader!"

"I am a leader, you stupid—"

"A leader in what? Sex? Women? I bet the reason you have so many is you can't satisfy any of them!"

"You never complained."

"Not to your lying, cheating face!" She reached for the knob on a huge unmarked door.

He slammed it shut with such unexpected fury that the woman jumped. "Hey, this face belongs to a man who—"

"Man! Ha! What do you know about being a man?"

"This conversation is over." He started to walk away.

"Oh, sure, run away, back to some lobbyist slut, some stripper—"

"You're out of your mind."

"Am I? What about the PR chick, the no-talent English actress, that skank ballerina in Saudi Arabia—"

"You don't know what you're talking—"

"I know a lot more than *Em-a-lee* does, you can be sure about that."

He spun and charged her, arm raised in a less-than-subtle warning, voice a whispered hiss. "You will not speak my wife's name, do you hear me? You will respect that woman."

"Or what?"

"Or else."

"Oh! Is that a threat? Are you threatening to kill me?"

"You're not worth the risk or the trouble." For some reason, that seemed to throw her, the beautiful face bunching up like a fist. His stare went dead as a statue's. "And I don't make public threats. I make private phone calls. That's all it takes for people like me to deal with people like you."

The lantern behind her bright green eyes suddenly went out. She took a series of short, quick breaths. A swallowed sob escaped her lips. "You would do that to me? Make that call?"

His features softened, but not enough to erase the menace. "I'd never do anything to hurt you, darlin'. You know that."

"Do I?" Part real, part for effect.

"Honey, my job is to protect Americans. National security. That's what I do."

"Okay." Nodding like a child.

"So unless you're some burqa-wearing terrorist—and as far as I can tell, you're not, because that is perhaps the finest ass I've ever seen on display—well, then, you are safe as a kitten in church."

Another nod, this one a little faster.

An oil-slick smile crept over his face. "Fine. So what say we forget this little tempest about other women who don't exist, and focus on the one who does, all right?"

"Me?" The hopeful voice nearly inaudible.

"Yes, sugar. We'll just go into my office, have us some adult liquid refreshment, spend a bit of time on those matters that, uh, unite us rather than dwelling on those that divide us."

He didn't wait for an answer, just opened the door to the unmarked office and began to usher her through.

She stopped two steps in. "Harry, when you're Secretary of Defense, will I get to go places with you?"

"Baby, when I'm Secretary of Defense, you and me are gonna go around the world and everything that implies." He winked and gently prodded her into the office.

"Senator Platte?"

The man turned toward the voice and frowned, contempt etching his expression. "Jesus. What is it, you commie prick?"

Tom Fargo gave him a grin that tiptoed right up to a smirk without crossing the line. "Change of plans."

FOUR

PENN MALLORY DRILLED Harry Platte with a look that was as hot and heartless as a branding iron. "Do you have any idea what's at stake here?"

"C'mon, Penn, you said yourself my nomination was gonna sail through."

Mallory just shook his head. "It will if you can just keep your pecker in your pants for the next month or so."

"I got needs, Penn." Almost a plea.

"So do I, Harry, except mine involve a large white mansion on Pennsylvania Avenue and not the twin peaks of a strip club waitress."

Sitting in a matching oxblood leather chair next to Platte, both of them opposite Mallory, Tom tried to force down a smile. When the Missouri senator and soon-to-be-nominated Secretary of Defense turned and scowled at him, he wasn't sure if he'd succeeded.

"You'd best respect me, you sanctimonious bastard."

It was part of Platte's routine, The Full Bully, known as widely in Congress as was his predilection for young blondes twice his height. "I meant no disrespect, Senator," Tom replied evenly.

"Radical fairy."

Mallory leaned forward and rested his hands palm down on the desk. He spoke slowly, deliberately. "That 'radical fairy' is a patriot who sacrificed everything for his country. You will treat him with the dignity he has earned, or I swear I will beat you like a rented mule."

"I'm entitled to my opinion."

"Not when it comes to my future, Harry, and the role that Tom Fargo's going to play in it. Are we clear?"

"I just meant—"

"Are. We. Clear."

The two senators glared at each other. Seconds passed, allowing the room temperature to drop a little.

Platte finally nodded. "Leopards don't change their spots, Penn. That's all I'm saying."

Mallory accepted his surrender without acknowledging it. "People change, Harry."

"This is Washington. Nothing changes."

"Hell, I did. Used to have hair." Mallory smiled and settled back in his chair. A football suddenly materialized in his hands. "President thinks you need to get out of town for a little while before the hearing gins up."

"Now?" Mallory nodded. "Why? Can't we at least hold off until the Memorial Day recess?"

"Nope." He started tossing the ball easily in the air. "We need some time to get our ducks in a row. The president wants that to happen more sooner than later, and thinks it's better if you're off being *diplomatic* rather than staying here catching the kind of grief you know is coming."

Platte waved off the concern. "Women and booze, so what? Name one person in this esteemed body who doesn't dance with those particular demons."

"Penn Mallory," Tom said without hesitation.

Platte's expression went tight with rage, but he said nothing, just staying eye-to-eye with his colleague. "Where?" he asked.

"Jordan, Kuwait, Saudi Arabia, and Israel."

Platte brightened. "Saudi Arabia?"

Mallory caught the ball one last time and slapped it on his desk. "Yep. You're gonna go there and you're gonna talk tough, Harry. You're gonna let 'em know, without actually saying it, that when you're SecDef, the war on terrorism will get a whole lot hotter. And you're gonna get prime time on CNN sayin' it, and the American people are gonna go, 'Right on,' and the Tea Party crowd is gonna jubilate, and *The New York Times* is gonna crank out editorials sayin' you're a Neanderthal, and you're gonna get confirmed with votes to spare." He smiled the sly, confident smile that had served him well in the courtroom as a federal prosecutor and better as a mainstay of the Sunday morning talk shows. "And most of all, you're gonna make me look like a genuine statesman for pushing you on the White House."

Platte considered that. "Well, Saudi Arabia, I guess that's something."

"Harry, listen to me and listen good: You're not going over there to get laid. Understand? You're going over there to send a message that anyone who doubts America's greatness will have made a serious, serious error in judgment."

It wasn't posturing, and Tom knew it. Mallory was someone who believed in his country, its security, and the obligations that came with global leadership. It was this undiluted passion that had originally led Tom to his Senate office, years earlier, before the sun had managed to pierce the dust and debris at Ground Zero, before the smoke had cleared at the Pentagon.

Reminded of what was within his grasp, Platte just nodded. "Who's going with me?"

"Just David and some people from the committee." Meaning David Diamond, staff director of the Armed Services Committee. "He's arranging your schedule."

"And I'll have some down time, right? In Saudi Arabia?"

Mallory looked at him like an annoyed father. "What part of *not getting laid* don't you understand?"

Platte's mouth curled into a cracked smile, and he glanced over at Tom. "Can't blame a fella for trying, huh?" His tone was playful, a vocal guy-to-guy jab in the ribs. Despite himself, and knowing he'd already pushed Platte harder than he should have, Tom chuckled.

Mallory's desk phone buzzed. He picked up and listened for a few seconds, nodded, and said only "Sure, I'll be right over," before dropping the receiver back in the cradle. He stood.

"Something up?" Platte asked.

"Strategy session on Vance's confirmation."

"Problems?"

"You wouldn't think so. You got a guy who runs a global security corporation who's spent his career protecting the lives of international businessmen and foreign leaders. There's not a person better suited to run CIA than Vance Harriman, and nobody would disagree."

Platte shot a look at Tom. "Unless you're a goddamned liberal."

"No argument here, Senator," Tom replied.

Mallory walked Platte to the door. "Just stick to the game plan, Harry. When you're at Defense and Vance is at Langley, we'll shock and awe those towel-headed bastards right back into the Stone Age."

"Hell, that'd be a step up for most of them." They laughed and shook hands. Platte left without acknowledging Tom.

"Hard to believe that guy knows more about national defense than anybody in the Senate," Mallory said after a moment. "Which may say more about the Senate than it does about him." He looked at Tom and chuckled, though without much humor.

"What's up with Harriman?"

Mallory sat back down at his desk. "The usual. Vance is a very strange dude, bordering on scary. You look at him and can't help but wonder what's going on in that head. And then you think maybe it's best if you don't know."

"But you still believe he'll be confirmed, right?"

Mallory let loose a lung full of air. "Let's just say I hope there isn't anything out there we don't know about."

Tom sensed real concern in Mallory's voice. "He's been vetted from top to bottom—the Senate, the White House, the media, the Internet—and we're already well into the confirmation process." Mallory nodded, but the gesture felt false, as if the senator knew the seconds were ticking down on some unseen time bomb. "What secrets could he possibly have?"

"The kind that people don't ask about, Tom. The kind that live in dungeons."

FIVE

VANCE HARRIMAN'S OFFICE at Territo International was a 50- by 50-foot glass-walled box with its own elevator, fastened to one upper corner of the building and overlooking an expanse that was the size of an airplane hangar and housed some of the world's most feared men and women.

For all the menace and dread that were his ultimate products (innocently packaged under the umbrella of "corporate security"), the wide-open floor beneath him hardly inspired trepidation. It was just a maze of bare cubicles where steely-eyed employees who could have been mistaken for corporate wage slaves worked to the low hum of unseen computers that captured data on suspected murderers worldwide.

"You're sure you want to do this?" The network security kid—geek stereotype personified, tall and exclamation-point thin, with a too-large white shirt, too-narrow gray tie, and too many pens in the pocket—was at the Territo CEO's desk, poised over his laptop as if waiting to throw some high-tech executioner's switch.

Harriman sat on a modernistic white leather sofa beneath an oil painting of Alexander the Great's victory over the Persians at the Battle of Issus, a bonus from a former Territo client, and crossed his legs. The cuffs on his Ferragamo suit inched up the calf, revealing Marcoliani cashmere and silk socks that cost $85 a pair. He raised his eyes from the open file folder in his lap, peering at the kid through narrow metallic black glasses that, while stylish, couldn't deflect attention from a 60-year-old face that had the texture of a pineapple. "Are we sure of anything?"

The voice was cold, bordering on merciless. Friends and enemies alike had said that in a dark room with no exit, Vance Harriman's voice was the most effective weapon America possessed in the war on terror.

The Geek gulped and nervously scratched the bridge of a nose that was bigger than a skinny guy deserved. "Because, you know, this is it. I'm gonna delete the partitions on the existing drive, and then create another partition on top of the deleted one, then add some new nonsense data on that, and—"

"I didn't summon you to give me an explanation of how to wipe the hard drive clean. I summoned you here to do it." A smile, tight as a coil. "So simply transfer the data to the discs—"

Which the Geek thought was odd, storing everything on CDs instead of a thumb drive, very end of the 20th century—

"And perform the service for which Mr. Loki employs you." Talking about Miles Loki, Harriman's famously reclusive No. 2 at Territo.

"Uh, yessir." He nodded fast, his head retreating like a turtle's into thin, bony shoulders.

Harriman went back to the file folder, which consisted of a single photo of a man and a woman.

He stared at the man, gaze severe and like an angry searchlight, then shifted to the woman. She was young and slender, with a beautiful smile, long lustrous hair, bright eyes. Hardly the type.

But then again, he knew that in this business, his business, the business of chaos and disorder, there really wasn't a type, not for these people anyway. They could be anybody, anywhere, and they usually were.

At the laptop, the Geek clattered away, his advanced-tech mumbling barely registering with Harriman, who was still considering the photo, trying to understand its subject.

Are you sane? he silently asked the girl's image. Do you live in a world of logic, rationality? Why is it that we Americans can be just as concerned socially, politically, economically, religiously, whatever, but we never resort to your extreme tactics, sending bomb-strapped maniacs into buses, or public markets, or schools, for the sole purpose of mass fear and human destruction?

Why is that?

Because we're free, he reminded the photo, and free people live by certain codes. It's what makes us human, and it's why you'll never be anything but a monster. Even with your long hair and beautiful smile and bright eyes that burn with whatever it is that drives people over the cliff of simple allegiance into the depths of fanaticism.

He closed the folder, massaged his forehead, and considered all that had happened and all that lay ahead, confirming in his own mind that what they were doing was right, that sitting back and waiting for this enemy to strike was not a strategy for security. It was a recipe for suicide.

"You wanna save emails and contact lists, right?"

Vance Harriman wasn't entirely certain of every piece of data that resided on the laptop. He could not, however, take the risk that somewhere inside the little box there existed something that could expose lies and schemes that, in the national interest, were best left buried in an unmarked graveyard of unspoken secrets. "No browsing history. No electronic road maps or paper trails. Nothing."

"Jeez, wouldn't it be simpler to just throw this one out and get a new one?" An honest question, asked without judgment.

Harriman's eyes got him in their crosshairs. "Electronic waste accounts for 70 percent of the toxins in landfills, but makes up only 2 percent of the volume." The Geek grinned, thinking Harriman was being sarcastic or ironic, maybe even funny.

He thought wrong on all accounts.

The Territo CEO broke the iron-hearted gaze after a moment. "And shatter the mirror as well."

"The mirror?"

Harriman sighed slightly in annoyance. In that moment, the Geek understood what a bad guy probably felt when he didn't provide the information requested by the feared Vance Harriman. "I am well aware of the backup system Mr. Loki has in place."

"Oh. Yessir." He swallowed hard and went back to work.

Harriman glanced again at the photo and shook his head, thanking God that democracy was stronger than terrorism. Then he rose and said, "Leave the CDs on the desk when you're through," and went into his personal bathroom to wash his hands.

The Geek nodded and watched him go, finished moving the data to the disks, and got out of there with the speed, if not the agility, of a greyhound.

When Harriman returned, he slid into the Eames executive chair behind his desk, which was glass and wood, sleek and soulless, large enough for a dinner party. Six CD-ROMs were stacked on top of the day's *Washington Post*. The data from his laptop.

One by one, he put them through the optical media destroyer slot on the level 6 high-security shredder. It was an overabundance of caution, but he wanted to witness the destruction of the data firsthand, not trusting what he couldn't see. Then he slipped the photo of the man and the woman through the infeed for paper.

He looked at the newspaper, open to the Metro section, and a headline:

"No clues in coffee bar shooting that leaves D.C. blogger dead."

He put that through the shredder, too. As he watched it reduced to particles that were 0.8 by 4 millimeters in size, a quote from Benjamin Franklin nudged his brain, "Three can keep a secret if two of them are dead," and he wondered how many more would have to die in order to keep theirs.

SIX

SARAH MORRIN BLEW into the bar in typical tsunami fashion, speed-walking past the happy hour crowd, on a mission, long red hair parted in the middle like a '60s bra burner, halfway down her back and flying around like an unraveling spool of copper.

"Sorry, sorry, sorry," she said, slipping onto the stool next to Tom, unsmiling. "One of the girls at the office, her brother got killed, a robbery or something." She caught her breath. "You don't want to know."

"Nice to see you." Forcing a grin, hoping to keep this as civil as possible.

"How's life in Limbaugh Land?"

So much for civility.

Tom said nothing, catching the bartender's attention and ordering a scotch on the rocks. Sarah asked for a club soda, explaining, "Have to get back, we got that thing going on, lotta work still to do."

He nodded, "that thing" being a multi-city march against U.S. global nation-building. "You expecting many people?"

She shrugged. "Half a million."

Tom laughed and shook his head. "You get a tenth of that, I'll buy you a small island in the Caribbean."

"I may need it. Mallory wins the presidency, and people like me will have to go into exile." She smiled falsely and looked away, surveying the room. When her eyes returned to his, they had softened. "There's a booth in the back, against the wall, if you'd like to move."

"I'm good." Sarah cocked her head slightly. "Yep. No more sitting with my back to the wall. No more nightmares. No more sweats on airplanes. Hell, I only use one of the locks on the door now."

"So you finally did go to therapy?" Her voice was tinged with an odd mix of hope and loss.

"No, Sarah," he replied, slowly and patiently. "I did not finally go to therapy."

The hope and loss instantly surrendered to disapproval. "Oh, no, that's right. You thought therapy was, how did you put it, for *emotional runaways*. So you went to Penn Mallory instead. Tell me, how is Daddy?"

"He's still dead."

The words were at once leaden and brittle.

Sarah caught it and threw her galloping superiority into reverse. "I didn't mean—"

"I know exactly what you meant."

The bartender brought their drinks. Tom went for his immediately, taking too much, coughing from the whiskey heat and the burning heart.

Sarah squeezed a piece of lime into her club soda. "Well, I'm glad you're okay, or doing better, whatever."

Tom raised his glass to her. "To my recovery." He glanced down at the end of the bar, seeing the editor of one of Washington's liberal monthlies, someone who'd not only jammed a journalistic knife into him years earlier, but who also seemed to revel in twisting it at every opportunity. He wasn't surprised to see her, this being a neighborhood hangout, the neighborhood being upper Connecticut Avenue, and the neighbors being a lot of media people.

He gave the woman a smile that oozed false warmth, and flashed a peace sign. She responded with a middle finger.

When Tom turned back to Sarah, she was holding a thick envelope. "It's probably time we did this," she said, dropping the envelope on the bar and sliding it toward him. "I met someone."

He stared at the thing for a second, then at her. "Anybody I know?"

Sarah bit her lower lip. "He, uh, used to work in the government. Defense Department. Information technology."

"I see." He forced a laugh. "Unable to bring me to my political senses, you simply recruit a replacement. Convert and conquer."

She stared at him, hard, for a full minute. "No, Tom. I found a guy who, when he opened his eyes, saw the world the way it could be, not the way it is."

"You getting married?"

She hesitated. "Just keeping my options open." He nodded and lowered his head. She sipped the club soda. "This can't come as any big surprise. It's been a long time. I mean, you've moved on, right?" He crossed his arms, said nothing. "You had to know this was bound to happen eventually."

Tom was struck by her voice, which was high and harsh and grating, like a chainsaw. He wondered if it had been that way when they were together, and he'd just mistaken it for the soundtrack of nobility. "I guess stranger things have happened."

"Like you going over to the other side."

He searched her expression for even a speck of humor, an indication that her reply was something other than a statement of betrayal—personal, emotional, political, ideological betrayal. He came up empty. Sarah believed what Sarah believed, and there was no debating it. Which was fine if the beliefs were shared, less so if they were questioned or, God forbid, renounced.

He drained the scotch, ordered another, gazed at his reflection in the mirror behind the bar. "You never understood. You never will."

"Oh, really? Which part didn't I understand? The part about you abandoning your commitment—"

"I never lost my commitment; it just changed—"

"Or the part about abandoning me?"

"I didn't abandon—"

"Becoming the poster child for the right wing's assault on our personal freedoms, you don't think that's—"

"We're at war—"

"You're at war, Tom. With your past, your fears—"

"Not anymore, Sarah, not anymore—"

"Right, I forgot, Dr. Mallory and his traveling medicine show, dispensing cure-alls to a terrified nation and the scared little boys who live there—"

"Enough!" Tom's fist hit the bar like an anvil, catching the attention and disapproval of customers on either side of them.

Sarah, not known for flinching in the face of anything, recoiled. "All I'm saying—"

"You have no idea what you're saying," he shot back. "But of course, that's never stopped you from saying it at great length." The second scotch arrived. He killed half of it. "You think you're always on the inside track of righteousness, and that if anybody dares stray from that path—goes over to the *other side*, as it were—they're somehow evil, traitorous. Can you not for one second recognize the possibility that not everything is black and white? That some gray areas exist?"

"You were a star in the movement, Tom, and then one day—"

"It wasn't just *one day*—"

"You walked away, out of the light and into the darkness, and if that's not black and white, I don't know what the hell is!" She exhaled deeply, and a tiny cry escaped. It sounded as if she'd been stabbed in the heart with a pin.

Tom's face was rigid with barely controlled rage, his eyes clouded with tragedy. "I did what I felt I had to do. You want to define that as treason, fine."

"And what would you call it?"

He just shook his head, sadly, maybe even sympathetically, and took the divorce papers out of the envelope.

"It's a clean break," Sarah said. "I'm not asking for anything."

He looked up at her. "Except out." He held her eyes for a moment before flipping through the pages, signing in the places designed by yellow stick-on arrows. He finished, refolded the document, stuck it back in the envelope. "The problem with you, Sarah, is that you think you're more of an American than I am."

"And the problem with you, Tom, is that you keep thinking that's what this is about."

"That's exactly what it's about. You believe that patriotism is just a convenient spasm of emotion. It's not, at least in my case. It's a responsibility I take damned seriously."

Sarah's face had the look of a funeral dirge. "You really did drink the Kool-Aid, didn't you?"

He took a couple of deep breaths. "We all drink the Kool-Aid. The only thing that's different is the flavor." He pushed the envelope in her direction. "Have a good life."

He stood and walked toward the door, neither glancing back at his soon-to-be ex-wife nor acknowledging the merciless stare from the liberal editor, who, when Tom was on the street and in a cab, looked at Sarah, eyes swollen with contempt, and mouthed, "What happened to him?"

He became someone else's idea of an American, Sarah thought, and never recovered.

SEVEN

THIS IS WHAT happened:

It's 9:25, and Tom has already been up for five hours, cracking out plans for a demonstration that will focus the world's attention on Vieques, a small Puerto Rican island that the U.S. Navy feels compelled to bomb into oblivion.

He's driven by rage—rage against the military, the application of power by the strong against the free will of the less strong, those whose only sin is that they lack money or access or connections or cold hearts or criminality, all the things that some people embrace to stay on top.

His hope, though, is to show that passion and commitment, in sufficient strength, are enough to fight the power.

So far, so good.

The past week has been totally productive, with mini-organizations set up on eight campuses in the Northeast—D.C., Boston, New York City—and groundwork put in place at another six. He's feeling optimistic. Still, there's work to do. A lot of it.

Sarah's been at the printer since about 8:30, getting fliers, petitions, signs, that kind of thing. Alex Boyce, a guy they'd met at the WTO protests in Seattle a couple of years back, has been a huge help, basically turning over his self-styled "guerilla ad agency" to create the work. It's very cool.

But that's Sarah's thing, the creative part. Tom's a word guy, a communicator, and this morning he's trying to find the message to persuade the event's biggest potential draw to join the party: Ruben Berrios, head of the Puerto Rican Independence Party, a man who wouldn't let cancer cripple his fight for the cause.

Back in 1971, Berrios squatted in Flamenco Beach, on Culebra, to protest the Navy's use of the island for military exercises. He was arrested and jailed for three months. But it worked. The protest. The Navy quit waging war on and against the island.

Then in 1999, he staged a 362-day protest on Vieques, which the Navy was using as a bombing range, and stuck it out through prostate cancer. Tom thinks that's the ultimate: being willing to die for your beliefs.

They finally arrested him May 4, 2000, a symbolic thing. Less than a week later, though, he was back camping out on the range, arrested again, and tried and convicted, getting six hours of detention time. Didn't put up any defense because he didn't acknowledge American jurisprudence.

Tom admires that, too.

The bombing runs still didn't stop, so there he was on the island again, five days this time before an arrest that was anything but symbolic, cuffed hands behind his back, spread out on a hell-hot gravel road for God knows how long. Still refused to mount a defense. The U.S. District Court gave him four months.

But he's out now, got out August 30, almost two weeks back, and Tom is angling to get him here for the demonstration.

That's what he's working on this morning, sitting at the computer: letters of support and encouragement.

Al Sharpton's on board already—and he should be; he got slapped with a 90-day sentence and a $500 fine for protesting the whole Vieques debacle—and Sharpton's got some state legislators and two members of the New York City Council lined up. He's also talking to Robert Kennedy Jr., a move Tom thinks is a slam dunk because Little RFK himself has already been arrested in one of the protests.

Tom's so caught up in drafting the letters, he almost misses the email from Sarah.

It's kind of cryptic, very unlike Sarah, who couldn't keep how she felt at bay if her life depended on it.

"Go to MSNBC," is all it says.

Tom does, punching in the web address on his computer keyboard.

At first, it doesn't register. From a distance, the towers look like a couple of smokestacks on a boat. Until the fire causes the structural steel elements to weaken too much, bringing one of them crashing down.

Tom can't believe it, can't believe what he's seeing.

Then a reporter comes, a stressed-out voice from Washington, saying something about a flight from Dulles, headed for LAX, plowing into the western side of the Pentagon, part of the building collapsing, big fire, no reports yet of how many inside, how many dead, how many injured.

"We're under attack," Tom hears someone say. "It's war."

He spins from the monitor, grabs a phone, hesitates, doesn't know the number because he hasn't called it in years, scrambles back to his desk, in the drawer, goes through papers and envelopes and notes and pads, looks for the direct line, finds it at last, dials, busy, dials again, busy, and again, busy busy busy busy—

Gets up, turns on the portable TV in the kitchen, watches as the world explodes and collapses and changes, all at once, and understands in an instant that no one will care about Vieques, not for some time, and as the nightmare unfolds, something tells him, something deep down in some unexplored place, something tells him that Lt. Col. Wayne Fargo works on the western side of the Pentagon, and fear starts to roll in and settle around him, a dark and dangerous cloud, and he goes to the front door in what seems like a frenzied dream, an out-of-body experience, and he locks it, checking and rechecking the bolt with growing dread, wondering who was going to protect him now and if he'd ever be safe again.

EIGHT

ANTOINETTE "TONI" ALLURA, the junior senator from California, looked up from the magazine and shot a poison-arrow glance at her press secretary over the top of Fendi reading glasses. "You call this good publicity?"

The aide, Victoria Chu, a 31-year-old former reporter who had been on the job less than six months, looked puzzled. "It's a profile of you in *People*," she said.

Toni Allura stared across her uncluttered Senate desk, eyes flaring like a matched pair of blue flames. "And I suppose this is when you tell me there's no such thing as bad PR?"

"Well, I mean, the circulation is three-and-a-half million."

She nodded. "And let's see what three-and-a-half million people are going to read about me:

"Long, lush, beautiful blond hair that looks fresh from a shampoo commercial . . . Features so perfect they would make runway models weep in envy, or binge on cupcakes . . . A lean and leggy body, toned to near perfection, that at a glance looks to be in even better shape than it was during her days as a college cheerleader."

The press secretary squirmed. "Senator, that's all pretty, uh, you know, positive."

"I don't want to date the captain of the football team, Vicki. I want respect."

"But, overall, don't you think it's good?"

The flame in Toni Allura's eyes got hotter. "Yeah. This paragraph is especially good:

"'The accidental senator from Rodeo Drive, as she is called by critics, strolls through the Capitol as if on a red carpet, draped in the latest couture, drawing admiring glances at every turn. While she has said repeatedly that she accepted the appointment to replace her late husband as a way to preserve his legacy and continue his work, and then defied expectations with a special election win whose margin of victory was slimmer than her hips, there is no mistaking the fact that Toni Allura, despite her thin resume and fondness for trim-fitting Armani suits, is the Senate's newest rock star.'"

Vicki Chu was thinking "rock star" was a serious step up from most of the whispered descriptions of her boss that wafted through the Senate hallways, but she wisely refrained from saying anything.

"Goddamnit, I have a master's in marketing, I had my first million-dollar year selling real estate before I was 25, and I'm on the board of seven nonprofits." She leaned back into the chair and threw her hands up in exasperation. "What do you need to be taken seriously in this town?"

Balls, Vicki Chu thought. Literally and figuratively. She refrained from saying that, too.

Toni Allura picked up the *People* again, rereading the profile piece, shaking her head. "When does this hit the stands?"

"Next week. That's an advance copy."

"I've got to counter this somehow. The story's got to be dead on arrival."

"I'll start working on it." She stood quickly, happy to be out of the hot seat.

"Where are you going?"

Vicki froze. "Uh, you know, to get the press team together so we can, um, start working out a plan."

Toni Allura raised one perfectly plucked eyebrow. "This would be the same press team that thought a piece in *People* would be a great idea?" No answer; none needed. "Make sure Kyle's in the room." Kyle Kendrick, her administrative assistant. "If history is any measure, your *team* could use some adult supervision." She massaged her wrinkle-free forehead, frustrated and resigned. "What's on the schedule today?"

The press secretary eased, relieved at the chance to field a straight-ahead question and give a straight-ahead answer. "Ten a.m. with the state Spelling Bee champion. Eleven o'clock photo op with kids competing in the Special Olympics. Lunch briefing with the Congressional Bike Caucus."

She groaned. "God, is there anything, of any substance, anywhere? I've got to have an issue, something to run with."

Vicki cleared her throat. "Well, there's the Harriman nomination. But since, uh, you decided to stay kind of, um, low-key on that and all, we just assumed you'd still be taking a pass on the hearings."

"Well, you assumed wrong." The reply came thunder-like, fast and sharp and out of nowhere. Vicki could see the calculation behind her boss' eyes, whose rage had turned to sparkle, and when the brief silence lifted and the senator began talking through a strategy to blunt the magazine article, even the press secretary had to admit that Toni Allura was about to show some balls.

NINE

"YOU MIGHT WANT to get over here," Tom half-whispered to Penn Mallory over the cell phone outside the Intelligence Committee hearing room on the second floor of the Hart Senate Office Building.

"She's been asleep at the wheel on Vance for weeks. Now you're telling me she's interested?"

"Interested and not toeing the company line."

"She's not a member of the company, son. She's a goddamned RINO." An acronym for Republican In Name Only, someone who doesn't rubber-stamp the party's preferences or, in this case, those of the president and Mallory. "A RINO from the left coast, and they ain't like the rest of us."

"I understand."

The senator paused. Tom could feel his paranoia starting to growl. "She's up to something. What do you think?"

"I think we need to show the flag."

"On my way."

Mallory broke the connection. Tom stepped back into the hearing room, where Toni Allura, not known for her interrogation skills, was sounding very much like a prosecutor.

"Could you explain to this committee exactly what *Territo* means, Mr. Harriman?" she asked.

Vance Harriman took a sip of water, more to chill his irritation than to soothe his throat, asking himself, again, just what an aging prom queen was doing grilling him on matters of national security.

"Mr. Harriman? It's not a trick question." A false smile.

At his side, Harriman's attorney clamped a hard grip on the Territo CEO's forearm:

Don't take the bait.

Harriman neither took the bait nor acknowledged her with the courtesy of eye contact. Instead, he focused on the large seal of the United States Senate that was affixed to the marble wall behind the chairman.

"It's Latin, Senator," he said as the photographers who were staked out on the floor in front of the committee started shooting the CIA nominee, their cameras filling the hearing room with high-pitched clicks that reinforced Harriman's belief that media people were nothing more than a flock of locusts whose specialty was noise rather than knowledge.

"And what is it Latin for, Mr. Harriman?"

"It means, 'I terrify.'" Voice flat as an aircraft carrier deck.

Toni Allura nodded. "So, just to clarify, you are the chairman and CEO of, what, a terrorist organization?"

A barely detectable smile creased Harriman's face. He understood that the confirmation process was a necessary evil, a political pageant, a circus. But he would not permit this Style section pinup from Orange County to put him in the center ring.

"What we do, Senator, is provide security services to individuals whose safety, for whatever reason, may be at risk." It was a well-rehearsed response, shaped during the weeks of preparation from White House vetters and handlers that had preceded the hearings. Harriman delivered it as instructed, without even a hint of emotion.

"Have you ever murdered anyone, Mr. Harriman?"

"You mean, out of anger?" Laughter rippled from the standing-room-only crowd.

The committee chairman, a short round man whose advanced age and ever-more-frequent mental lapses forecast a decline into Alzheimer's that his staff worked overtime to hide, rapped the gavel sharply. "Order, order." His voice and hands shook in equal measure.

Harriman appeared to be seriously considering the question. As he did, Penn Mallory slid into his seat on the panel. Toni turned to him. "Good to see my colleague from Florida could join us," she said, not meaning a word of it, then returned her attention to the nominee. "Mr. Harriman and I were just discussing the fine art of murder."

Mallory smiled easily. "Ah, but we are in Washington, Senator. I believe the appropriate term in this shining city on a hill is character assassination." They locked eyes before Mallory turned to the chairman. "I feel this line of questioning is not only inappropriate, but insulting to the nominee's integrity."

"Please," Harriman interrupted. "I want to answer the question."

The room went quiet, silence hanging in the air like a balloon ready to burst. Mallory's eyes found Tom standing in the back, behind the audience. Tom shrugged slightly, a no-idea-where-this-is-going gesture. Mallory looked oddly unconcerned.

"Classical music," Harriman said at last, almost dreamlike.

Toni Allura's blue eyes widened, then narrowed. "I'm sorry?"

"There was classical music playing, in the car. It was Berlin, a few years ago. A sunny day, simply beautiful, and we were in the Kurfürstendamm. Are you familiar with that part of the city, Senator?"

Toni Allura cleared her throat. "I've been to Berlin, yes."

Harriman nodded. "Then you know. It's the Champs-Élysées of Berlin. Shops and restaurants and hotels. Elegant homes. Very upscale."

"We appreciate the travelogue, Mr. Harriman, but can we cut to the chase? Or, in this instance, the murder?"

Vance Harriman smiled serenely, at peace with himself, like a man with a clean conscience. "We were in a large SUV, two of my employees in the front seat, one driving, myself in the rear seat with a client, an American executive with interests in the international defense industry. It was black and tinted." A brief pause. "The SUV, I mean. Not the client."

A slight, good-humored murmur in the crowd.

"In any event, the client wanted to stop at Chanel to buy his wife a gift. As we drove along the boulevard, which is very long and broad, I noticed a young couple pushing a baby in a pram. She carried a small satchel. He wore a wine-colored cardigan that was a bit too large."

"Let me guess," Toni Allura said. "Burberry."

Vance Harriman shrugged indifferently. "I'll have to take your word for that, Senator. I wouldn't know a Burberry from a blueberry."

It was a clear shot at her fashionista reputation, and Toni drilled him with a look of searing disdain. "That's okay, Mr. Harriman; I don't know the difference between a .22 and a .45."

"Perhaps one day I will show you, Senator. Times being what they are, one's security is as important as, well, life itself." His voice was level, betraying not so much as a syllable of derision. "But we digress."

He took another sip of water, setting the glass down and staring at it for a moment.

"As this couple passed our vehicle, I remember being struck by how perfectly happy they looked, so full of hope and love and optimism. Just a nice young family, out for a stroll." He took a moment to allow the image to crystallize. "And then the woman veered and pushed the pram in front of our vehicle."

A full 30 seconds of total silence. No one in the audience breathed.

"The driver applied the brakes, but the SUV struck the pram, sending a thick spray of blankets all over the avenue. It was at that point my employees made a fundamental error."

"As if striking a baby carriage wasn't mistake enough."

Harriman didn't rise to the challenge, just continued his story, picking up the pace slightly. "No. They assumed what they had witnessed was, in fact, what was occurring. As my employees exited the SUV, the woman reached into her satchel and the man behind his back, into his trousers, under the cardigan, and each produced single-action Hungarian FEG FP9 handguns, which they promptly used to shoot my driver in the forehead, his colleague through the heart. Twice through the heart, actually."

Mallory glanced quickly at Toni for a reaction. Other than tapping her well-manicured fingernails on the desktop, she was impassive.

Harriman pressed on.

"Within seconds, the back doors of my SUV swung open to reveal the young man and young woman, neither of whom, it seemed, expected to see me there, armed with a 9-millimeter HK P2000. Limited Edition, German Police Model. Such was their surprise that they hesitated. I did not. I fired until there was nothing left in the chamber. Then I got into the driver's seat, told my client his shopping excursion would have to wait. One hour later, I put him on a private jet at Tempelhof Airport and he returned to the United States."

"I see," Toni said. She looked down at her notes, shuffled four or five sheets of lined yellow legal pad papers. Mallory dropped his head and put a hand over his mouth to cover a smile. She was stalling for time. She'd asked a question she didn't know the answer to, and was paying the price for not being prepared.

"This executive, was his name Edward Irving?"

Mallory's head popped up. The smile vanished.

"Yes, Senator," Harriman replied evenly. "It was."

"And would this be the same Edward Irving who was the CEO of Defensor Industries?"

"Yes."

"The same Edward Irving who was murdered in Paraguay two years ago."

A moment. Then: "Yes, Senator. In Ciudad del Este."

"The same Edward Irving who—"

"Mr. Chairman, please," Mallory jumped in. "If my esteemed colleague from California has a destination in mind for these questions, could I respectfully ask that she get there?"

Toni Allura replied with a smile that was at once dazzling and contemptuous. "Certainly, Senator, since you asked so . . . respectfully." She looked down again at her notes, but Mallory knew it was pure theater. "Edward Irving died in a terrorist bombing for which Hezbollah took credit. Is that correct?"

Harriman nodded, saying nothing.

"And this occurred while you were still in his employ as a provider of, what did you call them, security services?"

"Mr. Chairman, I repeat my request," Mallory said.

Toni ignored him. "I was just wondering, sir, if you cannot protect one man from the awful consequences of terrorism, how can we realistically expect you to protect the entire nation from similar acts of violence?"

Even from where he sat, Tom could feel the fury rising off Harriman like steam. But when he glanced over at Mallory, the senator was just staring at Toni with a cruel, confident expression, one that said I know something you don't know, and I'm going to use it against you to inflict maximum damage, the kind of damage that's so severe you will never, ever recover.

TEN

"SENATOR, SENATOR, OPEN the door."

Harry Platte looked at his watch—3:17 a.m., Riyadh time—then at the lithe, long-legged creature snoring softly on the king bed next to him, her long dark hair splayed halo-like on the pillow, a reverse image of the blondes with whom he usually amused himself.

More urgent knocking on the door. "Senator? It's important."

Platte didn't have a great deal of personal affection for David Diamond, who ran the Armed Services Committee staff, but he did respect him. The man was a patriot, which mattered a lot in a dangerous and uncertain world. But beyond that, and maybe even more important, Diamond walked the halls of Congress like an unspoken threat. People like Harry Platte needed people like Diamond by their side.

Except at this particular moment, as Platte watched the small breasts of this gorgeous young dancer rise and fall with each breath, recalling the previous few hours of noisy bliss and hoping whatever Diamond had to say would not deprive him of a few more. "Awright. Jesus."

He dragged himself from the bed, grabbed a robe from a walk-in closet the size of Manhattan, and strode through the dining area into the large living room with its gold-toned wallpaper, elegant sofa-settee combination, and crystal tea set on a modernistic marble coffee table. A stunning vista of northwestern Riyadh peeked through the beige vertical blinds on the 42nd-floor window of the Four Seasons Presidential Suite at Kingdom Centre, the 99-story futuristic, bottle-opener-shaped skyscraper that cast a long shadow over the otherwise flat city landscape.

Platte cinched the robe sash and opened the door.

"They want you back in Washington," Diamond said bluntly. He was somewhere between short and average height, always looked like an unmade bed, and had dark eyes that shone with intrigue. His high forehead served to emphasize eyebrows that were thicker than his hair.

The news jerked Platte out of his half-sleep, and turned him instantly wary. "Why?"

Diamond looked over his shoulder toward the bedroom. "Why do you think?"

It took a second for the question to register. "You got to be kidding. This is about her?"

"It's about *all* of them, Senator." He brushed by Platte and flopped onto the sofa. Platte followed but didn't sit.

"Jesus. They want me to be a monk?" Diamond was silent. "Well, I'm sorry, but that's not gonna happen. It's not who I am."

"Explain that to the White House."

"The White House knows. We had this discussion, the president and me, when we first talked about the nomination."

"He remembers. You apparently don't."

Platte's eyes turned to black ice. "You would be wise to remember who you're talking to, fella."

Diamond fielded the stare and hung on to it. "I know who I'm talking to. The question is whether you do."

"What is that supposed to mean?"

"It means, are you going to remain the junior senator from Missouri, or become the next Secretary of Defense?"

Platte considered the question briefly before dismissing it and waving Diamond off. "They wouldn't walk the nomination back."

"The nomination hasn't been announced yet."

"They wouldn't do it. Not over a piece of ass. Never happen."

"How can you be so sure? Do you have any idea who she is?"

"She's a dancer. So what?"

"What do you mean, so *what*? She's a foreign national. She comes from someplace we could be blowing up tomorrow. She could go on Al Jazeera and say you're the father of her little Arabian love child."

"She wouldn't do that."

"How do you know?"

"Because I use protection."

Diamond dropped his head in his hands, rubbing his temples. "You have to know there are about 7 million possible outcomes here, and not one of them is good for you."

Platte's mouth screwed itself into a twisted grin. "Or for you."

Diamond stood to face him. "Yeah, for me. I'm attached to your star, Senator. I know it. And as long as I got a dog in this hunt, you can be very sure I'll do whatever it takes to protect your interests when they intersect with mine."

Platte stared at him long enough for the grin to dissolve into a sneer. "You are an evil, ambitious little prick, you know that?" Diamond nodded slowly, without hesitation. "I tolerate you because you got back-channel access to everybody in the government who matters, and probably half the people in the world. You know all the secrets, where the bodies are buried, my enemies, that kind of thing. But let me tell you this." He let the silence hang until the air between them hardened. "You are not gonna tell me who I can and cannot sleep with, you understand? You are not gonna tell me what to do."

Diamond didn't back down, didn't blink, didn't signal what he was thinking or feeling. He just stayed locked on Platte. "Here's what you're going to do, Senator. You're going to get dressed while I pack your suitcase. I have a limo waiting downstairs that will take you to King Khalid International, where you will board one of the Royal Family's private jets and fly to Munich. There, DOD will have a jet waiting for you."

"What? The White House is canceling the whole trip? And why Munich?"

Diamond ignored the confused anxiety working its way into Platte's voice. "Staff will remain here to conduct lower-level discussions with the government, and then proceed as planned to Kuwait. On your plane will be three ranking members of the Saudi defense ministry who have business in Munich. They have requested an audience with you."

Platte's expression shifted to suspicion. "Oh, did they?" Diamond said nothing. "And I'm guessing the details of this little airborne sit-down will somehow find their way to the president's desk." It was a statement, not a question.

"Let me just say that your talks will enable you to make an announcement of Secretary of Defense-like significance when you land at Andrews, and reinforce your credentials as the right man for the job."

Now Platte's expression arrived at admiration. "You rigged this, didn't you, covering my ass, keeping the White House from getting cold feet about nominating me."

"I did what I felt was best for my country, Senator. America needs you."

"Yes, it does."

"Harr-reeee?"

Over Platte's shoulder, Diamond saw the wonderfully nude image of an Arabic woman standing in the doorframe between the bedroom and the rest of the prodigious suite. She yawned and stretched, the muscles in her taut body rippling like a racehorse's. "You come back to bed?"

But Platte didn't acknowledge her, just stayed fixed on Diamond. "Get your clothes on, baby. I got a plane to catch."

David Diamond nodded and smiled, but his gaze remained on the girl, eyes so impassive and empty they bordered on dead.

ELEVEN

IN ANOTHER HOTEL, on another continent, 2,500 miles away, a slender, sharp-featured woman with eyes as black as a mineshaft sat on the balcony staring at her laptop, considering the most efficient way to send a jet into a nosedive.

On the one hand, she could shut down just the hydraulic controls. That would pitch the aircraft down at about a 30-degree angle, causing it to lose altitude at a rate of 350 feet per second and probably hit the ground at 500-plus miles an hour. She'd done that in Iran, killing a pair of Pasdaran leaders en route to a "weapons and support" meeting with the Taliban in Afghanistan.

On the other, she could initiate a full-on failure of the flight controls—the ailerons, stabilizers, elevators. The angle of descent would be more severe, close to 45 degrees, and the aircraft would be traveling at 600 miles per hour on impact. She'd done that in Israel, downing a Mossad cargo plane ferrying CIA contractors to the Gaza Strip for a dark-of-night tussle with Hamas.

She reached for the champagne that was chilling in a sweating stainless-steel cooler stand to her left and refilled the crystal flute, noticing, as she always did—even after all these years—that half her wedding-ring finger was gone, the result of an unfortunate incident in Yemen that had cost members of a small cell of Islamic fundamentalists not only their fingers, but also their arms, hands, feet, legs, and heads.

Beyond the balcony, Munich was preparing for evening's arrival.

In the distance were the spire of the New Town Hall in the Marienplatz, the twin church towers of the brick Frauenkirche, the neo-Gothic architecture along the Maximilianstrasse. On the quiet side street below, luxury stores began their slow fade into closed-for-business. Somewhere, the happy cries of children gave life to the dying light.

From behind her came the sound of a toilet flushing in the bathroom, with its Jacuzzi, steam room, heated floors, Swarovski chandelier, and television. She thought that was a bit over the top; bathrooms had no business being so luxurious. But she had enjoyed the Jacuzzi, and the Egyptian diplomat with whom she had shared it.

Speaking of whom:

"Ariella?"

She glanced at the small purse on the table next to her laptop, then pulled the thick, soft terry robe a little tighter. "Out here."

In a moment, the man wandered from the bedroom—which was a medley of creams and browns, cherry-wood nightstands framing a king-sized bed—and through the living area with its taupe-colored walls, handpicked art, plush chocolate-colored sofa, and low glass table accessorized by a 6th-century Chinese sculpture.

He stepped through the French doors onto the balcony and kissed her lightly on the head. "Are you going to be long?"

She shook her head. "Just a few moments."

"Don't delay." She took his hand and slipped it inside the robe. His breathing stopped for an instant. "Please."

After he had returned to the bed, she took another sip of champagne, thought for a few more seconds, and decided.

A full-on failure of the flight controls.

It was rare, but not impossible, and because multiple systems were involved, investigators would have a difficult time pinpointing the precise cause of the crash. By the time they did, if they ever did, she would be a ghost once more. It had worked to perfection in Ciudad del Este 18 months earlier. She was confident it would work again now.

With a few quick keystrokes, she accessed the cockpit controls, smiling slightly and shaking her head at the arrogance of the West—

"There is no way in the world you can hack into a flight control system," a NATO general had told her, *"and even if there was, you can be sure the technology wouldn't come out of Iraq"*—

But it had, and within moments, she had a virtual view of the instruments.

From there it was as simple as a dozen more keystrokes. Within seconds, at an altitude of 28,000 feet, the plane began to fall.

As it did, she rose quickly, shed the robe, slipped back into the form-fitting black dress draped over the sofa, put the mile-high-heeled red shoes on, and retrieved her laptop and purse from the balcony.

Thirty seconds after that, the plane was descending at just under the speed of sound.

At the moment the jet hit the ground and disintegrated, barely a mile and a half from where it had started to drop, she went into the bedroom, where she was greeted by the confused look of a man who expected to face something other than a woman in a dress that left little to the imagination and a matte black Bersa Thunder .380 pistol with seven rounds in the magazine, one more in the chamber—

All of which she emptied into him before going into the gaudy bathroom, checking her lipstick and finger-combing her hair, then returning to the bar downstairs where she and the diplomat had met less than two hours ago. She sipped and savored a glass of supremely expensive whiskey, walked easily out onto the street, and got into the back seat of a waiting black Mercedes, vanishing behind the opaque tinted windows as the car disappeared into the darkness that was coming over the city like a slowly unfolding nightmare.

TWELVE

CARI STAPLETON WAS medium height and wore skinny jeans and a form-fitting sweater, both of which amplified the effects of her daily aerobics regimen. "So," she said. "At long last I get to see your place. I was starting to think you had a gay lover roommate."

Tom laughed easily and ushered her into his living room. "He's out tonight."

She turned to him and smiled. Then her eyes—rimmed in black makeup, vaguely goth, which made her fashionably cropped blond hair seem almost blinding white—caught the inside of the front door:

Flush bolts mortised into the top and bottom edges of the door. A pair of double-cylinder deadbolt locks. Metal-based vertical deadbolt lock. Keyless entry lock. A pair of chain locks.

She looked back at him. The smile was still there, but it was dimmed by a sudden uneasiness. "Should I be worried?"

It took Tom a moment to get what she was talking about. "Oh." A semi-embarrassed grin. "A long time ago, in a galaxy far, far away." He went to the door and simply pressed the plunge lock on the knob. "If you need to make a quick exit, just turn it to the right," which he did, "and pull." He did that, too. The door swung open.

"Why would I want to make a quick exit?"

Tom reddened at the promise in her voice. "In case my gay roommate lover decides to come back unexpectedly."

The promise spread to her eyes. "Maybe you ought to go ahead and do them all," gesturing to the locks. "You know, just in case—"

She kept talking, but Tom's mind heard only Sarah, screaming, days gone—

"This is insane, Tom! You're turning our home into a fortress. Why? Just in case Osama bin Laden decides to come after you?"

When he returned to the moment, he had a haunted expression, and eyes that seemed to be peering over the edge of the world.

Cari noticed. "You okay?"

"Oh, sure, yeah. I'm fine," he said, less than persuasively. "Make yourself at home, please. Can I get you a drink?"

"More wine, sir." She dropped into a distressed-leather sofa, slid off the leopard-print flats, and stretched her legs onto the large, low, western-style coffee table that was topped in wood and cowhide. Anyone who didn't know her day job, which was legislative assistant to a congressman from Orlando, would likely mistake her for a model, or maybe an exotic dancer.

"Excellent, madam." He walked into the one-step-up kitchen—which was really little more than a wide hallway between the living room and bedroom, sink and counters on one side, bathroom opposite—and pulled a bottle of Pinot Noir from a cupboard over a microwave whose numbers were faded from repeated pressing. He poured two glasses. When he swung back to face her, he noticed she was staring at the rustically framed print over the sofa, *Flag*, by Jasper Johns.

"The artist said that working on something the mind already knows gave him a lot of freedom to focus his attention on actually making the painting," he explained, walking back into the living room and sitting next to her, putting the glasses on the table. "It's not even painted on canvas, but on strips of newspaper."

"So it's not a real flag?"

"It's an invitation to look more closely at a symbol the mind thinks it already knows."

"So what you see isn't what you get."

Tom nodded. "It never is."

Cari smiled. "Yeah. Kind of like you."

He shifted in the sofa, took a sip of wine. "I'm pretty transparent."

"I'm not so sure. Which means you're probably not." He didn't know what to say. She did. "I mean, what, six dates, and nothing more than a goodnight kiss? And this is the first time I set foot in your place? What is *that* about?"

"Good, old-fashioned respect. That's what it's about."

She leaned into him, so closely their noses almost touched. "Nope. You, my friend, have a dark side."

He laughed, but it rang false and had less life than a day-old soda. "I wish I were that interesting."

Cari sat back and took in the apartment. "Okay, then answer me this: Your place, it's very cool, very Santa Fe, and I so want *that* in my house." She pointed to a high, round turquoise-tile-topped breakfast table flanked by two tall, black cast-iron chairs. "But I look at this"—gesturing to him—"and at this"—then more broadly, to the room—"and I'm like, what's wrong with this picture?"

Tom acted like he was considering the question.

She answered herself: "I'll tell you what's wrong. You're nowhere to be found."

He shifted again. "Meaning?"

"Just that somebody's house, it's like a timeline of their life up to that point, okay? You see photos, books, diplomas, stuff that says, 'Here's where I've been, and here's who I am, and maybe here's where I want to go.' But you? Nothing."

Tom's eyes grazed the living room, from the breakfast table to the fireplace that didn't work, to the large bay window fronting a wooden privacy-fenced brick patio that had almost as much square footage as the apartment, to the door and its unlocked locks, and then back to Cari. He had to admit, she had a point. "I'm not sure what you're saying."

"The *Time* magazine cover. Where is it?"

His head snapped back, as if she'd threatened to punch him. "Wow, that was direct."

Her eyes widened with real curiosity. "No. It was an honest question."

Tom rubbed his hands together, staring at them, his mind seeing the image as clearly as if it, not the Jasper Johns print, was in the frame overhead:

The cover, a drawing, half looking like Tom as a long-haired radical, the other like Tom as a shorn Red State Establishment Type, all of it packaged under a screaming headline:

"The New Face of Patriotism."

And a subhead:

"I want to kill them all."

"Ancient history," he replied at last, reaching for another sip of wine.

Her eyes didn't leave him. "Can I ask you something?"

He cracked a smile that was rooted in actual amusement. "That hasn't been a problem so far."

"Why'd you do it?"

The smile remained, its amusement replacing the soft anguish of memory. "The world changed."

"It changed for all of us, and that's no answer."

"God, you are relentless."

"No. I'm just interested, that's all. We've been going out for a month, and you haven't said a word about it."

"That's because there's nothing to say."

"Was it your dad?"

Tom stared at the fireplace. That had been a none-too-subtle, between-the-lines theme of the *Time* article: Young antiwar radical honors estranged father and 9/11 Pentagon victim by taking up his mantle of national security. It had always struck him as too simplistic, too made-for-TV. But he hadn't come up with a competing narrative that was any more credible. "Can we move on to another subject?"

She moved closer to him, reached for his hand. "It's okay. You can talk to me."

He dropped her hand and flew off the sofa, saying, "Jesus, Cari, I'm not looking for a therapist, all right?" But the voice he heard, again, was Sarah's—

"You don't need any more locks; you need professional help."

Cari folded herself back into the sofa. "Okay, okay. Sorry."

He took a deep breath of self-reproach and sat back down. "No. I'm sorry. You didn't deserve that." Shook his head, let out a chuckle as dead as dried leaves. "Old demons, you know."

She nodded. "Can I ask you something else?"

"Yes, I really said it."

"Huh?"

"That's what you were going to ask, wasn't it? Did I really say what was on the cover, *I want to kill them all?*"

"No, actually, it wasn't." She smiled, warm and inviting, and moved closer to him. Their legs touched. She whispered into his ear. "I was going to ask if there was anything I could do to silence the demons."

He felt his heart start to sprint from the starting blocks. "I think they're already pretty quiet."

She took his face and turned it to hers. "Then what can I do keep them that way?"

He closed his eyes, and their lips met, and his heart picked up even more speed, and for a moment there were no images of magazine covers, no memories of dead fathers and smoking buildings, no replays of arguments in his head. There was just a sudden ache that wasn't mental or emotional, but physical, one that desperately needed to be soothed, and he let himself go for the first time since he couldn't remember when, and they were all arms and legs and hands, exploring each other with an intensity that felt new to him, unexplored, human—

Then his cell went off.

And as Tom uncoupled from Cari and caught his breath, an uncertain feeling started to creep up his back like frost, the rings from the phone sounding eerily like the unmistakable shriek of a demon resurfacing.

THIRTEEN

WHEN TOM ARRIVED at Penn Mallory's large brick home in the Embassy Row section of Washington, he expected to see his boss. What he didn't expect to see was his boss, and Vance Harriman, and Rep. Jasper Eddy, huddled at a computer, peering over the shoulder of a geeky-looking kid with a Territo ID badge whose every keystroke seemed freighted with meaning.

Tom watched for a few seconds in the door of Mallory's book-lined study, the three Wise Men so caught up in what was happening onscreen that they didn't notice his presence.

The Geek didn't notice either, just sat there power-tapping away.

Then he stopped, exhaled as if he'd been holding his breath for days, and announced: "It's clean."

"You're sure," Jasper Eddy said in his hammer-hard South Carolina accent.

The Geek looked up as if he'd never heard anyone speak Southern.

"He's sure," Vance Harriman said quickly, detouring any potential scenario that would end with blood coming from the Geek's nose, courtesy of Jasper Eddy's fist.

"Am I interrupting?" Tom asked, pulling a spare, all-right-angled wooden chair from the dining room and sitting down just inside the study.

Eddy and Harriman exchanged a quick look, but Mallory was unfazed. "Not at all, son. With this awful thing that happened, and the likelihood that we might be exchanging sensitive intelligence data in the next few days, Vance thought it might be a good idea if we ratcheted up the security on all our computers."

The Geek glanced at Harriman, who nodded once, then he stood and strode past Tom toward the front door, mouthing "Cuh-Ray-Zee" as he did.

Mallory went to a wet bar, poured himself a straight bourbon, and looked to the others, silently asking for requests.

Tom and Harriman declined. Jasper Eddy smiled and licked his lips.

Mallory poured a second Wild Turkey and handed it to the South Carolinian. "All right," he said, easing into an oversized brown leather chair and firing up a cigar. "Let's all understand one thing: This meeting never took place. It's entirely inappropriate for Vance, as a nominee, to give us even an informal briefing." He smiled and sipped. "But as we all know, he does have his own 'unofficial' avenues of communication, and I trust his over those that may be more regular in nature."

Harriman nodded slightly in acknowledgment of the praise.

"Okay," Mallory continued, as if gaveling the meeting to order, "what do we know?"

Harriman's face was gray and dispassionate. If he was feeling anything, it was locked deep down in some emotional vault. "We don't know anything with absolute certainty. I can only—"

"You know he's dead, right?" interrupted Eddy, Mallory's somewhat less cultured alter ego in the House, a member of the Armed Services Committee. Eddy was in his mid-50s but looked a decade younger. A former Navy pilot, he had never met a military program—or, his critics charged, a military adventure—that he didn't love at first sight.

Harriman dug at one of pits in his face. "Yes, sir. We have confirmed that Senator Platte's plane went down approximately four hours ago en route to Munich. Three on board. No survivors."

Jasper Eddy swung his head to Mallory. "It's the goddamned towel-heads, Penn. I'm telling you, they looked at Harry, knew he was an ass-kicker, and made their move."

"That makes no sense," Tom blurted, momentarily forgetting his place as staff.

Eddy, a bully who had earned and loved his nickname, the Velvet Blackjack, stared at him like a mad bull, then returned his attention to Mallory. "You need to keep your little dog on a leash, Penn."

Tom smiled a whatever-you-say-asshole smile, dropping his head to hide it, knowing it took very little to provoke Eddy. Still, the congressman caught the expression and snarled, "Love it or leave it, bitch."

"Shut up, Jasper," Mallory said, more of a warning than a demand.

"I'm just sayin'."

"Yeah, well, I'd appreciate it if you said a helluva lot less of it." He turned to Harriman. "Go on, Vance."

Harriman leaned back in a beat-up Chesterfield sofa that just missed matching Mallory's chair. He somehow managed to strike a comfortable pose without actually looking comfortable.

"Senator Platte was in a Saudi Learjet 25. These are high-speed aircraft, and they can be challenging to handle."

Jasper Eddy nodded his head. "The bird requires a ton of talent to fly. Not a whole lotta margin for error, even for a good pilot."

"How good were the pilots?" Mallory asked.

Harriman shrugged. "They were qualified in the Lear, but there is some question as to whether they possessed full operational knowledge of the aircraft."

"What?" Jasper Eddy howled. "You're tellin' us we put Harry Platte in an airplane with a couple of rookie ragheads who had no business even bein' in the cockpit?"

Impatience flared on Harriman's face without creeping into his voice. "What I am saying is that they may not have had the experience to deal with this type of situation." He paused. "But I don't think anyone, regardless of qualification, could have handled that particular vehicle in those particular circumstances."

Eddy frowned, shook his head. "Nope. I'll guaran-goddamn-tee you that those boys, the pilots, they got connections to bad people somewhere."

Penn Mallory ignored him. "What do you mean, Vance, *those particular circumstances?*"

"The Lear went into a 45-degree nosedive, and was nearing the speed of sound on impact. That tells me this was something more than pilot error."

"What?"

"Total failure of the flight controls, you ask me," Eddy answered. "Those things shut down, it's goodbye, Charlie."

"It is rare, but not impossible," Harriman said. "There have been only a handful of cases that I am aware of, perhaps three or four, all in commercial aircraft."

In the silence that followed, Tom could see Jasper Eddy spinning conspiracy theories in his overheated mind:

"Someone tucked away in the jet, breaks into the cockpit, somehow disables the controls?"

Harriman shook his head. "Doubtful."

"Could anybody have jacked around with the jet on the ground prior to takeoff?"

Harriman shrugged slightly, not exactly rejecting the idea but clearly not giving it much credibility, either.

"Maybe the dune coons flying the Lear weren't exactly who they pretended to be."

"Back off, Jasper," Mallory flared. "Nobody needs to be fishing for an excuse to invade somebody."

"Unless they got a reason."

Mallory dismissed him with a wave of the hand. "The last thing I need in the White House is another war chewing up taxpayer dollars and pushing our national ass deeper in debt." He looked at Harriman. "Vance, anything else?"

"Nothing that cannot be handled." Mallory spun his hand in a circular get-on-with-it motion. "There were supposed to be some Saudi defense officials on the plane. They canceled at the last minute."

That caught the senator's interest. "Coincidence?"

"No. My contact in Riyadh checked. Prince Salman convened an emergency meeting of his ministers. All official, all above-board, nothing suspicious."

Satisfied, Mallory instructed him to continue.

Harriman paused. "There is one more thing. Before the plane went down, one of the pilots screamed, *Allah Yela'an Platte.* It means, May the Lord curse Platte."

The study went silent, save for the ticking of a desk clock embedded in a triangular chunk of crystal, a gift to Mallory from the Chinese ambassador that sat on the senator's walnut desk, which was a 1739 model from Boston he'd wrangled for a song at auction.

Mallory glanced at Tom, whom he often depended on to bring debates like this back inside the gates of reality. "Thoughts?"

Tom cut his eyes to Jasper Eddy, who was staring at his bourbon, then began to speak, carefully, as if the wrong words could inflict some kind of harm.

"If I'm reading the Director right"—meaning Harriman, lack of final confirmation notwithstanding—"then what he's saying makes sense. It was an unfortunate tragedy caused by an equally unfortunate, unintended event. And while I agree that the issues he raised may encourage some alternative theories, they don't, individually or collectively, point to any larger crime."

Jasper Eddy popped out of his chair like a bottle rocket. "For God's sake, the pilot damned Harry Platte to hell! That points to something!"

"Probably that he was scared outta his mind and mad at Allah, or whoever, for delivering him to this particular fate," Mallory said.

Eddy considered that for a second and sat back down. "Or was pissed he wouldn't have 42 virgins waiting for him in heaven." He chuckled. No one joined him.

Tom continued, "But I also think it would be unwise to take any other scenarios, plausible or implausible, off the table. Everybody's going to be asking if this was terrorist-related. We better be ready."

Mallory nodded. "Okay. Let's run through the suspects."

They did, starting with the obvious possibilities, Al-Qaeda and its Iraqi affiliate, AQI—both of which Harriman rejected, saying, "There's no indication this is a suicide event, which is their preferred methodology"—and ending with a number of charitable groups in Saudi Arabia that had been known to channel money to terrorists. Of those, only Mercy International Relief Organization, another Al-Qaeda vessel, generated any serious discussion, mostly because it was involved in two 1998 U.S. embassy bombings in Africa and its membership once included no less than the late Osama bin Laden himself. But any lingering suspicion evaporated when Harriman reminded them the group had been pretty much off the grid since 2004.

After about an hour of war-gaming the terrorist potential, Penn Mallory slammed the door on further dialogue with a steely, "Flight controls failure. Case closed." No one objected.

With that, he officially adjourned the unofficial meeting, asking Tom to sit tight for a few minutes after the others had left. Back in the study, he poured them both a glass of bourbon. "Talk to me about the politics of this."

It wasn't an out-of-the-blue question, nor was it inappropriate. In Washington, the political context was the only context that mattered, and it could easily trump something as mundane as a friend's death.

"I think under these circumstances, meaning the plane crash, it doesn't matter whose name the White House sends to the Hill as the next Defense Secretary. They'll win in a walk. Hell, I'd get 60 votes."

Mallory ignored the sarcasm. "Yeah, yeah, I see that. My question, though, is about my politics, *our* politics. Does Platte dying do anything to hurt the presidential campaign?"

That, on the other hand, did seem slightly out of the blue.

Tom quickly reran the past hour or so in his head, trying to figure out if he'd missed anything. But for the life of him, he couldn't see a political downside. And for all the lunacy that ambition could engender, Mallory was less at its mercy than most. That made his question seem uncharacteristically anxious.

"No," Tom said at last. "I don't see it having any impact at all."

Mallory pumped a clenched fist. "Good. Because I need you here worrying about getting me in the White House, not in Munich doing damage control."

Tom nodded and went silent for a moment, then took one last sip of bourbon and turned to leave. At the door, Mallory stopped him. "Something bothering you?"

Tom hadn't made it this far into his boss' confidence by pulling any punches, and now was hardly the time to start. "Does it seem at all strange to you that Harriman knew an awful lot about a plane crash that only just happened?"

"Not even a little. Vance probably made three phone calls, logged in to the Territo security files, and got more answers in less time than it'd take me and you to brew a pot of coffee." Tom looked unconvinced. "It's his job. It's what he does."

Tom rubbed his eyes. "I guess."

"And I'd be willing to bet you, dollar to a donut, that when the official report comes out, it'll back up just about everything Vance Harriman said here tonight."

"You think there will be an inquiry?"

Penn Mallory's laugh exploded like a howitzer. "Hell, son," he boomed, clamping a hand on Tom's shoulder and squeezing just hard enough to invite a wince, "you know as well as me that in this town, if it ain't in an official report, then it never officially happened."

FOURTEEN

SIX DAYS LATER, the man sometimes known as Keios stood in the living room of his high-rise, high-priced condo in Crystal City, slipping his arms through a sky-blue Armani dress shirt whose sleeves covered matching tattoos on both forearms:

Eight black arrows in a radial pattern, emanating from a perfect circle, equally black, the design slightly larger than a silver dollar.

He heard a slight, shrill beep.

A 48-inch plasma television set woke up. It was 6:55.

Other than a tan sofa, long and boxy, there was no other furniture. Nothing on the walls but the television and paint so white it looked digitally enhanced. The pale wood floors were unmarked.

Keios walked to the kitchen, poured steaming water from a metal carafe over about two inches of ground coffee at the bottom of a round glass beaker, inserted the mesh-bottomed plunger. He let it sit for a moment before slowly pressing the plunger down.

The French roast was exactly the way he liked it: black and strong, consistency just a step or two away from mud.

Back in the living room, he looked through the large picture window, down to the Potomac River and beyond, to the District skyline, from the Washington Monument to the Capitol dome, wondering what the day would hold.

The answer came quickly.

"Breaking news," Matt Lauer said under the self-important music that announced the 7 a.m. arrival of the *Today* show. Keios paid no attention. These days, "breaking news" could be about anything from the split-up of Hollywood's latest "it" couple to the birth of a two-headed goat.

On this morning, though, it was about neither.

"*Today* has obtained the final report of the investigation into the death of Senator Harry Platte, the president's presumed nominee for Defense Secretary, and a member of the Intelligence Committee is raising questions about both the conclusions and the speed with which they were reached."

Keios stared at the screen, ran a hand over his slickly shaved head, and watched.

Television loved Toni Allura. She gave it no choice.

Unlike those whose youthful appearance had been eroded by the years, nothing about her seemed faded. She wasn't going soft, like a piece of fruit past its expiration date, or wrinkled, like a Barbie doll on the wrong side of 40. Her beauty was at once sublime and subtle, dazzling but not overwhelming to the camera.

And on this morning, seated in the studio of NBC's Washington affiliate, with her chorus-line body tucked into a tailored black suit and her long blond hair arranged strategically, but just barely, off the face, Toni Allura's natural appeal—sex and otherwise—was more powerful than usual, lit up by a sense of urgency that crackled like a distant fire somewhere inside her.

"No, Matt, I'm not suggesting a cover-up. That would be irresponsible." Even her tone, somber and bordering on troubled, would not allow the camera to look away.

"I'm simply saying that the government's official conclusions regarding Senator Platte's death don't vary in the least from the conventional wisdom that emerged within hours of this tragedy. That doesn't make them wrong. But coming just six days after the crash, I am concerned that we may have moved too quickly, that this report is perhaps not as thorough as the American people need it to be."

"How do you propose making it more thorough?"

"Well, I have requested that we open an official Senate investigation of the incident, and have offered to lead it. The Senate looks into everything from executive compensation to ethics transgressions, wrongdoings of all sorts. I just believe we owe the death of an American leader, in a foreign country, in hostile times, the respect of an exhaustive probe."

Tom was standing in his living room, channel surfing the morning television news shows—all Toni, all the time—when the call arrived.

"You watching this crap?" Penn Mallory barked.

"How'd they get the report?"

"Who knows? She probably leaked it."

It wasn't beyond the realm of possibility, Tom thought. "You think she'll get any traction?"

"She's gonna be the lead story on every newscast, on every network, for the rest of the day. On top of that, every liberal newspaper in the country is going to praise her for this truth, justice, and the American way act, and the conservative rags will fall right into step, thinking it'll turn up some dark conspiracy that'll give us an excuse to bomb the piss outta three tents and a camel in Afghanistan." He took a breath. "So, yeah, I'd say there's some potential traction here."

"What about her investigation? Is that going to happen?"

Mallory let out a long, impatient sigh. "What, am I talking in tongues? I just said she's got the left, the right, and the media. You know anybody in this great deliberative body with the stones to take on *that* coalition of the willing?"

"You think she'll find anything?"

"There's nothing to find. Everything Harriman told us at my place is true. There was no bomb. No explosion. No monkey business. Nothing. This was a straight-up systems failure."

Which was exactly what was in the report, Tom knew, having seen an early copy.

"She's running," Mallory said, his voice suddenly coarse, like he'd swallowed gravel.

"She's what?"

"I'm telling you, she's running for president."

Tom had to beat back the urge to laugh out loud. Power made men paranoid, and he understood that, and he fully recognized that the more power they accrued, the more paranoid they became. People were out to get them, steal their authority, humiliate them, whatever.

But Toni Allura for president? That was way out on the paranoia limb, even for Mallory.

"I'm serious," the senator said, as if reading Tom's mind. "This is her opening salvo."

"With all respect, that's—"

"What? Crazy? Well, let me tell you something: A lot of times it's the crazy ones who see things like they really are."

"You can't really believe this is about the presidency."

"That, or a spot on the ticket. My ticket."

Tom let him simmer for a second. "Look, if you're sure there's nothing there—"

"There's not," Mallory said quickly, almost as if he were trying to convince himself or Tom or both, "not a damned thing."

"Fine. Then let's just let her go. She'll waste a lot of Senate time and taxpayer money, nothing will come of it, and she'll drop off the media radar once her 15 minutes of self-promoting fame are over."

"Should I say anything publicly?"

"Just that you're confident in the official findings, but if Senator Allura believes an independent investigation would help to put any potential conspiracy theories to rest, she has every right to pursue one, and you fully support her efforts. And I'd punch *conspiracy theories*."

"Make her look like a crackpot." Tom could almost see Mallory nodding. "You know what worries me, though? If you look at anything long enough and close enough, put it under a big enough microscope, you're gonna find something that doesn't look exactly right, doesn't add up."

"So what? Like I said, if you're confident there's no fire— "

"None," he said again, quickly. "Absolutely none."

"Then let her stumble through the smoke. By the time she figures out all is exactly as it appears, she'll have inhaled enough to choke her ambitions."

Mallory murmured something that sounded like he agreed. "But I don't want any surprises. This little deal caught us all off-guard. No more bolts from the blue."

"Staff can handle it."

"No. No staff. Just you." The words were as hard and firm as set concrete.

"Me?"

"I'm gonna conduct my own investigation of Harry's death and whatever the Cheerleader's up to, and you're gonna head it."

"Me?" Tom repeated, having a hard time processing any of this.

"You."

"Why?"

"Because you're the only one I can trust to do what's best for me, that's why. And I need you to start right now."

"How? What?"

"By getting on a plane."

"A plane to where?"

"The scene of the non-crime, son."

The what?

"Munich."

Twenty minutes later, on the 33rd floor of the Crystal City condo, Keios listened carefully to his instructions, not asking any of the questions Tom Fargo had raised because he already knew most of the answers, burying his outrage at Toni Allura even though he'd been prepared for something like this, some unexpected turn, to happen ever since they had terminated the blogger at the coffee bar. "Where do you want me to start?" was all he needed to know.

And when Vance Harriman said, "From whence cometh evil," Keios knew that while he was going to Munich, the "evil" resided not in the German city but in the one person there who had it in her power to destroy them all.

PART TWO: **TREACHEROUS INFIDELS**

FIFTEEN

HALFWAY OVER THE Atlantic en route to Munich, Tom Fargo noticed an Arabic-looking man a few rows in front of him stand and pull a backpack from the jet's overhead compartment.

The passenger had a straight-out-of-Al-Qaeda look: wiry, dark complexion, tar-black hair with matching three-day beard. When he turned one way and then the other, looking toward the front and rear of the aircraft, Tom saw dull, deep-set eyes the color of onyx and a scowl cemented onto a face that belonged on a cyanide bottle.

The man removed something from the backpack. In the nighttime sky, with the cabin lights dimmed, Tom couldn't tell exactly what it was. A smallish metal thing, the size of a cell phone, with a wire attached to one end.

Stuffing the backpack into the overhead, the man again glanced up and down the aisle, his wary gaze bouncing off the laptop-tappers, book readers, restless children, and sleeping contortionists wedged against the fuselage with makeshift pillow-and-blanket beds. He seemed nervous, as if possessed by the fear of discovery.

Tom watched without expression as the man shoved whatever it was he'd retrieved into the pocket of his khaki pants and sat back down. There had been a time when the sight of a dark-skinned man with facial hair furtively rummaging through a backpack in search of a metallic device with wires would have sent him reaching for anxiety meds or racing for the emergency exit. Sarah had added that to the list of psychological wounds inflicted on him by 9/11, which was her answer to pretty much everything she said had doomed the relationship.

That wound had healed, though. They all had.

His gaze rested on the man for another second, but that was all. Then he went back to reading the briefing book, a quick history of every terrorist, terrorist organization, or terrorist act that Mallory and Harriman believed could have been—but likely weren't—in any way connected to Harry Platte's death.

There was the failed 2006 regional train bombing plot in Germany that would have killed hundreds had the explosives, which were built based on plans found easily on the Internet, not failed to detonate. That struck Tom as a dead end. The ringleader, Youssef Mohamad El Hajdib, was in prison, and his brother and co-planner Saddam was killed in Lebanon a year later.

In 2007, German authorities arrested three men at an apartment in Medebach, where they discovered 1,500 pounds of a hydrogen peroxide mixture and more than two dozen military-grade detonators. Cooking up car bombs. Apparent targets were Ramstein Air Base, the Frankfurt airport, and "a hotel bar filled with American sluts." The three suspects confessed.

Another dead end.

Then there was Hamburg, the host city of Mohamed Atta and his comrades, the 9/11 ringleaders who ushered in a whole new world disorder. In the aftermath of the attacks, a small but significant cell had emerged there, what newspapers called the second generation of terrorists. Local officials believed that its attacks would not be aimed at external targets like the United States, but within Germany.

Killing Harry Platte on a jet bound for Munich would not only qualify, but serve as a kind of twofer: create fear on the home front and take out a high-visibility symbol of The Great Satan in the process.

These guys, though not the amateurs of the 2006 and 2007 plots, didn't feel right to Tom. They talked and threatened, released videos, the usual method of operation. But even with Al-Qaeda training in Pakistan, they never followed up. All bluster, no blowup.

On top of that, no one in the so-called Hamburg Cell had taken credit for Platte's death. For that matter, no one in any cell, in any movement, in any country, had taken credit.

None of which meant that any of the 80 or so trained jihadists in Germany were beyond suspicion, Tom knew. But to scare the world into becoming something it never dreamed imaginable, terrorists needed to make noise that went beyond the sounds of explosions and agony. They needed to manufacture, in the minds of their prey, potential scenarios that justified tactics previously unjustifiable. They needed to unravel the fabric that held cultures together.

Silence achieved none of those objectives.

The simple fact was, nothing indicated that the crash was the result of anything other than a total failure of the flight controls, and no one really expected Tom to discover anything different. His mission, Mallory said, was basic: "I want to know whatever the Cheerleader knows before the Cheerleader knows she knows it."

He closed the briefing book, and then took another distant, unaffected look toward Backpack Man. Hell, he mused, maybe that guy was the culprit. Strange behavior, looks the part, fits the profile. Maybe he even knew Tom was on the plane and was going to blow it out of the sky before the evil truth could be exposed.

A small, easy smile flickered on Tom's face, and he shook his head at the absurdity of the thought. This wasn't a terrorist hunt. It was a fool's errand, and Mallory was counting on him to play the fool. He had no problem with that. Munich, he was already convinced, held no secrets.

He was sure of it.

SIXTEEN

DEPLANING AT TERMINAL 2 of Munich's airport, a half-groggy Tom Fargo wandered through the broad, bright, high-ceilinged steel-and-glass structure. He was struck by how wide everything was—the common spaces, check-in areas, passenger thoroughfares—and the conspicuous lack of tension. There was none of the angst or panic he'd seen in places like Atlanta, where sweating fliers loaded down with boxcar-sized carry-ons raced from one gate to another in a futile effort to make their connection.

No, this place was calm, comfortable. Maybe it was the lighting, the airiness. Even the passport screening process and Customs were a snap, no small achievement in an insecure world.

Tom had been advised by one of the legislative aides in his office to take the S-Bahn into the city center, a 45-minute train ride that was far less stressful than navigating Munich's clogged roads. But he'd always found rail travel oddly unfamiliar, possessing its own rules and conventions, all of which were as elusive as the wind to him. So he opted for a cab. In search of a taxi stand, he made a wrong turn in Terminal 2 that led him to the bustling business-and-retail Munich Airport Center—open air, big as a jet hangar and modern as a spaceship, with a tent-like semitransparent roof—and eventually to the expansive apron outside Terminal 1.

Where he saw something totally unexpected:

A swarthy man in a suit, standing in front of a large black car, holding a plain white sign on which had been hand-lettered, "Tom Phargo."

Tom stopped, waited, looked around.

Phargo. A mistake?

No one had said there would be a car waiting, either, and Mallory had been insistent that he have a wallet full of euros for the cab ride in.

Something wasn't right.

He took another second to weigh his options and quickly decided that the best place to be was back inside the terminal, where he could keep an eye on the man with the sign and see if some other Tom *Phargo* turned up or the driver just got impatient and left.

What he'd do after that was anybody's guess, but this was starting to feel like a one-step-at-a-time strategy. He'd figure out the next steps if and when the time came to take them.

Glancing quickly at the sign guy one more time, Tom tried to dam up the adrenaline flow by taking a deep breath and then walked back toward the doors into Terminal 1. With each step he felt a little better, even starting to think this was not some spy game, that his safety extended only as far as his paranoia allowed, and he wasn't ready to surrender to imaginary villains just yet.

Five feet from the door, a man with a bullet head and a kickboxer's build materialized.

He smiled and said softly, "I'm afraid that's the wrong direction, Mr. Fargo."

Tom froze, eyes alive and active, like a hostage looking for some way out.

"There's no reason for alarm," the man said. "We just need a few minutes of your time." The voice was as soothing as it was threatening.

Tom looked around at his fellow travelers, none of whom seemed aware of his presence, as if he were invisible. He tried to speak, but nothing came out, his mouth suspended in a silent O.

"We have a car for you."

Over his shoulder, Tom saw the man with the sign. *Phargo*. The guy shrugged easily and grinned broadly.

"Please, Mr. Fargo." Bullet Head gently pulled Tom away from the door, away from human traffic, toward the vehicle.

Not having any idea what his next move was—so much for the one-step-at-a-time strategy—Tom numbly went along. But as he approached the car, the shock and confusion gave way to a dread that gripped him like a seizure.

Bullet Head noticed.

Opening the door, he said, "Relax, Mr. Fargo. Your death does not serve our current purpose."

Current purpose?

Tom felt his dread spike, and it was so intense, so suddenly relentless, that when the man said, "We mustn't keep your date waiting," he thought he'd lost his mind, that the fear had already consumed him, pushed him beyond the limits of reason, into a maze of irrationality as dark and bewildering as a dream of death.

SEVENTEEN

"DO YOU KNOW who I am, Mr. Fargo?" She took one final draw on the unfiltered Gitanes Brune and stubbed it out in a square glass ashtray.

Other than the black-fading-to-gray hair, a face that was as thin and sharp as a knife blade, and dark eyes that were puddles of eerie ambivalence, Tom had no idea. But on a continuum between intimidating and seductive, she somehow managed to hit the extremes of both.

He shook his head, apprehension and confusion on full display, and mopped a trickle of sweat from his forehead.

She smiled, though not in triumph, and caught the eye of a waiter. "The whiskey list here is quite good," she said to Tom. "Expensive, but good. Shall I order for both of us?" Not waiting for a reply, she chose Jameson Rarest Vintage Reserve and, looking at Tom's still-stricken expression, added: "Make his a double." She had a vague accent that seemed more of the world than of any nation in it.

The bar was one of those out-of-the-way places that was a favorite of Munich's in-crowd, dark wood and dense with cigarette smoke, accented by muted lighting that made anyone look good. Low-key, too, not a lot of glamour, cozy in a way that suggested discretion was a specialty of the house.

A place, in other words, where secrets were safe.

"Call me Anath," she said when their drinks arrived. They each took a sip, Tom's a bit more ample than hers. Around them, the sounds of Thelonious Monk cut subtly through the room, Anath's right hand with its purple-polished fingernails tapping an accompaniment to "Between the Devil and the Deep Blue Sea" on the square wooden table. "I trust your flight was good." He shrugged. "Jet lag?"

Unlike Tom, whose nerves were electric, she had a certain peace about her, a calm, like a still lake. It was unsettling. He took another slug of the whiskey and shrugged again.

Anath smiled and nodded.

At the bar, a martini-drinking woman threw an occasional glance in their direction. In her tailored, dark-blue, short-skirted suit, she looked like a corporate hooker, which may have explained why the well-dressed businessman was chatting her up so intently.

"It is perhaps good that I am a stranger to you. It reduces, how shall I say it, your . . . exposure," Anath said. Tom's nerves sparked a little hotter. "Do you know why you are here, Mr. Fargo?"

"In Munich?"

Her eyes flashed. "Do not make this any more difficult than is necessary."

A sudden tightness gripped Tom's rib cage, as if a too-small elastic band had been wrapped around it twice. His hands began to tingle. "I'm sorry, I'm sorry, I didn't mean anything."

Anath took a sip of her drink, savored it for just a moment, and pulled another cigarette from the black, blue, and white box whose cover bore the silhouette of a tambourine-playing gypsy. "You are here, Mr. Fargo, because I would like you to take a message to your government."

Alarm and bewilderment chased each other across Tom's face. "A message?"

She nodded. "A personal message, from me."

"I'm not authorized to do that," he sputtered. "It's illegal for me to engage in anything that resembles foreign policy-making or negotiations on behalf of—"

"I know exactly who you are, Mr. Fargo," she interrupted, the anger in her eyes shifting to her voice. "And as to this issue of legality versus illegality, well, let us say we are both on a somewhat perilous perch."

Tom just stared at her. "I don't understand."

"Given the task before us, that is one of your better attributes."

His hands stopped tingling. They started to burn. His eyes wandered back to the bar, where he caught the corporate-hooker woman of interest looking at him again. The hand that wrapped around her martini glass was adorned with a diamond bracelet worth twice the gross domestic product of a mid-sized African country. She toasted him, ever so slightly, and turned back to her businessman suitor.

Tom turned back to Anath. "What's the message?"

She shook her head. "In a moment." For the first time, Tom noticed that half of her ring finger was missing. "Do I look like a murderer to you, Mr. Fargo?" The question came out of nowhere. "Humor me, please, and be honest."

"You scare the hell out of me," he blurted, wanting to reel the words back as soon as he heard himself speak them.

Anath's laugh was deep, and reeked of cigarettes and alcohol. "I am very grateful for the compliment, but in your best political fashion, you have avoided the question. So I repeat: Do I look like a murderer to you?"

"No," he replied after a moment of considering if there was a right or a wrong answer.

She nodded. "But in some circles, including those in which you occasionally travel, I am labeled as such. A cold-blooded killer of men and women and children."

"Are you?"

"Do I appear as one who could harm a child?"

Tom said nothing.

Anath smiled, finished her drink, and ordered two more. "Do you know what terrorism is?" she asked after the waiter had come and gone. "It is the last refuge of people for whom honor is no longer an option, people for whom the threat of ideological perversion or political persecution is so serious, so severe, that they feel compelled to embrace the very means they might otherwise deplore in order to achieve, how to put it, how to put it . . . " She paused, maybe for effect, Tom couldn't tell. "A balance of interests. The lesser evil. The greater good." She shrugged. "However one defines that."

He just stared at her, the sweat starting to flow more freely, an unmistakable warning from deep within his once-tortured soul that the fears he'd left behind years ago were now racing to catch back up with him.

"When those of us in the, oh, the *underground*, engage in such acts, regardless of intent, we are immediately cast as instruments of terror. But when you in the *over-ground* engage in parallel acts, it is considered an instrument of policy, even patriotism. Why is that?"

Their drinks arrived. Anath sipped hers. Tom's went untouched.

"I have a philosophy about that," she said, answering her own question.

Her comparison of terrorism and patriotism hit Tom's brain like acid, momentarily burning off any dread. He held her stare. "I'm not surprised."

She leaned in toward him, and spoke in a harsh whisper. "The underground, with all of its bombs and hijackings and beheadings, is so much more open about its activities. So thoroughly democratic."

"That's bullshit." Not worrying about what he said or wanting to reel the words in.

Anath was unfazed by his directness. "I prefer to say it is ironic." She pulled away from him. "But I am, after all, a member of the so-called underground. So my comments must be taken with as many granules of salt as you feel appropriate."

"Grains," he corrected her, more out of spite than anything else. "Grains of salt."

Another smoky, whiskey-drenched laugh. "Such precision of language. Would that your politics have such clarity."

Tom said nothing, feeling oddly liberated, as if firing back at Anath had rejuvenated him and crippled the inevitable return of his anxiety. He tented his hands in front of him on the table and looked toward the bar, where the businessman was showing his new $500-an-hour friend something on a cell phone, then back at Anath. "So why am I here?"

"Ah, the very question with which our little rendezvous commenced."

Tom felt like she was toying with him and, worse, enjoying it. "And apparently the one," he shot back, standing, "with which it's gonna end."

Two men, the bullet-headed kickboxer and the Mercedes driver, appeared as if conjured from the air.

Anath sighed wearily. "Sit, Mr. Fargo. Please."

Tom looked at the two men, and despite his surge of defiance thought it better to choose common sense over bravado. He sat. The two men vanished as quickly as they had come.

At the bar, the businessman and the girl had swapped seats, apparently so he could get a better shot of her from his camera phone. She laughed and posed.

"So are you going to answer my question," Tom asked, "or are we just going to sit here, pleasantly discussing actions that are anything but pleasant?"

Anath eyed him coolly. "You are very assured in your beliefs, are you not?"

He didn't flinch. "I am."

She kept his gaze. "You are a true believer, then?"

"Is there any other kind?"

An odd, caustic smile screwed its way onto her lips. "Beware, then, as beliefs are a moral act for which the believer must be held accountable."

"I'll gladly take that responsibility."

The caustic smile slid into sympathy. "Of course you will. But tell me, your belief, is it based on evidence? Truth? Or do you believe simply because you have a blind need to do so?"

"What difference does it make? Why do you believe whatever you believe?"

She wagged a tut-tut-tutting finger at him. "I never said I was a believer, Mr. Fargo."

"Then what are you?"

"A capitalist." She saw the disorientation on his face, the inability to align what he thought about her with what she'd just said, and reached out to pat his arm with unexpected gentleness. "Now, Mr. Fargo, I want you to go back to America and advise your superiors that this ornamental investigation of Senator Platte's death must stop immediately."

It was hard to say what stunned Tom more—the order, the description of Toni Allura's probe as "ornamental," or the sudden injection of the plane crash into the discussion. But in that instant, a sky of confusion opened up and shock rained down. "Uh, I'm afraid I don't have that kind of pull."

The gentle pat became a blood-constricting grip. "Then I suggest you find it."

Tom swallowed hard and bit the inside of his right cheek.

Anath stood. "My driver will now take you back to the airport."

"No, no, wait," he sputtered, "I've got work to do here, a job—"

"Your job is done," she said coldly, turning and walking toward the door and the Promenadeplatz outside, nodding indifferently to a seductive blonde in a matching leather skirt and vest. Tom hesitated and then followed, grabbing Anath's shoulder from behind, knowing instantly he'd made a mistake when she spun and looked at him with a depth of hostility he'd never before seen.

But he didn't buckle. "I still don't understand."

"Of course you don't, Mr. Fargo. That is why you are here." With that, she disappeared into the Munich night.

At the bar, the man with the camera phone watched her go, then looked at Tom, then smiled at the girl in the short-skirted dark-blue suit and asked if she knew where the men's room was.

EIGHTEEN

FROM THE FAR end of the bar, Keios watched the businessman smile and say something to the girl in the dark-blue suit. The man leaned in to hear her words over the music, which seemed to have grown louder with the hour.

Keios hated jazz, thought it was a pretentious art form embraced by smug people who believed it gave them a veneer of cultural superiority. He preferred opera, liked the fact that it was more white noise than music, loud but somehow comforting, filling the silence without making any demands on his attention.

The businessman slipped off the barstool and made his way through a thickening crowd into a dark hallway that led to the restrooms. Keios tracked his movements, wondering if this was as it appeared or something else, something to do with the photos he had not so casually taken of Fargo and the terrorist.

At his feet, an oversized messenger bag concealed a 9mm Welrod Mark I, a later version of the vintage World War II pistol that had been the preferred handgun in places like Korea, the Falkland Islands, Vietnam, and Northern Ireland. Basically a steel tube with a barrel, single-stack magazine, and bolt, the Welrod had a twofold advantage:

First, it was clean, without any markings that could identify its manufacturer or nation of origin. Second, it was built around an integrated suppressor that delivered a quiet kill even in the absence of direct contact with the target.

The perfect assassin's pistol, so deadly that Great Britain still classified it under the Official Secrets Act. Although out of production, it had been the wet-work handgun of choice for Keios since the first Gulf War.

As he watched the man turn down the hallway, the leather-clad blonde who'd aimed a come-on look at Anath slid by, smoking a cigarette like it was a sex act. She caught his gaze briefly and opened her brightly painted red lips in a slim smile, no mystery in the expression, just a silent hint of what could follow.

She paused briefly at the opposite end of the bar, whispering something to a thin girl in painted-on jeans who had the gaunt look of someone in the second month of a hunger strike. The girl laughed, the two exchanged a quick kiss, and the woman disappeared around the corner and into the hallway.

Keios rose and followed—the man, not the blonde—the messenger bag in hand.

Passing the businessman's martini-sipping hoped-for evening conquest, he lowered his head to avoid eye contact. He was reasonably certain she was uninvolved, her role in the picture-taking notwithstanding, but there was no point giving her a full-on view of his face.

He reached the hallway, turned into it, began walking toward a heavy door beneath a sign that read *Ausgang.*

Exit.

Keios stopped in front of the door. To his right, another door, *Manner* posted in raised chrome lettering. To his left, *Frauen.*

He glanced back toward the bar to see if he'd been followed, intentionally or otherwise.

Satisfied no one was paying him any undue attention, he opened the flap of the messenger bag, wrapped his hand around the designed-for-comfort rubber pistol grip, and pushed into the men's room.

It was small, three urinals opposite three stalls with wooden doors that nearly stretched to the ceiling. Soft mood lights threw a subtle glow onto black- and white-tiled floors. The walls were dark and marbled. By the shallow silver sinks, linen-like hand towels sat stacked on longish ceramic plates. No jazz came through the speakers, just a woman's voice, sultry yet mechanical.

"*Guten tag,*" it said. "*How do you do?*"

Keios removed the Welrod, carefully pushed open the first stall.

"*Was ist dein Name? What is your name?*"

Empty.

"*Wo ist der Bahnhof? Where is the train station?*"

He stepped toward the second stall, nudged it ajar with the Welrod's barrel.

Nothing.

"*Kann ich Ihnen helfen? Can I help you?*"

Keios paused in front of the third stall, fixed his grip on the pistol, inhaled slightly.

"Suchen jemanden für spezielle?"

Except the voice that asked if he was looking for someone special was neither mechanical nor sultry, and there was no translation, and Keios kicked in the stall door in to see the blonde, bright red lips tightened into a toxic smile, standing on the commode, in one hand holding a cell phone, in the other a 9mm Smith & Wesson Sigma.

She straddled the businessman, who sat slumped on the toilet seat, a single bloody hole in his chest, eyes and mouth wide open in a terrified I-can't-believe-I'm-about-to-die expression.

"Stellen Sie den Welrod hin."

Keios set his pistol on the floor, as ordered.

"Machen Sie einen Schritt zurück."

He again did as told, taking a step back. The woman, still smiling, got down from the toilet seat.

"Irgedwelche anderen Waffen?"

Keios gestured to his coat pocket.

She nodded once, signaling him to remove whatever remaining weapon he had.

With his left hand in the air, Keios slowly slipped his right hand inside the jacket, and into the pocket, wrapping it around the small cigarette-package-sized device, which he pulled out with the speed and suddenness of a meteor shooting across the sky, jamming the side button with his thumb, releasing a million volts of electricity, stunning the woman, dissolving the smile, sending her into unspeakable pain, turning her legs to wet noodles, her entire body quivering and then collapsing.

Just as quickly, he grabbed the Welrod and fired once. The woman's head came apart like a melon. The cell phone clattered onto the tile floor.

Keios picked it up and spun around, and in three steps was out the door. With a quick look to be certain his would-be killer didn't have any backup, he turned to his right, pushed through the *Ausgang* into a dark alley, then strode with a careful but easy purpose onto the Löwengrube toward the U-Bahn at Marienplatz and into the brightly lit orange passenger tunnel. He waited at the platform, trying to blend in. After a minute or two, rumbling filled the air, announcing the blue train's arrival. Keios stepped into the second car, dropping into a seat halfway back, behind a young couple encumbered with backpacks and hope.

Settling in, he pulled out the dead businessman's cell phone, which was open to the Sent window on the email program. One email had gone out in the past 30 minutes, to an address that had no name or recognized domain, just a3345161159@uggsrock.com.

While he knew it was pointless, Keios tapped the Write Message icon, typed in the address, and wrote *Confirm receipt* in the subject line.

Almost instantly, a Mail Undeliverable response kicked back, confirming what he suspected: Whoever received what the businessman had sent was using a temporary address that expired quickly, probably in 10 minutes, maybe even less.

The train slowed to a stop. The young couple exited. Keios eyed them distantly, then returned his attention to the cell.

He pushed a button that brought up the master screen, and

tapped the phone icon. A clock symbol appeared, taking him to a list of recent calls made.

At the top was a number he didn't recognize, but an area code he did: 202.

Washington, D.C.

Silent alarms started going off in every part of his brain.

He exited that screen, went back and quickly studied the phantom email.

It had been sent moments after the call was made.

Keios pieced a scenario together:

The businessman, or whatever he was, makes a call, gives the recipient a heads-up that he's sending the email, sends it, and then is murdered. In the absence of a subsequent email, logic would suggest that the next step would be a follow-up phone call confirming the message had been received.

He dialed the 202 number. Waited.

One ring—

Two—

Three—

Then a voice that came into his ear like a bullet—

"Talk to me, Bob—"

Searing his consciousness—

"Who's that Fargo is with, the woman—"

Sounding less cool and confident than it had just days before, talking to Matt Lauer on the *Today* show, in the announcement that had set this dark enterprise in motion—

"What's going on? I don't know what this means."

Keios stared at the cell as if it were malignant, thinking—

And you never will—

Then feeling an uncharacteristic surge of anger mixed with a betrayal he should have known would come eventually—

Because as of this moment, Senator Allura, our agreement is no longer in force—

And we are no longer co-conspirators.

NINETEEN

ON THE FLIGHT back from Munich, Tom tried not to stare at the man sitting a few rows up in the passenger seat across the jet's aisle. But he couldn't help it. Something about the guy wasn't right.

He didn't look like an Arab in the strictest sense, wasn't wearing one of those ankle-length dress things or a white knitted skullcap. But he was, he had to be, all his features were dark, the skin and the hair, and the beard would be, too, if he had one, but he didn't, which Tom thought was pretty damned suspicious for an Arab.

Tom adjusted himself, shifting his body this way and that way, trying to get comfortable, to tamp down the nervous energy, not having a lot of success, still feeling jittery, like he'd just mainlined a case of Red Bull.

The Arab wore a gray suit, a nice one, and when he'd come on the plane, he'd taken the jacket off and folded it carefully and set it in the overhead compartment on top of a small rolling suitcase. Again, it didn't feel right, just didn't fit—the Arab looks, the sharp suit—and that made Tom even more suspicious.

He inhaled deeply, trying to slow his pounding heart.

At the man's feet, tucked under the seat in front of him, was what looked like a computer bag, except it was a bit thicker, as if there was something else in there, something that wasn't a laptop—

"Sir, can I get you something to drink?"

The flight attendant's question startled Tom so much he felt dizzy. Tiny pinpricks of pain stabbed at his face. "No, no," he managed, throat dry. "I'm, uh, I'm good." He felt sweat start to pool at his hairline.

"Maybe some water?"

He forced a smile. "Just a little light-headed. Long day."

She didn't look convinced. "Well, if you need me, just ring the call button."

He nodded, looked at the Arab in the custom-tailored suit, and then back at the flight attendant. His eyes asked if she was seeing what he was seeing. Her eyes said she was looking at a basket case.

"You're sure you're okay?"

He nodded again, this time a little faster. "Yeah. Sorry. I get anxious on long flights, that's all. Feeling closed in. Claustrophobic."

She scanned the wide-bodied jet. "There's an exit row seat open, if you'd like a little more room."

Tom eyed the suit-wearing Arab and decided it wouldn't be wise to put any more distance between them. Another weak smile. "I'll manage."

"Okay, then. Let me know if you change your mind." She hit him with a look that straddled compassionate and get-the-straitjacket-now, and continued making her rounds.

The Arab reached under the seat in front of him and pulled out the laptop bag. If it was a laptop bag.

"Christ," Tom muttered. "This is bad." He glanced quickly at the girl next to him in the window seat, a thin, chirpy 20-something who'd told him in great detail about her Internet startup—scheduling exotic dancers in Des Moines—before falling asleep 45 minutes into the flight. She snored softly.

Not much help there, he thought.

Directly across the aisle, a huge black guy in a New Orleans Saints jersey grooved slowly to whatever was coming out of the Beats by Dre headphones. Tom caught his attention and threw a slight head gesture toward the Arab. The black guy shrugged and closed his eyes.

Tom closed his as well. But no sooner had the world gone dark than he felt as if he were floating away. He opened them.

The Arab unzipped the computer bag and reached in.

Tom's throat tightened. He glanced up at the call button, then leaned into the aisle and looked behind him, for the exit.

The Arab pulled something out, a sealed envelope—

The pinpricks of pain in Tom's face exploded into shooting pains—

Opened the envelope, looked around with a thin, calculating Arab smile—

The pain spread north to Tom's scalp, south to his neck—

Peered inside—

Tom's ears started to ring—

Turned the envelope upside down—

Tom closed his eyes again, seeing flashing lights in the darkness of his mind, unable to stand it, opening them, looking at the suit-wearing Arab terrorist as—

Something fell out of the envelope—

"Anthrax," Tom whispered.

Trying to be as calm as the crisis would allow, searching for the flight attendant, hitting the call button, unbuckling his seat belt, he'd be damned if he'd let the same thing happen to these people that happened to his father, reaching for his briefcase, undoing the snaps, finding a pen among the papers, thinking it wasn't much of a weapon but not caring, watching as the killer chemical slid from the envelope, white powdered death—

Except it wasn't white, and it wasn't powder.

It was shiny, and it sparkled, even in the dull light of the cabin.

Tom sagged back into his seat in relief—they weren't all going to die, the anthrax wasn't anthrax, it was only confetti in a birthday card—just as the flight attendant arrived.

She reached up and turned off the call button light.

"Can I get you something, sir?"

The ringing in his ears had grown so intense it nearly drowned out her voice. "Uh, yeah. I think I'll have a scotch. A double."

She nodded hesitantly and left.

Tom looked at his watch.

Five hours until they landed at Dulles.

Five hours.

Then he could make the call.

TWENTY

"I WAS A little surprised to hear from you."

Tom shrugged and looked warily around the diner. It was early Saturday morning, and the breakfast crowd was thin. One person was at the counter, a truck driver, drinking coffee and working on a Danish, chatting up the uninterested teenaged waitress between chews. Two booths were occupied, a pair of working girls in one, looking gray and exhausted, a guy in a wrinkled suit in the other, chin in his chest, half-asleep, like he was coming off a bad bender.

"Flashback," Tom said. "You know."

The man sitting opposite him in the booth nodded. "Been a long time."

"Yes. Yes, it has."

Nick Rousakis stared at him. He was 50-ish, medium height, naturally bald, wearing a black mock turtleneck and a gold chain necklace with a one-inch sacred snake pendant. His voice was soft, almost reassuring, but Tom knew better. "Something happen?"

Tom looked over his shoulder, toward the front door, then back at Nick. "You mind if, uh, we swap places, so my back's, you know, to the wall?"

Nick nodded. They changed positions. "Something did happen. Want to talk about it?"

"Is this is a therapy session?" He drummed the thumb and little finger of his right hand on the table.

Nick shook his head. "No. This is a transaction. But when your customer is someone who has the ear of one of the most powerful men in D.C., well, one likes to get the lay of the land."

"That wasn't a concern in the old days."

"In the *old days*, my friend, you were a troubled young man who was never more than a bad moment away from swan-diving off the Washington Monument."

The finger-drumming stopped. "I got through that. I'll get through this." Nick kept staring, with neither expression nor judgment. Tom took a sip of water. "What?"

"I do not know exactly what it is you do, Thomas. What goes on in your world, it has no meaning for me. Still, I have concerns."

"About?"

Nick picked at the remains of his breakfast, moving the scrambled eggs and orange slices around on the plate before taking the last bite of a sausage patty. "As I said, about whether I should be selling my goods to a man who now advises the man whose job it is to protect this country."

Tom let out a dismissive laugh. "C'mon, we're not talking crack here. It's not like I'm going to be trading state secrets for a piece of the rock."

"Yes, that is true."

"Then what's the problem?"

"Do you not find it odd that one such as yourself, a bright fellow who has an important part to play in the nation's security, must seek out personal security from an illegally obtained controlled substance?"

From across the diner, the two working girls whooped in laughter. The trucker turned toward them and unconsciously licked his lips.

"It's not an illegal substance."

Nick smiled. "I did not say it was. I said it was illegally obtained."

Tom sat back in the booth and crossed his arms. "Okay. Fine.

You got me."

"That is not my intention, Thomas. Not at all."

"Then what is?"

A long pause. "I simply want to be certain that you know what you are doing, that you understand there are consequences."

"I know exactly what I'm doing."

"And do you know the consequences?"

"You mean like, drowsiness? Relax, I don't plan on operating any heavy equipment."

The smile hardened but did not vanish. "That is a side effect, Thomas. Side effects are your problem, not mine."

"How is this your problem?"

"It is my problem because you are who you are, and you do what you do, and any erratic behavior might raise unwanted eyebrows and possibly, just possibly, bring unwelcome visitors to my doorstep."

Tom's eyes widened. "You think I'd give you up?"

Nick shook his head. "You are smarter than that."

"Then what are you afraid of?" Nick didn't answer, instead slipping his hand under the table. For an instant, Tom thought he was going for a gun. But what he fished out and put between them was a container of round, orange tablets, a large K engraved in the center of each. Tom could not hide his disappointment. "No Xanax?"

"It was short notice. You get what the medicine cabinet dispenses."

"I've never taken Klonopin."

"It works well. Dissolve one half-milligram tablet under your tongue, three times a day, the last before you go to sleep. You will begin to feel the positive effects in as few as 30 minutes, and they last a minimum of six hours. Not as strong as Xanax, but you will function perfectly normal. No feeling of being drugged up. No severe side effects."

Tom nodded lifelessly. "Sold." He slid three $100 bills, folded and paper-clipped into a tight square, toward Nick, and picked up the bottle and examined the label. It looked like a typical prescription from Walgreens, down to the dosage, expiration date, and physician name. One thing caught his eye. He looked up. "No refills? Are you sending me some kind of message?"

Nick pocketed the money and put on a small hat that reminded Tom of the one Rocky wore in the movies. "One day at a time, Thomas. One day at a time." He stood.

"Wait. You didn't tell me."

"Tell you?"

"What you're afraid of."

Nick sat back down. "I like you, Thomas. I do. You are interesting to me, much more so than suburban housewives in Manassas or night watchmen and security guards in Herndon."

"Do I feel a *but* coming on?"

"Yes. And it is this: But you are trying to escape from a world of uncertainty into a world of safety. And the harder you try, the more difficult the effort becomes. And at some point, it becomes so difficult, and your pursuit so zealous, that you lose your direction, and you can no longer see the line that separates the ranks of the sane from the ranks of the mad, and you step over it." He paused. "That is what I am afraid of."

Tom shook the bottle of pills. "This stuff doesn't make me crazy. It keeps me level."

He nodded sadly. "Just remember, my friend, that wherever there is life, there is danger. From that fact, there is no escaping."

The finger-drumming resumed. "Is there a threat in there someplace?"

Nick stood once again. "Do not lose your direction, Thomas. That is all I am asking." He turned and walked through the door, the tinny ringing of a bell announcing his exit.

Tom watched him climb into a yellow Cadillac and drive off. Then he unscrewed the container, pulled out one of the Klonopin tablets and slipped it under his tongue, looking at his watch and calculating, hoping that the desired peace would arrive before his next stop.

TWENTY-ONE

TOM SAT IN Penn Mallory's study, staring at the floor, grateful the anti-anxiety drug had smoothed out his edge without putting him down. He was a little sleepy, which wasn't unexpected. It had been years since he'd taken his last pill, and experience told him that the drowsiness might stick around for a day or so until his body adjusted.

Not that it mattered. This was a temporary thing. He just needed to get over the hump. A couple of good nights' sleep and everything would be back to normal.

"You look like stir-fried shit, son."

Tom looked up at Mallory, whose face was creased with concern. "I feel like I was born and brought up in an airplane."

"We can finish this later if you'd like."

"I'm good." He coughed.

The senator leaned back in the oversized old-English-looking swivel chair at his desk, took a sip of Wild Turkey. "So lemme get this straight. Two guys hijack you at the airport, stuff you in a Mercedes, and take you to a jazz bar for drinks with a terrorist."

Put that way, it sounded more than a little bizarre. "Pretty much."

"And her message to us, through you, was to end the Cheerleader's investigation into Harry's death?"

"I believe her exact words were *ornamental investigation*."

"On which account, she is of course correct."

Tom's head swung in the direction of the voice, to the door of the study, where Vance Harriman had materialized.

"I asked Vance to stop by and hear your story firsthand without me mangling it," Mallory said. "After all, he's the pro at this kind of thing."

Harriman nodded and smiled shyly, as if embarrassed by the compliment. Although Tom had assumed this would just be between him and his boss, he was too tired to care much about a third party in the room. "That's fine, it's okay. Thanks for being here, Mr. Director."

"May I sit?" Asking Tom, not Mallory, which was interesting. Tom shrugged his assent, and Harriman took a seat next to him on the semi-battered Chesterfield sofa. He handed Tom a folder. "Can I assume that this was your contact?"

Contact?

The word, and its baggage, jolted Tom to mental attention. He opened the folder, Anath staring back at him, her expression as cruel, cold, and ruthless as a Russian winter. "Yeah." He dropped it onto the antique table in front of them and looked up at Harriman. "And for the record, *contact* implies an agreed-to arrangement. This was not agreed to, and I got the clear sense it was either be there or be killed."

Harriman's right eye twitched. "Of course. An unfortunate choice of words. I apologize."

"No apologies necessary, Vance. Tom's tired as a dog, and probably a little bit shaky at the moment, and that's understandable. So why don't you go on and tell us what you know about this lunatic bitch who threatened my guy."

Tom didn't acknowledge Mallory's assessment of his condition or the undercurrent of protective concern in his voice.

"Her name is Seraphina Livini," Harriman began, "and she—"

"That's not what she told me," Tom interrupted. "She told me—"

"To call her Anath." Harriman nodded and stood, starting to walk the room, looking at the volumes in Mallory's bookshelves as he spoke, the whole act seeming to Tom like a none-too-subtle effort at casual misdirection that had been rehearsed to perfection.

"Anath is the name she has taken," he went on. "A goddess of war and fertility. A protector. A bloodthirsty agent of vengeance. In ancient Egypt she was called the 'victorious, a woman acting as a man, clad as a male and girt as a female.'"

"Sounds like a nasty piece of work," Mallory said.

Harriman nodded and continued the walking book tour as he ticked off the greatest hits on Seraphina Livini's resume. "Educated in Paris, the daughter of Zionist guerrillas. Began her career managing safe houses for Mossad hit teams and graduated to service in elite covert units that targeted and assassinated Palestinians throughout Europe."

"I take it back," Mallory said. "She doesn't *sound* like a nasty piece of work. She *is* a nasty piece of work."

Harriman grimaced. "And she is exceptional at what she does. While there is no proof, she is widely believed to have infiltrated an Abu Nidal splinter group and is credited with the systematic murder of its leadership. In the early days of the Iraqi atomic program, she posed as a prostitute to lure an Egyptian-born scientist who was working on the project to her bed. They made love for an hour. Then she slit his throat."

Tom shook his head, as if trying to clear some cobwebs. "Wait a second. So what are you saying? She's one of us?"

"Perhaps. Once." Harriman returned to the sofa and sat. "But for Seraphina Livini, there is no longer any *us*. Or, for that matter, any *them*."

"Which means what?"

"She is on nobody's side."

"A mercenary?"

"Mercenaries have no convictions. She has no soul. There is a difference."

Tom wasn't entirely sure what that meant, but it sounded ominous, and he chose not to pursue it.

Penn Mallory lit a fat cigar. "So you're saying she's a switch-hitting terrorist?"

The study was as silent as snow for about 30 seconds while Harriman considered the question. "I don't know what she is, exactly," he said at last. "I do know she left Mossad right after 9/11 under circumstances best described as murky, and has been underground ever since."

"She talked about that," Tom remembered, "about going underground."

Mallory leaned forward at his desk. "Anything in particular?"

"No, nothing specific. Just some boilerplate rhetoric about there being no real difference between what the underground and the 'over-ground' do, and how terrorists are more democratic because they do what they do in the open."

Mallory and Harriman traded a quick, guarded glance. Tom caught it, wondering if the look meant anything, then quickly attributed his reaction to a flare-up of the one or two nerves the Klonopin hadn't yet filed down.

Harriman did not set aside his own concerns quite so discreetly. "Why you?" he said to Tom, without warning or setup. His tone wasn't exactly accusatory. It wasn't exactly sympathetic, either.

Tom felt the subtext of the question and tightened, firing Harriman a look that all but shouted his irritation at the unstated but—at least to him—clear inference that he was somehow complicit in what had happened. "Your guess is as good as mine."

"I make it a habit not to guess. It reduces the likelihood of accuracy."

Mallory sensed the tension, again, and stepped in. "It's not an unreasonable question, Tom."

"I don't resent the question, Senator, just the way it was asked."

Harriman's right eye twitched once more. "Nothing was intended."

Which was a lie, and all three of them knew it.

Tom massaged his forehead and went to the bar, pouring himself a glass of water. "Look, I have no idea why she chose me. I mean, how could she even know I was going to be in Munich?"

Mallory dropped the cigar in an ashtray, picked up a copy of the *Post*, a 1-A headline trumpeting Toni Allura's investigation, and walked it over to Tom. "Eighth paragraph."

In the initial phase of the probe, Thomas Fargo, the top aide to Sen. Penn Mallory, the Florida Republican who reportedly played an essential behind-the-scenes role in engineering Platte's all-but-announced nomination as Defense Secretary, will travel to Munich.

Tom looked up, lost, and shook his head. "Where'd that come from?"

"You tell us," Vance Harriman said.

Tom's eyes dug into his face. "You want to make an accusation, make it. But otherwise, get off my back."

"Shut up, Tom," Mallory ordered, then turned to the CIA nominee. "For Chrissakes, Vance, it could've come from anywhere. This is Washington, remember, and Washington leaks like a baby— from both ends, the top, and the bottom."

"But never without an agenda."

"What possible agenda could I have?" Tom nearly screamed.

"Enough! Tom, go to the kitchen. Give me a moment alone with Vance."

Tom hesitated, unsure whether being banished from the room was punishment. Then he did as instructed, not looking at Harriman, who followed his exit with lifeless eyes.

"Listen to me, Vance, and listen good," Mallory said. "We need Tom Fargo."

"With all due respect, Senator, we need people we can trust to do what needs to be done."

"I understand that."

"Do you?"

Fury rose on Mallory's face like a radioactive flood. "Are you talking about Tom here, Vance? Or about me?" The words were clenched-fist hard.

Harriman's voice softened but did not entirely abandon its severity. "What I am saying, sir, is that we are already having to manage two rogues in this crazed Jew terrorist Anath and the junior senator from Prada. It is not to our advantage, to any of our advantage, should a third emerge."

"Jesus Christ, Tom Fargo ain't gonna go rogue. He's straight as a plumb line, and his heart and head are exactly where we need 'em to be. He'll do whatever I tell him to do, and he won't ask any questions, and once he gets a bone in his mouth, he won't let go. So you will cut him the necessary slack until events dictate otherwise. We straight?"

The qualifier, *until events dictate otherwise*, left enough doors open to satisfy Harriman, at least for the moment. "Yes, sir, we are."

"Good." Mallory nodded once and called out, "Fargo, get your ass back in here." Tom returned as ordered, sitting down without so much as a sideways glance at Harriman. Mallory went back to his desk and retrieved the cigar. "Now you two need to quit shootin' at each other and keep your aim on the real enemy."

"Anath?" Tom said.

"Senator Sis Boom Bah," Mallory said.

"No question," Harriman agreed.

Tom stared at them as if they'd suddenly turned into aliens.

"It's true," Mallory continued. "She leaked it. Had to. It gives her whole investigation the veneer of propriety, official-ness, the idea that Harry's biggest benefactor in the Senate—that would be me—has put his top guy on the case." More of the Deep South was migrating into his words. "I'm telling y'all: *She* is the enemy." He drained the bourbon, landing the glass back on his desk with a wooden crack.

Vance Harriman had spent his life navigating a world where things were often not as they appeared. It was his job to see what wasn't there, and even Tom had to concede he was good at it. But Mallory? To the extent that any politician could—and Tom thought most had a streak of psycho in them, some wider than others—Mallory existed in this world, the real world, and had been able to separate what was possible from what was paranoia.

Until now.

"And she's running for president," Mallory said, almost as an afterthought.

An odd sound came from Vance Harriman, equal parts chuckle, growl, and sneer.

Mallory fired him a look that was as grim as cancer. "Yeah, laugh. But she outflanked the fly shit outta all of us on this investigation deal."

He was sounding more and more Deep South, a clear signal that Penn Mallory was rattled. Which made Tom wonder if it really was Toni Allura, someone Mallory had always dismissed as a political lightweight, that had gotten under his boss' skin, or something else.

"All right, at least we know the landscape and the players, if not necessarily the game," Mallory continued. He'd shifted into full strategy mode, leaving Dixie and its voice behind. "Let's just stay on point, eyes open, heads down."

Harriman turned and extended his hand to Tom. "I meant no offense."

Tom took it without hesitation. After all, the guy was going to be the next CIA chief, and there was great value to the friends-in-high-places concept. "None taken, Mr. Director. I know it can seem strange, me going from one side to the other so fast, so completely, and I can see how it could raise some doubts. But you need to know"—a quick glance at Mallory—"you both need to know that my loyalties are right here in this room."

Harriman's face went thoughtful and serious, like he was trying to ease a spiritual crisis. "Then may ye also do good, that are accustomed to evil."

"Okay, let's leave the Bible thumping to the cult leaders and TV ministers, if you'll forgive the redundancy," Mallory said. "I think we can safely say that, for a lot of reasons at a lot of levels, it's in our best interests and those of the country to fold the tent on the Cheerleader's little flea circus. Agreed?"

Nods all around, Tom's more halting than Harriman's.

Mallory leaned back and propped his cowboy boots on the desk, drawing deeply on the cigar and exhaling. "Okay, Mr. Fargo, you went toe-to-toe with a terrorist and lived to tell the story. As a reward, I'm gonna give you a new toy to play with."

Tom groaned inside but said nothing.

Harriman's right eye twitched a third time.

A Cheshire cat smile blossomed on Mallory's face.

"Y'all ever heard of a fella named Hector Rubio?"

TWENTY-TWO

"SURE," KYLE KENDRICK said, stopping a forkful of crab cake halfway to his mouth, "I've heard of Hector Rubio. A defense contractor. Fled Castro's Cuba when he was 18, wound up in California, self-made businessman. Builds some kind of super-secret, black-budget radar component for the Air Force. Lives on a boat in Florida now."

"Major fundraiser and contributor," Tom Fargo said.

Kendrick put the fork down, glancing around as if trying to spot a tail. But they were alone in a private room on the second floor of a Capitol Hill hangout favored by House and Senate staffers, their bosses, and the lobbyists who picked up the tabs. "For *John* Allura, Toni's *late* husband." He adjusted a bow tie that didn't need it and took a sip of wine, his antennas fully extended. "Not that there's anything wrong with that."

"Nope," Tom replied, casually munching on a salad of smoked bacon, chopped tomatoes, and blue cheese dressing.

"Then why does that sound like an accusation?"

Tom smiled. "You're beautiful when you're jumping at shadows, Kyle. And today, you're radiant."

Kendrick forced a smile. "I'm sitting here with an agent of the sworn enemy of my boss, and he's making noises that sound vaguely captious."

"*Captious*? Everybody in Toni's office throw around $25 words like that?"

"*Senator* Allura takes pride in surrounding herself with the best and the brightest." One of whom, if he believed his own fantasies, was Kyle Kendrick, her administrative assistant.

Tom sat back and wiped his mouth with the linen napkin, which he then set on the empty plate.

Kendrick, round and red-faced, fiddled again with the bow tie and absently ran plump, pink hands through thinning hair. "I understand Hector's left the fundraising business anyway."

Tom nodded. "Went out with a bang, too. I mean, raising what, $2 million, for John Allura in the last cycle?"

"Something like that, yeah, $2 million and change." His attempt at nonchalance was undercut by a guarded expression that couldn't mask his wariness.

"Two million, four hundred eighteen thousand, seven hundred fifty, to be exact. Which, after John's untimely heart attack, was refunded to the donors, who in turn reinvested in the special election campaign of his grieving widow."

The fact that Tom had the fundraising numbers from a major donor to John Allura at his fingertips sent a bolt of anxiety through Kyle Kendrick. His eyes blinked rapidly for a couple of seconds. When they stopped, he took another sip of wine. "Nothing wrong with that, either."

"Didn't say there was. There's never anything wrong about raising money, not in this town."

"I mean, the law lets us do that, and we did exactly what—"

"Relax," Tom said, with the confidence of a gambler who held three aces in his hand and a pistol under the table just in case. "This doesn't have anything to do with your boss." A strategic pause. "Not directly, anyway."

Kyle Kendrick's anxiety meter edged a little closer to the red zone. He was an attorney from Sacramento who'd come to Washington with little in-the-trenches political experience. The guy was in over his head, and Tom knew it, so this whole exercise felt like a cat batting around a confused mouse.

But that didn't change the fact that Tom was here to bat.

"Rubio made a ton of money when John Allura was alive."

Kendrick shrugged. "Like I said, he's an up-from-the-bootstraps guy, built a huge company. He's a poster child for the American entrepreneurial spirit."

"Spare me the sound bites on the glories of free enterprise and capitalism, Kyle. This isn't CNBC."

"Then what is it, Tom?"

A bunch of words or phrases drifted in and out of Tom Fargo's head, ranging from "death knell to your boss' ambitions," which would have been too harsh by half, to "just a friendly heads-up," which would have been too soft by equal measure. He settled on something appropriately ambiguous: "It's an opportunity."

Despite himself, Kendrick laughed. "Penn Mallory is offering Toni Allura an *opportunity*?"

"Indeed he is."

Kendrick leaned back in the chair, his expansive, white-shirted gut protruding like a snowy tumor. He smiled. "Oh, I cannot wait to hear this."

Maybe it was the tone, maybe the attitude, maybe the fact that the anti-anxiety meds had put him back in charge of his life— or maybe he just didn't like Kendrick, thought he was a hack whose sense of self-importance was blindingly at odds with both perception and reality. But for whatever reason, Tom decided it was time to stop dancing.

"Yolanda Díaz."

Kendrick coughed slightly. "Uh, never heard of her."

Tom had to laugh. "God, Kyle, how have you survived in this city being such a bad liar?"

"I don't know what you're talking about." He alternately scratched his forehead, chin, back of the neck, tip of the nose.

"Yolanda Díaz. Worked the reception desk at a health club in San Diego. Retired now, living in a new condo, driving a new Mercedes, and struggling to get by on $40,000 a month. Not bad for a 28-year-old whose only apparent skills are the ability to manage sign-in sheets and say 'Sales to the front desk, you have a customer.'"

Kendrick looked like an exposed nerve. "What a man does in his personal life is of no—"

"Stop it." Kendrick's head snapped back. "Not all of the money Hector Rubio got in the defense budget went to those, what did you call them, 'super-secret, black-budget radar components' he built for the Air Force, did it?"

Kendrick stiffened. "Whatever Rubio got, however he used it, that was between him and Toni's husband."

"But Toni knew something wasn't quite right."

"I couldn't tell you what she knew, Tom. When we got here, she had a bunch of interns go over who was getting federal money. The numbers didn't add up on Rubio. He was out. Period. End of story."

Tom laughed. "That's an understatement."

"What?"

"The numbers didn't add up on Rubio."

Kyle Kendrick licked his lips. "I don't know what you're talking about."

Tom shook his head in mock sympathy. "I'm talking about money, Kyle, taxpayer money, hidden in the blackest corner of the federal budget. Money that was properly and lawfully given to Hector Rubio to provide defense services, but a percentage of which was redirected, shall we say, to non-defense services." Another strategic pause. "Unless, of course, your definition of *defense* includes putting three kids through Harvard, making cash payments to legislators in exchange for state contracts for his brother, and hiring seven lobbyists who disbursed their not-inconsiderable fees to 25 others who, in turn, gave the money back to John Allura in the form of campaign contributions. And here I thought we didn't have taxpayer-financed Senate elections." He took a second to check Kyle Kendrick's pulse. It was rapid. "Oh, and then there's the little matter of Yolanda Díaz."

For a moment, Kendrick seemed to find his spine. He leaned into Tom, jabbing a thick finger in his direction. "Toni Allura never, *never*, did anything wrong."

"I don't doubt it," Tom said easily.

"Then why are we having this conversation?"

"We're having it, Kyle, because no one cares whether Toni did anything wrong. All that matters is the headline in the *Post*, the one that says, 'Donor Linked To Allura Campaign Indicted.'"

Tom could almost see the steel in Kendrick's spine turn to oatmeal. "Indicted?"

"Yeah," he said slowly, stringing the word out, nodding. "Could happen."

Whatever mechanism passed for strategy in Kendrick's head started to whir. He dabbed his right temple with a napkin. "Is there, uh, any way to, you know, prevent such an occurrence from, uh, occurring?"

"*An occurrence from occurring?*" Tom smiled. "And here I thought Toni only hired the best and the brightest."

Although he tried to fight it, tried to put on a good show, Kendrick was coming apart like wet paper. "What do you want?"

"Stop the investigation into Platte's death."

Kendrick cocked his head slightly. "What?"

"You heard me, Kyle. This is a non-starter. You know it. I know it. She knows it. There's no fire here, and the only smoke is coming from your boss. This thing drags on, we all look foolish."

"She thinks there's something there." It was less a statement than a plea.

"I think there was a second gunman on the Grassy Knoll in Dallas."

"Tom, I can't, I mean—"

"Fine." He pushed his chair back and started to stand.

"Wait." Tom sat back down. Kendrick searched unsuccessfully for his composure. "Let's say, just for argument's sake, no guarantees, let's say I can, she will, call off the investigation. What's in it for us?"

An unseen smile broke out deep inside of Tom. One thing was sure in politics: The minute the other side quit arguing over the big issue and started negotiating the details—in this case, Tom's details—the war was over. He'd won. "It'll all go away."

"Define *all*."

"Senate Ethics Committee. Grand juries. Justice Department."

"But none of that is in the works now."

"I think the operative word here is *now*."

Threat made and received. "What about Hector."

Tom shook his head. "I don't care about Hector. He's not my problem. But your boss will get a pass."

Kyle Kendrick thought it all through for a moment. "And if she says no?"

"Bob Decker." He stood, asking offhandedly, "You know him?"

"No."

"He's a producer at *60 Minutes*." Tom could see the calculations going on behind Kendrick's eyes, knowing they added up to images of an ambush interview that would dominate the news for at least five or six cycles and God knew how long on the blogosphere.

"This is extortion. You have to know that." It was a last-ditch, Hail Mary response.

Tom Fargo's inner smile broke onto his face, warm and confident and friendly. "I'm looking forward to hearing from you, Kyle. My best to your boss."

TWENTY-THREE

AS TOM STOOD in the shower at his apartment, hotter-than-normal water pounding him, he couldn't get that line from *Patton* out of his head, the one where George C. Scott looks over a scorched-earth battlefield, sees nothing but death and destruction, and says, "I love it. God help me, I do love it so."

That's how he felt after strong-arming Kyle Kendrick. It was how he felt after strong-arming anyone at Mallory's behest: exhilarated by his ability to take the senator's fight to the opposition and win it in bare-knuckled fashion; regretting, maybe even hating, the fact that he was so good at it.

Which raised the question, again, as always seemed to happen in these steaming shower postmortems, of what was worse: having an elastic conscience or no conscience at all.

If there was an answer anywhere out there, it was on the other side of the horizon. These days, he wondered more and more if he was getting closer to or farther from the line that separated blind acceptance from responsible suspicion.

After about 20 minutes, the water started to cool, cutting the deep-thought processes short. Tom toweled off, climbed into a pair of jeans and a vintage Bruce Springsteen concert tour T-shirt, and grabbed a Michelob Ultra from the near-empty refrigerator. He drained about a third of the beer and walked over to the sofa, grabbing the remote and turning on the TV, switching to the Fox

News Channel because that was part of his job.

"Now I will be the first to admit—well, admit is not the right word, perhaps agree—I'll be the first to agree that Toni Allura, the junior senator from Dior, is nuttier than squirrel poo," one of the planet's angriest white men brayed. "And I'll agree that she's an airhead, a lightweight, a back-bencher who is more suited for a centerfold in Milf Monthly—wait, can I say that on TV? Well, I did, let her sue me, because I promise, you put that little muffin on the stand, nobody's gonna disagree with me. My point, friends and fans, is this: While I believe that she's about as far from being a leader as a pig's butt is from a pork chop, I cannot dispute that there's some merit to what she's doing. If Harry Platte's death was terrorist-related, then we owe it to his family and to the country to follow every lead, to whatever cave it leads us in the Middle East. Then we need to kill whoever was responsible so thoroughly and so swiftly that their entire family tree withers up and dies."

Tom hit the mute button and picked up the day's *Post*, which was still giving Toni's investigation a decent ride on both the front and the editorial pages.

Reporters played up the fact that she was taking on the Senate powers: "Ever since Allura came to Washington, the California Republican has not only refused to blindly follow her party, but also to walk in lockstep with convention or expectation. Senate sources said that her questioning of the 'official story' of Platte's death is consistent with her willingness to ignore the risks of political independence, a willingness that her staff and supporters believe Washington is sorely lacking." In a column headlined "Where Will Platte-Gate Lead?", a noted liberal opinionator wrote, "We have always viewed Sen. Allura as something of a media star. With her investigation, however, and her recognition that truth is the imperative of service and something we cannot allow to become a casualty of challenging times, we may be witnessing the birth of a true leader."

Penn Mallory nailed it. Toni Allura had become a hero to both the right and left.

Of course, the coverage and commentary were spiced with speculation about her political ambitions, ranging from a down-the-road run for governor to a power play in the Senate. But there wasn't so much as a veiled, trial-balloon murmur about a presidential bid. Tom found that odd. This was, after all, Washington, and in Washington—and especially in the Senate—lust for the White House was a virus that got into the blood quickly and stayed forever, the only cures being an inability to raise money and an ill-considered affair with someone whose gender you shared or whose last name you didn't.

So while Mallory may have been on top of the whole Toni-as-a-darling-of-the-press thing, Tom couldn't decide if the lack of presidential chatter confirmed his boss' paranoia or reinforced the senator's reputation as someone who knew what was coming before it arrived.

Probably a little of both, but that didn't matter. Tom was pretty certain the meeting with Kendrick had done what it was supposed to do—the elasticity of his conscience notwithstanding—and that Toni Allura and her quixotic mission, regardless of its political intentions, would soon be yesterday's news, bringing his brief but unsettling relationship with both Anath and the anti-anxiety drugs to an end.

He put down the paper, unmuted the television, finished the Ultra, and went into the kitchen for another, sifting through a drawer full of takeout and delivery menus. In a moment, another angry white man was on the TV screen, basically agreeing with his brethren on the right that there was merit to Toni's investigation, but still not missing a chance to skewer her as a "wannabe who will never be," and then—perhaps forgetting her home state—predicting the Californian would soon find herself inside a "personal Alamo, fighting along side the illegal immigrants she cares for so deeply, besieged and eventually falling not to Santa Anna and the Mexican hordes, but to the regiment of rectitude, of which yours truly is a proud commander."

Tom narrowed the evening's dinner choices down to Chinese and deli, finally opting for a turkey sub, salad, and fruit bowl from a place in Old Town. Ten minutes, the bored-sounding order-taker told him, which Tom figured gave him enough time to check emails and see if anything pressing had cropped up since he'd left the office.

He uncapped the beer and turned on the laptop that sat on the high-rise Santa Fe table, logged into his email service—

And heard a noise outside. A rattling of the gate on his back patio. Like someone was trying to get in.

Was his food here already?

He looked at his watch. It hadn't been two minutes since he'd placed the delivery order, let alone 10.

He stepped into the center of the living room, eyeing the gate.

The pick-proof, hard-to-bolt-cut, steel and chrome-plated shackle lock was off, Tom suddenly remembering he'd removed it that morning so the termite guy could come in, leaving the black patio door latch as the only line of defense.

He glanced quickly at the front door. The chains and flush bolts were in place, knob on the vertical bolt twisted left, red activation light glowing on the keyless entry pad, everything back to assuming their intended duties after idling for years.

Outside: more rattling and shaking.

The only thing that passed for a weapon in the place was a bat he used during the summer Senate League softball games, and he slid out of the living room, through the kitchen and into the bedroom, opened the closet, pulled out a 34-ounce Mizuno that retailed for $250, went back into the living room, gripping the Mizuno like it was an ax, unsure if it made him feel brave or foolish, the idea that even with an elaborate security system, there was no such thing as absolute protection, it was an illusion, and what now shielded him from a terror that arrived unseen and unexpected was not anything of the modern world but something as primitive as a metal club.

The rattling and shaking had gone way past insistent, becoming so aggressively unrelenting that Tom thought the gate might collapse.

He looked back toward the kitchen, at the phone, thinking 9-1-1 wasn't such a bad idea, the Mizuno more of a fallback position—

Then seeing a pair of hands over the top of the gate—

No time for 9-1-1, the Mizuno moving back up to Plan A, deciding not to wait, this was no time for hesitation—

Grabbing his house keys off the Santa Fe table, speed-stepping to the front door, bat in one hand—

Fumbling to get the chains off—

Struggling to disengage the locks—

The deadbolt locks—

Vertical lock—

First kicking himself for falling into this trap again and then for making it all so complex, the irony not lost on him that if he died, the reason would be not be for lack of security but the presence of too much, the thought that he'd never considered offense, just defense, and that all the money in the world, and all the locks it could buy, could never replace a misguided plan—

Seeing the hands get a solid hold on top of the gate outside, noticing they were small and not having much success hoisting the body up and over the top and onto the patio—

Punching in the code for the keyless entry system, jerking the mortise locks out of their catches, throwing open the front door—

Hearing labored breathing and oomph-oomph-oomphing, stepping out onto the brick-red-tiled patio, fired by adrenaline and fear, raising the Mizuno, Fargo-at-the-bat—

Unhooking the latch—

Launching a kick into the gate—

Stepping into whatever unseen threat awaited on the other side—

Starting to swing—

"No no no no no no no—"

Stopping at the sight of a young woman in a defensive crouch, arms over her head—

Tom sputtering nothing but single syllables: "Who are you? What do you want?"—

The woman, mid-20s, more of a girl, slim, dressed all in black, eyes soaked in terror and rage behind black-framed glasses, finally standing up when she realized he wasn't going to crush her skull, words tumbling out like blood from an open wound—

"My name is Liberty Dash, and I work with Sarah, and I need to talk with you about my brother and why I think someone killed him."

TWENTY-FOUR

"ARLO WAS JUST an awesome guy," Liberty Dash said, sipping a cup of tea at Tom's Santa Fe table while he nursed a coffee mug half full of scotch. "Kind of a political cyberpunk, y'know? Someone who thought he could use his technical skills to fight the government's evil plan to control us." A shy smile, bordering on sad. "As if anybody could do that, right?"

She shrugged and took off the glasses. It made her seem about 10 years old.

"Anyway," she went on, "he had these grandiose ideas of, I don't know, like self-importance. It was the Internet, I guess. It gives people this sense of security, this idea they can hide behind some invisible but impermeable wall of anonymity." Her voice went up at the end of each sentence, turning statements into questions.

"Except you believe someone got through the wall."

The smile ventured closer to sadness. "I don't think there's anyplace to hide. Not in this world. If they want to find you, they're gonna find you, and there's not a wall on the planet that's going to keep them out."

Tom glanced at the newly re-employed locks on the door.

His eyes caught hers for a moment. The fear that had greeted him at the gate was gone. They were now softer, and gray, and absorbed the room's light like pieces of cut glass.

On the other hand, everything else was black:

The hair, straight and landing at the shoulder, bangs hiding the forehead. The leggings and mid-calf biker boots. The either too-long top or too-short skirt, dark skull imprints barely visible.

She looked like either the lead singer in an all-girl rock band or maybe the vice president of social media for an ad agency.

"You're sure it's okay, you know, that I'm here." Tom nodded, again. It was the fourth time she'd asked. "Because, I mean, with Sarah, things between you guys being kind of sketchy and all."

He took a bigger-than-necessary slug of the scotch, feeling the heat go down his throat, into his chest, burning his heart, and tried to cool it off by sucking in a lung full of air. "We're fine," he wheezed, exhaling, the sound not unlike a deflating tire.

"She said you were cool"—Tom doubted those were Sarah's exact words, but he appreciated the translation—"and when I saw your name in the paper, about going to Germany on the whole Platte thing, I thought maybe you could help, so I asked her, and she told me she'd said something about Arlo to you—"

Remembering the bar, Sarah blowing in late, crisis at the office, someone's brother killed in a robbery—

"So I figured just go for it, right?"

Tom smiled, neither brightly nor sadly, just plainly, as if his face had nothing better to do, and said, "Right," because he really didn't know what else to say.

Her soft gray eyes darkened with defiance. "I'm not crazy."

"I didn't say you were."

"But you don't believe me."

Tom half shook his head. "Twenty minutes ago you appear out of nowhere and tell me your brother's death was related to Senator Platte's. I'm still waiting for you to connect the dots."

"You told me to start at the beginning."

"Let's move on to Chapter 2."

She seemed to consider that for a moment, reaching some decision and putting her glasses back on. "You mind?" Gesturing to the laptop.

Tom nodded his permission. "Liberty is kind of an interesting name."

"Oh, yeah, *very* hardcore," she said, spinning the laptop around so they could both view the screen. "Born Elizabeth. Nicknamed Libby. Rechristened Liberty by my Uncle Fred after 9/11."

"I see."

"I don't." She punched in a few keystrokes and pulled up a web page with an image of the Bill of Rights in the shape of a sort-of dinosaur; a banner at the top reading *The Veracitaurus. Because Truth Should Not Be Extinct.*; and under that a series of text blocks with various headlines, most of which railed against the war in Afghanistan, the current administration, and pretty much anything Red State or Republican.

One caught Tom's eye, *9/11: The Day America Went On Sale,* accompanied by a paragraph that read:

To paraphrase H. L. Mencken, patriotism is the favorite device of people who have something to sell. And on 9/11, when a handful of too-true believers got the product they needed, America went on sale. My question is: When will the rest of us stop buying?

"Your brother was a blogger."

Liberty nodded. "The Veracitaurus was his identity. His online veil."

Tom sat back in the chair, arms folded tightly across his chest. She caught the body language. "Yeah, I know, I know, I get it. You're probably not one of his regular readers."

"I'm not a huge fan of blogs. They're instruments of arson that give people an opportunity to start fires."

"Sometimes fires need to be started," she replied, soft but rebellious, a clear signal she had no intention of giving in, either to him or to her situation. "The thing is, Arlo had a following in D.C. Mostly liberals, sure, young Democratic staffers on the Hill, left-leaning advocacy groups."

"The usual suspects."

"Yep. Just like the racists and misogynists and philandering focus-on-the-family freaks that follow Bill O'Reilly. Except Arlo had a heart and a sense of humanity."

Tom nodded slightly, acknowledging her point without conceding it.

"So with all of his online connections and followers and friends, Arlo would get his stuff picked up and passed around. Mostly other bloggers, shared stuff on Facebook. Retweets. But every once in a while, he'd get a hit, a mention, in the mainstream media."

He just stared at her and reached out in a half-pleading, give-me-something gesture.

"Okay, okay, okay," she nodded, getting the message. "All I'm saying is that regardless of what you think about his opinions, or the way he expressed them, Arlo had a following, okay? People read his stuff, and they shared it so other people could read it, too."

Tom leaned back into his chair. "That's fine, but what are you asking me to do?"

"I'm not *asking* you to do anything."

He recrossed his arms. "Then why are you here?"

Liberty squinted at him like he was fine print. The look was less confusion than it was Clint Eastwood, though, and when she spoke, the words rode in on a wave of just-under-the-surface rage. "Somebody murdered my brother, okay? I want you to help me find out who and why."

"As opposed to just going to the police."

"Been there, done that." She reached into a backpack—black, naturally—and pulled out a cell phone that was safety-cased in thick tire-treaded rubber. "But go ahead, give it your best shot, see if you get anything besides 'It's an ongoing investigation.'"

"What else would you expect them to say?"

"Nothing, if they were covering something up."

"A cover-up? And you have evidence of this how?"

"Hey, the complete lack of evidence is abso*lute* evidence that there *is* a cover-up, and that it's working."

"No, the complete lack of evidence suggests that if you're going for a dip in the conspiracy pool, you had better be careful."

"Why? Because someone will pull me under?"

"No, because you may get swept away by a current of reality."

"God, whose side are you on?"

"Nobody's, because there are no sides here."

"There are always sides, man. Always. Choose one, or lose."

"Ah, the wisdom of youth." Saying it offhandedly, trying to mask a growing impatience, walking into the step-up kitchen to top off the glass of scotch.

"Better than surrendering before your time's up."

Tom finished pouring and set the bottle down. He felt the anger begin to bubble up. "What does that mean?"

She spun her head toward him, gray eyes now even darker, the color of a winter sky. "When you surrender your beliefs, your ideals, that's when you really get old. And that's what you did, dude. Gave up. Took Easy Street. Fight the terrorists, and fuck the people."

That sounded familiar. "Did Sarah say that before or after she told you I was cool?"

Liberty shook her head sadly and grabbed her backpack. "She warned me, Sarah did, said you wouldn't help, you were too far gone." She headed toward the door, propelled by a short burst of laughter. "Far gone. Is that like the past tense of Far-go?"

"Stop." She did, but didn't turn. "If you have proof of anything, tell me. Let me see it. Then we'll continue this conversation."

After a moment, she dug into the backpack and pulled out a folded piece of paper, finally looking at him. "You want proof? Here's your damned proof." Not moving, just holding it up.

He crossed to her, took what was the printout of an email:

To: Liberty4All
From: Veracitaurus1
Subject line: I GOT HIM!!!!

Sis, I'm on to something huge, gonna make The Big Penis go soft. This evil prick is goin down, and the greedy multinationals, too, and there ain't enuf Viagra in the world gonna get him up again!!!!

Tom read it twice and looked up. "This is your proof?"

She swept past him, back to the laptop on the table, where Arlo Dash's website was still on the screen, and tapped a couple of keys. "Check this out."

Tom came over, reading a month-old blog entry over her shoulder—

"Rumor has it The Big Penis, the Biggest Prick in the Senate, is moving up the right-wing food chain"—

Accompanied by a picture of—

"Harry Platte," Tom whispered.

"Yeah," Liberty said. "The late, great Harry Platte."

His eyes fastened themselves onto hers and narrowed. "That's what your brother called Harry Platte. The Big Penis."

She nodded and inhaled, deep and fast.

Tom was suddenly alert, as if some invisible, intangible force had taken possession of his mind. He looked again at the printed-out email, reading it this time with a surge of anxiety—

"Sis, I'm on to something huge, gonna make The Big Penis go soft"—

Then recapturing Liberty's gaze, seeing the fear, getting the sense that telling him about this, whatever the hell *this* was, made her dread all the more real.

Tom's voice went fact-finding flat. "What are you saying?"

"I got that email from Arlo a week before Platte died." She hesitated, looking small and fragile, like she was about to break. "I'm saying he found out something about Harry Platte, something bad, and he was going to write about it, and someone murdered him to make sure the secret never got out."

Tom softened, but kept his focus. He knew he had to tread

lightly. "Okay. Let's say you're right. Let's say the secret, whatever it was, is safe. Then—"

"But what if it's not safe?" she interrupted. "What if they hacked his email account? What if they know I know something's going on?" Her eyes filled with tears. "What happens to me?"

Tom hesitated before reaching out and wrapping Liberty in an embrace he hoped felt more secure to her than it did to him. "Nothing's going to happen to you," he said. Then he looked at the front door again, and wondered if some new terror had suddenly invaded his life, and whether he had enough locks to keep his promise to her.

TWENTY-FIVE

TOM HADN'T DREAMED of his father in six years. Until tonight:

He is lost, unable to solve this five-story, five-ringed, five-sided puzzle.

He walks along what he knows is the building's outermost ring, the E Ring, past Corridor 2 and the south parking entrance, toward Corridor 3.

He knows it's the E Ring because there are windows, and he can see outside.

It's a clear day, a little before 9:30.

People dressed in fatigues or uniforms, blues and greens, looking at him and his long hair, unshaved face, jeans, T-shirt, looking at him like he was a zoo animal who'd escaped from the cage.

Tom doesn't care. He's on a quest.

The place is huge, millions of feet of office space, three times the size of the Empire State Building. Somehow he knows this.

It's a bitch to navigate, too.

Offices that were once small had morphed into offices that are now huge, screwing up the whole hub-and-spoke setup, the five rings, A to E, the 10 corridors, designed to be efficient, but now, at this moment, anything but.

Secure areas block passageways, armed guards looking stern and fearsome, eyeing Tom warily, not like a zoo animal now, more like an enemy of the state.

Tom smiles at that. He likes the idea.

Then he reminds himself why he's here. He's searching for an office. The smile evaporates.

He sees an open door, sticks his head in, says, "Excuse me," thinking he is going to discover people analyzing budgets or buying weapons or figuring out what country to invade next.

But he only finds people with their backs to him, watching television.

"They're here," a man in a flight suit says without turning from the TV, his eyes glued on the images, which Tom now sees:

The Towers, smoking.

Tom ducks out fast, heart pounding like a high-speed sledgehammer, reaches into his pocket for the pills, pulls out the bottle, the thing is empty.

No refills.

Starts to sweat.

Pushes on toward Corridor 3.

It's 9:32.

He stops a handsome-looking woman, green uniform, gray hair. She's a colonel, wears the eagle on her blouse. Army. Maybe she knows.

"I'm looking for my Old Man," he says.

"Got an office number?" she asks. He shakes his head. "Sorry. Can't help you."

"Please. It's important. He's in danger."

A line of more men and women in fatigues and uniforms races by him. They have huge guns and determined, angry faces.

The colonel smiles like she is the only one who knows the answer to some essential cosmic riddle. "Don't worry, this is the most secure building on earth. He's safe." She drifts off, like a ghost, feet barely touching the floor.

It's 9:34.

"Please," he calls out. "I have to find him."

Instantly, she's right back in front of him, like she'd never left.

Except now, she's not in uniform, hair isn't gray, no blouse, no eagle.

"Hello, sweetheart."

His mother.

Tom feels the tears coming. She looks so young, like she did before—

"You're alive," he says.

She lets out one of those sparkling laughs of hers, the kind that made a room brighter. "Oh, no, silly. Cancer doesn't work that way."

"But—"

She puts a finger on his lips. "Why?"

The question throws Tom. He blinks rapidly. "He's in danger." She cocks one eye, and he feels busted like only a mom can make a child feel busted. "He's lost."

His mother smiles, warm and fresh and alive as a spring dawn. "He's always been lost. To you."

This stings, the reminder of the lifelong disconnect. He gently moves her finger away from his face. "That's why I have to find him."

More people run past, dressed like extras in a Wild West show, cowboys with six-guns and rifles, Indians with bows and arrows, spears.

"You can't, sweetheart."

"I have to try. I need to try."

"It's too late."

"It can't be," he whispers.

Her eyes, which look violet, hold his. "He's not the one who is lost, Thomas. You do understand that, don't you?"

Tom nods. "That's why I have to find him."

She sighs. It is hesitant, as if she is about to reveal the truth about Santa Claus to a wide-eyed innocent.

"I need to try," he says again.

He sees a decision arrive on her face. "It's 1B526, past the next corridor and around to the right."

"Will you help me?"

The sadness on her face is her only answer.

It's 9:36.

Tom turns and races away.

Past people with slingshots and swords, people dressed like Roman warriors, shouting, "Run, run!"

Tom speeds past Corridor 3, around the corner, then past Corridor 4, seeing the heliport out the window, construction equipment, a chain-link fence, stopping anyone, everyone, asking, begging, "Where's 1B526?" but never getting an answer, never getting anything, until one man, not in a uniform, not in anything but a loincloth, all hairy, like he'd just been hunting saber-toothed tigers, until this one man points and says, in an English accent, "Can't you see it?"

Tom looks through the window and freezes, seeing it, treetop level and descending, coming at him, 500 miles a hour, coming at him like a monstrous bullet—

An airplane—

But all he can think of is 1B526, where is it, where is it, going from office to office, none marked—

The plane's right wing hits a generator, and there's a fireball—

Grabbing at the doorknobs, all of them locked—

The left wing almost at ground level—

"Where are you, goddamnit?" Tom cries out. "Somebody help me!"—

But he's alone, everyone has vanished, they're all gone—

The right engine tears through a series of fence posts—

He sees a door, half ajar, and he knows, he just knows, it has to be 1B526—

Both wings break apart—

He pushes it open, feeling suddenly safe, secure—

Pieces of metal slice through the morning air—

But no one is inside—
Then 14 feet above him, the impact—
In a voice he barely recognizes, loud enough to be heard in his head, above the boom, he stares into the emptiness and hears himself say—
"I want to kill them all"—
And then come the explosion, the fire, the screams.
It's 9:37.

TWENTY-SIX

THE BLAST THAT filled Tom's sleeping brain nearly threw him out of the bed. He bolted upright, hugged himself tight and shivered, trying to catch his breath, sweating like a snowman in hell.

The same dream, he thought, almost frame for frame, image for image, character for character, right down to the backward history of warfare, from 21st-century soldiers to English-accented cavemen.

And the Old Man. Missing in action. Still.

He shivered again and peeled off the Springsteen T-shirt, dark at the neck from perspiration, and walked into the kitchen. A full moon threw a glimmer of light onto the counters, revealing the bottle of scotch right next to the bottle of Klonopin.

What'll it be, boy, the lady or the tiger?

Tom looked at his hands, seized by a slight tremor, and clenched them into tight fists.

He decided on the tiger, the scotch, because refills were easier to get and a lot cheaper, and he still had two hours of run time on the last pill.

After the third sip, he felt something that bordered on calm begin to settle in. After the fourth, he heard the sound.

It was a slight but insistent pinging, coming from the bedroom. Even though the liquor was burning off his dream-induced daze, for a moment he couldn't decide if the sound was in his head, a remnant of the nightmare, or something more real.

He went back into the bedroom. On his nightstand, next to a stack of books that would likely never get read—bios of Steve Jobs and Robert Redford and Lyndon Johnson, a year-old Swedish mystery, an award-winning literary novel that seemed like a good idea at the time—he saw that the screen on his cell phone was illuminated.

Liberty, he thought. He had insisted that she text him to say she'd gotten home safely. When she asked if that was really necessary, Tom replied, "Caution is the father of safety." To which Liberty replied, "That may be, but over-caution is the mother of wackos."

Tom smiled at the recollection, took another sip of the scotch, sat down on the edge of the bed, and reached for the cell.

Except the text wasn't from Liberty.

He rubbed his eyes into sharper focus and stared at the message: *There's a package for you on the patio.*

He shot a puzzled, uneasy look through the darkness toward the bay window in the living room, then returned his attention to the touch screen on the phone. No identification of the sender, just a number, 780-04.

He typed *Who is this?* in the text box at the bottom of the screen and hit the Send button.

Almost instantly, he got a response:

"Error invalid number. Please resend using valid 10-digit mobile number or short code."

He stood and walked tentatively into the kitchen, avoiding the moonlight, able to see the patio while cloaking himself in shadows, a sense of uneasiness morphing into anxiety.

The phone pinged again. A second message:

What are you waiting for? If I wanted you dead, you would be dead.

Tom's eyes swung rapid-fire around the apartment, to the ceiling, the floor, the walls, the windows, the bookcases, the kitchen, the furniture, the doors, anyplace there might be some sign he was being watched.

Nothing, but he wasn't surprised. Instinct told him this was no innocent online adventure, that whoever the mystery texter was, he or she knew the game. Meaning Tom could spend all night probing every light fixture, electric socket, shoe sole, or crack in the wall in search of a micro-camera. Or he could go out to the patio and stare into whatever abyss awaited.

He glanced at the Mizuno bat leaning against the bathroom door and wondered if it would make any difference at all in what was about to happen. Probably not. Mystery texter was a pro. And, strange as it sounded, Tom found some comfort in the fact that whoever was at the other end of the text could have killed him but, for whatever reason, had chosen not to.

Security redefined: You're safe, but only if they allow it.

He took a deep breath and moved from the kitchen to the front door, undid all the locks, released the chain, opened it, quickly scanned the patio, looked into the sky—maybe the camera was a drone, watching his every move—then turned to check out the three floors above him. He had no idea what he was searching for, though the weird image of men in black jumpsuits suddenly appearing and rappelling down from the roof came to mind.

Then he stepped on something slick, his left leg nearly sliding out from under him.

It was a 9-by-12 manila envelope. *Thomas Fargo, Office of U.S. Sen. Penn Mallory* was written in neat, clean, felt-tip lettering on the front.

He picked it up, unfolded the clasp, pulled out the contents. His eyes went wide as two moons when he realized what he was looking at:

A photo.

Munich.

Him.

Anath.

The bar.

Tom felt the sweat start to rush back.

He turned the photo over.

In the same neat, clean, felt-tipped lettering:

Parking garage, 22nd & Eye, roof, 10:30. Many lives in the balance. Yours is the least important of them.

TWENTY-SEVEN

TOM TOOK THE Metro from Alexandria to the Foggy Bottom-GWU station that fronted 23rd Street West. The area, typically a collision of med students, construction workers, and kiosks hawking everything from antiwar T-shirts to pretzels, was quiet. The only sign of life was a dreadlocked man in shades who could have been 40 or 140, sitting on an upside-down bucket at the mouth of the subway entrance, mumbling for money.

A small army of college kids, loud and drunk, fresh from pouring themselves out of a pub on Pennsylvania Avenue just around the corner, seemed to mock the guy as they stepped onto the escalator going down to the platforms.

On the sidewalk, Tom watched them without expression.

After a moment, he pulled a $20 bill from his wallet, walked over to the guy, and stuffed it in his callused hand. The man turned his head in the direction of where the drunks had just disappeared.

"Mooch-ass grassy-ass, my brother." He smiled, revealing teeth that looked surprisingly healthy.

No acknowledgment of Tom, just an assumption his benefactor was headed underground to catch a train. Thrown for a moment, Tom suddenly got it. The man was blind.

Tom said nothing and walked across 23rd down Eye. A major construction project ate up most of the block to his left. To his right was the Jacqueline Bouvier Kennedy Onassis Hall, then Munson

Hall beyond that, then a concrete wheelchair ramp zigzagging up to glass doors that opened onto a stairwell entryway into the garage.

Tom hesitated, looked around. Alert. Anxious.

A couple approached him, tall black guy and a thin girl with red hair and tight jeans that tapered at the ankle.

The black guy raised his eyes at Tom and nodded slightly as they passed. The girl paid him no attention, just talked earnestly and passionately about some new cancer treatment, which she described as "like a car bomb that blows up the malignant cells."

Tom watched them fade into the night.

He turned, went another five or 10 yards, walked past a pair of barrier gates into the garage, looked for an elevator.

If one was there, he didn't see it.

He did see a door into the stairwell, pushing through it and taking the steps two at a time until he hit the second floor, which was maybe three-fourths full of cars.

He glanced around quickly, wondering if this was such a good idea, then asked himself if not showing up would be an even worse idea, because he'd end up spending the rest of his days—however numbered they might be—in the grip of a lurking, unseen peril.

He saw the elevator.

Glanced around again, another last-minute check, making sure nobody was about to burst from some dark place, and hit the Up button, which seemed to awaken the lift from a mechanical sleep. It arrived almost instantly, the metal doors straining open, creaking and labored, sounding like the chains in a dungeon torture chamber.

He stared at the empty elevator car for a couple of seconds, then muttered, "Hell, in for a dime, in for a dollar."

Entered and punched the 7 button, the highest floor, assuming it was the roof.

On the street outside, the wail of police sirens punctured the city's ambient sound.

The doors closed. For a moment, the elevator didn't budge.

Tom's heart rate ticked up a beat or two. He licked his lips, absently patted his hands against his legs, asking himself again just what he was doing here.

The elevator started to rise, a few seconds later delivering him not to the rooftop but, as advertised, to the seventh floor.

More empty spaces than cars.

To his immediate right he saw more stairs, which presumably led to the roof.

Tom did a quick mental checklist, pros and cons of continuing—

Remembering the photo, and the note—

"Lives in the balance"—

Wondering if the only "pro," which was getting some answers, was enough to trump the big "con," which was him never getting off the roof alive.

In for a dime, in for a dollar.

Quietly, carefully, he walked up the two short flights of steps and pushed through a heavy black door, finding himself in a dimly lit, tight, block U-shaped rectangular space that was a kind of reception area opening onto the roof.

He stood still for a moment, listened.

Nothing but the sounds of the city.

He stepped into the night.

What struck him first was not the sight of the Washington Monument behind him, the National Cathedral far off in the distance, or the American flag flapping angrily in the wind at the end of a massive crane that lorded over the Eye Street construction site.

No, what struck him was there was no place to hide.

The roof was large and flat, populated only by a red Ford Focus in front of him and a silver Toyota SUV at the far end.

Down where the Toyota was parked, at the corner of the roof, was a blocky white building.

Unmarked.

No sigh of activity.

Above him, two dozen metal-grate steps led to what looked like a maintenance shed whose floor doubled as the roof of the

U-shaped reception area.

It was padlocked.

No place to hide.

Tower lamps spaced at intervals along the edge of the roof threw some light onto the expanse, but it didn't make Tom feel any safer, any more secure. He got a vague, unsettled feeling as his anxiety began to rise.

His eyes flashed from the Toyota to the Ford, from the white building to the maintenance shed, back to the black door, the exit, thinking of the stairs that descended to the street, to safety.

Suddenly a horn sounded, followed by the screeching of tires.

Tom ducked down and pressed hard against a waist-high brick wall that rimmed the rooftop.

More screeching, another blast of the horn.

Not as loud this time, like off in the distance, moving away from him, and down, out of the garage.

Tom eased slightly and stood, ran his hands through his hair, looked around again, checked his watch.

Ten-thirty on the dot.

Showtime.

And just like that, the black door opened—

Two beeps, the Ford's lights coming on—

Tom going into a crouch, trying to see who was coming for him, looking for that one clue, the one piece of knowledge or understanding that would somehow pierce the uncertainty and give him a roadmap to What Happens Now—

But seeing only a coed, car keys in hand, wide-eyed and twice as freaked out as he was, who let out a small but terrified yip and didn't waste a second before doing a 180 and flying back down the steps.

Tom wondered how long it would be before the cops showed up looking for a would-be rapist, and then whether having the cops around would be such a bad thing anyway.

He shook his head rapidly and walked over to the Ford, opening the door, reaching in to hit the automatic lock, the least he could do for scaring the coed—

When a small, short pop cracked the air—

Glass raining down on him—

Tom falling to his knees, looking up—

The tower lamp above shot out—

More mini-blasts, the lamps along the edge of the rooftop exploding, one by one—

Pop—

Pop—

Pop—

The night getting darker with each burst—

His eyes ricocheting off every corner, every shadow, every wall, every door—

Nowhere to hide—

Nowhere to run—

No escape—

Seeing nothing—

Nothing except—

A $20 bill blowing across the rooftop, like a tumbleweed—

And then seeing nothing at all, as a curtain of total blackness descended upon his face, and a voice at once familiar and frightening rasped—

"Mooch-ass grassy-ass for coming, my brother."

TWENTY-EIGHT

TOM WAS ON his knees, head jammed into a corner, hands bound, entire body trembling, slightly but uncontrollably, as if the brain had sent out a stop-shaking order that had been only partially received, swimming in sweat, breathing heavily, the hood rising and falling against his face, clinging tightly to his nose and mouth, but never tight enough to choke or smother him, just enough to keep the thought of impending death close, like torture, an all-too-real sense that the end could arrive at any moment, with the awful swiftness of a sudden blast of wind—

"This was a great country once."

The homeless street-hipster voice had vanished, replaced by something cold and empty and brutal and angry, a lethal mixture of emotions that Tom instinctively knew had been used as a weapon of human destruction in places far darker than a garage rooftop.

Then, with some added sadness:

"And a great city." Tom tried not to drown in the panic. "Do you know the story of Fort Davis?"

A history lesson? Tom shook his head, haltingly.

"Of course not. Why would you?" A touch of menace now, laced with disdain. "It was the site of the only attack on Washington during the Civil War. On July 12, 1864, President Lincoln and his wife went there, to the fort, and he stood on a parapet watching the Union troops beat back the treacherous infidels. It is difficult to imagine such courage, such inspiration, today."

Even in his fear-soaked state of mind, Tom could not help but register the phrase:

Treacherous infidels.

Not Confederate soldiers.

Not Rebels.

Not Sons of the Goddamned South.

Treacherous infidels.

"It was a time when our leaders well protected this glorious city," the voice continued, detached, as if talking either to himself or to the past. "There were 68 forts here. Ninety-three batteries, with 807 cannons and 98 mortars. Twenty miles of rifle trenches. Thirty miles of military roads. And we created this power not to serve as a bludgeon to intimidate and frighten and oppress the people, and force them to follow the path of our desires. No, we did it because . . . "

He didn't stop speaking so much as his voice ran out of life.

Tom waited.

"We did it because our democracy was under attack then, as it is today. And we did what we had to do to defend ourselves, to repel those who had dared revolt against the principles of greatness. We built fortresses. We fought like men, like the heroes we, Americans, like the heroes we were put on this Earth to be. And on that day in 1864, at that fort, Fort Davis, 41 Union troops died upholding an idea—an idea!" He stopped suddenly, as if catching himself and his rage, and realizing it was somehow disrespectful to those 41 to display such fury. "An idea," he repeated, so low the night almost swallowed the words. "And today, our leaders uphold only lies. And self-interest is the currency of their deceit."

The brief silence that followed melted into an unmistakable omen.

"Much as it is the currency of yours, Mr. Fargo."

With a brain-searing clarity, Tom instantly saw the future, the final chapter in his transition from antiwar activist to pro-America poster child:

One of the disembodied phantoms whose threats had once populated his nightmares—"You're still one of them, boy, I don't care what kinda little pin you wear in your sport coat, or who you work for, or what you do, you're still one of them, and we're gonna get you, and you're gonna pay, you terrorist traitor"—one of them had found form at last, and had found him.

He was the one who had turned his back first on his country, then on a movement that had invested in his leadership.

He was the one trapped in some bleak netherworld of his own choosing, a world of questions for which the only answers came in the extreme, black or white, good or evil, right or wrong, a world he had entered with honorable intentions but whose realities conspired against anything so high-minded.

He was the one nobody could believe.

He was the one nobody could trust.

He was the treacherous infidel.

In that moment of epiphany, when he saw what was on the rapidly approaching horizon of his life, he expected that death was as near as dusk is to darkness.

What he did not expect was this:

"But I am giving you a second chance to be a patriot, Mr. Fargo. You would be wise to take it."

TWENTY-NINE

TOM'S FEAR EBBED slightly but didn't vanish, creating a void in his emotions that a sudden surge of intense curiosity quickly filled. It was accompanied by an odd understanding, the realization that he was in this place, with this person, for a reason, and he needed to know why.

"Who are you?" Trying to control the tremble in his voice.

"I am the one who will determine the fate of this government, and the pretenders who pose as its leaders, in the days to come." The answer was forceful and without hesitation, underscored with raging disgust.

In the air, a police siren wailed, growing less sonically harsh as it swept past, consumed by the night.

"How did you find me? Is my apartment bugged?"

"No, Mr. Fargo. That would be illegal."

The answer was so unexpected, so off-the-wall, that Tom took a second to mine the voice for humor. Not a trace. "What do you want with me?"

Silence, as if they'd come to the brink of something and the right answer or the wrong word could knock the world from its axis.

"I want you to disregard your instructions from Anath—"

In the insanity, Tom had forgotten about the picture—

"And do exactly as I tell you. Are we clear?"

Tom's mind raced like a runaway train. "Did you take that photo?"

"No, I did not."

"Then who did?"

A pause followed that seemed to last eons, creating a moment so still Tom thought he'd been left alone, accompanied only by the sound of his short, anxious breathing.

"I am not here to satisfy your need for understanding, Mr. Fargo. What you know, how much you know, is of no concern to me. Because I know more."

Under the hood, in the artificial blackness, Tom wondered what someone who spoke with such cold detachment looked like. He imagined blazing, crazy eyes, hair short and the color of steel wire, a face as hard and chiseled as a blood diamond.

An abrupt calm settled in, as if attaching a voice to a face—however envisioned—somehow made the man more human, and less fearsome.

"Then what *is* your concern, and what does it have to do with me?"

Out of nowhere, Tom heard two sets of sounds.

The first was a dull but insistent thud-thud-thud, clearly the pounding of a fist on the door that led to the rooftop, followed by the metallic shudder as whoever was on the other side tried to force it open, accompanied by a weary and frustrated, "Son of a bitch!"

The second was a bullet being chambered in a pistol, the barrel of which found Tom's temple, accompanied by a menacing, "Do not even think about it—"

Tom's abrupt calm abated—

"And if that door does not hold, and whoever that is pushes it open, you both will die"—

And then vanished altogether.

More pounding and profanity, Tom holding his breath, the hood so dark over his eyes he couldn't tell if they were open or closed.

Then the pounding stopped, replaced by an exhausted, "This is bullshit."

But the handgun didn't budge.

Tom heard the swooping, buzzing whir of a helicopter overhead. The noise seemed to give his captor a shove, like an electric prod.

"There are treacherous infidels inside this government today, Mr. Fargo, just as there were treacherous infidels who attempted to fracture our democracy 150 years ago at Fort Davis, and I will not allow them to go unexposed." The words, tone, and voice spilled out, colliding in a fierce urgency that left Tom frozen in confusion and feeling as if he was about to start spinning down some rabbit hole of unknown depth and destination.

"So you will go to Senator Allura, and you will tell her, forcefully, that she will *not* discontinue her investigation, and that she will pursue it to whatever end without regard to the consequences. Do you understand me?"

Tom thought of Penn Mallory and Vance Harriman and Kyle Kendrick and Hector Rubio, all he had done to derail Toni Allura, and tried to think of some way to get out of this, some sane, logical escape route.

But there was none, and he knew it, and all he could manage was, "I'm not sure I can do that," to which the voice replied with razor-edged sharpness:

"Not only will you do it, Mr. Fargo, but you will say nothing to Senator Mallory about this request nor any related matter you may uncover as part of it."

Request?

"Are we clear?"

It was a question that had only one answer, and Tom knew it, and his body went bowstring tense.

He nodded the hooded head.

"Because if you do not, if for some reason, intended or otherwise, my instructions are not followed to the absolute letter, I will find the blogger's sister, bind her hands and feet to a chair, take a rather small knife and slit her throat, severing the carotid arteries and jugular veins, the trachea, and the esophagus. She will bleed out within a minute. Then I will sever her head with a machete."

Tom tried to speak—"How do you know about her?"—but couldn't find his voice, the words choked off by nausea that began rising from his stomach, like a volcano about to explode.

"And I will capture the entire episode on video, and email it to you, so you will forever understand and remember the collateral damage that can result when a patriotic American refuses to commit an act of American patriotism."

"This isn't patriotism," he gasped, breathing fast, fighting back against the rushing bile, "it's insanity."

"I am glad we understand each other."

There was some shuffling, and Tom heard a sharp clipping sound.

The tightness at his wrists vanished as the plastic restraints fell away, leaving a hot sting in their wake.

"Count to 10, Mr. Fargo. Slowly. If the hood comes off before you finish, the girl will be dead within the hour, and you within two."

As Tom counted, he heard stealth footsteps moving away from him, and the sound of something—a piece of wood, a metal bar, whatever had pinned the door closed—being jerked away, and the heavy creaking of the door opening and closing—

Getting to 10, pulling off the hood, struggling for air—

Looking around, making sure he was alone—

Which he was, seeing nothing but the night, the darkness, the place where fear lives—

Trying to picture in his mind some chain of events that didn't end with the triumph of his dread—

Along with its chief collaborator, evil—

But nothing came, nothing except the horrible realization that there was no way out—

And he could no longer stanch the nausea—

Doubling over—
Retching in dry, shuddering heaves—
Panting, trying to catch his breath—
Swallowed by his own terror.

THIRTY

TOM HAD SEEN Toni Allura more times than he could count, mostly in the context of politics and her thorn-in the-side opposition to anything Penn Mallory said, did, or tried to do. So he was struck, while sitting in one of the two armchairs in her hideaway Senate office, by the recognition of just how stunning the woman was.

"You are a very conflicted young man," she said.

You have no idea, he thought, Dreadlock Man and Anath with their threats, Liberty Dash with her suspicions, all fresh as a gunshot on his brain. "I'm just trying to do my job, Senator."

"You're also out of your mind." She smiled—a slight expression, more like her face had cramped—and eased back into the chair. "Yesterday, you told Kyle Kendrick that if I didn't stop my investigation, you'd have the guillotine of *60 Minutes* lopping off my political head for a relationship that ended the moment its impropriety came to my attention. But today you come to me asking that I continue. It leaves me wondering if your left hand is even remotely acquainted with your right."

Tom had always thought her toughness was a put-on, what she did to hold her own in the Man World of the Senate, a shield against the perception of her as intellectually and politically out of her depth. But looking into the unyielding blue eyes, he began to sense that to underestimate Toni Allura would be to make a crippling error.

"I understand," he nodded, refusing to break her stare, trying to send a message that if this was battle for control of the moment, he was happy to engage.

Toni Allura gave it right back to him. But despite its beauty, her face looked at war with itself, ambiguity on one side, vigilance on the other. "Well, I don't. So you'll forgive me if I greet your every syllable with a healthy dose of skepticism."

They had been talking for about 15 minutes, most of which Tom had spent trying to get around a years-long wariness of all things Mallory that was strapped to her hip like a pistol. "As I said—"

"I am well aware of what you said. But what puzzles me is why Penn Mallory sent you here to say it."

"Senator, I told you, he doesn't have—"

"Don't bullshit me. I get enough disrespect in public. I will not tolerate it in private."

Her tone was icicle sharp, and Tom looked away at last, his eyes grazing over the high-ceilinged office. The walls were a soft yellow, the trim white, freshly painted by the smell of it. No windows, a conference table with six chairs, a couch, a fireplace, a television, a mini-bar, a bathroom. Great location, too, just off the Capitol rotunda—

"I know what you're thinking. And no, I didn't sleep with anyone to get this place."

His head snapped back to her as if she'd jerked it on a string. "I wasn't—"

"If you weren't, then you'd be the first." No self-pity in the voice, not even anger, all the inflection of a street sign. Her eyes hardened. "I want to start again. And be warned: If I find out you're holding anything back, or that you're just a stalking horse for Mallory's political scheming, or this is just some scam designed to sidetrack my future, or make me look foolish, or get me to back off on Harriman, as God is my witness, I will end your career in this town."

Tom nodded, but her "sidetrack my future" reference rattled around noisily in his head, making him wonder if maybe Mallory was right, maybe she was making a play for something. But he bookmarked that mental discussion for another time.

"Senator Mallory has given me carte blanche on this," he began. "He wants answers, and I've been instructed to get them, regardless of where the questions lead." It wasn't entirely true; the carte blanche thing was a statement of convenience. But it wasn't a stretch to translate his adventure in Munich as an order to find answers.

Not much of a stretch, anyway.

"You're conducting an investigation," Tom continued. "I'm conducting an investigation for Senator Mallory, so it just makes sense for us to follow our respective paths, and to compare notes at some points."

"That's not going to happen, Tom, and we both know it." She folded her hands into her lap. "Penn Mallory is going to take whatever you give him and run with it, kill it, or leverage it for his own ends. And me? I'll just be another casualty of his ambition. So please don't insult me by suggesting I have something to gain from this little partnership."

Tom rested his hand lightly on the lower part of his stomach and took two quick breaths. "I'll give you a copy of my final report 24 hours before it goes to him."

Toni Allura's well-developed mistrust flexed like a muscle on her face. But the eyes shone with possibility. "Go on."

The tension that had handcuffed Tom's body eased. She'd taken the bait.

"All I ask is that you don't do anything with it until we do."

She laughed contemptuously. "The second-day story is always on Page 22. And no one reads Page 22."

Tom considered that—pretended to consider it, anyway—and then said, "Fine. Do with it what and when you will." It was no concession, because there would never be a report.

Her lips twisted into a suspicious smile. "My, that was easy."

A tactical error, Tom thought, report or no report. He felt her gaze on his skin. "As I said, Senator, I'm just trying to do a job."

Toni Allura's smile went from suspicion to scorn. "I'm a blonde, Tom, not a mathematician. But I don't need a solar-powered calculator to tell me that one and one isn't adding up to a lot of confidence that any of this has the ring of anything other than duplicity."

Tom's mouth went dry. "I told you I'd give you the report. What else—"

"There's not going to be a report, so let's just stop the pretense." She cocked her head slightly. "I must say, if you were my staffer, and went to Penn Mallory, and had a discussion like this without my knowledge, I'd have you drawn and quartered on the Mall."

He shifted in the chair. "So I'm disloyal."

Toni shrugged easily. "I don't know what you are, or who you are, or why you're doing whatever it is you're doing. The logic of it all escapes me."

"I'm just trying to do what's right, Senator."

"Still the idealist, are you?"

"Yes, ma'am, I am." No hesitation.

"So am I," she said with a curt nod of the head. "And like any good idealist, I believe that everyone in the world is corrupt except me, and every agenda suspect except mine."

Before Tom could ask what that meant, she plowed on.

"So you keep your nonexistent report. I'll keep my investigation moving forward at a pace to be determined. And I won't advise Penn Mallory of this conversation. I ask only one thing in return." Tom just looked at her. "Not a word about my late husband's association with Hector Rubio. To anyone."

Tom felt his right eyelid start to twitch. "Senator, that's uh, I mean, I'm not sure I can—"

But she waved him off, and produced a black satchel-like Prada bag, from which she pulled a white mailing envelope, and opened it, and produced a photo, and slid it in front of Tom, and said, "You might want to think twice before telling me what you can and cannot do, Mr. Fargo."

Tom stared at the picture, feeling the air leave his lungs—

He and Anath at the bar in Munich—

"Because if so much as a whisper of Hector Rubio's past should find its way into the public dialogue, then this will find its way to Matt Drudge, Fox News, Rush Limbaugh, and everyone else who bows and scrapes at the altar of Penn Mallory." A brief, strategic pause. "And then the question facing your boss will no longer be about how Harry Platte died, but about why his top aide was—oh, how do they say it—palling around with terrorists."

Tom could only stare, wondering why Toni Allura and Dreadlock Man possessed the same photo, unaware that in another room, in another building, in another part of the city, unseen men were listening, and they had the photo as well, and were plotting accordingly.

THIRTY-ONE

"*BECAUSE IF SO much as a whisper of Hector Rubio's past should find its way into the public dialogue, then this will find its way to Matt Drudge, Fox News, Rush Limbaugh, and everyone else who bows and scrapes at the altar of Penn Mallory. And then the question facing your boss will no longer be about how Harry Platte died, but about why his top aide was—oh, how do they say it—palling around with terrorists.*"

Vance Harriman hit the Off switch on the small digital recorder and said to no one in particular, "Comments?"

Jasper Eddy, the congressman from South Carolina, spoke up first. "I think we need to neutralize that left-wing faggot now."

Harriman smiled, softly but noxiously, at the word. *Neutralize.* "What possible good would come of that?"

"The guy's off-the-wall unpredictable. He protests against America one day, supports it the next, suckin' up to Mallory one day, sneakin' around behind his back the next. Christ, who knows what he and the Cheerleader are cookin' up."

"Or he and Mallory."

For a moment, Eddy's eyes went foggy with confusion, then became angry and hot as a stovetop burner. "You think Penn's got something to do with this? That he knows about it?" Harriman just shrugged. "Due respect, Vance, but that's crazier than a sack of squirrels."

"As you are well aware, stranger things have happened."

Eddy considered that. "Then maybe you and me stage another little brain-trust session, like the one at Penn's the night Harry's plane went down. You know, to smoke Fargo out, see what he's up to. He fell for that one hook, line, and sinker."

Harriman shook his head. "He didn't know anything then. There was no competing narrative."

They were sitting in a conference room at Lang & Bird, a K Street firm whose managing partner had overseen Harriman's vetting in preparation for his confirmation hearings. Eddy was in a starched white shirt and off-the-rack suit of dubious fabric; the CIA nominee looked as fresh-pressed as ever. On the huge round table were three Styrofoam-boxed lunches—tuna, chicken salad, and turkey sandwiches, all untouched—a sterling coffee service, three cups and saucers, small bottles of water, a silver ice bucket.

Eddy stared at the digital recorder. "Tell me again how you bugged a conversation in her private office."

"Her Blackberry," Harriman replied evenly. "We remotely downloaded a spyware program into the device. It is controlled via an encrypted SMS command that we send." His explanation was matter-of-fact, as if describing how to change a tire.

"But they weren't talking on the phone."

"The software is voice-activated. It captures personal conversations as well as calls."

"And she's got no idea?"

"Not a clue, and everything that implies."

Eddy made a noise that sounded impressed and uneasy. "Whatever. I don't trust her, and I especially don't trust Fargo. He's a loose end, and—"

"And tying him off now," Harriman interrupted, impatient, "when he has been publicly linked to the investigation, would only invite the turning over of stones that are better left unturned."

Eddy couldn't disagree. "What about Rubio? Somebody pushes him, will he talk?"

"He's living in Florida on a yacht paid for by the United States government. He understands the consequences of disclosure."

"We gonna let Penn know? About Fargo and the Cheerleader, Rubio, any of this?"

Harriman shook his head. "It's in everyone's interest to keep him at a distance. We'll continue to monitor Fargo; should any matter of concern surface, we will consider bringing Senator Mallory into the conversation at that point."

"And you don't think conspiring with the Cheerleader is a matter of concern?"

"I think it is the act of a traitor, and will be dealt with in the appropriate manner at the appropriate time. But this is not that time."

"Penn still needs to know."

The scars on Harriman's face went strawberry red. "Let me be clear. Once Penn Mallory becomes president, and we have the full force and power of the United States government at our disposal, we will focus on Mr. Fargo should that be necessary. Until then, however, it is essential that Senator Mallory be kept as much in the dark as is prudent."

"Nope, sorry, Vance, you're wrong on this. Penn deserves to know the landscape, and if there's something out there than can trip him up, sidetrack his campaign, we have to tell him."

"No, if there's something out there that puts his campaign at risk," Harriman replied in a voice that could scrape off skin, "our duty is to manage the problem."

"And if it comes back to bite him on the ass later?"

"It will not."

"How do you know? You a fortuneteller now—"

"We must protect him—"

"A soothsayin' gypsy—"

"This is, has always been, a need to know—"

"A damned county fair card reader—"

Harriman came at Jasper Eddy with the explosiveness of

floodwaters, strong right hand pinning the congressman back in the chair by the throat, his expression blazing like a black torch.

Eddy tried to say something, but the words couldn't escape Harriman's grasp.

"Vance, leave him alone."

Harriman leaned closer into Jasper Eddy, saying nothing, the bulging blue vein that bisected his forehead doing all the necessary talking.

"Vance?"

Eddy's eyes looked as if they were about to burst from their sockets.

"Damnit, Vance, back off. That is not the act of a Christian gentleman."

Harriman shook his head ever so slightly, confused, as if he'd woken up in a stranger's bed, and did as ordered. He took a step back.

"Crazy bastard!" Jasper Eddy rasped.

And another step.

"I oughtta have you fuckin' arrested!"

And one more.

Then, after a full-body shudder, Harriman straightened himself, and the anger evaporated, replaced by genuine righteousness and false humility. "I apologize, Congressman. Sometimes I know not what I do."

Jasper Eddy glared at him, massaging the front of his neck. "I just don't want anything blowing up in our faces."

"Nor do I," Harriman replied, barely above a whisper, miles from contrite.

"Then I'm tellin' you, this may not be national security, but it sure as hell is our security, and we need to engage Unde Malum and clean up this little mess before it buries us all."

"Unde Malum is not yet in my portfolio."

Eddy eyed him skeptically. "Vance, you were one of its daddies, present at the creation. I think that gives you some, uh, operational flexibility on this type of thing."

"Listen to me. Both of you." Harriman and Eddy turned toward the voice. "Nobody touches Fargo, and Mallory stays in the dark about his dalliance with the Cheerleader. Rubio is insignificant. He hasn't said anything yet, and if he opens his mouth, he dies, and he knows it. So we're going to just let it play out. Once Vance is at Langley, we'll revisit the question." A pause to light a cigar the size of a battleship. "And for the record, I do have some operational flexibility on this type of thing."

With that, David Diamond, former aide to Harry Platte, smiled like the proud father of the Antichrist.

"And I need to exercise it by arranging a date with a dancer."

Vance Harriman looked at Diamond but saw the photo in his mind, the one with the girl, the one he'd shredded that day before all of this became what it had become. He nodded without feeling. "Keep it ordinary, David. A robbery gone wrong, automobile accident, drowning. Something small. This is not the time to be making a statement or sending a message."

"I know what I'm doing," Diamond replied. "This won't be on CNN. Trust me."

"I distrust anyone for whom the impulse to punish is all-consuming."

"Don't worry. This isn't about punishing anybody."

Harriman frowned. "Tell that to your agent of punishment."

THIRTY-TWO

THE CROWD WAS young, beautiful and young, all of them moving on the smallish dance floor like a throbbing, manic wave to the DJ's pulsing beats, Western music, heavy on the bass.

Laughing and smiling and sweating, their swaying arms overhead, rhythmically stabbing up and down through the thick haze of cigarette smoke—Parliaments, made in Switzerland, no one caring about Lebanon's ban on smoking in closed places— their bodies gyrating and jumping.

Lights going from red to green to yellow to white to blue and then back again, in perfect sync with the music, throwing a momentary flash of color on their faces that for an instant made each of them an individual, something more than just an anonymous face in the pulsating crowd:

One, in her tight designer jeans and high heels and long black hair. Psychology student at the American University of Beirut.

Another, thin and brooding despite the happy mayhem. A coffee-shop poet, maybe a member of the Arab Spring Youth Federation.

And another, too-tight shirt, too many buttons not doing their intended job. Gold smuggler.

And another, red hair, dress shorter than it needed to be, sandwiched between two brown-skinned 20-something men in black suits, white shirts, no ties. Rich American girl on holiday. A pair of hustlers.

And another, plaid cowboy shirt with stitching at the shoulders, white faux-jewel buttons, thick mustache. Middle East mob.

And another, mid-calf cotton skirt, long-sleeved linen blouse, hair tied back, respectful. Australian tourist.

And another, slight beard, older than the other men by maybe five years, and taller, draped in Armani, shiny shoes and serious eyes and steady hands. Surgeon at Clemenceau Medical Center.

And another, three-piece suit out of the disco era, gaudy rings and bracelets and chains, heavy, thinning hair. Drug lawyer, or dealer, or both.

And another and another and another.

Until:

At a corner table, a woman, sitting with three friends, also dancers, smiling and laughing as she read through a program from the evening's show at Al Madina Theater—*Serenade*, choreography by Balanchine, music by Tchaikovsky—pointing excitedly at something on the page, her friends shrieking with glee.

She was young and beautiful, more so than anyone else in the clamorous room.

Serenade. How appropriate, Balanchine often being accused of hiding a story in the ballet, but always saying no, it was just beautiful people in motion to beautiful music, a dance in the light of the moon.

The bartender, dark-skinned and all in black, approached and leaned in to the red-haired patron in the horned-rim glasses, shouting in English over the electro-dance din, "Another whiskey?"

She nodded. "Yes, please. I have a credit card. Celia Lampson. And can you tell me where the ladies' washroom is?" He made a vague gesture toward the back wall.

The young woman at the corner table looked at her watch, suddenly leaping to her feet and moving gracefully through the crowd, around the lip of the dance floor, pure liquid ease, toward the front entrance, talking briefly to a heavyset man in a long black leather jacket who monitored everyone coming in or going out.

He nodded as she spoke. She brushed his cheek with a light kiss of gratitude and returned to the table, where her friends greeted her with applause and champagne toasts.

At the bar:

A man in a turtleneck and jeans, sitting alone, wearing frameless glasses tinted light purple, sipping a 961 Beer, Lebanese pale ale.

"Pardon me?"

The man turned to Celia Lampson but said nothing, as if trying to be heard above the music was not worth the effort. He just stared.

"I need to go to the ladies' washroom, and was wondering if you would keep an eye on my package." Pointing to the floor.

The man's eyes followed.

A shopping bag from Aishti, the luxury department store sometimes called "the Barney's of Beirut."

His mouth curled into a dismissive sneer. "Fendi?"

Celia Lampson replied with a noncommittal shrug.

"Dior? Gucci?"

"It's a gift, a surprise."

"A surprise," he nodded. "I am so sure." He didn't refuse the request, just turned away, studying his reflection in the mirror behind the bar, muttering "Surprise, surprise, surprise" as if it were code for Materialistic Western Whore.

"I'll only be a moment."

His eyes didn't leave the mirror. "Whatever."

Looking back down at the Aishti bag, she used her toe to edge it a bit closer to the bar, farther under the steel-rod footrest, slightly less in view, then got up and walked toward—

The young woman at the corner table, who was now talking to a slight but muscled man in a horizontally striped T-shirt that clung to him like a second skin. He said something to her. She nodded in agreement and laughed happily.

The music seemed to suddenly get louder, and as it did, the dance-floor gyrations grew exponentially faster and more crazed.

The man in the striped T-shirt tried to get the young girl to join him on the dance floor, but she refused, saying, "I've had my fill of dance for the evening," the words flecked with some Nordic dialect, because the ballet troupe had been re-created in Denmark after its dismantling in the wake of the chaos that followed Saddam's downfall. She glanced again at her watch. "And I must keep an eye out for my little sister."

The lights leaped and flashed and careened to keep pace with the higher-voltage beats, landing on the faces of this man or that woman, illuminating them for just a moment, their mouths moving but drown out by the music. They looked like mimes.

"Excuse me?" Celia Lampson said.

The young woman faced the pleading man in the tight T-shirt and couldn't hear.

Celia Lampson tapped her shoulder. "Excuse me, didn't you dance one of the leads tonight?"

She spun around. "I'm sorry?"

"Who are you?" the man demanded.

"I just, I mean—"

"This is famous ballerina, famous dancer, hero to freedom-loving Iraqi people," he yelled.

Heroism, like so many other things in these twisted times, was a matter of perception.

"I understand, I know. I just wanted to tell her, you, how much I enjoyed your performance this evening."

With that, everything seemed to melt away. The suspicion, the swagger, the nationalism.

"Thank you," the young woman replied, loud without screaming. Up close, her eyes were dark brown, almost black. The cheekbones were high and perfect, the neck like a swan's, the hair in a tight knot at the crown of her head.

"Well, goodbye," Celia Lampson said.

The dancer looked past her and erupted in joy. "Safa!" she squealed, standing and throwing strong-but-slender arms around a child, 12 or 13, who had her same beautiful features, but eyes swimming in innocence and a face as pure as an angel's thoughts. "You came, you came, you came!" The man in the striped T-shirt grabbed an empty chair and ceremoniously invited the little girl to sit.

No longer a part of the conversation, Celia Lampson stepped out of the dancer's orbit, watching the sisters chattering happily, asking herself why fate had delivered this poor child to this place at this moment, recalling what Disraeli had said, that we make our own fortunes and call them fate, and wondering what the British prime minister would say to this baby girl, who at such a young age had not had the opportunities to make fortunes of any sort, and never would.

She took another step back. She lowered her head and looked to the floor. Her mouth slipped into a tight smile.

Then she finally turned and walked in a direction opposite the washroom, past the sullen Aishti bag watcher, through the thick crowd of doctors and druggies and students and smugglers and tourists and mobsters, away from the pounding beats, out of the flashing lights, into the dark, semi-industrial La Quarantaine neighborhood in the northeast part of the city. Almost instantly, her nose rebelled against the stench from a nearby slaughterhouse and waste disposal and treatment center.

Once outside, Celia Lampson slowed and thought once more about the child, allowing the hesitation to anesthetize her humanity, waiting to be embraced by the cold, reminded again of how in fighting monsters of all ideologies she had become one.

The detachment returned, as she had hoped, though faster than she preferred.

Picking up her pace again, she took a cell phone from her leather satchel purse.

Opened it. Punched in a number. Let it ring.

Once, twice, three times—

A ringer in the receiving phone was wired to a pair of detonating caps, the incoming call completing an electric circuit and setting off

20 pounds of gelatinous dynamite packed with nails and screws—
Concealed nicely and neatly in an Aishti shopping bag.

The explosion cracked the nighttime sky wide open, throwing building and body parts over a hundred yards in every direction.

Celia Lampson pulled off the red-haired wig, dropped it on the ground, crushed the horned-rim glasses underfoot, and started walking again, ignoring the carnage and the terror and the screams, no longer thinking about the lovely young ballerina and her innocent baby sister, but of what would happen next. Because she knew that no matter how well Tom Fargo followed her instructions in Munich, things were spinning out of control, and she would likely go from hunter to hunted, and that meant she had to send a message, so she did, and she had no doubt it would invite a response.

When it came, she'd be ready.

THIRTY-THREE

VANCE HARRIMAN SIPPED an espresso at a small coffee shop about a mile from the Territo office, staring at the flat screen on the wall, horrific images of bodies being pulled from the ruins of a Beirut nightclub, flames knifing into the black sky, wailing women and crying children and angry men, flashing lights, firefighters and police, all of it to the soundtrack of a grave-toned CNN reporter detailing the destruction—

A favorite gathering place for locals and tourists—

Shortly after midnight—

Explosion—

At least 125 dead—

Death toll expected to climb—

No group has taken credit—

Widely assumed to be terrorist-related—

Members of an exiled Iraqi dance troupe believed to be among the victims.

Harriman finished the coffee, put $10 on the table, stood, and walked outside, smiling at his waitress, a sweet-looking girl of maybe 20 who, he could tell, recognized him from the news.

This was one of those moments that had the potential to alter everything, he thought, waiting for the early morning traffic to pass so he could cross the street to his car. He knew that. He also knew it was no time for caution. A challenge had been put to them, and any perceived weakness in response, any perceived uncertainty, would only invite further defiance.

Keep it ordinary, she had been told. No statements. No messages.

Except she had sent one. And Vance Harriman simply could not allow that to stand.

Once in his car, he punched David Diamond's number into the secure satellite phone. "I take it you've seen the news."

"Yeah." Diamond's voice was lifeless and without anger. Harriman sensed he knew what was coming.

"I think it's time we concluded our arrangement with the Jew."

THIRTY-FOUR

IT DIDN'T FEEL like the end of the world.

There was no desolation or chaos, no roving hordes of crazed and feral survivors scavenging the countryside in search of anything that could keep them alive one more day, no permanent midnight in either the literal or the figurative sense.

Instead, there were barbecue restaurants, a casino, expensive jewelers, high-end clothing stores, cruise ships, chocolate shops, boutique hotels, and at least one big blue double-decker bus that was a coffee bar on wheels.

That was why Anath so loved Ushuaia, the last city on the globe, at the southernmost tip of South America: It was at once foreign and familiar, like being on another planet that still felt strangely like Earth.

And it was a good place to hide from those who, at this moment, 6,500 miles north in Washington, were no doubt plotting her death.

She lit a cigarette and looked up at the low, snow-dusted mountains that ringed the city. The day was drifting toward sunset, and the clouds were settling in. The temperature, now in the mid-40s, would soon drop, freezing the fine mist in the air.

She strolled easily down Avenue San Martin, Ushuaia's Rodeo Drive, a block from the bay and the Beagle Channel, which after 150 miles opened into Drake Passage, the shortest direct route to Antarctica, and which, because of its high winds and currents and waves, was generally considered one of the planet's most perilous bodies of water.

She'd taken the trip once, to Antarctica, traveling with an English scuba diver who had been a contractor with the Turkish National Intelligence Organization. She had loved the man for two weeks. He had taught her the efficient use of a KA-BAR knife that a Navy Seal had given him. On this day, the knife rode just under her armpit, strapped tight to her body, concealed by the Aztec blue Gore-Tex North Face jacket.

Every so often she stopped to look into a storefront window. Avenue San Martin reminded her, in a strange way, of lower Manhattan, with its incongruous mix of trendy retailers like Timberland, cheap souvenir stores that trafficked mostly in penguins—stuffed, ceramic, or otherwise—and tucked-away gems of restaurants, the shops and eateries under gaudy awnings that would make a Canal Street bodega proud. One of her guilty pleasures, a store that appeared to cater to rock stars and their fans, would be at home on St. Mark's Place. Her hotel, sleek and warm and very European-feeling, looked like it had been airlifted from Lexington Avenue.

From somewhere in the ether she caught the pounding beats of "Venus," by the Bangles.

Crossing the street, she heard the sharp wail of a car horn. It was perhaps the only real danger in Ushuaia, the lack of stop signs, which empowered tiny little toy-like cars—Saabs, Fords, Chevrolets, Toyotas, Peugeots, a lot of them cabs—to go blazing along with little regard for the safety of pedestrians.

She stepped quickly back on the sidewalk. A city policeman, dressed in a neon-orange vest and paramilitary black jumpsuit, looked at her, shook his head, and smiled as he passed. She knew that crime was not a huge concern here, making his presence mostly ceremonial. Still, he carried a working semi-automatic light combat pistol with a wooden handle—wooden so it wouldn't freeze in the winter.

Two little stray dogs raced by, both of them looking happier and better fed than a lot of the natives, as did most of the strays in the town. Her eyes followed them up a sloping side street—Ushuaia in a lot of ways felt like a Maine fishing village without the fishing industry, San Francisco with smaller hills and no sprawl—and landed on what looked like a husky-shepherd mix lolling in the middle of the road. The two strays traded secrets with him then took off. Anath climbed the 25 yards to the big dog, who rolled over on his back as she approached. She stroked his ear.

Wondering how much attention the Beirut incident had generated, she walked back down to Avenue San Martin and wandered into an electronics store that offered public Internet service and everything from MacBook Pros to PlayStations to Wiis. She was surprised to find it open. Ushuaia merchants had a kind of laissez-faire attitude about commerce, with store hours being more of a whim than a requirement.

To her right was a row of pay-by-the-minute computers on a long table. In front of her, at the back of the store, were stacks and stacks of liquor bottles. To her left, two teenagers were rough-housing at the register under the dim eyes of a thick-set graying man who looked like an extra in an Argentine version of *The Godfather*. He smiled at Anath, revealing crooked teeth and questionable intentions.

She smiled back and left. She was here to be anonymous, if just for a few days, until the cards of her fate were played. This was no time to attract unwarranted attention from unknown eyes.

As expected, the weather suddenly changed, the temperature dropping into the high 20s, and the mist in the air crystallizing. Anath wrapped a black scarf around her throat and put on a pair of black neoprene gloves. As if by magic, her breath suddenly began to take form.

She considered walking a block down to Avenue Maipú, mostly because she liked the architecture of the buildings that fronted the bay. It was a mishmash of every conceivable style, one building looking like faux Taos, the next like an Alpine A-frame, the next like a flat in Prague, the next nearly art deco with right angles and clean lines and pastels that had lost their luster if not their life.

But she changed her mind, suddenly craving a Patagonia, the Argentine beer that came in a bottle the size of an Atlas missile. One wasn't enough. Two were too many.

She thought of the Irish bar where she'd first met her scuba diver, with its wood interior, tall stools, satellite televisions showing soccer, looking like someone's idea of Dublin except the menus were in Spanish and the waiters couldn't speak English on a bet.

She smiled at the memory and headed in that direction—

Past graffiti that was as diverse as the architecture, black silhouetted men captioned by *Justicia*, or rainbows and clouds and *Buenos Vibros* written in the bright blue skies above them, or musicians in striking reds and yellows and greens, one on the sax, one on the guitar, one on an upright bass—

Past a high-def billboard that sat atop the taxi depot, advertising a bank—

Past a street protest, a mini-shanty town, nurses demanding a living wage, signs all in English, which was interesting—

When, a block from the Irish bar, she saw another Ushuaia police officer approaching her, a woman, late 20s, dark hair pulled back, could have been a former Miss Argentina, maybe even a former Miss Universe.

Anath stopped for a moment to catch her breath, to focus, get her bearings.

The cop kept walking toward her.

Anath smiled, thinking of the possibilities.

The cop smiled, looking for all the world like a promise, a dream—

Until Anath caught sight of the gun—

Olive drab, definitely not a police pistol—

Not a wood handle, but plastic—

The cop not noticing what Anath had seen or what she now

knew, picking up the pace just a bit, smile wide and enchanting—

Anath picking up hers as well—

The cop breaking into a trot, reaching for the Fabrique Nationale Five-seven, a 5.7mm semi-automatic that could blow a man's head off, or a woman's—

Anath matching her stride for stride, reaching under the Aztec blue North Face jacket—

The cop getting the FN 5.7 clear, keeping it hanging at her side—

Anath doing the same with the KA-BAR, keeping it hanging at her side—

The cop still not noticing, her eyes locked on Anath like she was big game, coming at her faster—

Anath in a full run—

The cop starting to raise the pistol—

Anath reaching her and wrapping strong arms around her before she could get the pistol in firing position—

Then kissing her, deep and passionately—

Feeling the cop's knees start to dissolve—

Loving the warmth of her mouth—

The gentle sweetness of her breath—

Then plunging the KA-BAR into her belly—

Once, twice, three times, four times, rapidly and relentlessly—

The cop's eyes going wide, drowning in shock and unexpected agony—

Anath never breaking the embrace, or the kiss—

Jamming the knife into her one final time, twisting it hard and jerking it up into the ribs, brushing her tongue briefly over the dying woman's lips, thinking not of what might have been, but of what was going to be—

That those in Washington who had been plotting her death would soon pay the price for this blundering attempt on her life—

And for their crimes—

And it would be at her hand.

She stared into the dark and now-dead eyes of the gorgeous woman, kissed her one more time with a fury that would frighten the devil himself, then dropped her in a bloody heap on the street, looking at no one as she disappeared into the dusk, the growing chill in the air nothing compared to the ice that wrapped her heart and the merciless desire for vengeance that froze her blood.

PART THREE: **ANGEL IN YOUR POCKET**

THIRTY-FIVE

TONI ALLURA GLANCED at her notepad, flipped through a couple of pages, jotted something down, and looked back up at Vance Harriman over the top of Versace reading glasses. "If we could, I'd like to shift my focus to outsourcing. Is that all right with you?"

Harriman smiled coldly at the put-on politeness. "Of course, Senator."

"Your company, I believe it is called I Terrify—"

"As I made clear the other day, Madam Senator, it's called Territo."

"Which means, 'I terrify.'"

At the center of the panel, the chairman barked, "Let's move along, please."

Toni nodded toward him with deference, and returned her attention to Harriman.

"This company of yours, has it received any contracts from the United States government?"

He nodded, confident, having been well-prepped for this line of inquiry by the White House. "Yes, we have."

"What would you say the value of those contracts is?"

Harriman feigned plumbing his mind for a number. The answer to this particular question had been a subject of some debate, the White House arguing that he should not provide the specifics—

he was, after all, Territo's CEO, not its accountant—Harriman arguing back that she could find out easily enough if she desired. "Probably $75 million, in that range."

Toni raised an eyebrow. "Impressive."

"Not really," he shrugged. "It is only a portion of our business, and a relatively small one, comparatively speaking. Other third-party security professionals have arrangements worth five to 10 times that amount."

"Should the American people be concerned that an issue as vital as national security is being outsourced to 'third-party security professionals'?"

Harriman looked at her like he'd swallowed a fishhook. "Senator, third parties such as Territo bring a different set of values to the task. We are corporate entities. Our job, simply stated, is to do the job. Period. We do not engage in intra-office squabbling. We do not try to protect turf. We steer clear of political intrigue. We perform essential, prescribed functions with a high degree of efficiency and a superior level of quality."

Toni took off the Versaces and glared at him. "So your answer is no, the American people should not be concerned."

"My answer, Senator, is that we're at war. I would assume the American people would prefer that we win it."

"At any cost?"

His face went hard as concrete. "Freedom does not come cheaply."

In the third row, an anonymous White House aide softly whispered, "Boom."

But Toni Allura was enough of a performer to know she could not allow Harriman's sound bite to stand, and she rolled right over it. "I should say not, Mr. Harriman, not when we're talking $75 million." She did not wait for a reaction, either from the nominee or the audience. "But that $75 million, it's not a real number, is it?"

"Excuse me?"

"That's just what we know, what's public." She cocked her

head. "What about what we don't know, what's hidden?"

"Hidden?"

"You are aware, I'm certain, of the so-called black budget, are you not?"

"I have seen news accounts, yes."

"So you know that approximately $56 billion appropriated to the Department of Defense is to be used for intelligence-related programs that are neither overseen nor regulated, and basically free of congressional oversight and public scrutiny."

Harriman put a hand over the microphone and had a quick exchange with his attorney, something the White House had told him not to do, fearing it conjured images of a mob boss giving testimony before some special committee on organized crime.

He leaned in closely to the attorney, nodding in agreement with the near-silent instructions.

"Senator, I do not have the appropriate government clearances, so any comment would be purely speculative."

"Oh, go on," she said with a pronounced just-among-us-girls smile. "Speculate."

"I'd rather not. It would be inappropriate."

"I appreciate your penchant for secrecy, Mr. Harriman. It is an important quality in a director of Central Intelligence." He nodded. "But this top-secret slush fund of yours—"

"Senator," the attorney interrupted, "for the record, my client does not agree with your choice of words, and it is irresponsible to suggest he has now, or has had in the past, any possession of any government budgetary authority for any purpose."

She sat back in her chair, looked left and right to the other committee members, and refocused on Harriman with an astonishment that was as real as a campaign promise. "Wow. So that's what an $800-an-hour attorney sounds like."

"Actually, it's $1,000 an hour," Harriman retaliated.

They locked gazes in what the next day's paper would refer to as "a visual smackdown."

"Did you and Harry Platte ever discuss the black budget?"

Harriman sat up straight, unmoving as a granite statue. "No, we did not."

"I ask, because with you and he being associates, and with so much of the Pentagon budget being redirected to activities undertaken by the CIA or its private-sector contractors, it seems—"

"Harry Platte is dead, Senator, and I find any effort to soil his legacy to be distasteful at the minimum."

She inhaled and exhaled deeply, as if resigned to the idea that this was all heading toward a dead end, and rifled again through her notes. "So you have never heard of Controlled Access Programs?"

"No."

"Special Access Programs?"

"No."

"Special Evaluation Programs?"

"No."

"Classic Wizard?"

"No."

"Chalk Angel?"

"No."

"Black Light?"

"No."

"Link Plumeria?"

"No."

"I ask, Mr. Harriman, because these are all programs in the Defense budget that, frankly, nobody knows about because none of them are explained."

"Perhaps if you went to the Department of Defense, Senator, and—"

"Mythic Thunder?"

"No."

"Red Badge?"

"No."

"Unde Malum?"

"I'm sorry?"

Toni Allura focused on Harriman like a drawn bayonet. "Unde Malum, Mr. Harriman?"

Harriman stared straight ahead, smart enough to recognize that his "I'm sorry" response, coming after a litany of "No's," likely sent an unintended message.

"Unde Malum," she repeated. "It's Latin. Loosely translated, it means, 'From whence cometh evil.' Did you know that?"

Vance Harriman remained stoic.

She smiled. "And here I thought you were facile in the language of Caesar." The smile hardened. "I guess we won't make that mistake again, now, will we?" Then, to the chairman: "I have no further questions for the nominee at this time."

As he watched his interrogators exit the stage, a narrow smile, brutal as truth, elbowed its way onto Harriman's face. "Damnant quod non intelligunt," he muttered—

They condemn what they do not understand—

While in the back of the committee room, Penn Mallory seemed to teeter ever so slightly, as if trying to keep his balance while the ground shifted beneath him.

THIRTY-SIX

WHEN TOM STEPPED into the second-floor private dining room of Mallory's favorite French restaurant, he expected to find the senator seated in one of the ergonomic chairs at the granite conference table doing business as usual—papers and notes and briefing books spread everywhere, maybe a glass of bourbon— occasionally glancing at Fox News on the 42-inch flat-screen TV on the wall.

But there were no papers or notes or briefing books, and the television was dark.

The bourbon was there, however. A bottle.

And Mallory.

And sitting across from him, David Diamond.

"Hey, son," Mallory said, smiling broadly, standing and shaking Tom's hand. "Sit, please. I think you know David."

Diamond extended his hand as well. "Good to see you again."

Tom took it and nodded in silence, trying to get his bearings, knowing the greeting was a complete lie. Diamond had said maybe 500 words to him over the years, most of them soaked in thinly disguised disdain. He slipped into a chair next to Mallory, eyes flicking back and forth between his boss and Diamond, still saying nothing, smart enough to know that you never talk until you know the shot.

He knew the shot was coming. He just didn't know he was the target.

"I'll just get straight to the point," Mallory said. "The presidential campaign is starting to make some moves, and you two are a big part of them. So I needed to get the both of you in the same room to make sure we're all on the same page."

Tom felt suddenly light-headed. Diamond looked unsurprised.

Mallory poured bourbon into three short glasses. He and Diamond drank, Tom left his untouched, feeling the sudden need for something more pharmaceutical. "I have it on good authority that the Cheerleader's gonna run for president."

Tom was so knocked back by Mallory's pronouncement that it barely registered when Diamond said, "The woman is to unbridled ambition what New York is to liberals."

Even in his cloud of confusion, Tom couldn't help but wonder what it was about Toni Allura that robbed powerful men like Mallory and Diamond of their ability to think rationally. His eyes once again bounced between the two of them. "Did I miss something?"

The senator's expression went grim. He stared squarely at Tom. "I'm afraid we got an enemy within, somebody who's secretly feeding her information about me."

Tom's mouth fell open slightly. Instantly wondering if this was about his clandestine meeting with Toni Allura, he summoned every milligram of strength—psychological as well as physical—to keep from sending the wrong body-language message to Mallory. "Who?"

Mallory shook his head. "That's why we're having this little get-together."

Beneath the table, Tom clenched and unclenched his fists, trying to steer the anxiety away from his voice and face. "What can I do?"

"David's coming on board as a principal of Patriot's Blood," Mallory said matter-of-factly. Tom's eyes widened in disbelief. What in the hell was a shill for the military establishment doing in charge of the group that would support the senator's White House bid when the time came? Mallory saw the question in his face and put both hands up in a calming, don't-worry-about-it gesture. "It just makes sense. He's got a ton of contacts in the defense industry, and those folks got a lot of money to give, and a good reason to give it to yours truly."

Tom paused and set his elbows on the table, fingers laced tightly. He flattened his voice. "What's this got to do with me?"

"I need you to take a leave of absence, a short one, and go over there. To Patriot's Blood."

Tom's face felt like a red pepper. "I don't raise money, Senator. It's not what I do. My job is to—"

"We don't need you to raise money," Diamond interrupted. "We need you to find out who the leak is."

Tom tried giving him his best stony gaze. "Assuming there is one."

Diamond gave it right back to him. "Assuming there is one."

"Why me? Why not you?"

"Because I *do* know how to raise money. That's *my* job." A small, toxic smile.

Tom unlaced his fingers and laid them flat on the table.

"It'll be a temporary leave, all on the up-and-up," Mallory reassured him. "No big announcement. You'll be back in a week, 10 days tops."

"Who's going to replace me?"

"Nobody, because there's no need."

Right, he thought. "When do I start?"

"No better time than the present, huh?"

Tom surveyed his boss' face looking for a hint that this was something other than what it appeared to be. He got nothing. Unsure whether that was good or bad, he just nodded slowly, without a lot of conviction, and said, "Whatever I can do."

Mallory grinned and turned to Diamond. "Meet your new No. 2, Mr. Principal."

Diamond took a cell phone from his pocket, punching in some data. A swooshing sound followed shortly after he stopped typing.

"I just sent you my contact info. It'll download automatically onto your phone when you open the email. My private numbers are included. I expect we'll be spending a lot of time talking."

Tom's Blackberry vibrated. He pulled it out, opened his email program, and downloaded the information into his list of contacts. The business at hand concluded, the three of them sat in an uncomfortable silence—Mallory and Diamond finishing off their bourbon—until Tom looked at his watch, the act a little more obvious than he would have liked. "Well, I guess I need to get the transition process going."

He stood to leave. Mallory rose with him, grabbed both of his shoulders, fixed him with a meaningful stare. "This is temporary, Tom. You gotta believe me. We have a problem. I need you to solve it. Don't read anything into it."

"I serve at your pleasure, Senator."

"Find my leak, son."

"I will, sir."

Mallory watched in silence as he left, eyes lingering on the door after it closed. "How long have you known?"

"A few days."

"You should have come to me when you first found out."

"Frankly, Senator, his meeting with the Cheerleader, secret though it may have been, was on its face no real cause for concern." Diamond paused. "But when she asked Vance about Unde Malum, well, the threat level went from guarded to elevated."

"He doesn't know about Unde Malum. He can't."

"With all respect, I'm not going to make that assumption." Mallory, still staring at the closed door, shook his head. "It was the right move," Diamond continued. "We need to keep an eye on him."

"I still don't believe there's a connection."

"We'll find out soon enough. If he runs back to the Cheerleader, we'll know."

"He's been loyal to me for years."

"Beware the face of loyalty, Senator. It is often the mask of betrayal and the secret weapon of one's enemy."

Mallory returned to the conference table and sat. "That boy isn't my enemy."

"As I said, Senator, we will see," Diamond replied, holding up his cell phone, reminding Mallory that it was now the vessel of virtually everything Tom Fargo would say from that moment forward. "We will see it all."

THIRTY-SEVEN

A TALL, SOLIDLY built man in a fedora and large oversized glasses sat at the French restaurant's zinc-topped bar, sipping club soda and lime, cell phone at the ready, watching a dazed Tom Fargo work his way through a crowd thick with the city's elite—

Lobbyists, senators, congressmen—

Watching as one or two of them acknowledged him with a smile and a handshake, others with a glare, noticing that Tom returned both the pro and the con gestures with a frozen expression that was neither receptive nor defensive, more lost than anything else, as if he'd been suddenly dropped into this place from another world.

Watching as Tom walked past the tall round columns, high-end fixtures, framed Taittinger poster art and newspaper front pages on the walls—

Past couples sitting on wood-and-black leather chairs, squarish granite-like tables between them, leaning close to each other, smiling, conspiring—

Past the booths, brown leather and wood, fine white tablecloths, not a lot of them occupied just yet, more activity at the bar—

Past the cherry-wood walls, turning at the hostess station toward the glass doors onto the street, face a ball of confusion, the disorientation coming off him in waves.

The man in the fedora thought that had its advantages and disadvantages.

Severe distraction was good. It blurred the lines of logic, brought down the guard, created a mental state that made manipulation easy. But it also increased unpredictability. And right now, at this moment, he needed Tom Fargo to be anything but erratic.

The man in the fedora glanced at the Rolex on his left wrist, thinking there were probably five hours or perhaps seven until Tom Fargo's world would begin to collapse like the World Trade Center on the day that had brought them to this moment. He found an odd solace in the fact that the dreadlock wig was no longer necessary, that from now on there would be no more disguises or deceit, just the path to a final truth. And although he knew where all this would ultimately lead, where it had to lead, he did not know what the destination would look like when they arrived, or who would be left standing in the end.

He picked up his cell phone and pushed the Send button, dispatching a two-word message:

"Now, please."

THIRTY-EIGHT

AS TOM TRIED to make an inconspicuous escape from the restaurant, ideas and thoughts and intrigues caromed off every corner of his brain, each of them a pinball of paranoia.

This made no sense on any number of levels:

He had done political work for Mallory in the past, like the whole Kyle Kendrick thing, Hector Rubio, the Munich trip, and he'd still held his staff position. None of that had ever been an issue. Hell, politics *was* the job.

Mallory had never liked Diamond, never trusted him, thought he had too much influence over Platte.

Defense industry ties and his own claims aside, Diamond wasn't a professional fundraiser, didn't have real access to wealth and wealthy people, seriously wealthy people, which was one of the basic requirements of running Patriot's Blood, because, let's face it, groups like Patriot's Blood let billionaires determine who wins elections.

No, it made no sense at all.

Did something happen that forced the decision to move him out of the Senate office?

Had Toni Allura betrayed him to Mallory?

Had Harriman finally convinced the senator that Tom truly was the enemy?

Did Mallory have some deep dark secret, some closeted skeleton, which Diamond found out about and put to his own advantage?

And on the subject of secrets, again, had Mallory somehow discovered his newly re-emerging reliance on mind-balancing pharmaceuticals and decided it was too risky to keep him in a sensitive position?

Tom pushed through the glass front door and stood on the street, a little shaky, the world seeming a lot less certain than it had just hours ago, murkier, the darkness and light coalescing, giving him a sense that his once-clear core, his substance, was becoming indistinct, spawning shadows that now entwined him like black ivy.

He shook his head, trying to silence the mental thunder, and turned without looking—

"Whoa, dude!"—

Ramming straight into the Geek, from Vance Harriman's office, who was toting a green canvas messenger bag and wearing an expression that appeared lit up by a controlled substance.

Tom raised his hands in apology. "Sorry, sorry, sorry."

"You look like you're cruising first class on a freak flight, man."

Tom nodded. "Lot of things on my mind."

"Tell me about it, bro. I work in the mystery mansion, remember?"

Tom nodded again, trying once more to quiet the storm in his head, masking the effort with small talk. "And how are things there?"

The Geek gave that more than a few moments of deeper-than-necessary consideration, the process crumpling his pasty face like a piece of wadded-up paper. Then he replied, "Mysterious."

In the strange context of a strange moment, it seemed like a perfectly appropriate reply.

"Well, I'm late for a meeting," Tom said, impatient and agitated and not up for a conversation, starting to back away, accidentally brushing shoulders with an anonymous-looking young woman, dressed for the bureaucracy except for the running shoes, offering a quick "Excuse me" that was drowned out by whatever was blasting through her iPod earbuds.

The Geek eyed her as she disappeared down the street. "Steve Jobs," he muttered, shaking his head, turning to Tom: "If he hadn't made cool toys, he'd be sipping firewater in hell with Osama as we speak."

Then he did the strangest thing:

Pulled Tom into a quick but not perfunctory hug that lasted a good 15 seconds. "Vaya con Dios, bro," he said. "These are some very strange dudes you are dealing with."

With that, he broke the embrace—

And winked—

And smiled—

And said, "Angel in your pocket"—

And was gone—

Leaving Tom to watch him melt into the hustling, bustling after-work crowds, thinking how odd it was to just run into him like that, unaware that new shadows were tightening around him and they were getting darker, and there would be no sun on the horizon to vanquish them.

THIRTY-NINE

AFTER HER BROTHER'S death, Liberty Dash had made a list of what to do in order to close the official book on Arlo's life.

It amounted to a compendium of little things, each one not meaning much on its own, but together providing an aching reminder that where there was now a void, there had been, just weeks ago, a presence that however routine had constituted a young man's day-to-day existence, one that though lonely—the blessing and curse of the Internet age—never robbed him of passion and an eagerness to talk about whatever hooked his mind at any given moment.

She cried a lot during this closure process.

Cried when she sold the only furniture that was sellable from his Dupont Circle studio, a decent mattress and a three-piece, L-shaped, glass-topped desk set that amounted to his Veracitaurus "office." Cried as she watched the Salvation Army truck cart off the non-sellables, everything from clothes to fraying, mismatched chairs to sparkling-clean dishes. Cried when she told his landlord about what had happened, halfway ready for a fight, grateful when she was met with understanding rather than with a greed-driven "not my problem." Cried when she talked to the power company and the phone company, the *Post* subscription people and the bank people, all of whom would simply hit a key on a computer and Arlo Dash would cease to exist.

Cried because she thought there were other measures of a man beyond the mundane, and especially this man, her brother, who was of the belief that while the truth could set you free, it should also make you mad, and he never feared the consequences of the anger it provoked in him or those of its pursuit and discovery.

Consequences, she was convinced, that included his murder, which made her cry, too, but with a rage that accompanies the helpless conclusion of knowing that no matter what the Higher Powers, however defined, told you to believe, this was a world fraught with peril, where safety in the end was little more than a superstition.

Through it all—the tears, the terror, the fury—she stayed focused on the list, checking off the to-do items one by one because it was her responsibility. There were no other brothers or sisters; their parents had been only children, both of them dying from heart failure within six months of each other. It was just her, keeper of the family name and flame, custodian of Arlo's memory, a solitary and uncertain survivor, alone.

And that life, Arlo's, had brought Liberty Dash to a Starbucks on M Street in Georgetown, a place where she liked to hang out because it was close to the basement apartment she rented with two grad students and because it had enough electrical outlets to make plugging in her laptop a non-issue. A place where, in the final act of closing the book on her brother's too-short tenure on Earth, she was sifting through an envelope full of mail from the post office box she'd canceled earlier that day.

Most of it was trash, junk, postcards offering to sell him real estate in Virginia, credit card solicitations, come-ons for Caribbean cruises, domain name offers from Internet companies.

Magazines: *Washington Monthly, Wired, Fast Company, The Atlantic, Fantasy & Science Fiction, Macworld.*

Two or three thick packages, a book of restaurant coupons, something from an insurance company, a white bubble-wrapped envelope—

Addressed to Arlo—

In Arlo's handwriting—

With Arlo's return address on it.

Carefully, she tore open the gummed flap at one end, glancing around to see if anyone was watching. This late in the day there wasn't a lot of activity, just a handful of people sipping coffee, reading newspapers, taking advantage of the free Wi-Fi, none of them appearing especially suspicious, the thought flashing through her mind that it's the ones who don't look the part you really have to watch out for.

Peering inside the envelope, trying to look like it was no big deal, her performance sandbagged by a nervous tucking of hair behind the right ear.

She reached in and pulled out a small black rectangular device, ultra-slim and light, maybe four inches by three and a half, not even an inch thick, rounded edges, a USB port at one end, no markings or brand name, just a circular logo.

Her heart began to pound, but softly, as if the discovery had cranked its engine.

She glanced around again. Everyone in the place suddenly looked like a suspect in some global scheme. So when a voice in her head screamed *"Get out,"* she listened, sticking the device in the envelope and the envelope in her backpack, heading for the door, pulling out her cell phone, thinking as she dialed that she might be about to uncover something that would give Arlo's life meaning that extended beyond a checklist of the humdrum and maybe, just maybe, find a clue that would restore the possibilities of consequence.

FORTY

TOM WAS ON the Yellow Line Metro train, two stops from King Street, righted by a Klonopin, trying to stay focused on the *Washington Times*, doing his best to put the past couple of hours and all their curiosities out of his mind, when his cell phone started to vibrate.

Liberty Dash, excitement pulsing through the connection like electricity—

"I was going through Arlo's stuff, his old mail, and I found a 1-terabyte portable drive, storage, backup, encryption, everything—"

"Wait, wait, slow down."

"And he sent it to himself, he was a security freak, kept backups all over the place, online, offline, in the cloud—"

Tom having no idea what *in the cloud* meant—

"And this package, the one with the backup drive, it was sent three days before the thing that happened, you know—"

He knew—

"And I'm telling you, whatever we're looking for, whatever that is, it's on this drive."

She took a gulp of air, providing a window of silence that Tom quickly climbed through.

"Do you have any idea what it might be?"

"I dunno, there was no USB cable with it, but I've got one just like it at home, a drive like it, I mean, with the same cable, so I can hook it up to my computer, and we can see what's there."

The train slowed to a stop at Reagan National Airport. A young couple got off, dragging impossibly large suitcases toward the terminal.

"And you think what, again?"

"You know that email I showed you, about The Big Penis?"

Platte. "Yeah."

"I'll be willing to bet you that was just a part of a thread, and if it was, then whatever came before it, and maybe even after it, might be on that drive."

The train's doors closed and with a smooth lurch, it started moving.

"And they would be on there? His emails?"

"Who knows for sure? But don't you think it's a little weird that just before, you know—"

He knew—

"That just before, he'd send himself a hard drive? I mean, it's like he had this idea someone might come after him, and this was his insurance, his protection, right?"

Protection, Tom thought. In this world. Right.

"It can't be a coincidence," she said. It was a statement rather than a plea for his approval or agreement.

He took a moment to consider what she was saying, wondering if she could be right, if maybe this wasn't mere happenstance or cosmic tomfoolery, if sometimes when worlds intersect, they do so under the direction—intended or otherwise—of someone, somewhere.

The trained slowed, approaching Braddock Road.

"So what're you going to do now?" he asked.

"I told you: I've got the right cable at home. I'm heading there now. I'm gonna hook this thing up, see what's on it, see if there's anything there about, you know—"

He knew—

"And if there is, we're gonna figure out what to do next, where to go, who to take it to, the cops, whoever."

We're gonna figure out what to do next.

The train stopped.

Tom was exhausted. He felt like someone had put his brain through a meat grinder.

The doors slid open.

This didn't have to be tonight, nobody other than he and Liberty had an inkling about the portable hard drive, and he needed some decent rest like a fish needed water.

Over the train intercom: "Next stop, King Street—Old Town."

His stop. Home. Sleep.

Just as the doors were closing, he bolted from the seat, briefcase barely making it out with him, cell phone still in hand.

"Give me your address."

"It's a block away from the main Georgetown campus, right by the track, there's some steps at ground level, inside a black iron fence and some garbage cans, that go down to the front door. I'll be there in about 10 or 15 minutes."

In the Patriot's Blood offices just east of the White House on New York Avenue, David Diamond puffed on the ever-present cigar and listened as the secretly downloaded eavesdropping software played the conversation between Tom and Liberty as clearly as an FM channel.

He, too, was exhausted. The circles under his eyes were darker than usual, and razor blades of discomfort sliced into a stomach that had become immune to Maalox.

He looked at his watch.

Ten or 15 minutes, she'd said.

Somewhere deep inside his black fatigue, a light went off, a warning:

This could rapidly get out of hand.

David Diamond picked up the secure phone on his desk and dialed.

"I think we may have a problem," he said to the voice that answered.

FORTY-ONE

LIBERTY'S MIND WAS running full throttle as she walked through the darkness to her apartment, fueled by a combination of anger and excitement and anticipation, the thought that the answer to whoever or whatever had killed her brother was somewhere on the portable drive, and soon she'd know, and then—

What?

What would she do, exactly? Who would she go to?

Who *could* she go to?

If Arlo was dead because he knew something he wasn't supposed to know, something secret and dangerous that threatened powerful people, then there were no safe havens or sanctuaries. People like that, they chased you and they found you, and you never saw them, and then it was over, and sure, the cops or the government could talk about protecting you, try to make you feel better, but what if—

What if it was all just a mirage?

What if the shield they promised really didn't shield you from much of anything?

What if they, whoever *they* were, what if they were going to win no matter what, and trying to outrun them or outsmart them or outfight them was nothing more than swimming upstream against the inevitable?

What then?

Lost in that somewhat ominous thought, Liberty found herself at the front door of her apartment. She took a quick breath, but it felt more deep and desperate than calming, like she'd been underwater too long and had just come up for air.

She pulled her keys from a side pouch of the backpack, thinking about how nothing seemed certain anymore, wondering when events had become so random, coming out of nowhere, the fear of the unknown gripping you like some terrifying convulsion—

Unlocking the door, opening it, hanging the keys on the little hook just inside—

Reaching to turn off the alarm—

Except the alarm wasn't on.

Liberty froze for an instant, trying to process what was happening, the sudden fear so thick in her head she couldn't remember where the light switch was, so paralyzing she couldn't run, so real she could almost touch it—

When a shadow seemed to explode from the air, slamming her to the floor, Liberty's head bouncing off the hard wood like a croquet ball, the terror replaced by chaos and confusion, a daze—

Then a shard of moonlight, sneaking through the half-drawn drapes on the glass door that opened onto a tiny back patio, captured the glint of a gun, not aimed but raised overhead, starting to arc down, a man on his knees ready to crush her skull.

In an instant, the confusion evaporated.

She twisted away, the gun crashing to the floor and from the man's grasp, followed by a muffled whisper of pain and profanity, Liberty thinking for a nanosecond whether she should go for the pistol, deciding flight not fight, scrambling into the small dining area just off the living room, knocking over the table, the chairs, a vase of linen flowers, clinging to her backpack like it was a life preserver because somewhere, somewhere deep in her mind, she knew, just knew, that whoever this was—

God, was he wearing scrubs?

Whoever this was, he wanted what was inside of it, Arlo's portable drive, and there was no way she was giving that up, and all she had to do was get to the kitchen and to a knife, something, and she could fight back, take charge—

Crawling on all fours, in the kitchen, remembering a barbecue set, in the cabinet, under the sink, long fork—

A hand grabbed her ankle, Liberty kicking wildly, the attacker either not expecting her to be so aggressive or surprised by the strength and speed of her legs, which were driving back at him like crazed pistons, firing fast and furious, and faster and more furious until—

She heard a gasping groan of agony and the sharp expulsion of a lung full of air—

The man rolling into a near-fetal position, one hand blindly waving the gun, the other gripping his bruised testicles—

Liberty rolling to her left, no-go on the barbecue fork, out of the kitchen into the living area, up on her feet—

The man rising, too, angry and huffing—

Liberty bolting to the bedroom, backpack still in hand, slamming the door, remembering there was pepper spray somewhere in the nightstand, going through its drawers like a madwoman—

Harry Potter paperback—

Hand lotion—

Socks—

The bedroom door suddenly bursting off its hinges, Liberty panicked but barely turning, thinking pepper spray pepper spray pepper spray—

Postcards from Rome—

Kleenex—

Cough drops—

Suddenly more terrified than she thought possible, the idea that her last hope, her only hope, the only thing that could keep her alive, it wasn't there—

At the sound of the gunshot, muffled, silenced, feeling her heart just stop—

Turning full now, back against the wall, the man walking toward her, waving the pistol more than aiming it, a dead look on his face, no emotion or expression as he raised his free hand, opened it—

Liberty feeling herself starting to shake—

The hand coming at her, reaching for her throat—

On her throat—

Pressing—

The air passages starting to narrow, coughing—

Raising the gun now, against her forehead, the silencer warm and cold at once—

The room, the world, seeming to go sideways under his tightening grip, the dead look on his face mutating into a malevolent smile, her eyes wide, knees turning to noodles as he lifted her from the floor, by the throat, first a few inches, then a few more, Liberty struggling like a fish on a hook, arms and legs flailing, but the man was too strong, his hand too big, wrapped halfway around her neck like a chain, squeezing the life out, the flailing slowly stopping, the puzzle of existence at last giving way to life's final solution—

When she suddenly felt a thud and heard a grunt and a crash—

And fell to the floor, freed from his hold—

Clutching her throat, gasps coming as if pushed out by a machine—

The man in scrubs on his back, another shape on top of him, hammering away wildly, all whirling fists and arms—

Through the blur of motion, Liberty saw the gun, beneath the window that looked out onto the patio, and slid in its direction—

The man in scrubs somehow sensing what she was doing, throwing off her savior, grabbing her by the hair, jerking her up, flinging her like a rag doll onto the bed, picking up the gun and turning, looking at the other man, who was searching for breath against one wall—

Raising the gun—

The evil smile back—

Until he heard, "You kill me, and Penn Mallory won't stop until he finds out why—"

And realized it was Tom Fargo—

The smile evaporating, eyes dissolving into questions, *Should I or shouldn't I*, finding no answers—

Hearing only Vance Harriman's voice: *"If Fargo is there, he is not to die, do you understand me?"*—

Leaving only one option, a hard right that didn't full-on connect because Tom turned his head at the last second—

Looking quickly at Liberty, pure malice—

Making a quick and quiet and angry escape—

Backpack and its contents in hand.

FORTY-TWO

"LIKE THE POLICE are really going to help us, Tom." Liberty gave him the look of a mother who'd just caught her kid in the dumbest lie ever. "They're probably in on it."

"All I'm saying is that if there is a connection between what happened tonight and what happened to Arlo—"

"There is no *if*. That guy *knew* about the drive. That's what he was after." She sat back stiffly in the taxi's rear seat, annoyed and impatient, arms in a tight fold, black-booted foot tapping on the floorboard.

Tom rubbed his right cheek with hands that had only just started to quit shaking, the reddening spot under his eye sensitive to the touch but not badly swollen. He looked into the cab's rearview mirror to see if the turbaned driver was listening. All he saw were a pair of eyes as distant as Jupiter and twice as mysterious. "There are processes, Liberty. Accepted channels. Proper ways to get things done—"

"Dude, come on, seriously," she nearly screamed, eyes branding him with outrage. "You think, what, that your *processes* and your *channels*, that they're gonna somehow come to our rescue, somehow save us?"

"Yeah, I do."

"Then I feel sorry for you, man, 'cause there isn't any cavalry, and the Indians are kicking our asses—"

She caught herself and glanced at the driver, hoping he didn't hear what he could construe as a slur. But his gaze stayed forward, unblinking.

"And the only ones who're gonna get us out of this are us, me and you, The People, fighting the power."

"For Chrissakes, you sound like Sarah," he shot back, suddenly more angry than tired or sore.

"Yeah, well, somebody's got to. Because if you think for one second that going to the cops, just because they got uniforms and hardware, if you think that's the solution, then you're more whacked-out than I thought you were."

She refolded her arms in a huff. Tom wondered what she meant by that—*you're more whacked-out than I thought you were*—because she barely knew him. Probably Sarah talking again. When she quickly added, in a half-growl, "How's that *established order* thing working out for you so far," he was pretty sure he was right.

They rode in silence from Georgetown, past the Kennedy Center and Lincoln Memorial, over the Arlington Memorial Bridge, a handful of committed runners on either side. When they passed the Pentagon, Tom briefly closed his eyes, surrendering to a sudden gust of sorrow that he forced out of his mind to concentrate on plotting their next move.

For all his arguing that they needed to go to the police, Tom wasn't sure he believed his own case. Not because of Liberty's suspicions, necessarily—*They're probably in on it*—but because the pieces of the puzzle, at least the ones they knew, defied being put together into some cohesive picture. They just didn't fit:

Arlo's murder. Platte's jet going down. Toni Allura's crazy investigation. Anath and her demand to stop the probe. Dreadlock Man and his demand to keep it going. The attack on Liberty. The stolen portable hard drive.

And if some picture eventually did come into focus, Tom thought as the cab slowed to a stop at his apartment, he wasn't entirely sure he wanted to see what it revealed.

Then there was the matter of Liberty. With Dreadlock Man's threat to kill her, and the possibility, however remote, that she was right and Arlo's death was related to Platte's, Tom felt he couldn't risk opening any door that could slam behind the both of them. Of course, Liberty had the advantage of knowing nothing about any of that, and he wasn't about to tell her, so she was free to maintain the no-holds-barred, "us vs. them" diatribe.

"You gotta put your faith in you, not in some symbol, some false god of authority," she barked after they'd exited the cab, trailing Tom as he walked up the narrow driveway that bordered his apartment. "Because if you talk about this to the cops or somebody else who's got any control over us—"

He ignored her, reaching the gate onto his back patio—

"They're gonna come to your house one night, and the next day you're gonna wake up in Abu Grabu or whatever that prison is called—"

Found the key to the high-security, stainless-steel shackle lock—

"And nobody'll ever hear from you—"

Slipped the key into the base of the lock, twisted it, the hardened metal loop at the top opening—

"And the bad guys will win again, just like they always do, because you were singing 'The Star-Spangled *Fucking* Banner' while those bastards murdered my brother!"

Tom paused at that, but only for a moment, then took the lock from the door.

"Hey, Fargo, why didn't that guy kill you?" He turned to her, and even at a distance could feel the disappointment, the distrust. "Back there, at my place. The burglar could've killed you. Easy. But he didn't. Why?"

Tom didn't have an answer and didn't try to find one. "Just my lucky day, I guess." He gave her an empty smile, pushed open the gate, and went into the patio.

"Yeah, well, I don't think you were lucky at all," she said, marching toward him, all purpose and attitude, jabbering away. "I think that guy knew who you were, and knew he wasn't supposed to shoot you, which means you're somehow involved in all this, whether you know it or not, maybe even smack in the center of it—"

Following him onto the patio, stopping at the sight of Tom on his cell phone—

"Boss, I need a favor—"

And then seeing a manila envelope on the patio floor, *Thomas Fargo, Office of U.S. Sen. Penn Mallory* written neatly on the front—

And then a single sheet of white typing paper in Tom's hand, identical penmanship, neat black block letters—

Letters that read:

Tonight. Same time. Same place.

FORTY-THREE

THEY WERE ON the second floor of Penn Mallory's two-story home, in a family room that was awash in beige—furniture, carpet, curtains, wallpaper—and seemed oddly delicate, almost feminine, made more so by the soft lighting overhead. Liberty Dash didn't know a lot about the senator, other than Sarah's descriptions, which ranged from "war-mongering fascist" to "right-wing asshole fascist" to "tool of the fascists."

But she did know this:

"Delicate" and "feminine" were not qualities she would attach to Penn Mallory.

"It was my wife's favorite room," he said, as if reading her mind, a sad smile seizing his face.

Liberty shifted in the oversized chair, with its wide tan-and-beige stripes and pillows that had a different design but the same colors. Her eyes went to the wall behind where Mallory sat on a matching sofa, to a semi-contemporary portrait, framed in pale gold wood, of a woman. "Is that her?"

He shook his head, the smile shifting to full-on amusement. "Crate & Barrel." He gestured broadly to the room. "Most of this is."

Liberty couldn't keep from shaking her head. Penn Mallory, Crate & Barrel guy. Who'd have thought?

"Warm that up for you?" Pointing to a half-full mug of tea that sat cooling on a beige marble-topped coffee table with white-painted cast-iron legs.

She shook her head. "You have any kids?"

Any sign of joy or amusement or life fled his eyes. "A son. But he, uh, died with his mother. In the automobile accident."

Liberty felt like crawling under the coffee table. "I'm sorry."

"Summer of 2001." He shrugged slightly and paused, as if wondering what more he should say. "I almost quit, resigned from the Senate. The leadership persuaded me to put off any decision until, I don't know, the emotional dust settled."

"How long did that take?"

Another shrug. "It still hasn't settled."

"So why'd you stick around?"

"A bunch of crazy Islamic extremists hijacked passenger jets and flew them into the Twin Towers, the Pentagon." His voice went as soft as the room. "And my problems, personally painful as they may have been, seemed less significant in the larger context." She eyed him carefully, trying to decide whether the statement was political or personal, but saw no evidence one way or the other. "I guess my point is, I know what it's like to lose someone close to you."

"Yeah, it pretty much sucks."

Mallory nodded. "Yeah, it pretty much sucks."

"Is that why you like Tom so much?"

He shot her a look that could melt glass. "No one can replace my son."

Liberty blinked rapidly and pulled one of the chair pillows in her lap. "I'm sorry, I didn't mean—"

"No," he interrupted, "I apologize for my tone." His eyes took a forced march over the room, searching for what to say next. "I love Tom like a son—not like *my* son, but like *a* son. I grieve for him, his loss. I admire what he's done; it took a lot of guts to come over to"—a devilish smile—"the *dark side*. I think he's made the country a better and a safer place."

"You think we're safer?"

"Absolutely. Don't you?"

"My brother was murdered, and someone robbed me and tried to kill me tonight. I'm not feeling real secure these days."

To her surprise, he didn't push back, didn't even debate. "Bob Dylan once said that democracy doesn't rule the world, violence does." Liberty's eyes got a little wider. Mallory laughed. "Yeah, even right-wing assholes can like Dylan."

"I don't think you're an asshole." A beat, really for effect. "I mean, not a *total* asshole."

"But not nearly as cool as somebody like Toni Allura." It was an easy comeback, not defensive, adorned with a Hallmark card smile.

She rolled her eyes. "Yeah. I am *so* into fashion."

"Ah, then you know her." He stretched back into the sofa, rested his long legs on the coffee table.

Liberty set the pillow aside. "Not really. We met once, a long time ago. Arlo was an intern in her office the summer after her husband died, the first year she was there."

Mallory looked almost startled. "Your brother worked for Toni Allura?"

She gave him a slight no-big-thing nod, missing his surprise altogether. "Something to do with computers. I think he updated email lists, maybe was an admin for her webpage. Nothing, you know, like state secrets or anything."

"That was it? Just the one summer?"

Suspicion swelled in her eyes. "Why is that so strange?"

"It's not. It's just that this being Washington, and Senate staff jobs being what they are, I'm a little amazed he didn't turn an internship into a career."

The suspicion drained away. "Arlo thought of himself as an outsider. It was part of his whole 'rebel with a blog' thing."

He nodded. "Easier to be on the outside of the tent piss—" he caught himself, coughing to cover the mild profanity.

Liberty laughed. "Right. That."

A relaxed silence hung in the air for a few seconds, Mallory breaking it with a question that seemed both off hand and interested at once. "So what do you think they were after, at your place? The burglar?"

She hesitated, thinking back a half hour ago, when she and Tom arrived, Tom not saying a lot, just telling Mallory they were friends, had met through Sarah, her place had been broken into, and her brother had been killed recently. Nothing about Platte or the emails or Arlo's portable hard drive or her theories. She'd made a mental note at the time to ask why he'd given Mallory just the broadest of strokes rather than the details, but assumed there was some reason. So she stuck with their story.

"I don't know. I got home, this guy was there going through my stuff, and Tom showed up."

"Just like that, huh?"

Something in his voice, a touch of skepticism, pinged Liberty's mental defenses. "Uh, Sarah had actually called him, and asked him to stop by, you know, check up on me, make sure I was okay."

"Of course." His face was a curtain, and she couldn't tell if there was belief or disbelief behind it. When he smiled, it felt forced. "So they're still speaking, I guess. Tom and his wife."

"Soon-to-be ex-wife. And yeah, they are."

He rested his head on the back of the sofa, looking up at nothing in particular. "I actually liked Sarah. Obviously, we're from different planets politically, but there's no arguing her passion."

"She's thinking about getting remarried."

Mallory grimaced. "How's Tom with that?"

"You know him better than I do."

Perplexity creased his face. "I'm not sure anyone knows Tom, not really—"

Which Liberty thought was strange after the love-him-like-a-son remark—

"But I do know he feels some things deeply, and I can only assume Sarah is one of those things. And to lose someone close . . ." He stopped, and a muffled, faraway sound filled the hush that followed, like the cry of an abandoned baby, and after a moment, when he again said, "This was her favorite room," the only thing Liberty Dash heard was the unmistakable melody of despair.

FORTY-FOUR

TOM STOOD ON the roof of the Eye Street garage, every nerve on full alert, scanning the shadows, looking for someone, something—Dreadlock Man, a sign, a message, anything—that would bring some answers, knowing equally well that whatever was lying in wait could just as easily, and maybe more likely, compound the unknown, and bring with it an even greater danger.

But if any menace lurked, it was invisible.

He saw only the tower lamps, the lights Dreadlock Man had shot out, still dark and unreplaced.

Three cars, a small black Honda, years past its prime, and two VWs, a green Passat and a red Jetta, the latter with Colorado tags and a bike rack, each parked alone in the extremes of the rooftop.

The American flag still snapping in anger on the crane over the construction site.

The white block building at one end, not a sign of life or activity, looking like it hadn't been opened since the Nixon administration.

The maintenance shed, at the top of the metal steps overhead, padlock still in place.

Nothing had changed, it seemed. Yet here he was.

Somewhere above, in the distance, he heard the insistent chop-chop-chop of a helicopter.

Tom took another long look across the nightscape, and then

began to cautiously walk the perimeter, first along the waist-high brick wall toward the street, focused, anxious, wary—

At the far end, he turned left toward the block building, the construction site quiet across Eye, running his hands along the wall, the touch of brick a coarse reminder that this, whatever it was, this was all too real.

In the darkness to his left, a sharp, sudden, metal-on-metal creaking noise pierced the silence, just for an instant, and was gone as fast as it had arrived.

Tom stopped, heart beating like a racehorse's. He searched for the sound, the source, the cause, but all he saw was the near-empty roof, bathed in a dim gray light that illuminated everything and nothing.

He took a deep, calming breath and then a second and a third, trying to restore his imagination to its rightful recess in his head, reminding himself to stay sharp, this was no time to be feeding his hallucinations or anxieties.

He continued past the white block building, refusing to look inside the windows or try the door, preferring the peril he couldn't see to the one he might unleash.

Walking on and on, back toward the opposite end of the rooftop, with each step feeling the calm of the previous moment slowly evaporate, the hallucinations returning, the tension stirring, his body going increasingly rigid, as if expecting an ax to suddenly materialize in the night and deliver a fatal blow.

He somehow beat it back, though, the rising fear, and moved to the center of the rooftop, just standing there, halfway resigned to face whatever consequence lurked hidden in the night, halfway challenging his fate to step up and reveal itself.

Then a thought torched him like a flamethrower, an awful realization born of his troubled mind—

What if this was a ruse?

What if the whole idea was to get him out of the picture, away from Liberty because he'd done something Dreadlock Man saw as a betrayal, something unintended or random, something that would take her death from an unimaginable horror to an absolute certainty?

Tom slammed his eyes hard in anger.

How could I be so stupid?

But she was with Mallory, he thought, and safe, and the foreboding quickly eased, though only for a second before roaring back, driven by his growing sense that real safety was a cruel fantasy, there was no way to make life orderly and it was pointless to try because the way the world works, you never see the end of anything, so terror would always be a fact, always present, and that made security on its best day a sunny deception.

Tom decided instantly that he had to get back to Liberty.

He turned quickly and ran toward the exit that led down to the street, his thoughts focused only on Liberty and her protection, nothing else mattering—

Past the black Honda—

Into the rectangular-shaped area with the low-overhang roof that fronted onto the parking lot—

Seeing for the first time a sign advising that the garage was unmonitored after 10 p.m., and a warning painted on it, *So Beware MoFos*—

Reaching for the door, pushing it open, mind in overdrive, when—

Something reached out and grabbed the corner of his eye.

Something so unexpected, so out of the ordinary, he thought it was a vision, another delusion in a night saturated with them.

But it was real, so real he could only stop and stare.

Sitting there, just to the right of the door:

A laptop computer, 15-inch screen, dark, with a black cell phone next to it, no trademark or logo.

He crouched down and eyed the laptop warily.

Looked behind his back, over his shoulder, hearing the helicopter again, undetectable except for its rhythmic thrum, which at that moment seemed like it was closing in on him.

Tom shuddered and returned his attention to the laptop. After a moment, he touched the space bar on the keyboard.

The computer came alive.

He pulled back like the thing was going to chew his throat out.

Then the screen went black, and four words appeared:

Angel in your pocket.

FORTY-FIVE

TOM STARED AT the message as if were in code.

Angel in your pocket.

Remembering Vance Harriman's guy had said that when they bumped into each other outside the French restaurant, the statement seeming just odd then, but now it felt over-the-top crazy, baffling, like sanity had died and these words were etched on its gravestone.

Angel in your pocket.

The night had suddenly become silent, the air still, time suspended, thoughts of riding to Liberty's rescue now distant.

It was just Tom and the darkness, alone together, again.

Angel in your pocket.

Eyes still fixed on the computer screen, he thought for a second, trying to find his bearings, then decided to follow the only concrete clue that had made itself known:

He began going through his pockets.

First the left one inside his blue suit coat, a 9/11 commemorative pen from a veterans' support group that he always carried with him.

The right one, a "security edition" of the Bill of Rights, the size of a playing card, metal with rounded corners, whose presence and purchase was a job requirement of working for Mallory.

A smaller pocket, bottom inside left, a plastic envelope with a spare coat button in it. Nothing out of the ordinary, angels or otherwise.

He shoved his hands into both pants pockets, just a set of keys and some change, and started patting himself down, like the cops Liberty couldn't or wouldn't or shouldn't trust, pressing, searching for something, finding nothing, wondering if someone was just playing a game with his head, surrounding him with unknown things, looting his subconscious—

Until he found it, in the outside right pocket of his jacket:

Thin and oblong, sleek finish, almost cool to the touch, blue aluminum, with a ridged plastic slide on the bottom that he knew, if pushed to the left, would reveal a retractable USB plug-in.

A thumb drive, for storing data.

Tom stared at the device for a moment, then flipped it over. Against the blue background, in strong, bold, white letters, no fancy type or logo:

"Territo."

An ocean of questions surged through Tom's mind, the first of which was the most improbable—

Was it possible the Geek from Territo was Dreadlock Man?—

The next ones focusing on Vance Harriman and his demonstrated dislike of all things Fargo and whether this was some elaborate setup, some way to once and for all banish the turncoat to his rightful place on the margins of America, where he would be of no concern to those with higher callings.

Higher callings.

Whatever the hell that meant, Tom thought, a bit of anger flaring in him, momentarily sidetracking the uncertainty, anxiety, and foreboding, leaving in their wake the knowledge that whatever questions the thumb drive raised, there was only one way to answer them.

He crouched back down in front of the laptop, slipped the drive into one of the USB ports.

In a moment, *Angel in your pocket* dissolved into a blank screen that contained a single folder icon labeled Territo Secure.

He clicked it.

A window popped up, revealing two files.

The first was a photo, slugged simply unk.jpg. He clicked that. A pinprick light on the thumb drive illuminated, and a low, muffled, mechanical hum followed as the computer went to work.

The image popped up:

Harry Platte, with a slim, beautiful young Arab-looking woman, under a brightly lit marquee that read, "Danish Dance Theatre Presents National Ballet Troupe of Iraq, Performing Serenade."

Tom stared at the photo, leaning in a bit to the screen, as if physical proximity would bring him closer to an answer.

But it didn't, so he closed the file, thinking that maybe the second document, slugged "Platte," might.

The sudden thrumming of more helicopter rotors pierced the nighttime silence.

He looked up, saw a chopper swooping overhead before fading into the darkness, then went back to the screen and clicked on the "Platte" file.

In a few seconds, a document appeared, the title page heralding its content:

"Final Report on the Death of Sen. Harrison D. Platte"—

And under that, "Senate Select Special Investigations Committee"—

And under that, the date of release, May 27, which was 11 days after the crash that killed Platte.

Tom's tension eased. It appeared to be nothing more than a copy of the publicly issued report.

So why all the cloak-and-dagger crap? he wondered. If this was what it seemed, there was nothing new here. Once the report had confirmed the emerging consensus and with Toni Allura's probe seemingly going nowhere, Platte had fallen off the front page, the speculation among an attention-challenged media shifting to whom the White House would now choose for Defense.

It made no sense.

Unless he was missing something.

Tom quickly scrolled through the document, but it didn't take long to realize that there was nothing here, that what he was seeing was in fact the report with the findings of the official investigation: total failure of the flight controls, tragic accident, no connection to terrorists anywhere in the Mideast.

Again, why all the cloak-and-dagger crap?

But before he could come up with even the germ of an explanation, a reply arrived, as if prompted by his brain: The unmarked cell phone next to the computer began to vibrate, its Caller ID window reading only Secure Incoming.

Tom hesitantly picked it up and listened as an all-too-familiar voice gave him an order he knew he had no choice but to follow, an order he also knew would take him down a path he had never anticipated but, he sensed, one that had already been paved for him by some unseen and sinister presence.

"Do exactly as I tell you," Dreadlock Man said. "Because time is not on your side."

Just as Tom started to ask what that meant, the words in the document began transforming themselves into numbers, and line by line started to vanish from the screen.

FORTY-SIX

"LISTEN TO ME carefully," Dreadlock Man said, low and calm and about as soothing as crushed glass. "The entire file, the document as well as the code behind it, is written to self-destruct if accessed by an out-of-network computer."

"How long do I—"

"Four minutes."

Frantically, watching the line-by-line, words-to-numbers-to-nothing process on the screen, Tom began following each of Dreadlock Man's commands, first getting a wireless connection, then seeing the Password box, typing in XREAQZZ4P, hitting enter.

"What are you seeing?"

Tom told him a new window had popped up over the vanishing text, titled TGS-EXE V5.1, with three tabs: Photos, Documents, and Options.

"Click Documents." Tom did. "Three minutes and 30 seconds, Mr. Fargo."

Two boxes appeared inside the window, the top one saying Source Folder, the bottom one, Destination Folder. Dreadlock Man gave him a series of numbers, which Tom typed in. The Source Folder window was suddenly populated with a data string that ended in territosecurity\documents\Platte.

"Three minutes."

Dreadlock Man told him to click the Options tab now, then the Date-Stamp command, and again asked Tom what he was looking at. "Uh, three sets of windows: Create Date, Modified Date, Last Accessed Date."

"What are those dates?"

Tom said the Create Date was May 18, two days after the crash; the Modified Date was May 26, the day before the report's release; Last Accessed was blank.

"Two minutes and thirty seconds."

Tom tried to ignore the lines of text that were disappearing like smoke in the wind as Dreadlock Man told him to go back to Options, click the Track History tab. Tom did, seeing a window labeled Path and below that, a larger, empty window with columns that read Name, Type, Size, and Date Modified, typing carefully as Dreadlock Man slowly instructed him to enter another string of data: D\TGS-EXE_Files\documents\Platte\date-time-values\path_start\disable-security\run.

"Do you see a Run Program command?" Tom said he did. "Click it, please." Tom did that, too. "One minute, 45 seconds. What do you see?"

The larger empty window filled with streaming lines of data, one after another after another, maybe a couple of hundred with all the revisions, all of them named Platte, all of them identified as Word documents, the size of each growing with every subsequent revision. The streaming suddenly stopped.

"Seventy-five seconds. What do you see now?"

"A bunch of files, I'm guessing variations of the Platte report as it was being written from beginning to end."

"What else?"

Tom scrolled down the lines of data, no idea what he was looking for, groping in the digital darkness. "Jesus, this is no time for games. What am I looking for?"

"Sixty seconds. When did Harry Platte die?"

"May 16."

"Fifty seconds. When was this document released?"

"May 27."

"Forty-five. When was this document created, Mr. Fargo?"

"Oh, man, come on," Tom shot back, exhaustion and confusion trumping logic and personal safety. "Will you just stop the spy games and tell me what I am supposed to find?"

"Thirty-five seconds."

"If there's something I need to know, tell me!"

"Thirty. Scroll to the bottom of the window."

Hands shaking more from adrenalized frustration than alarm, Tom sped down the window, through all the file names and types and revision dates, all the way to the bottom, when he discovered a line that contained no information about the files, just a pathway to more data—

"Twenty seconds. What do you see now?"

"Previous History—"

Which seemed odd, given that the entire history of the report had just been laid out in 200 or so lines of data, but he hit it anyway, and the window was suddenly depopulated of all content, then new information streamed in, faster than the first set, and in greater volume, maybe two, three times as much, Tom unable to do anything but sit back, watch it stack up, the concept of information overload all too clear—

"Ten seconds."

And then all that stopped, too, Tom seeing the first entry in the entire stream of Previous History data—

"Five seconds. Again, Mr. Fargo, when was this document created?"

And everything he'd been feeling, all the fear and dread and anxiety and confusion, it all collided again, a big bang of discovery—

"Four."

Because when he looked at that first line, the very first piece of information associated with the special report on Platte's death—

"Three."

It showed that the Document Created Date read May 13—

"Two."

Meaning that the report was already being written three days before the Learjet carrying Harry Platte crashed en route to Munich.

"One."

Tom just stared, barely hearing Dreadlock Man telling him to leave everything and go—

But still grabbing the thumb drive—

Barely noticing the phone dying—

Just watching as the computer went blank, the document and the codes that held its mysteries slipping into oblivion, disappearing like the ghosts in Tom Fargo's waking nightmare.

FORTY-SEVEN

TOM WALKED BACK to Mallory's home, taking advantage of the 45 or so minutes to clear his head, calm his nerves, and navigate his mental maze.

But standing there, at the senator's front door, bathed in light from a Colonial-looking brass lamp, he knew he'd struck out on all accounts. There was no clarity or calm, and he sure as hell couldn't find any way out of the puzzle palace in his head, so when Mallory greeted him, his boss' voice didn't register at first—

"Tom? You all right?"—

And then the after effect settled in, halfway jarring him back to the moment. "I'm good. Just a little tired."

Liberty came into view behind Mallory. Her face was a mask of concern. "Is everything okay?" Saying it slowly, as if she were leading him on, trying to pull some secret from deep within.

Tom gave her a slight, cobweb-banishing nod. "Really."

"You look lost as a goose in a snowstorm, son."

The comment struck Tom as strange, Mallory going full-on Southern only when he was mad or worried, and there was no reason for either at the moment, at least that he could see. A few more cobwebs were swept away. He brushed at the slight bruise on his face. "Just a weird night."

"Tell me about it," Liberty chimed in, smiling, sensing Tom's uncertainty.

"You want to come in?" Mallory asked.

Tom feigned giving the offer some thought, buying a few seconds to determine if he should say anything about the vanishing report. His eyes shifted to Liberty, and Dreadlock Man's warning came roaring back. He snap-decided her safety was still paramount at the moment. Besides, there was no real downside to holding back from the senator. The less Mallory knew, the more he could deny—assuming there was something to deny, a big assumption given that all Tom had was a bunch of loose threads, and even with the night's discoveries, there was nothing solid to tie them together. He'd have to do that on his own time, in his own way, for Liberty's sake. "No, thanks. I just need to crash."

Mallory nodded, looked briefly at Liberty, smiled. "And you?"

"I just want to go home."

"Because this is a big place, lotta room, if you'd feel safer."

Tom detected a quick hit of sadness on Liberty's face and sensed something had passed between them during the evening. "I'm fine," she said. "But thanks."

She tried to shake Mallory's hand, but he would have none of it. Instead, he wrapped her in a fatherly hug that seemed intended to say everything was going to be okay, then stepped back and asked, "Would you give us a second?"

Liberty looked at Tom, then at Mallory, then back at Tom, who nodded slightly. She headed down the brick walkway to the street.

"What's going on, son? Is this about the Patriot's Blood deal?"

That, Tom thought, and Platte's death, and Arabic-looking dancers, and Geeks bearing thumb drives, and seemingly faked reports, and a scary man in dreadlocks. Pick your poison. "Just tell me one thing."

"Shoot."

"Why am I at Patriot's Blood, really? I have done this kind of thing a hundred times for you from my desk in your office. How come all of a sudden it is so critical that I handle your politics from the outside instead of the inside?"

Mallory glanced at Liberty, who was fiddling with her cell

phone, paying no attention.

"Diamond," he said, simply, tersely, like the name was rotting meat. "I don't trust him."

"Then why—"

"Keep your friends close, but your enemies closer, that's why."

Tom tried to prevent the shock from catapulting off his face. "You think Diamond's the enemy? Your enemy?"

"I think he was Harry Platte's enemy." There was no preventing it this time. Mallory saw Tom's expression and nodded gravely. "Who arranged for that jet to take Harry to Munich? Who got him on the plane? Who didn't tell him those three Saudi defense guys that were supposed to be with him bailed at the last second, making sure Harry didn't know he was going solo until he was on board?"

Before Tom could even process the question, Mallory pressed on.

"Diamond, that's who." The senator gently tapped a finger on Tom's breastplate. "So I need you to watch his every move. He takes a piss, you zip him up. He hires a blond hooker, I want to know if the drapes and the carpet match. He wears ladies' underwear, you tell me if they're lace or cotton."

Tom started to say something, but Mallory cut him off. "When we said today that there's a leak in our operation?" Tom nodded. "I still believe there is, and I think David Diamond is up to his ass in whatever's goin' on. He's the enemy, son, and I got him right where I want him."

"And where's that, boss?"

Mallory smiled like the sole star in a black sky. "Under the thumb and in the crosshairs of the only person in his troubled world I can trust."

Me, Tom nodded, glad to be let in on the charade but not entirely comfortable with its meaning or burden, wondering if Mallory's natural paranoia had shifted into high gear.

The thought put events of the evening a million miles behind him.

They wouldn't stay there long.

FORTY-EIGHT

IT WAS LATE, Tom was tired, and he just didn't care.

So when Liberty—who, after a brief argument agreed to sleep on his sofa rather than go home, for her own security—asked him about the bottle of pills on his coffee table, Tom gave her a smile better suited for a mourner and said, "I've got a secret."

"Apparently."

He held up his hands—busted—and got them a couple of glasses of Chianti, served in unmatched coffee cups.

"So, you're like, what?" she asked after he sat back down on the sofa. "Bipolar?"

"Wow," he said, not unkindly, "she's tough *and* she knows her pharmaceuticals."

"Arlo had panic attacks as a kid."

Tom leaned back and crossed his legs. "I don't panic. It's just general anxiety, that's all. Easily managed."

"Which I guess is kind of good, you know, since your finger's on the button and all that."

"There is no button in my life at the moment, but there are sure as hell a lot of *all thats*."

She looked at him closely, eyes lit by twin fires of interest and interrogation. "Is that where you went tonight? To deal with one of them?"

He knew that surrendering anything—what he'd been through,

what he suspected, what he feared, and she'd pretty much asked it all on the Metro ride back to Alexandria—would only put her in Dreadlock Man's sights. He rubbed a finger behind his left ear, deflecting the question. "So, what did you and Mallory talk about tonight?"

"Ah, artfully played, sir." A smart smile, almost parental in its understanding. She took a sip of wine, her gaze unwavering. "You know, Sarah was right about you." Tom rolled his eyes. "No, really. She said you were like the most buttoned-up guy she'd ever known."

Which made Tom laugh out loud. "Yeah, leading a hundred thousand people in an antiwar march, that pretty much qualifies as buttoned-up."

"I think she meant after." Said it softly, as if to lighten the blow.

It still landed. His jaw tightened. "I think that's Sarah-speak for, 'He went to the other side and I'll never forgive him, so I need to just hit the road and find someone I'm politically compatible with.'"

Liberty shook her head. "Guys. Jeez. Everything's so black-and-white to you. You look for an easy answer, then you convince yourselves it's the truth."

"Sometimes the easiest answer is the right one."

"Sometimes it is," she nodded, sitting up and leaning toward him. "But this isn't one of them."

"Wow, she's tough, she knows her pharmaceuticals, *and* she's a relationship expert to boot."

"You are such a jerk." She pulled back from him. "But that doesn't mean I'm wrong."

"Sarah left because I became ideologically impure."

"Sarah left because you checked out, dude," she replied sharply. "You shut down emotionally, kept putting distance between the two of you."

"That's not even close—"

"Really? You ever ask her about it?"

"What was the point? Her answer to everything was for me to get help, go into therapy."

"Did you?"

"Hell, no."

Liberty picked up the bottle of Klonopin. "And how's that working out for you?"

He toasted her with the coffee cup of wine. "So far, so good."

She toasted him back with the meds. "Couldn't be happier for you."

Tom gave her a caustic look and glanced at his watch. It was almost 2. "I'm going to bed. I'll get you a blanket and pillows."

He started to stand, stopped by Liberty's hand on his leg. "Listen, I didn't mean anything, you know, what I just said. About you and Sarah. It's none of my business."

"It is what it is. Or was."

She pulled herself into a cross-legged position on the sofa. "Wanna know what I think?"

He took a sip of wine and leaned back. "I'm guessing that's not a rhetorical question."

"I think you and Sarah are true believers, and there's nothing wrong with that. That's because you're true believers in a good way. You guys believe what you believe because you really believe it, okay, not because it's some crutch, something you need to hang onto just to make it through the day. What's wrong with that?"

"What's wrong is that sometimes it's easier to believe than it is to doubt. Doubt can make people talk. Belief can separate them." It was a clear reference to Sarah, and he made no effort to hide it. "How about Mallory. You think he's a true believer?"

"Oh, I think he's probably a complete tool." They shared a quick laugh. "But yeah, I'd say he's a true believer. That whole deal about his family, why he stuck around, it's not about getting votes. That kind of epic sadness is tough to fake."

"Took a lot of guts to do what he did. He could have just walked away from it all. But he chose to tough it out." Tom paused before adding, almost as an aside, "I wish I had that kind of strength."

She cocked her head. "What, you don't think you're strong?"

He shrugged. "Sometimes, in the deep, dark hours of the night, I wonder if I walked away, or at least took the easy way out."

"You mean, the whole patriot act thing."

He chuckled without humor. "Yeah. The whole *patriot act thing.*"

"I didn't mean—"

"No, no, it's fine. Really. I just ask myself if I chose the easy fight instead of the right one."

"Everybody did back then, didn't they?"

"My point exactly."

"But at least you're fighting for something. That's more than most people I know can say."

"I guess."

"And hey, if it brought you and Mallory together, and if he's president, you can write your own ticket. That has to account for something."

Tom put his hands up in a half-surrender. "I'm not sure I'd go. I've been with him a lot of years, and I'm not getting any younger. It could well be time to move on, find some new passion."

"Right. I want to be a fly on the wall when you have that conversation with him."

Tom looked at her as if he'd missed every third word she'd spoken. "What does that mean?"

"Nothing. I was just telling him about Arlo tonight, how he didn't want to turn his internship with Senator Allura into a career, and Mallory couldn't believe that anybody in Washington—"

"Wait," he interrupted. The light in his eyes flickered for a moment as he processed what she'd just said, and then he blinked four or five times trying to get it back. When he did, his look was half-wild with discovery. "You're saying Arlo worked for Toni Allura?"

She read his expression, and felt a sudden shudder. "Uh, yeah."

"And you never told me this?"

"It was like a hundred years ago; he was an intern. What's the big deal?"

"The *big deal*, Liberty, is that he worked for a United States senator who is leading the opposition to Vance Harriman—one of the most secret, scariest people God ever created—and he was murdered, and he may have had something on his computer that was important enough for someone to steal, and maybe even kill you. Christ, can you not put two and two together?"

"Yeah, I can," she shot back. "The problem is, I get four and you get 27. God, who's swimming in the conspiracy pool now?"

He got off the sofa and started pacing, back and forth in the small living area, up and down into the kitchen. "You don't understand. In Washington, everything happens for a reason. Nothing is unconnected."

She shook her head, but there wasn't a lot of conviction. "I don't see any connections."

"That's because the hidden reasons are a hell of a lot stronger than the obvious ones."

"You're being way too paranoid."

"And you're not being paranoid enough."

"Paranoid about what? You think Toni Allura had my brother killed?"

He stopped pacing, and Liberty could see the confusion evaporate, replaced by a sudden composure, the calm of a lake at sunset, a clear message that some plan had taken shape. And when Tom walked over to the door and began to meticulously check and recheck the security of every lock, she felt a slight chill, and couldn't tell if it was caused by what was going on inside the apartment or what was lurking on the outside.

FORTY-NINE

TONI ALLURA'S EXECUTIVE assistant had been doing her job exceedingly well, preventing Tom from gaining any kind of access to the senator, until she agreed, after about 10 minutes of badgering, to pass along the message that he was calling about Arlo Dash.

Less than an hour later, he and Toni were at the conference table back in her hideaway Senate office, which still smelled vaguely of fresh paint.

"I think your paranoia is getting the best of you, Mr. Fargo," she smiled after he'd tried to find a through line between Arlo's internship with her and his murder.

"Yeah. I get that a lot these days."

"Runs in the political family, I see," she replied easily, a shot at Mallory.

"You know what they say about paranoia."

"By all means enlighten me."

"It's being aware of all the facts."

"One of them being that I have some information regarding Arlo's death."

"Do you?"

Toni shifted slightly in her chair. After a moment, she stood and walked to the mini-bar. She moved with a gazelle's grace and a gunslinger's confidence, the long legs and slender body enhanced by a precision-cut black pinstriped Armani suit. She returned with a single glass of grapefruit juice, sat, took one sip, and drilled Tom with a look that could incinerate rock. "Frankly, I don't have the first idea what you're talking about, but I don't appreciate your inference."

"Senator, I wasn't infer—"

She held up a hand. "Stop." He did. "Every time you move your lips, all I hear is the sound of deception."

"I'm sorry if—"

"Stop."

Tom hadn't been entirely sure how the sit-down with Toni was going to play out, although her gaining the offensive position—especially now that he had discovered the link to Arlo—had been pretty far down the list of possibilities. But here they were.

"I am assuming," she continued after letting him squirm for a few seconds, "that your boss is unaware of this visit, am I correct?"

"Yes, ma'am."

"So our little arrangement—my silence on all things Thomas Fargo in return for yours on all things Hector Rubio—I can trust those terms are still in force?"

"You can."

"Then what does any of that have to do with the death of an obscure intern?"

"He wasn't obscure to his sister."

She nodded but didn't soften, and took another drink of juice, blue eyes never leaving his face. "If you want to ask me something, ask me. But as God is my witness, if you suggest, however slightly or subtly, that I had anything to do with Arlo Dash's death, I will find a way to have you charged with threatening a federal official, and I will hold a news conference on the Capitol steps waving that picture of you and the terrorist and asking the world to consider why a presidential candidate would employ a delusional young man who consorts with international murderers."

Tom could feel his body go rigid with anger. "Nobody will ever believe you."

"This is America, Mr. Fargo. The charge always trumps the truth." Toni sat back, laced her fingers and rested them easily on her lap, smiled. "So, ask away."

He didn't waste a moment. "How'd you get that picture of me in Munich?"

She didn't waste a moment, either. "I was conducting an investigation. You were, too. It seemed perfectly appropriate to see what leads you pursued." Not a trace of uncertainty in her voice.

"And where is your investigation now?"

She sat up straighter and cleared her throat. "It's ongoing."

"What happened?"

Her eyes ricocheted around the office before coming back to his. "Off the record?" He shrugged his assent. "I don't think there's anything there." She hesitated before adding, carefully, choosing the words with the caution of one making her way through a minefield, "I thought I had a source. As it turned out, I did not."

Tom skipped the obvious question—Who was your source?—knowing full well she wouldn't give up a name, and went for the bottom line: "So are you going to fold the tent, shut it down?"

She pierced him with a long, tough stare that felt like the prelude to a declaration of war, accompanied by a smile that dripped with contempt. "If and when I do, be assured, you will be the *first* to know."

Tom didn't need a translation, and moved on. "Then it's safe to assume, at this point, that you believe the official story?"

"Apparently, it's never safe to assume anything. I came into this meeting assuming you wanted to talk about Arlo Dash. But you seem to be more interested in circumstantial events surrounding Harry Platte's death." She stared at him without seeing him, too busy doing mental calculations of some kind. "You think they're somehow related, don't you?"

"I think you're not telling me everything."

She leaned back and crossed her legs at the ankles, left foot bobbing with agitation. "I'd be very careful if I were you."

Tom knew she was right; he was skating on some seriously thin ice. But he was just as sure she was hiding something, and decided to make one more run at her. "You start your investigation with great fanfare, great assurance—almost like you knew something from the get-go—and now you're going to just let it dry up and die. You have a tenuous history with Hector Rubio, whose activities, however separated from you, have the power to cripple your ambitions. And you have a photo that has the potential to do the same to my boss—who, not incidentally, is your tormenter-in-chief—but you sit on it."

"What does any of that have to do with Arlo Dash?"

"You tell me."

She leaned forward, palms down on the conference table, patting its surface four or five times. "Let's cut through the nonsense, shall we? You show me yours, and I'll show you mine."

Deciding this was the moment the meeting was about, Tom didn't back down, leaning forward as well, matching her iron gaze. "I'm not sure I follow, Senator."

"Then let me be more explicit: What do you know that suggests Arlo's death and Platte's were not two independent occurrences?"

Tom couldn't tell if she was pumping him for information or trying to find out how much he already knew, but he figured he had maybe 10 seconds to decide what to say, how much to say, and whether Toni Allura—as opposed to Penn Mallory—was the right person to say it to. He took every one of them, and then tried to straddle the line between truth and lies. "I'm going to tell you something, Senator, that no one else—"

"Spare me the caveats and qualifications. Just say it."

He took a deep breath. "I have reason to believe that Arlo Dash knew something about Harry Platte, and whatever that was somehow led to his murder."

She stared at him without expression, then pulled a tube of lip balm from her small Fendi bag and applied it lightly. "And what might that be?"

"Nothing concrete. A communication that suggests something."

A moment, while she put the balm back in her purse. She suddenly seemed distant, removed from the conversation. "What does it suggest?"

"I don't know."

"Guess." The word hit him like a wrecking ball.

"Honestly, Senator, I don't know. I was hoping that you might know."

"Me?" She gave a small chuckle that Tom felt was a bit defensive.

"Yes. Because he worked for you." Toni nodded and said nothing. "What exactly did he do?"

She remained silent, but Tom could see a conflict boiling inside her. It dissipated quickly, however, replaced by the trademark Allura coolness. "I am afraid that what Arlo did for me was not especially exciting. After my husband died, I wanted to know how much federal money was being spent in the state, where it was going, and for what purposes. It was pure in-the-trenches work, poring over agency budgets, requiring no skill other than the ability to pay attention and stay awake."

"The perfect job for an intern."

"And that's all he was. An intern."

"Unless maybe he was an intern who discovered something he shouldn't have. About Hector Rubio."

The Allura coolness went full glacier. "I believe we're done here." She got up from the chair. "But let me say that you would be wise to think twice before wandering into the wilderness of your imagination. You might end up in a place other than your intended destination."

Tom didn't know if that was a warning, or a threat, or a bit of friendly advice. He didn't care. "I appreciate it, Senator. But I know exactly where I'm going."

"I hope so, Mr. Fargo. For your own sake. I truly hope so."

FIFTY

THAT NIGHT, TOM dreamed again of the Old Man:

Outside the empty office, 1B526, Tom watches like an eyewitness to the apocalypse:

The jet's fuselage shrivels into a metallic wad, its aluminum exterior melting like wax in the heat—

The tail bursts—

The walls around him tumbling, the ceiling above collapsing—

Doors blown off hinges—

The air on fire—

Then he sees it:

Fuel, spewing from the tanks in an angry, violent stream, racing in his direction.

It's red-tinged with blood, body parts surfing on its wave, arms and hands and legs and feet and heads.

Tom wonders if any of them belong to the Old Man.

He turns and runs from the swell of death, going left from Corridor 4 to Corridor 3, passing firefighters in protective gear running straight into the blaze—

Military personnel and civilians yelling for people to get out of their offices—

Zombie-like men and woman with blistered skin and shredded clothing and blackened faces and missing shoes—

People climbing through rubble, looking for friends, colleagues, survivors—

The heat rising, rapidly becoming unbearable, thick enough to choke on, and from what Tom hears, a lot of that is happening—

And just when he thinks this could not get any more surreal, the black smoke that has taken over the corridor suddenly parts to reveal—

Four men, all in uniform, inexplicably standing at a water cooler, talking as if the world was not coming apart around them.

Tom starts running faster. "Dad?"

Three of the men turn and look at him without expression, their faces indistinct. The fourth doesn't.

"Dad, you're not safe!"

"Don't be a fool, boy," the three say in unison. "Everybody's safe. This is America."

Tom looks over his shoulder to see the wave of bloody fuel and human remains coming toward him like a tsunami—

Tries to catch his breath, but spits the air back out, gagging at the taste of fuel, burning metal, seared flesh, barely getting out the words as he says—

"I'm gonna get you out of here!"—

Which gets a hearty collective chuckle from the three men whose faces he now sees clearly, and they're—

Penn Mallory, David Diamond, and Vance Harriman—

"No way out of this, son," they reply. "No way out."

"I'm gonna find one, don't worry!"

"We're not worried," he hears Mallory-Diamond-Harriman say.

Then the fourth one turns, and Tom sees instantly that it's the Old Man wearing a cracked grin and staring at him with glowing eyes that feel mischievous and knowing at once.

"But you should be, boy," the Old Man says.

"Don't believe him," Mallory-Diamond-Harrison say.

"Believe me, Tom, because there's something you need to know."

"What, Dad? Tell me! What do I need to know?"

Then an eardrum-bursting blast fills the corridor, blowing Mallory-Diamond-Harriman into some unseen place, the river of bloody fuel suddenly igniting.

The Old Man just shakes his head sadly and repeats, "You should be awfully worried," before turning and walking away without a word of explanation, as if immune to the unfolding catastrophe.

"I'm sorry," Tom says, almost cries.

But the Old Man just keeps walking away, disappearing into the black haze, his vanishing form the last thing Tom sees before being engulfed by the rolling fire, and Tom holds his breath as he's pulled under, struggling bravely against the inevitability of his fate, but still knowing, deep down, that the fight is futile.

FIFTY-ONE

THE FOUR MEN sitting around the small conference room table at the Patriot's Blood office represented almost $186 billion in annual revenue. All their companies ranked among the *Fortune* 500. Two manufactured aircraft, one produced jet engines, the fourth focused on defense technology and cybersecurity. They owned their respective segments of the military market, and were known as feared competitors who would stop at nothing to win a contract.

And David Diamond was shaking them down like they were corner grocers caught in a local hood's protection scheme.

"Penn Mallory will be elected, gentleman," he said, leaning back in one of the six chairs that ringed the round table, blowing out a cloud of cigar smoke. Tom Fargo sat in the sixth, saying nothing, there at the insistence of Mallory, who wanted a firsthand assessment of Diamond in action. "The polling says it. Our contributions say it. And most of all, every corner of the Republican Party, from the evangelicals to the fiscal conservatives, they say it, too."

He sat up straight and leaned forward, set the stogie on an ashtray, propped both elbows on the table's walnut surface and laced his fingers. "And you guys need to belly up. Because if you don't, I'll have four more companies in here tomorrow, and they will, and you gentlemen will be totally fucked when Mallory's in the White House. I personally guarantee it."

The four men, each a vice president for public affairs, their haircuts and suits and ties suggesting that all emerged from the same pod, glanced uneasily at each other before one of them, from the jet engine maker, a company called AMC, spoke. "You can't bully us, David." He was in his late 50s and had a red, veiny nose that suggested a lot of late nights and vodka breakfasts.

Diamond smiled. "Okay."

"It's not that we don't back Penn. We do. We all do." Nods everywhere. "We're just not comfortable giving the kind of money you're talking about."

"You've given in the past."

"Not in these amounts. And this is about the presidency."

"What's the difference?"

"We're just concerned there'll be more scrutiny, that's all. None of us wants to be under a media microscope." More nods.

"No one's going to know."

"How can you be so sure?"

"They haven't so far, have they?"

"No, but the law—"

"The law lets us set up a not-for-profit advocacy organization, which we've done with Patriot's Blood, and says the contributors to that entity can stay secret."

"Some of us are public companies. We have to report—"

"And some are private. But you're all run by billionaires who have a lot of cash to give. And you've all got lawyers and accountants that, at least so far, have figured out ways to keep contributions to Patriot's Blood off the radar."

The AMC executive looked at the others around the table, all of whom seemed to have the same question on their mind. "But what if the rules change?"

Diamond snorted. "The first rule of Washington is, there are no rules. The second rule is, if there are rules, you figure out a way to get around them. Besides, do any of you really think Congress is going to vote against its own interests and bite the hand that passes it cash under the table?" He turned to Tom. "You're the legislative guy, Fargo. Am I right about that?"

Tom was only halfway paying attention, still running the previous day's discussion with Toni Allura over and over in his head, trying to find a link between her and Arlo Dash and Hector Rubio and Harry Platte, convinced it was there but lurking just inside the shadows of his consciousness.

"Fargo?" Diamond repeated.

Tom snapped back to the moment, taking a second to collect his thoughts. He looked at Diamond, then scanned the other four faces at the table. "David is right. People in power build a system that allows them to stay in power. They need people like you to help maintain that power. It's a pretty simple equation."

"And an expensive one," the man from AMC said.

"Yes," Tom agreed. "But influence isn't cheap. And let's be honest, David was also right when he said you are replaceable." He was revolted by the calm certainty in his voice. Yet he had a role here, and he had to play it. He glanced over at Diamond, whose dark eyes bled suspicion.

Diamond returned his attention to the bags of money disguised as good corporate citizens. "Let's just get to the bottom line, gentlemen. Your companies have generated a lot of profits thanks to a mutually beneficial relationship with Penn Mallory. Now I am giving you the option to make more. A lot more. You'll get promotions. Your bosses will look good. Your shareholders will be happy. Everybody wins."

Tom could see the AMC representative's growing agitation. "This feels vaguely like extortion."

"No," Diamond replied easily. "This is democracy at work."

"Does Mallory know you're doing this?"

"By federal law, the candidate and the independent social welfare organization can neither collude, communicate, nor coordinate," Diamond said, bored and robotic, as if reciting the words from a policies and procedures handbook.

"You didn't answer my question."

"He doesn't," Tom said, firing a sharp look at Diamond, one that accused him of not standing up for the guy at the top of the pyramid. "That would be illegal."

"And Lord knows, there's no room for illegality in presidential campaigns." Diamond's grin had all the humor of gall bladder surgery. "So here's the drill. You will each be contacted by our surrogates, like-minded supporters and contributors who are similar to yourselves and who believe that the best America is a secure America."

"I'm going to assume we'll be dealing with the same like-minded supporters and contributors we've been dealing with in the past," one of the jet makers asked.

"Yes, except for you," Diamond said, gesturing to the AMC executive. "You'll have a different contact than we originally discussed. The Cuban is no longer serving our South American interests."

The Cuban?

Tom, still trying to connect the dots between Arlo Dash and Harry Platte, swung his head toward Diamond, who, fortunately, was so wrapped up in playing the power broker he didn't notice, Tom's mind flashing back to the lunch with Kyle Kendrick—

"Sure, I've heard of Hector Rubio. A defense contractor. Fled Castro's Cuba when he was 18, wound up in California, self-made businessman. Builds some kind of super-secret, black-budget radar component for the Air Force. Lives on a boat in Florida now"—

And in an instant that connection revealed itself, and Tom knew exactly where it would next lead.

FIFTY-TWO

"*FLORIDA? CHRIST, TOM, what the hell's in Florida?*"

"*Hector Rubio, boss.*"

"*What's he got to do with anything?*"

"*Did he ever raise money for you? For Patriot's Blood?*"

"*Hell, I don't know. I don't know Rubio, except for the whole skimming money deal.*"

"*I think he did.*"

"*How do you know?*"

"*We were in a fundraising meeting today with some corporate guys, and Diamond said he had a new point man in South America, that the 'Cuban' was no longer part of the operation.*"

"*And you think he was talking about Rubio?*"

"*I do. And the fact that Diamond knows Rubio, and Rubio is connected to Toni—*"

"*Means Diamond is connected to the Cheerleader—*"

"*Uh-huh.*"

"*And that could prove Diamond's the leak.*"

"*If I'm right, boss, and Rubio is who I think he is, maybe he had a falling out with Diamond, and maybe it was something that'll give him a reason to talk.*"

"*I dunno, son, seems like a stretch.*"

"*Maybe. But it's worth a shot.*"

"*Why would Diamond line up with the Cheerleader?*"

"Diamond doesn't do anything that doesn't benefit Diamond."

"She thinks she's got something on me, and he gave it to her, and she thinks she can use it as leverage against me in the campaign."

"Let me ask you this: What if Rubio had been raising money for you, and was pulling the same thing he pulled with John Allura, except he was skimming campaign contributions?"

"That's a crime."

"Yeah. And what if Diamond found out and fired him, but still fed it to Toni?"

"Doesn't make any sense. Why not let Rubio keep doing whatever he was doing, dig my grave a little deeper?"

"It makes perfect sense: Once Rubio broke the law, he broke the law. There's no matter of degree here. And by getting rid of him, Diamond can take the high ground and say he acted as soon as he found out what was going on."

"Goddamn, we are smack in the middle of a nest of vipers, son."

"We are."

"You really believe they're working together, Rubio and Diamond and the Cheerleader?"

"That's why I want to see Rubio."

"Diamond got any idea what you're thinking?"

"Absolutely not. I'm keeping him way in the dark."

"That little prick. I am gonna rip his head off and shit down his throat."

"So you're good with my little fishing expedition?"

"Yeah, sure, go. But Tom?"

"Yes, sir?"

"When you get back from Florida, you better have more than just a suntan."

The digital recorder clicked off.

"Keeping me in the dark," David Diamond chuckled, sitting in his chaotic, dimly lit office at Patriot's Blood. "That is rich." A few seconds of silence settled in as he further considered the recorded conversation and its implications. "Fargo is way off base. He's all puzzle and no pieces. But Hector, well, he's got some pieces, and even though they may fit a completely different picture, I'm not sure it's one we want Fargo to see."

The silence returned. Diamond sucked on a dead cigar.

"Not that I think Hector will talk," he continued after a moment. "He hasn't yet, and it's been more than a little while since he became a born-again moralist." He opened the desk drawer, found a wooden matchstick, and fired up the cigar. "Still, this probably isn't the time to be taking any chances."

What little light there was in the room seemed to dissolve.

"Then none will be taken," said Miles Loki, the second-in-command at Territo, Vance Harriman's combination strategist-fixer-conspirator, knowing full well that Diamond had just painted a target on Tom Fargo's back and plotting a second strategy on a second front to make sure it wasn't hit. "None will be taken."

PART FOUR: **UNDE MALUM**

FIFTY-THREE

NOBODY PAID THE well-dressed man any attention.

He pulled the black Cadillac coupe into a parallel parking spot in front of an art gallery on the palm-lined street, absorbing a final blast of air conditioning before venturing into the sticky, wet-blanket afternoon heat.

Leaned easily against the driver-side door waiting for a couple of cars to pass, thick briefcase in hand.

No rush, no big deal.

A pair of tourists, barely out of their teens, the guy in baggy cargo pants and a too-red polo shirt, the girl in a flowered skirt and a tourniquet-tight halter top, walked past and disappeared into an imitation Italian bistro at the corner.

He checked his watch, let another car cruise by, winced a little at the jackhammer action on the other side of a Road Closed sign, where an orange-striped wooden barricade sealed off the street adjacent to the bank building.

The bank building.

Five floors of offices, the exterior pale pink and glass.

On top of that, 20 floors of condos, slightly-darker-than-tan brick, each with a balcony.

On top of that, at a front corner of the tower, a hexagonal cupola whose six sides were half-glass, about waist-high from the ceiling. A clock, metal strips instead of numerals, sat just underneath the cupola, overlooking the bay and marina 100 or so yards to the west.

The man strolled across the steaming macadam, carefully staying within the white crosswalk lines, and took the three steps from ground level to the building's shaded sidewalk level in a single motion, instantly feeling the cooling effects of the grayish concrete overhang.

Walked past a brokerage house, which looked closed, and then a resort real estate office, its window display showing seniors smiling and playing golf, the place empty, nobody buying the dream of golden-years security.

Then into the bank, where frigid air hit him like a shot from a meat locker.

It felt good, but he didn't show it, didn't take a moment to cool off or make a snappy remark to some anonymous passerby about how he could take the heat, but not the humidity.

He just eased past the handful of desks in the wide-open lobby, acting like he belonged, another businessman with a briefcase, off to another meeting.

Pushed through a set of glass doors on the far side of the lobby that led to the elevator.

Which he'd take to the fifth floor and then get on another one.

Which he'd take 20 floors higher, to the top of the condo section, where he'd get off and climb two short flights of stairs.

Which would lead to the glass hexagonal cupola, where he'd unload his briefcase and go to work.

Nobody paying him any attention, in his lightweight gray-blue suit and ultra-pale lime-green shirt, tie awash in understated blues and greens, a dash of yellow, festive but muted.

Just blending in, like he usually did, all the other times.

Except all the other times, he wasn't usually this well dressed.

He was usually in scrubs.

FIFTY-FOUR

WITHIN 30 SECONDS of pulling his rented Ford into the marina's crushed-seashell parking lot, Tom Fargo knew which of the moored yachts belonged to Hector Rubio.

It was in the fifth slip from the dock walkway, in the fourth row of boats, the row closest to Sarasota Bay, the one dedicated to really serious pleasure craft.

Of which Hector Rubio's was, unquestionably, the most serious, a 92-foot Argos Gulfstream, 800 square feet of deck space that was split into two levels, the upper one home to a folding-wing, Glasair sportsman float plane.

Tom didn't know the first thing about boats, and would rather sit through a classical music recital than go sailing. But that didn't quell his sense of awe, or the thought that for Hector Rubio, there had once been good money in defense contracts.

The air was wet and the sun intense, and while a soft breeze blew off the water, it was warm bordering on hot, not so much easing the conditions as reinforcing them. Tom had barely made it from the parking area through the arched, very-Florida marina entry gate that announced the Gulf Coast Marina and Yacht Club when sweat began to darken his off-white three-button T-shirt.

He took his time, not wanting to give the perspiration any more incentive, heading slowly past Docks A and B, where the smaller boats bobbed easily on the surface. Dock C, lodging for a combination of mini-maxis and maxi-minis, sat across the walkway from a green-awninged outdoor bar, which even in the sauna-like heat was half full of patrons, middle-aged men outfitted in Tommy Bahama shirts, too-young women corseted in long, lightweight dresses.

At Dock D, Tom stepped onto a slatted walkway that led to an iron gate. Beyond the gate was a line of yachts the size of battleships.

There was a small, narrow box attached to one of the bars on the gate, next to a sign that ordered contractors to check in with the dockmaster before beginning any work on any of the vessels. Tom opened the box, revealing a keypad.

He punched in the sequence of numbers Hector Rubio had provided.

The gate clicked open.

He approached the Argos Gulfstream almost timidly, as if it were going to pass judgment on him.

Or maybe it was because of the two mountain-sized men standing on either side of the yacht's stern, dressed in black despite the sun, staring straight ahead behind aviator shades, wearing linen jackets loose enough to hide something dangerous.

The craft was named *Love and Respect*, which Rubio had told him came from a quote in a Hemingway novel, *The Old Man and the Sea*: "Fish, I love you and respect you very much. But I will kill you dead before this day ends."

Tom stopped five feet from the boat.

"You Fargo?" one of the behemoths asked.

"Yeah. Mr. Rubio's expecting me." He began walking again.

The other behemoth held up his index finger. It was both an order and a threat. He spoke into some unseen device, low, not quite a whisper, then nodded once. "Follow me."

The bodyguards exchanged a quick look before one peeled off. Tom followed.

In a minute, he was in the huge second-deck master stateroom. It had light-brown granite floors and countertops, a king-sized bed, a walk-in closet, rounded mahogany cabinets along one end with a built-in workstation opposite the bed, an entertainment center complete with a 52-inch widescreen, and his-and-hers bathrooms.

Tom wondered how much this thing set back the federal government and its taxpayers.

"Six million dollars," a voice answered, in what sounded like lightly accented Spanish, but Tom knew to be Cuban.

Hector Rubio, who then wondered something himself, the question coming unexpected, out of nowhere, sending a surge of electricity into Tom's brain:

"And how is Mr. Penn Mallory's presidential campaign going?"

FIFTY-FIVE

HECTOR RUBIO WAS short and round, and wore a black tent-like guayabera shirt with intricate white stitching on either side of the buttons. His thin hair was combed in a way designed to preserve its past glory, without success. A few chins migrated into his neck, which was almost nonexistent, so the head looked like it was attached to the rest of him as an afterthought. He wore a carefully trimmed moustache. His eyes bulged.

"Sit. Please."

But the voice was soft, even friendly, and when he spoke, it was with an odd mischief, the words accented by a nod and a wink.

Tom sat at the workstation, his back to a battery of three computer screens. The chair was modern and stylish, its off-white upholstery and mahogany frame matching the stateroom's décor.

Rubio took a place at the foot of the bed, which was covered in a tan comforter as thick and soft as a pastry.

"So, uh, what's your interest in American presidential politics?" Tom asked.

A warm smile fanned out across Rubio's butterball face. "You first."

"I'm sorry?"

"Tell me why you are here and what you want from me." He spoke with the precision of someone who had learned English from an audiotape. "Then we will discuss matters related to Senator Mallory, his campaign, and other issues of significance."

Tom rested both elbows on the arms of the chair and tented his hands, as if in prayer, and instantly decided to try misdirection, thinking maybe he could surprise Rubio into giving up some dark secret. "How do you know David Diamond?"

It didn't work. "As I said, Tomás. You first."

The voice was still soft, but some of its friendliness had ebbed. Tom got the point and figured he could tell Rubio everything he knew because, well, Rubio probably already knew it.

So he more or less passed through the information about campaign contributions to Toni Allura's late husband, payoffs to lobbyists and legislators, college for the kids, Yolanda Díaz and her needs.

Rubio listened quietly, occasionally nodding, the big eyes and blank expression revealing nothing. When Tom finished, he smoothed his moustache and shrugged. "This is a truth, but a half-truth." His eyes drifted to the windows around the suite that provided a near-panoramic view of the bay, then returned to Tom. "And like most half-truths, it is a total lie."

"Why is it a lie?"

Rubio ignored him. "Do you know for what purpose wood is utilized, Mr. Fargo?" The nod and wink had returned to his words, confirmed by the knowing, bemused grin.

Tom paused, not because he didn't know the answer but because the question didn't track with anything they were talking about. "Uh, construction, I guess."

"Precisely!" Rubio replied. "And yet in the past 25 years, your government has spent approximately $100 million on wood utilization research. Apparently, senators and representatives do not possess your deep understanding of the purpose of wood."

Just as Tom began to answer him, throwing out the standard this-is-the-way-government-works response, Rubio pressed on.

"Oh, and have you ever desired to enjoy the lush beauty

of a tropical rain forest?" Tom felt like he had stumbled into a foreign language film without subtitles. "Now you may do so without leaving home, thanks to a $500 million indoor rain forest in Indiana, courtesy of the United States Senate." He shook his head in mock disbelief. "Who says America is destroying the rain forests?"

"I'm not here to discuss the ins and outs—"

"And $2 million for a water taxi service to a community that is located two miles inland and has a population of precisely zero."

"What's your point, Mr. Rubio?"

"My point is that the wood industry contributes large sums of money to 17 senators and congressmen who apparently do not understand the composition of a two-by-four. The developer seeking to bring an Amazonian adventure to the Middle American heartland personally interceded to assure acceptance of the sponsoring senator's niece into a college that had previously rejected her application. As for the water taxi, I will just say that it is the enterprise of a woman with whom a prominent member of Congress is currently engaging in an inappropriate relationship, a woman whose husband, not incidentally, is the chief fundraiser for the congressman to whom I refer."

Tom took a deep, impatient breath. "Okay. I get it. The system's screwed up."

"Oh, no," Rubio said in protest, as if apologizing for some misunderstanding. "No, no, no. That is, how do you say it . . . the way of the world in Washington. How things works. *That*, I understand. I admire it, in fact. And, yes, it had been very good to me."

"Until John Allura died and his wife ended your deal with the government."

"She did. But this also is a half-truth. And the lie that resulted is larger, and more shameful, and without conscience."

"Listen, can we just cut through the cryptic doublespeak, and maybe get to—"

"Those matters to which I referred, wood and rainforests

and water taxis, they were public, open for all the world to see, transparent, accountable, the essence of democracy, so very American." A pause. "But the money that found its way to me, it was not quite so, how shall I say it?" Another pause. "Well, it was not very American, at least in principle, though I suppose one could make the argument that it did pay for acts of American patriotism." A third pause. "*Extreme* acts of American patriotism."

"I see. And skimming from government contracts to bankroll your girlfriend, put your kids through college"—a sweeping gesture to the yacht—"buy yourself a nice little houseboat, those would be extreme acts of American patriotism?"

"No, Tomás, no. But using money from your federal budget to pay assassins to secretly murder terrorists? That would be."

FIFTY-SIX

ANYBODY WATCHING WOULD have thought her small for this kind of work, hauling large boxes of beverages off a truck in the marina parking lot, stacking four of them onto a dolly, wheeling the dolly down the marina walkway.

Sweating through the khaki uniform—multipocketed shorts and matching shirt, Southside Distributors logo patch on the left pocket. Khaki-colored visor as well, same logo on the front. Ankle-high socks, black Reeboks, scanner attached to her belt.

She walked past the outdoor bar, angled her way down to the front of Dock D, slowly, not wanting the dolly to tip over. Stopping in front of the box at the gate, she punched in some numbers on the keypad.

A click. The gate opened.

She removed the Oakley shades and looked into the sun, almost daring it to fry her retinas. Took off the visor and ran a hand through short-cropped hair that perspiration pasted to her head. Put the glasses and hat back on, turned around, pushed through the gate with her back, turning to face forward when it shut with a metallic clank behind her.

Once inside, she stopped and pulled the order form out of one pocket, a yellow sheet of paper that told her where to make the drop-off:

Adventure Capitalism.

She scanned the dock, guessing that it was six slips up, just past that mother-of-all-yachts that looked big enough to host the World Cup.

She folded the order form and stuck it back in her pocket, started pushing the dolly toward the customer's boat, stopping when a big guy—one of two, both of them in black—stepped in her way and said, "Whoa."

"Just making a drop-off, man." Her throat was dry, and the words scratchy, like a well-worn 78-rpm record.

"What's in the crates?"

"Something that belongs to someone who's not you." Not the best answer, but she didn't care. It was hot, and she was drowning in the sweat running down her neck, back, and arms.

"Who?"

Quickly deciding this wasn't worth the effort, she pulled out the order form, which was limp with dampness, and read, without enthusiasm, "Juice boxes. Grape. Orange. Apple. Cranberry." As if anticipating the next question, she handed him the piece of paper. "The order is for Mr. and Mrs. George Atkinson, to be delivered to a 65-foot Fleming yacht, *Adventure Capitalism*." Boredom in her voice.

The Big Guy looked over at his double, who stood eight or 10 feet behind them. The double shrugged.

"I haven't seen the Atkinsons lately," the Big Guy said.

"They're arriving tomorrow."

"Arriving from where?"

"Denver."

If that set off any alarms with the Big Guy, he didn't show it, just tossing a head gesture at the dolly. "Lot of juice."

She folded her arms in annoyance. "Yeah. It's a lot of juice. Maybe the Atkinsons go on extended juice fasts. Maybe they're prone to colds. Maybe Mrs. Atkinson has chronic urinary tract infections, Mr. Atkinson is always constipated, and Little Boy Atkinson is anemic. I don't know, I don't care, I just deliver." She pulled the scanner out of its holster and shoved it in his face. "So let me do my job before I get heat stroke."

The Big Guy looked again at the crates on the dolly, suspiciously, like they were boxes of snakes that he couldn't decide were asleep or dead. He glanced back at his double. "Lot of juice," he said again, this time shaking his head.

"Lot of juice," the double nodded.

"Screw this," she said, slamming the scanner back in its holster, spinning and walking away. "I'm leaving it, and goin' to the dockmaster, and I'm gonna tell him about the delivery. I've done my job. You dickheads can take it from there. I'm gonna go shoot pool and get wasted." As she pushed through the gate: "Assholes."

Except she didn't go to the dockmaster, didn't get back into the truck, the one marked Southside Distributors, didn't go shoot pool or get wasted.

Just walked out of the marina, past the parking lot, toward busy U.S. 41.

Waited patiently at the crosswalk for the light to turn green.

Reached into the deep right pocket of the cargo pants, grabbed a cell phone, tapped out a quick text message and sent it, gauging how much time she should allow for it to be received and register.

The light turned green, and she began to cross, pulling the scanner from its holster as she did, resting her finger lightly on the Power button, ready.

FIFTY-SEVEN

RUBIO HAD INSISTED they leave the cool elegance of the suite to go outside to the yacht's front deck, where, inexplicably, under the blazing sun, he sat shirtless and flabby at the edge of a hot tub, pants rolled up to the knees, legs dangling in the steaming water, a bottle of Cristal beer next to him.

"If you can't stand the heat," he smiled, "don't tickle the dragon."

Sitting in a deck chair directly opposite of him, Tom returned the smile, thankful Rubio didn't insist he join in the body boil, even more thankful that a canopy overhead provided a shield from the unremitting afternoon sun. He sipped from a bottle of Evian. "And that dragon would be what, exactly? This supposed covert anti-terror strategy?"

Rubio leaned back on both hands, face full into the sky. "Ah, Tomás, the question is not *what*. The question is *whom*."

Tom sat up a bit straighter. "Go on."

The Cuban's expression turned curious and playful at once. "Do you know what I do?"

"You're a defense contractor. You build secret radar components, something like that."

"Yes, I have a factory," Rubio said, slowly, nodding with each word, "and yes, I make, uh, *aparatos*—gadgetry—of a sort." He paused. "But that gadgetry was not, strictly speaking, my primary contribution to the safety and security of the United States."

Tom tried to flatten his voice, drain it of apprehension. "Then what were we paying you to do?"

"Again, Tomás, that is not truly the question."

"Then what is the question?"

"The question, my young friend, is why your government is no longer paying me for my services."

"Then by all means, enlighten me."

"Illusions may be shattered."

"About what?"

"About everything."

At which moment Tom Fargo's cell phone, which he'd put down on the deck next to his chair, began to beep.

In the six-sided glass cupola overlooking Sarasota Bay, the well-dressed man eyeballed Tom Fargo and Hector Rubio through the flip-up Leupold scope on the Barrett 82A1/M107, whose parts he'd taken from the briefcase and assembled in less than a minute. He kneeled on a small mat, resting the rifle and his right elbow on the inside ledge, the semi-automatic's 29-inch barrel thrust through a 12-inch-diameter hole he'd cut into the glass.

Occasionally, he glanced at a small SMS-only device, half the size of a business card and almost as thin, an invention of the child geniuses at Territo, that was propped next to the Barrett.

Watching the message screen.

Waiting.

Beneath Territo's warehouse-like headquarters, in a spare secure room, David Diamond and Vance Harriman sat at a polished-to-a-shine maple table and listened as Diamond's cell phone broadcast the conversation through a Bose mini-speaker system.

"Are you familiar with what is known as the Tri-Border Area of South America, Tomás?"

Diamond and Harriman exchanged a quick look that was

neither concerned nor panicked. This was not unexpected.

"*It is where the borders of Paraguay, Brazil, and Argentina meet. There is a belief in your government that this area is also a, what do you say . . . a breeding ground for radical Islamic activity that will be targeted at America. There has been much talk of militias and training camps and bombings and the support of Iran. Also, the military commander of Hezbollah is known by your FBI to work frequently out of Ciudad del Este in Paraguay.*"

"*What's that got to do with you? Are you some kind of undercover killer of terrorists?*"

Some lighter-than-air laughter came through the speaker.

"*Me? An assassin? Oh, goodness, no. I was, how do you say it, I was the* hombre de la bolsa—*the bagman!*"

In the brief pause that followed, Diamond glanced at his SMS-only device on the table next to one small speaker, Harriman catching it and shaking his head ever so slightly:

Not yet.

"*The bagman for who?*"

"*Your phone is beeping, Tomás.*"

"*A bagman for who?*"

"*The question now, Tomás, the question now is not for whom, but for what.*"

Diamond glanced at Harriman, who was listening with eyes closed and lips moving slightly, as if in prayer.

"*Who, what, when—I don't care about the questions anymore. But I'd appreciate an answer—to something, anything.*"

"*And you shall receive one. But, if you will, permit me one more inquiry.*"

"*One more.*"

"*Thank you.*"

David Diamond's finely tuned instincts told him what was coming next, and he knew what had to happen.

He picked up the SMS device and pushed the Send button, then turned off the speakers just as Hector Rubio said:

"Tomás, are you familiar with a programa presupuesto negro, *a black-budget program, known as Unde Malum?"*

In the cupola, the well-dressed man saw a one-word message appear on the touch screen of the SMS device:

Go.

He aimed, cross-hairs on the back of Tom Fargo's head, recalling his training as he sometimes did at these moments, having to hit a football-sized target from 800 yards, thinking this was nothing, a piece of cake, by comparison.

The Southside Distributors delivery driver walked easily across U.S. 41, not too fast, not too slow. The rented Mustang, angle-parked a few blocks up on Main Street, wasn't going anywhere.

To her right, a large bank building—condos stacked on top of five floors of office space—loomed over the bayfront, the adjacent street under construction.

She saw a concrete overhang and considered ducking under it, anything to get out of the heat.

Instead, she looked back over her shoulder, toward the marina, considering again if sufficient time had passed for the message to be received, gripping the scanner, which wasn't a scanner but an encrypted GRMS radio that operated on the same frequency as the electrical firing circuits buried inside six of the juice boxes in the crates that sat on Dock D, the radio being the transmitter, the circuits the receivers, which would trigger a firing impulse when she hit the Power button.

Maybe a few more seconds, she thought. But only a few.

Hector Rubio spoke softly, almost as if talking to himself. "Unde Malum was an honorable creation, birthed in the wake of September 11th, fathered by John Allura, that financed a global campaign against terrorism."

Tom's eyes widened. "What does that mean?"

Rubio held up one hand. "Tomás, your phone. Please. I find the constant beep-beep-beep highly annoying."

"Tell me what you're saying."

"My contracts with your government, steered to me by John Allura through Unde Malum, were not for the purpose of building gadgetry. And yes, some of the money I kept for myself, as payment. And yes, some was returned to Mr. Allura in ways that were not entirely proper. But I delivered most to dead-eyed, cold-hearted assassins in Paraguay for the purpose of murdering terrorists in the Tri-Border Area."

Tom's brain did a quick backflip, landing on concerns about his boss. "What's that got to do with Mallory's campaign? Did he know?"

"Your phone, Tomás."

"Christ," Tom muttered, showing his own annoyance, bending over to find out who was so insistent about reaching him, probably Mallory—

But it wasn't Mallory, and there was no Caller ID, just an onscreen message—

GET OFF THE BOAT NOW—

As Rubio continued—

"Many in your government knew. But after John Allura's passing, the mission of Unde Malum changed, and the money was no longer used to murder terrorists, and the half-truth became the bigger lie, the more shameful lie, the lie with no conscience—"

Tom was still bent over, staring at the screen—

"Oh, there was still murder, but Unde Malum was reborn in a new spirit, the spirit of capitalism, although some might say greed—corporate and human—and while I may not be pure of action, I could serve neither its new mission nor its new master, because what they were doing, and why, it was not of American principle—"

Rubio stopping suddenly, the words replaced by a harsh, croaking sound, like he was gagging on a mouthful of gravel—

A hole exploding in his neck, the force so great it nearly decapitated him—

A second bullet shearing off the top of his skull at the forehead—

Tom, freezing momentarily, everything looking and feeling as if it were in slow motion, swinging his head in every direction, trying to see where the shots were coming from, where he could escape, if he could escape—

GET OFF THE BOAT NOW—

Blood erupting from a fresh hole in Rubio's chest, big enough to put two fists through—

Tom seeing Rubio's two bodyguards coming at him, waving pistols—

The hot tub's water turning red, the pristine white deck spackled with brain matter—

GET OFF THE BOAT NOW—

Tom absorbing the message—

Just as the two behemoths started firing and firing and firing—

Just as he went over the side into the warm bay water—

Just as the GRMS radio signal sent by the delivery driver triggered the firing impulses—

Vaporizing the yacht, Hector Rubio, and whatever secrets he held.

FIFTY-EIGHT

DAVID DIAMOND SET the secure phone down gently and stroked his chin. "What is it?" Harriman asked.

Diamond said nothing, but the stroking began to rise higher on his face, from the chin to the nose to the eyes.

"At the risk of being repetitious," Harriman said, biting down on the impatience, "what is it?"

Diamond shook his head slightly. "We missed him."

A fire erupted on Harriman's pitted face. "Fargo is alive?"

"Yeah. And Rubio's dead." He swung his eyes to the CIA nominee. "It seems his boat blew up."

Both were thinking the same thing, though neither said it, as if verbalizing their fears might make those fears real and, therefore, demand a resolution they knew would be messy.

After a brief silence that was burdened more by puzzlement than concern, Diamond recounted what the sniper in Sarasota had just told him: Fargo and Rubio on the boat; Fargo leaning over at precisely the wrong time; Rubio taking shots to the neck, head, and chest; Fargo going into the bay; boom.

Harriman mulled it all with the focus of a chess master, concerned less with where the pieces were situated on the board at the moment than with what the board would look like in six or eight or 10 moves. "Perhaps it's not such a bad thing, Rubio being dead."

Diamond shot him a hard look. "Fuck Rubio. Fargo's still alive, and that's a huge loose end."

Harriman nodded. "And Rubio's dead. That is one uncertainty that has been effectively resolved. What he was about to tell Fargo, that toothpaste could not be put back in the tube."

Diamond nodded, the heat in his eyes cooling. "But I still have some questions." Harriman moved in more closely to the wooden table, drumming his fingertips lightly to a song that only he heard. "Like why was Rubio targeted, and who gave the order?"

"Penn Mallory had quite a lot to lose if Rubio got unexpectedly talkative."

"Not Mallory's style."

"But it did save Fargo's life." Diamond just shook his head. "Senator Allura?"

"I don't think it's the Cheerleader's style, either, unless there's a line of designer-label assassins."

It was a throw-off line—*designer-label assassins*—but not without meaning to either of them. "You know her better than any of us," Harriman said slowly. "What do you think she is doing?"

She.

They had acknowledged their unspoken fear:

Anath.

Diamond considered the question carefully. "I think she's become an avenger."

"Because of the mishap in Ushuaia?"

"Yeah," Diamond chuckled darkly. "The *mishap* in Ushuaia. But that's not what's bothering me."

Harriman's finger-drumming stopped. "Then what is?"

"If it was her, then how did she know? How did she know Fargo was going to see Rubio?"

Harriman's face turned into a stone carving, blank. Diamond took a second to revel on the great and feared and invincible Vance Harriman's sudden attack of bewilderment. "Are you saying we have a traitor within?"

"That's exactly what I'm saying," Diamond said.

"Impossible."

"Then give me a plausible alternative." Before Harriman could reply, he leaned forward and propped his elbows on the table, hands in a here's-the-church, here's-the-steeple grasp. "Somebody told her, Vance, and it was somebody who could get to her. That's the only explanation. Who knew about the plan? The specifics, time and place."

Harriman was silent for a moment. "You, myself, Miles Loki, our man in Florida."

"Nobody else?"

"No."

"And if it wasn't me, and it wasn't you, and it sure wasn't the man with the gun, then . . . "

"Impossible," Harriman repeated, barely above a whisper. "I have known and trusted Miles Loki for 20 years."

"Disloyalty is the secret weapon of our enemies, Vance. You told me that once."

"But why would he do it?"

"Why does anybody do anything? He's got his own agenda."

"Which would be?"

"No idea. But I'm guessing it looks a lot different from ours, and that means he has to be stopped, and soon, so we can get back to the business at hand."

Diamond took out a cigar. Harriman eyed him with borderline distaste. "This is a no-smoking facility."

A smile, cold as death, curled onto Diamond's lips. "I'm sure it is." He fired up the stogie with a lighter that could have doubled for a welder's torch, sucked in a mouthful of smoke, and released it with a slow exhale. "But it now appears that someone on the inside—someone, I don't need to remind you, who knows everything—has gone off the ranch. That being the case, I'd say that lighting up a fine Cuban, with all due respect to the late Señor Rubio, is the least of our worries."

FIFTY-NINE

Tom sat upright in his bed at the Hampton Inn adjacent to Sarasota's airport, laptop on a pillow in front of him, reading a brief story on the local paper's website that reduced his near-death experience to a mere six paragraphs:

Yacht explodes at Sarasota marina

Firefighters said three people were killed and one person was missing after a yacht exploded in a Sarasota Bay marina.

The explosion occurred at about 3:30 p.m. Fire crews said they arrived to find the 92-foot yacht virtually destroyed, with its remnants engulfed in flames.

The names of the victims were being withheld pending notification of their families. Officials are searching the waters for a fourth person, who was seen jumping into the bay right before the explosion.

There were unconfirmed reports that the yacht was being refueled just before a loud explosion and ensuing fire rocked the marina, a portion of which was also engulfed in flames.

Six other vessels suffered damage.

The state fire marshal and the Florida Fish and Wildlife Conservation Commission are investigating the incident.

He just stared, and thought about the convenience of it all. No bodies, so no way to know that Hector Rubio was dead before his yacht disintegrated. An "unconfirmed report" that he knew full well would eventually morph into a final conclusion because it was easy and explainable and anyone who could deny it had been reduced to bite-sized pieces of fish food.

And then there was the message on his phone—

GET OFF THE BOAT NOW—

The one that made him a missing person instead of a dead one.

Who had sent it?

Who wanted him alive?

And why?

He rubbed his eyes, replaying as best he could what Rubio had said before the explosion, but getting little more than fragments— Hezbollah, Tri-Border Area, Unde Malum, global campaign against terrorism, greed, Paraguay—bits and pieces of information that simply added to the mystery rather than providing any clear path toward its solution.

Shifting windows to Google, he typed *Hezbollah* and *Tri-Border Area* into the search field, and got 313,000 hits. He clicked the first link, landing on a global security consulting firm's page that read:

"In South America, there is a region known as the Tri-Border Area, where the borders of Argentina, Brazil, and Paraguay intersect. After the 9/11 attacks, it caught the attention of the U.S. intelligence community. There have been confirmed reports that terrorists have met there to plan strikes against U.S. targets throughout the Western and Southern hemispheres. Those meetings were held in Ciudad del Este and were attended by members of Hezbollah and various other groups believed to be sympathetic to or affiliated with Al-Qaeda."

Ciudad del Este.

His mind flashed back to Vance Harriman's confirmation hearing, and the nominee's tale about saving the life of a corporate executive, who later died in a terrorist attack in Ciudad del Este.

He added *terrorism* and *Ciudad del Este* to the search terms, knocking the list down to 88,000 hits. One caught his eye, a blog headlined "Tri-Border Area: A lawless region, an illicit economy":

"This lawless region is basically made up of three cities: Puerto Iguazú, Argentina; Ciudad del Este, Paraguay; and Foz do Iguaçu, Brazil. It is widely known as a home, and a sanctuary, for illegal activities that range from intellectual property theft to counterfeiting to drug trafficking. This has become of increasing concern to U.S. policymakers because of their belief, though unsubstantiated as of this writing, that Hezbollah operatives are engaged in illicit activities to fund terrorist acts against the West, including the murder of selected corporate executives in an attempt to destabilize the regional economy."

Tom reread the paragraph and rewound in his mind something Rubio had said—

"Cold-hearted assassins in Paraguay"—

"The spirit of capitalism, although some might say greed"—

"Corporate and human."

He typed *Paraguay* and *corporate executives* into the search field. It produced just seven hits. Crime and safety reports out of Brazil, a white paper on cigarette smuggling, a book chapter on global terrorist tactics that focused on the kidnapping of business people, something from Air Uganda, nothing that shed any light on anything.

Until, on the next to last entry, he saw:

"Manufacturing executive dies in air tragedy."

Tom brought the story up on his screen, dated 18 months earlier, and read the first paragraph:

"John G. Maxwell, Vice President and General Manager of Systemos Integrados Avenzados (SIA), based in Ciudad del Este, died today in an airplane incident that also killed the pilots and two other corporate executives. It was the third tragedy in recent months affecting officials of the U.S.-based company, coming on the heels of two incidents believed to be terrorist-related. These have led to the announcement that SIA would exit the South American market in the interests of the safety of its employees."

But it wasn't the first paragraph that pushed him closer to the edge of some unseen cliff. It was the second:

"Although investigation into the accident is ongoing and a third terrorist act has not been ruled out, U.S. air safety investigators, assisting Paraguayan officials, believe that the cause may have been a total failure of the flight controls, a rare but not impossible event that disables the stabilizers, elevators, and ailerons, sending the plane into a nose dive."

The words came at him like bullets.

Total failure of the flight controls.

The same "event" that, according to the official story, had led to Harry Platte's death. The same "event" that, according to the all-knowing Vance Harriman, had happened only a handful of times.

What was it Hector Rubio had also said, something about Unde Malum being reborn, shifting from a secret program that murdered terrorists to a new mission that was "not of American principle"?

He went back and reread the blog, its content—"*the murder of selected corporate executives*"— taking on sudden new meaning.

Tom glanced at his watch. It had been only five hours, but what the hell, if any circumstance could be described as extenuating, this was it. He reached for the bottle of Klonopin on the nightstand and slipped one under his tongue, asking himself what Harry Platte and the victim of a South American plane crash had in common, and thinking that the distance between coincidence and conspiracy was beginning to shrink.

He shook the bottle of pills, a dozen or so left, more than enough to get him through the next few days. Which was good. Because after a quick visit to the Delta website, he booked himself on a flight leaving Sarasota at 10:31 the next morning.

For Paraguay.

SIXTY

TOM SAT AT what passed for an outdoor café in the dense, five-block-by-five-block center of downtown Ciudad del Este, sipping a Cossab Red Ale, the streets choked with people—Asians, Arabs, Africans, as well as the natives—watching as they conducted commerce in one of the blackest of the world's black markets:

A Subaru station wagon, rear gate open, three men perched on it, the car flanked on either side by mountainous racks of soccer balls.

A card table piled high with bootlegged DVDs, another with laptop parts, another with car accessories, others with fake Mont Blancs, fake perfume, fake watches, fake NFL jackets, and fake Viagra.

A gaggle of old women, fighting among themselves over who was going to buy the Incredible Hulk action figure, occasionally turning their attention to the bemused vendor, who knew demand when he saw it and had no intention of dropping the price.

Small booths with ragged-looking children hawking fruit.

Banners and billboards lording over the rolling sea of humanity; images of olive-skinned, vaguely feminine-looking young men advertising Dolce & Gabbana and Asian models hawking Euro-trashy-looking clothes and gangster jewelry.

Shotgun-toting security guards, some of them barely into their teens, roaming the street.

The droning buzz of motorbikes, driven by unhelmeted riders trying to navigate the masses.

An impossibly beautiful woman, slender, the color of caramel, with long shining black hair and gleaming white teeth, drawing a crowd at the stall where she was selling knockoff Ray-Bans.

Fat moneychangers sitting off to the sides, in the shadows, with their equally fat genuine leather wallets, watching it all, sipping chilled beverages and smiling benignly, ready with U.S. dollars, Paraguayan guaranis, or any other currency that could oil the market.

Multicolored umbrellas, dulled by the sun, that shaded cages of small animals of indeterminate breed, a wooden sign leaning against one of them, hand-painted, *Mastocas Exóticas*.

Con men. Criminals. Entrepreneurs. Opportunists.

"You seen *Star Wars?*" a voice asked. Tom turned to find a thin, sweating man in his 40s who had the pale appearance of someone recovering from dysentery. "This place makes that cantina scene look like the Ritz-Carlton." The man extended his hand. "Ricardo Garza. Call me Rick." Despite his Spanish-sounding name, there was no trace of an accent.

"Tom Fargo. Thanks for seeing me on such short notice."

Garza sat down in a black-metal-mesh chair next to Tom, and pulled it a little closer to the matching table—one of just six at the café—to get as much of his body as possible underneath the rusted awning overhead, out of the unforgiving sun. He gestured half-grandly to the chaos on the street. "So what do you think of our little freak show?"

"It's, uh, different, I have to say."

Garza laughed. "That's a diplomatic way of putting it. But then again, you're a politician." He caught the waiter's attention and ordered a beer, after a moment fixing a suspicious eye on Tom. "So what brings you to our little corner of the world, Mr. Fargo?" He asked as if he already knew the answer.

Tom saw the expression and took a second before answering. "I was doing some research on companies here in Ciudad del Este—"

"The legal ones, or all of them?"

"I don't follow."

"The city has only authorized 11 to do business, but another 40 or so operate illegally. The illegal ones, they're mostly money launderers, drug fronts, that sort of thing."

"How come the city doesn't shut them down?"

"There's a lot of money in those unregistered businesses," he said, smiling, offering no further explanation because none was really necessary. "Speaking of which." Tom swung around to find two beefy men standing behind him, thick moustaches, their eyes somewhere between dull and dead, hair as black as their dispositions, one with a toothpick in his mouth, the other with a machine gun in his hand.

"M21E," Gun Handler said. "Top model. Great accuracy. Burst fire. Six hundred U.S."

Garza motioned for him to pass the weapon over. The men exchanged a glance. Toothpick nodded.

Flashing a watch-this look at Tom, Garza gave the gun a once-over, inspecting it with the care of a jeweler seeking flaws in a diamond. He handed it back and shook his head. "It's not the real thing." The thugs looked at each other. If they were surprised, it didn't show. Tom felt his spine begin to tighten. "It's one of those handmade jobs from Brazil."

"Three hundred," Toothpick said.

"No deal."

"Fifteen free bullets."

Garza's lips coiled into a smile. "What good are the bullets if the firing mechanism doesn't work?"

"One twenty five and 50 free bullets." Garza shook his head. Tom waited for the shooting to start. But after leveling a stare at Garza that was equal parts puzzled, disappointed, and angry, they simply moved on to a man sitting a few tables away, and started the sales pitch anew.

"You seem to know your guns," Tom said.

"It's part of the job description." The server brought Garza's beer. "This can be a dangerous place."

"Especially for U.S. companies with divisions down here." He waited for a reaction that didn't come. "Like SIA. Systemos Integrados Avenzados."

Garza blinked, cut his eyes quickly to the right, then refastened them on Tom. "Don't know much about them."

The guy was a lousy liar. "How about Unde Malum. Does that ring any bells?"

Garza seemed almost relieved that the discussion had moved into different territory. "Unde Malum," he repeated, running it through his head. "No. What is it?"

Tom looked into his eyes and decided that on this one, the lousy liar was telling the truth. No point in pressing it. "Nothing. Just Washington stuff." When he steered the conversation back to business, the temporary relief drained from Rick Garza's face. "I do find it a little odd, though, that you're unfamiliar with SIA, since they were a competitor and pulled out of Paraguay after their general manager died in a plane crash."

"What's so odd about that? Accidents happen. And, like you said, this can be a dangerous place to do business."

"It's odd because your company picked up most of their work. You're pretty much the go-to guys for jet engines in Latin and South America now."

He shrugged. "We're good at what we do, and besides, everything was put up for bid." He took a sip of beer, trying to look casual. It didn't work. He was tense as a guitar string.

"But you were the only bidder." It was an empty statement, Tom pulling it out of midair, a shot in the dark he assumed would go nowhere.

He assumed wrong.

"I wouldn't know anything about that. Contracts, bids, all that, it's handled at AMC's headquarters in the States."

Tom just stared at him. "AMC?"

"Yeah. Aircraft Machinery Corporation. That's our parent company, up in Seattle."

Tom's mind slingshotted back to a few days earlier, in the Patriot's Blood office, recalling the guy from the jet engine manufacturer—

"We're just not comfortable giving the kind of money you're talking about."

He managed to say, barely, "AMC is your corporate parent."

Garza nodded. "I just assumed you knew that. AMC's given a ton of money to your boss in the past. Frankly, that's why I thought you'd called me. To shake us down for more, for that political action committee David Diamond's running for the presidential campaign."

Hearing Diamond's voice in his own head—

"Your companies have generated a lot of profits thanks to a mutually beneficial relationship with Penn Mallory."

"You know about Diamond and Patriot's Blood?"

Garza's eyes narrowed. "Why wouldn't I?"

Remembering, once more, Hector Rubio—

"Some might say greed—corporate and human."

"I just didn't think those decisions trickled down this far."

"They don't. AMC skims my profits and gives it to Patriot's Blood, then sends me a memo saying I've got to work harder to earn it back."

Tom nodded, but he wasn't listening. He was still trying to find the thread that connected David Diamond, Hector Rubio, Patriot's Blood, AMC, and a pair of too-similar-for-coincidence plane crashes that killed an anonymous U.S. businessman and Harry Platte.

And as strange as it sounded, the search kept bringing him back to an unlikely source.

SIXTY-ONE

ARLO DASH, TOM thought. Arlo was the key.

He was slumped on a chair in the passenger gate area at Bush Intercontinental Airport in Houston after a brutal 10-plus-hour flight from Asunción, exhausted, his body feeling like it had been run through a blender.

But his mind wouldn't shut down, because it wouldn't let go of that single line in the email from Arlo, the one Liberty had shown him the night she first crashed into his life:

"This evil prick is goin' down, and the greedy multinationals, too."

Greedy multinationals. Like AMC?

Arlo had apparently discovered some connection between Platte and whatever Hector Rubio was going to reveal about Unde Malum. Tom had made a connection between the crash that killed Platte and the one that killed a U.S. businessman, and between the crash that killed the businessman and the sudden contract success of AMC's South American division. And Rick Garza had handed him a connection between that contract success and David Diamond.

If he were plotting this on a straight line, it would start with AMC's newfound profitability in the South American market and lead to Platte's death, with Arlo somehow in the middle.

He fired up the laptop, letting his eyes graze the terminal as it came to life, checking out faces, seeing if any of them was taking an inordinate interest in a sleep-deprived guy who looked lost and was drowning in conspiracy theories.

It was early morning, and his flight to Dulles didn't leave for a few hours, and there wasn't a lot of activity—harried businessmen, teenagers with tennis rackets, moms pushing strollers, a lot of guys who were too old and too white to be wearing baseball caps turned backward. They all just looked past him or through him or didn't see him.

Satisfied he wasn't on anyone's watch list, he went back to the laptop, to search for . . .

What?

He'd already checked out AMC in South America, and found precious little he hadn't already discovered. Further research into Ciudad del Este only confirmed reports that it was home to a thriving illicit economy and an under-the-radar terrorism architecture. Other attempts to find incidences of plane crashes due to failure of flight controls turned up nothing. There was no mention of Unde Malum anywhere, even in the congressional budgets he'd accessed online, but that was no surprise given Rubio's description of it as a secret, black-budget program. He even cross-referenced Toni Allura, Vance Harriman, and David Diamond with every conceivable search term, from AMC to Ciudad del Este. Nothing.

The answer, he knew, was with Arlo's emails. Not the one he'd seen from Liberty that, while intriguing, proved nothing in and of itself. But he knew it hadn't been sent in a vacuum; there had to have been others, before and after, and they were likely on the portable hard drive that Arlo had sent himself and that was now in the hands of a guy in scrubs.

All of which left him more than a few miles short of nowhere.

"Goddamnit," he muttered, staring at but not seeing the laptop screen, ransacking his brain for anything resembling a strategy, getting nothing until a solution arrived in the unlikeliest of forms:

One of those traveling businessmen, overweight, thinning

hair, Bluetooth device jammed into his ear, screaming at the poor secretary or aide or partner at the other end of the line as he walked toward Tom.

"I don't care, do you understand me? I. Don't. Care. That's your problem. All I know is that this piece-of-shit computer crashed—I swear I'm going to come after whoever bought it with a grenade launcher—and it took the document with it, and I have to be with the client in two hours, and the client is expecting a strategic plan, and there's six million in billings riding on this, and unless you're gonna write me a commission check, you better figure it out!"

He paused to catch his breath, listened, and said, with a lot less anger and a lot more hope, "What, exactly, is a remote server?"

Remote server.

With his cell phone shredded in Sarasota Bay, Tom fired up his email program and typed in Liberty's address, writing, "Would you know if Arlo used a remote server, and if he did, how to access it?"

Thirty minutes later, he got her answer:

"There's good news and there's bad news."

SIXTY-TWO

IN LATE 2009, the U.S. Department of Defense began training people to hack into its computers.

Employees got 40 hours of instruction, studied 4,500 pages of written material—most devoted to the latest and greatest strategies being used to take down computer networks—and emerged with what the consultants called a Certified Ethical Hacker designation.

The goal, simply stated, was to find weaknesses in the Pentagon's systems that could make them vulnerable to attack, and then increase security in order to remove the potential threat. It was the classic "to fight a hacker, you have to think like a hacker" theory.

Of course, the government took issue with any such description.

"Our technology professionals are not learning to hack," a Defense spokesperson was quoted. "They are learning the skills and strategies necessary to defend networks against hackers."

That distinction may have been fine. It may have even been true. But it was lost on Paul Moody, a former technology wizard at the Department of Defense, who had used his taxpayer-funded skills—$2,500 per employee—to hack into Arlo Dash's remote email server.

That was the good news.

The bad news was that Paul Moody was involved with Sarah Morrin, Tom's ex, and they were all sitting at a desk in her radical chic 14th Street apartment, with its framed *Ramparts* covers on the wall and progressive journals—*Mother Jones, The Nation, Utne Reader*—piled or scattered everywhere.

In one corner, Liberty Dash was in a brown corduroy-upholstered chair, watching them and wondering if and when the weird dynamic would go upside down.

"I'm going to tell you both this one more time," Tom said, looking at Sarah. "Whatever happens in the next few minutes, whatever we find out, it stays here. Are we clear?"

Paul Moody—strongly built, easygoing, hair starting to go gray and get long, and more ruggedly good looking than Tom would have preferred—merely shrugged. "I'm just Hacker Boy."

Sarah, on the other hand—

"Not a chance. If we come up with something, and it is in any way illegal, immoral, or unethical, I'm running with it, and there's no way you or anyone—"

"Just listen—"

"No, I'm not gonna listen, or hold on—"

"You don't understand what you're dealing with—"

"I understand you sold out, and now you're trying to protect the guy—"

"Sarah. Shut up. Now." Tom's tone was flat, hard, and hot. It split her self-righteous anger like a meat cleaver.

Even Paul, who up to this point had shown no evidence he saw anything strange in this dysfunctional homecoming, sat up straight and tensed.

"I'm sorry," Sarah said quietly. "That was unfair."

Paul looked at her, and then at Tom, and then at Liberty, and then back at Sarah. "Uh, you guys need a minute or two alone?"

Liberty popped up like a jack-in-the-box. "I'll make some coffee."

"No," Tom said sharply, unblinking eyes not leaving Sarah's. "This has nothing to do with the past." She started to say something, but stopped. "What?" he asked. The word snapped like a whip.

She didn't look away, and after a second began to nod her head slowly, an Okay-you-asked-for-it gesture Tom had seen on more than a few occasions. "You know, when you walked out—"

"Let's be clear, Sarah. I walked out on this"—hands sweeping across the room—"not you. And if memory serves, you were the one who took the hike."

Paul and Liberty exchanged an uh-oh glance.

Tom and Sarah exchanged a stare that could have blown up an armored tank. "I did what I had to do, what I felt I had to do, Sarah," he said, slowly, deliberately, almost dispassionately. "I apologize deeply if it did not conform to your view of the world." He looked briefly at Paul, then back at her. "You've clearly moved on, and I respect that. But this is neither the time nor the place to refight lost causes or reopen old wounds."

"Causes are never lost, Tom. Not the right ones."

"And wounds are never healed, Sarah. Not the deep ones." He kept his eyes on hers for another couple of seconds, then blinked. He kneaded the bridge of his nose.

Liberty sat back down. Paul focused his attention on the desktop computer, mostly because it felt like neutral ground.

"Now, as I was saying," Tom continued, "I don't know what we might find. But here's what I do know. People are dead, and it may have something to do with this"—pointing to the computer—"and if whatever we learn leaves this room, you two might be next. Understood?"

"Jesus, Tom, are you threatening—"

"Do. You. Understand." Eyes nailed to Sarah's.

"Yeah, yeah," Paul jumped in, a one-man peacekeeping force. "We get it."

Tom nodded, but did not look at him, staying fixed on Sarah. "Because this is not a rally. It's not a march or a protest. Signs and banners and leaflets don't matter."

"They can if you have enough people carrying them," Sarah shot back, unable to stop herself.

"Not when the other side has secrets. There's not enough moral outrage in the world to overcome the need of powerful people to protect their secrets."

Paul's eyes got a little wider. Sarah's fell to her lap. Tom's roamed the room, settling for a moment on one of the *Ramparts* covers, an American flag redesigned by Mark Twain in 1901, with red and black stripes, and skulls and crossbones instead of stars.

"Okay," he said, turning back to Paul. "Tell me what you got."

SIXTY-THREE

"IT'S ACTUALLY A pretty basic remote email server," Paul Moody said, using a chewed-on BIC pen as a pointer, aiming it at the screen, looking at Tom like he was the only person in the room. "Kind of surprising, given what Miss Dash told me about her brother, his penchant for secrecy and all."

"Just out of interest, how long did it take you to hack into his account?" Tom asked.

"Ninety seconds." No pride, no ego, just a wry smile. "Your tax dollars at work."

Tom thought that in another world, under other circumstances, he might actually like this guy. "Okay."

Paul glanced at Sarah, who replied with a stiff nod. He ran a hand through his hair. "There are two things that strike me as significant. The first is, the email address is relatively new, about a month old."

"So he set it up right before—"

Liberty, who had pulled up a chair next to the desk, finished Tom's sentence. "Right before he was killed."

Paul smiled tightly. "Yes."

Tom exhaled, dropped his head, lowered his eyes. "So there's a possibility he set up this account just to deal with this, I dunno, this thing, this conspiracy, whatever the hell it was he was dealing with."

Liberty touched his shoulder.

"Yes," Paul said again. He gave Tom's frustration a moment to ebb, then added, "That's probably exactly what happened."

Tom looked up.

Paul tapped in a quick command on the keyboard. An email came to the screen. "Here's the first of the three messages in his mailbox. It suggests pretty clearly that this was a designated location."

Tom leaned in to the monitor:

To: VeracitaurusRex123
From: DDDc1102tQwazMa@noreply.us
This will be our channel of communication. Do not attempt to respond or initiate messaging. I will contact you as required.

That was it.

"Do I assume the sender used a dead or disposable email address?" Tom asked.

"Yes."

"Which you can buy online, I'm also assuming, like throwaway phones?" Paul nodded. "So there has to be a return email box, right, something you can hack into, or some record of the user?"

Paul hesitated. "I tried, but it's not, uh, quite that simple."

"Meaning?"

"Meaning this is beyond anything I saw at DoD." He shot a quick glance at Sarah, then looked back at Tom. "The secrecy. The security. It's just light years beyond."

Tom stared at him. "What does that tell you?"

Paul's voice lost some of its ease. "We're not in Kansas anymore."

"All right. Let me see the second one."

Another quick keystroke, and message No. 2 was revealed:

To: VeracitaurusRex123
From: DDDc1102tQwazMa@noreply.us
There are roads out of secret places that we all must travel, regardless of where they lead. You will be both the vessel of transport and the messenger of truth. Then you will know from whence cometh evil.

"From whence cometh evil," Tom half-whispered. "Any ideas?" His eyes went from Paul to Sarah to Liberty, met each time with a puzzled headshake. "This guy, whoever it is, sounds like some kind of religious zealot."

"If it's a guy," Paul said.

After another minute or so of thought, which took him to one more dead end, Tom asked to see the last email.

To: VeracitaurusRex123
From: DDDc1102tQwazMa@noreply.us
I am an individual of my word. You have the dancer. Upon execution of our agreement, I will show you from whence cometh evil. After that, there will be no further contact.

"In the absence of any other message," Paul spitballed, "I'm wondering if Arlo got spooked, or for some reason didn't hold up his end of the bargain—"

"And maybe that's what got him killed," Liberty said.

"No," Tom said faintly, not listening, staring into space, off in a world that at that moment had a population of just one, him, and recalling a hallway shouting match, a tall, young, very unhappy blonde, shrieking at Harry Platte—

"That skank ballerina in Saudi Arabia"—

Saying, "That's not what got him killed at all," as he re-entered the current world, getting up, going to his laptop carrier/backpack, hands flying through every little storage space, every zippered pouch, every netted compartment, running up and down and front, back, sides, until he found it:

A small thumb drive.

He looked at Paul.

"Can you get me access to some kind of facial recognition program?"

"Can John Ford make a classic Western?"

Oh, yeah, Tom thought, *I really could start to like this guy.*

"What's going on?" Sarah asked.

"Not holding up his end of the bargain didn't get Arlo killed." Tom handed the thumb drive to Paul, and turned to Liberty. "This did."

SIXTY-FOUR

IT DIDN'T TAKE long for Paul Moody to access a facial recognition program or to identify the young Arab-looking woman in the photo with Platte that Tom had seen on the laptop computer in the garage.

"Her name is Jamilah Sabeem," he read in a slightly droning voice from a biography posted on Wikipedia. "She is 23, studied at the Music and Ballet School of Baghdad . . . Instilled at an early age with a passion for movement . . . Rehearsed in her slippers for fear she would wear out her pointe shoes, and there was no place in Baghdad to buy another pair . . . While other young women dropped out of the school in their early teens out of fear of Muslim extremists who found music sacrilegious and have been known to kill for far lesser 'crimes,' she never stopped showing up for class and defiantly wore a leotard in front of men . . . Jamilah attributes her devotion to dance to her mother, Fadilah, a seller of fabrics on the streets, who along with Jamilah's father died in the violence that followed the American invasion of Iraq . . . Became a principal dancer with the National Ballet Troupe of Iraq when it left Baghdad in 2009 and relocated to Scandinavia in a partnership with Copenhagen's Danish Dance Theatre, one of Europe's foremost contemporary dance companies."

He stopped, looked over at Tom. "That's it."

Tom stared at the screen, silent.

"So on the one hand, you have a young dancer who defies culture, custom, and the fundamentalists," Sarah said. "And on the other, she's hanging out with Harry Platte, Mr. Nuke Baghdad Into Ruin, who's probably just as happy her parents are dead."

"Do you think she knew who he was?" Liberty asked.

"After the invasion, they carried signs in the streets in Baghdad that read 'Death to the War Criminals,'" Tom replied, talking more to the room than to any of them. "They had pictures of Harry Platte on them." He turned to Liberty. "She knew who he was."

"There's no guarantee," Sarah said. "I mean, artists live in their own world, and a lot of times it's insulated from politics."

Tom shook his head. "She knew."

Sarah started to say something, but Paul shot her a silent-alarm look, accompanied by a brief half-shake of the head that got her attention. "You're probably right," she said softly.

Tom leaned back in the chair. "See if you can find anything else."

Paul clack-clack-clacked on the keyboard, found a review, and read:

"In an evening of standout performances, Jamilah Sabeem was incandescent as the Dark Angel figure. She is beautiful, both in form and face, and brings more depth to the role than most of her contemporaries. One can understand why, when her strong, handsome partner enters, he leaves blinded by this Dark Angel, whose slashing leg extensions, commanding arabesque, and feline smile were precisely what the evening required, and may be among the most glorious the dance stage has seen in years."

"So she can dance," Tom said, impatiently. "She's a dancer. What do you expect?"

"Maybe a little less attitude," Sarah shot back, "and a little more gratitude."

"It's Google, Sarah. A blind goat could manage Google." To Paul: "No offense."

"None taken."

"You mind giving it another try?"

Paul looked at Sarah, then at Tom, then smiled broadly. "Well, since there don't seem to be any blind goats around . . . "

Liberty laughed, and, once again, Tom tried to beat back the urge to like this guy.

A few more keyboard clacks, and Paul suddenly straightened up. "Whoa."

"What?" Tom and Sarah asked, almost in unison.

"This girl, the dancer, she just died. A nightclub in Beirut blew up. They're saying it was a terrorist bombing."

While Paul kept clacking away, Tom's mind went into stream-of-consciousness freefall. "Okay, so we have this dancer, and her parents are killed in the Iraq invasion, an invasion Platte all but suited up for, and she's not afraid of the extremists, and she hooks up with Platte, and then she's killed in a terrorist bombing." He stopped, looked at Sarah. "It doesn't add up."

The silence was pierced only by Paul's investigatory typing.

"Maybe terrorists killed her because she was having the affair with Platte, like for revenge," Liberty offered.

"Or because she defied Islamic custom," Sarah chimed in, though without much conviction.

Tom shook his head. "If you're gonna kill anybody, it's Platte."

"Maybe they did," Sarah said softly. "And she was just in the wrong pace at the wrong time."

He turned to her. "You really believe that? It's just that simple?"

"Sometimes the simplest answer is the only answer."

"Nobody's taken credit for it. I'm telling you, if this was a hit on Platte, half the crazies in the universe would be doing Internet videos claiming victory."

He drifted back off into thought.

More silence.

Paul clattering.

"We're missing something," Tom said, his voice distant, swallowed by confusion. "There's a link here."

"Arlo?" Liberty asked.

Tom nodded, but for everyone's good he kept what he knew about AMC, Diamond, and dead executives in South America to himself. "At some point, all of this has to intersect."

The clattering suddenly stopped. "Uh, guys?"

The anxiety in Paul's voice had the ring of an air-raid klaxon. Sarah turned to him and saw nothing but raw apprehension. She followed his eyes to the computer screen.

Tom was still freefalling. "We have all these threads—Platte, the dancer, Arlo, the plane crash—and somehow, some way, they're woven together, they have to be."

"Tom," Sarah said.

Liberty looked at the screen, and put her hand over her mouth.

"I refuse to believe any of this just happened—"

"Tom," Sarah repeated.

"That one day the planets lined up in a particular order, and set off a series of accidental events—"

"Tom!"

"Jesus, Sarah, will you just let me think out loud for a second? You know that's how my mind works. I have to speak—"

"No, Tom, you need to shut up and read this." Pointing at the monitor.

"Read what?"

"Something I'm guessing would have escaped even a Googling goat."

Tom faked a laugh, then saw she wasn't joking, and in that moment felt the room start to close in on him.

"You need to see this, man." Paul sounded like he was announcing a cancer diagnosis.

Tom looked at the monitor, knowing instantly that Paul had hacked into the bare-bones FBI Terrorist Screening Database, which was used to compile everything from no-fly lists to the Interpol Terrorism Watch List.

Every day, an estimated 1,600 names were suggested for

addition to the database, and 600 recommended for removal.

It contained more than 1 million records.

There were over 400,000 unique names in the system.

But the only one Tom cared about, the only one that mattered, belonged to the face that looked back him, a face whose chiseled, classical beauty could not be obscured by an expression that seemed devoid of humanity, full of hardened hate.

Jamilah Sabeem.

"What is a dancer doing in the FBI's terrorist database?" Tom asked, as much to himself as anyone.

Paul took a slow, deep breath. "It seems she's not just a dancer."

Tom unhooked his eyes from the screen, fastened them on Paul. "What is she?"

"According to, uh, according to this, she's, uh . . . "

"What is she, Paul?"

"She's been associated with the Ministry of Intelligence and National Security of Iran."

Tom's hands tightened on the arms of the chair. "The secret police."

"She was sent to Iran in 2007 by the Supreme Council for Islamic Revolution in Iraq for a month of training in intelligence gathering," Paul said. "Then she returned to Baghdad, presumably to put her newfound skills to work against the American interlopers." He paused. "U.S. officials who know about these things believe that after the war in Iraq ended, she may have returned the favor of her training by going to work for the Iranian secret police."

Tom's eyes grazed over Sarah, then Liberty, settling on Paul, trying to catch his breath, to shake a sense of doom that was as real and tangible and inevitable as death. "What does that mean? Tell me exactly what that means."

Paul tried to collect his thoughts, but quickly gave up, choosing instead to just lay it out there. "It means that Harry Platte was probably sleeping with an Iranian spy."

"And Arlo must have found out," Tom said darkly, sensing in that moment that the road to finding out who killed Platte had just taken another turn, and knowing exactly where and to whom it now led.

SIXTY-FIVE

IT WAS AN odd place for an ambush.

Twelve blocks from the White House, overlooking the C&O Canal, a couple of steps from Rock Creek Park. Dark Escalades with tinted windows choking the driveway out front, joined by the occasional Mercedes with diplomatic license plates. Men armed with earpieces and unseen weaponry peering through blacker-than-black sunglasses, scanning the landscape, alert eyes searching for anyone or anything that might throw this otherwise sunny morning into a state of emergency.

None of them saw or suspected the man in the suit, sipping complimentary coffee in the dripping-with-luxury lobby of the Four Seasons, pretending to read the *The Wall Street Journal*, his attention never straying from the stairs that went down to the Seasons restaurant.

As power breakfast locations go, they didn't get any more powerful than this.

Within five minutes of arriving, Tom had seen a columnist for *The Washington Post*, the Secretary of State, the head of the Republican National Committee, and the minority leader of the House go in, and the vice president's chief of staff, a Supreme Court justice, and the Washington bureau chief of ABC News come out.

The parade didn't stop over the next half hour, either, as the stairs disgorged a who's who of the political elite. The mayor of Washington, the host of network television's most popular Sunday morning talk show, the chairman of the president's second re-election campaign, the governor of Virginia, and on and on and on.

But still no sign of—

Then there she was, in full de la Renta, a trim white sleeveless dress that stopped at the center of the knees, black polka-dot design, the design reversed on the waist-length cardigan, black with white polka dots.

Toni Allura.

Accompanied by a man he'd never seen, shaved head, strong-looking in an older Navy Seal kind of way, eyes that even at a distance Tom could tell communicated intensity, or insanity, or both.

Tom jerked the paper closer to his face, demonstrating all the subtlety of a strip show, and watched them walk through the lobby. They were wrapped up in a serious discussion, Toni pretty focused, the bald man shaking his head, either not agreeing or telling her not to worry.

When they had left the hotel, Tom dropped the paper on a side table and followed them outside, where they waited for their cars, still talking. He held back a comfortable 15 or 20 feet, picking up bits and pieces of their conversation.

Toni saying, "—about to come apart—"

The bald man replying, "—it can still be managed—"

"—biggest mistake of my life—"

"—acting as a patriot—"

"—your fault, all of it—"

"—deviated from our agreement—"

"—come back to haunt me—"

"—right thing to do, the intended consequences—"

"—there are intended consequences, and then there is what happens—"

"And what was it that happened, Senator?"

Their heads swung to him in unison.

"Why, Mr. Fargo, what a pleasant surprise," Toni said, seemingly not in the least shocked by his appearance, a megawatt smile burning off any fears or concerns or anxieties she might have been feeling.

For his part, the bald man wasn't shocked, either. But Tom saw the anger in his face and thought the air between them might detonate.

Toni grabbed her friend's arm and pulled him a step in Tom's direction. "Do you know Miles Loki? The *mysterious* Miles Loki?"

Tom suddenly felt himself spiraling down a mineshaft of disorientation.

Miles Loki?

"He's Vance Harriman's No. 2," Toni went on, glancing quickly at Loki, then back at Tom, "the director-in-waiting's consigliere, as it were."

She smiled. The bald man didn't.

"Anyway, if you would like some entertaining coffee chat on American history, I would strongly recommend a session with Mr. Loki. His discourse on the Confederacy as a traitorous band of, what was the term—"

But Tom knew, in that instant, he knew—

"Treacherous infidels, that's it"—

His mind blazing back to that first encounter on the Eye Street garage rooftop, the night made even blacker by the hood covering his head, remembering with utter clarity—

"On July 12, 1864, President Lincoln and his wife went there, to the fort, and he stood on a parapet watching the Union troops beat back the treacherous infidels. It is difficult to imagine such courage, such inspiration, today"—

Recalling again, that phrase, *treacherous infidels,* and trying to wrap his head around the question of why Vance Harriman's No. 2 had disguised himself as a dreadlocked blind man, pushed him to continue the probe of Platte's death, given him the dancer-spy—

Standing there in a daze as the door to one of the Escalades opened—

Hearing Miles Loki say, "Give you a lift?"—

Imagining what terrors might await if he said—

"I guess"—

Getting in because he felt he had no choice, knowing the terror would always be there, exhausted at fearing its inevitability, ready to look at it straight in the eye, dead-on, wondering what would happen if he flinched first or, maybe worse, if he didn't.

SIXTY-SIX

THEY SAT ON the steps in front of the Lincoln Memorial, a setting Tom thought appropriate given the chiseled inscription that hovered over the larger-than-life statue of the president who preserved the nation—

"In this temple, as in the hearts of the people for whom he saved the Union, the memory of Abraham Lincoln is enshrined forever"—

A sentiment shared by Miles Loki, or Dreadlock Man, or whoever he was, a true believer in all things America, whose belief had been dented, perhaps even shattered, by actions that Tom sensed he himself had in some way set into action.

They sat in silence for a few minutes, paying no attention to the tourists going up and down the steps, Loki seemingly focused on the National World War II Memorial on the other end of the Reflecting Pool, or maybe the flag-rimmed Washington Monument beyond that, until he finally said:

"You are in significant danger."

Tom nodded and squinted into the bright midmorning sun. He took off his suit coat, folded it, and set it down next to him. "Yeah."

"I cannot tell you exactly what kind of danger, or how the associated"—he paused, searching for a word—"retribution might be exacted."

Tom half-smiled. "Can't tell me, or won't?"

For the first time, Loki turned to face him. "I will answer whatever questions I feel that I can."

At this point, there were thousands of them, buzzing like bees in his mind. But Tom started with the big one, the one that had gotten him here, wherever that was, in the first place. "Who killed Harry Platte?"

Miles Loki's tough exterior cracked, just slightly. "We did."

"We, as in Territo?"

"No. The government of the people of the United States." His eyes hardened. His voice was at once sad and angry. He pushed his shoulders back. "*Our* government. *We* murdered Harry Platte."

"Because of the girl, the dancer."

Loki nodded. "Because he was about to become an embarrassment."

Tom broke the eye contact. "Who set it up?"

"Anath."

Which explained why she wanted the investigation stopped. "How do you arrange a complete failure of the flight controls?"

"Carefully." A pause. "But in this case, it appears, not carefully enough."

"Who gave the order to kill him?"

Loki considered the question for some time before shaking his head. "No."

"Did it have anything to do with Toni Allura?"

A long pause. "You'll get nothing from me regarding Senator Allura."

Tom wondered why he was protecting her, thinking that maybe they were an item, then rejecting the thought almost instantly. Opposites may attract, but these two were as different as a hurricane is from a gust of wind. "What's the connection to her? Anath."

Loki answered simply, without hesitation. "She managed a global assassination bureau, created in the aftermath of 9/11, funded by the American taxpayer, that targeted terrorists."

More or less confirming what Hector Rubio had said. "Unde Malum." Loki nodded. "Was Platte a victim of Unde Malum?"

"We are all victims of Unde Malum."

"Including American businessmen in South America?"

Miles Loki's face reddened with a rage that only barely crept into his voice. "What John Allura did, forming and funding a network whose purpose was to murder the world's most abhorrent criminals, it was an honorable thing. But when he died, and his widow gained the seat, everything changed."

"So she is involved."

"You will get nothing from me regarding Senator Allura," he repeated, devoid of emotion.

"Then what changed after she inherited the seat?" Loki did not reply. He reached into his suit jacket pocket and pulled out a sealed envelope, which after a second of hesitation he handed to Tom. "What's this?"

"This is how it ends." He stood and began walking down the steps toward the Reflecting Pool.

Tom looked at the envelope, then up at Loki. "Who killed Arlo Dash?"

Loki stopped and lowered his head. "Not that it matters anymore, but I did. I am directly responsible for the young man's death."

Tom got up and approached him cautiously. "Because he was about to blow the whistle on Platte?"

"No, Mr. Fargo. Because I was his source. I provided him the intelligence about Platte and the dancer." Tom leaned back slightly on his heels, as if pushed by Loki's confession. "Now may I ask you a question?" Over his head in confusion, Tom could only nod. "Do you have any personal affairs?"

"Personal affairs?"

"I ask because if you do, you would be well-advised to get them in order." He gestured to the envelope in Tom's hand. "I doubt very much that you will survive the week." Then he smiled cheerlessly and walked away, dissolving into a clot of tourists at the base of the steps.

Tom watched him, trying to get his world back on its axis. He returned his attention to the envelope and tore it open.

A single page, 12 names, nothing else, listed in alphabetical order.

Starting with Aircraft Machinery Corporation.

AMC.

SIXTY-SEVEN

MILES LOKI WALKED along the Reflecting Pool toward the World War II Memorial, feeling an acid-like anger rise within him as he thought of how the contributions of 16 million Americans could be soiled by the acts of a few men whose only interests were self-interest, men for whom the national good was secondary to personal ambition, men who murdered Harry Platte because exposure of the senator's tawdry secret would have tarnished reputations that had been lifetimes in the making.

On any other day like this one, with its cloudless sky the color of bluebonnets, the surrounding green spaces seeming greener than usual, he would have shown his respect. Perhaps he would have run his hand gently over the Gold Star Wall, 4,048 stars, each representing 100 lives lost in the war, or taken a moment to simply gaze into the Rainbow Pool at the heart of the plaza, contemplating the horrors that might have followed had so many not decided so selflessly that we, the people, were more important than they, the individuals.

But not today.

Today he could not bring himself to even enter the memorial, instead choosing the footpath along its outer edges, around and down to 17th Street, where his driver was waiting.

Except the car wasn't there.

Miles Loki tensed.

He had made the call just minutes ago. The driver had assured him that he'd be in the front of the memorial, at the entrance on 17th.

Traffic was flowing smoothly along the street, no sign of congestion, no snarls, nothing that would have prevented the Escalade from being where it was supposed to be, when it was supposed to be there.

The sun suddenly felt a little warmer, the day a little darker.

Miles Loki's eyes roamed up 17th Street toward Constitution, which he knew could be a nightmare at certain times of the day, tourists and traffic making it a mess.

He watched for a minute or so, but saw nothing, then started moving toward the intersection, thinking maybe the driver had been swallowed up by the gridlock.

There were three sharp blasts of a car horn.

Loki turned to see the Escalade, as promised, sitting on the other side of 17th, opposite the entrance to the memorial.

He briefly held up his hand in acknowledgment, crossed the street, and approached the car. From a distance, he could see the shape of his driver, behind the wheel, leaning over to open the door.

A young woman passed him, walking a Labrador retriever accessorized with an American flag bandana around its neck.

Miles Loki smiled at her.

Two aging, slow-moving veterans, one wearing his VFW hat, the other a mesh Navy baseball cap emblazoned in gold with USS Arizona, walked solemnly toward the memorial.

The Escalade door swung open.

A father leaned down at his son's level, pointing variously to the Lincoln Memorial, the Washington Monument, and the memorial dedicated to the signers of the Declaration of Independence, explaining the history, the boy nodding and taking it all in eagerly.

Miles Loki stepped into the car, seeing a warning flash in his driver's eyes—

The first silenced gunshot cutting a bloody trench through the top of the man's skull—

Loki dropping to the ground a moment after a second bullet grazed his right shoulder—

Rolling under the car, reaching for the Glock 33, nine .357 rounds in the magazine, squeezing off three through the floorboard—

More muffled shots blasting at him from overhead, back through the floorboard—

Slithering on his back to the other side of the Escalade, the driver's side—

Another burst from inside the car—

Loki firing twice more, grabbing the running board at the base of the door, pulling himself out and up with one hand—

Getting to his feet fast—

Firing once into the tinted back-seat window, the glass shattering, his would-be killer's right bicep rupturing, the Czech CZ 75 semi-automatic pistol flying from his grip—

Seeing the shooter for the first time, dazed and staring at the jagged gash in his arm, Loki not recognizing him but knowing instantly what this was about—

Slamming the Glock into the man's temple, a sharp crack—

Then shooting him again, twice more, once in each thigh—

Hearing someone yell, "Carjack!"—

And someone else, "Call 911!"—

And someone else, "Terrorists!"—

Pushing his dead driver to the passenger side, jumping in, cranking up the ignition, spinning around, squealing down 17th to Independence, then 14th—

The man in the back seat moaning—

One round left in the Glock—

Taking the George Washington Memorial Parkway, heading toward Alexandria, negotiating the traffic—

Finally arriving at the parking lot in front of the building, stopping, getting out of the Escalade, jerking the rear door open, yanking the wailing gunman onto the macadam surface—

Crouching, Glock in one hand—

Jamming the index finger of the other into one of the thigh wounds—

The man screaming—

Painting a circle in blood on the killer's forehead, then eight crude arrows emanating from it, a rough match for the tattoos on his forearm—

The man crying, gasping for breath—

Leaning into his face—

An unsparing whisper, "I am the chosen curse who will blast the man who owes his greatness to his country's ruin"—

One round left—

Firing it into the man's stomach, knowing death would follow, but not immediately, confident the whispered message would be received before the blackness descended, prepared for whatever peril that fate might deliver to his doorstep.

SIXTY-EIGHT

TOM WAS SURE from the second he saw AMC's name on the list from Miles Loki that all 12 names had something to do with Patriot's Blood. The question was what, and how that was connected to Platte, Unde Malum, Arlo Dash, David Diamond, and any of the other riddles whose solutions seemed at once tantalizingly close and frustratingly distant.

Back at his desk in the Patriot's Blood office, he fired up two computers: a desktop to access donor information and his laptop to fill in the blanks.

Typing in his username and password on the desktop, he quickly got to the screen that displayed data for AMC. At the top of the page was a brief description:

"Seattle-based company. Manufactures jet engines for primarily military clients. Strong presence in U.S. and Asia; seeking foothold in Latin America and South America. Key competitor: Systemos Integrados Avenzados (SIA)."

The company had given $585,000 in two installments. The first had been two years earlier, the second 15 months ago. In between those contributions, Tom knew and Rick Garza had confirmed in Ciudad del Este, AMC had indeed gained a foothold in Latin and South America when SIA had left the market.

After its top executive had died. In a plane crash. Attributed to a total failure of the flight controls.

A black chill began to slowly sweep over him.

He paused for a moment, clenched and unclenched his fists, and typed *Blackthorne Technologies*, the next name on the list:

"Berkeley-based company. Provides navigation and guidance systems and support services. No. 2 in sector in U.S., seeking entry into Mexican markets. Key competitor: AeroDynamics Corp."

Two contributions, $250,000 each, the first a year ago, the second three months ago.

Tom spun from the desktop to his laptop, typed *AeroDynamics Corp.* and *Mexico* into the Google search window, 3,013 hits, but he didn't have to go past the fourth, clicking through to the story, an item from the San Diego newspaper:

"Robert Ellsworth, president of the Mexican subsidiary of California's AeroDynamics Corp., was killed Monday in a car bombing police suspect was carried out by Hezbollah terrorists associated with and financed by the drug cartels. Ellsworth was the second company official to be assassinated in what officials see as a heightening campaign targeting U.S. companies in the region."

It was dated a month before Blackthorne's second $250,000 donation.

Tom added *Blackthorne Technologies* to the search string. The top link was from an English-language website based in Mexico City, posted a week later:

"Blackthorne Technologies said today it had secured a contract with the Mexican government to provide advanced navigation systems to the Fuerza Aérea Mexicana. Although the amount was not announced, sources say it is likely in the range of $75 million to $100 million, which is believed to be the value of the Mexican air force's previous contract with AeroDynamics Corp."

The chill that had gripped Tom suddenly became tighter, and got blacker and colder.

Two companies, each making two huge contributions to Patriot's Blood, each winning major contracts after their competitors' top executives had died.

Tom tried to convince himself it was coincidence, just an odd confluence of timing and events. But that was crazy, and he knew it. His mind told him that coincidence was only someone's way of staying anonymous, and that the probability of all these things coming together in this way was too small to be accidental.

He returned to the desktop, typed in *InterSatt*, the next name on Miles Loki's list:

"Boston-based company. Provides hardware, software, and communications services for satellites used in intelligence-gathering. Strong presence in Europe, with the exception of Germany. Looking to expand into South America. Key competitor: Defensor Industries."

Tom froze, the black chill landing on him like a falling piano.

Defensor Industries?

The same company Toni Allura had grilled Harriman about during his confirmation hearings, the one whose executive the Territo CEO had protected against the two German assassins in Berlin, the same executive who later died—

In a terrorist attack in Ciudad del Este.

"Son of a bitch," Tom whispered.

He quickly entered *Defensor Industries* and *InterSatt* into the Google search window, the first link reinforcing his rising dread:

"U.S. company InterSatt has been awarded a joint contract to provide technical services to intelligence agencies in Argentina, Brazil, and Venezuela after the prior contractor, Defensor Industries, was destabilized by the deaths of its corporate executives in presumed terrorist attacks that led the company to leave the market."

He went back to the desktop.

Two contributions, totaling $1 million, the second one coming barely a month after the Defensor official, Edward Irving, was murdered.

Tom didn't have to look at the remaining nine donors, or review their contribution histories, or check out their backstories.

He knew.

Companies were being strong-armed into giving to Patriot's Blood, and Unde Malum made the donations pay off by killing the leadership of their competitors in foreign markets, with one contribution coming before the act, the second when it was completed. And the murders continued until the competitors either fled the market altogether out of fear, or lost the contracts because they were perceived as being crippled. In either case, the Patriot's Blood donors filled the void and took over the business.

That was what Hector Rubio had been talking about, the "new mission":

Unde Malum had gone from murdering terrorists for revenge to murdering Americans for campaign contributions.

And it was all as secret as silence. Unde Malum was classified and buried in the black budget. Federal law prevented disclosure of the contributions. The perfect cover.

But in addition to the truth behind Unde Malum, he now also knew two other things:

First, the people who were behind the conspiracy, the anonymous creators of coincidence, were no longer anonymous. They were David Diamond, who had clearly decided that the rules of the game, such as they were, didn't apply to him. And Toni Allura, because she rattled Harriman at his hearing by grilling him on Edward Irving's death, something there was no logical reason she should have known.

The second thing he knew was this:

Possessing this information gave him a bargaining chip that could well extend his lifespan beyond the week that Miles Loki had predicted.

He quickly shut down the laptop and packed it up, then began printing the histories, donation and otherwise, of the 12 companies on Loki's list. He tried to stay focused and not let his growing alarm mutate into something more disabling, but still felt suspended in the murky waters of his own anxiety. When he finished, he quit the desktop, grabbed his laptop and the cell phone that Patriot's Blood had provided him, and walked as casually as possible to the printer.

Where he found Doris Steinkeller, Diamond's older-than-dirt, thin-as-a-reed secretary, glaring at him with a sour expression and tapping her foot in disapproval. She held the copies out. "You cannot print this. It is confidential information."

Tom had neither the time nor the inclination to come up with a justifying lie, thinking only that he had to get out of there, and fast. "I can if Mallory says he wants it."

"Why would he want it?"

"Ask him."

"Why wasn't I informed?"

"Ask him that, too."

If her accelerated foot tapping was any indication, the Mallory card wasn't having a lot of effect on Doris Steinkeller. "I don't think I can allow this."

Tom's patience was evaporating. "Take that up with him, too, Doris. All I can tell you is that Mallory asked for the information, and unlike some whose names shall remain unspoken, I do what the boss tells me to do."

With that, he snatched the copies from her hand, a move that both shocked and offended the secretary, and walked from the office into the elevator without another word.

Out on the street, he dialed Mallory's private number on the cell, getting a recorded message on the third ring. "Boss, we need to talk," he said. "You were right about Diamond and Toni, but it's bad, worse than we could have imagined. Get back to me as soon as you can."

Above him, in the Patriot's Blood office, Doris Steinkeller stared out the window at Tom on his phone, her anger rising like steam from a teapot. "If you think you're the only one around here who does what the boss says to do," she half-hissed, half-muttered, "you are sorely mistaken, mister."

Then she picked up the first phone she could get her hands on and made the call that would change everything and everyone in the coming days.

SIXTY-NINE

"IT APPEARS THAT Loki delivered Unde Malum to Fargo on a platter," David Diamond said.

Harriman shot him a look that could start a wildfire. "This is unacceptable."

"Yeah, Vance, I get that. But it doesn't change the facts."

"What else does Fargo know?"

"Besides the 12 names? It's just a guess, but he probably knows whatever Loki wanted him to know."

"And you think Loki told him everything?"

"I don't care what Loki told him. I care that he has a stack of papers that open a window to Unde Malum. And I think that makes a pretty good argument for not waiting any longer to push the button on this thing and get it behind us."

They were in the safe room under Territo's headquarters. A speakerphone sat on the maple table in front of them. They looked at it, waiting for some response, some instruction or guidance, from the other end of the line.

They heard only breathing. Nothing else.

"How about you, Congressman?" Diamond asked, turning to Jasper Eddy. "Any thoughts?"

"We are in a position," the South Carolinian replied slowly, carefully choosing his words, "to move toward endgame when so authorized."

Diamond smiled, thinking the guy had been nominated as Secretary of Defense only a few days ago, and already he'd dropped the profanity and picked up the lingo and cover-your-ass phrasing that would have made a career bureaucrat proud. He'd no doubt be a tremendous addition to the Cabinet and an asset to freedom-loving people everywhere.

"Will Loki go underground and stay underground?" Jasper Eddy asked.

"I just incinerated the body of a dead contractor who had the symbol of chaos painted in blood on his forehead," Harriman shot back angrily. "Loki was sending us a message we would all be wise to heed. He is not going away."

Eddy let Harriman's fury sit for a second before asking, "And what does your gut tell you he's gonna do, Vance?"

Harriman drew little invisible circles on the table that, with the four chairs and phone system, was the only thing in the 15- by 15-foot room. "My gut tells me this is not over."

"Then I agree with David," Eddy said. "We need to end it, and we need a plan to end it now."

Ever the strategist, Diamond leaped in. "We actually have a plan, Congressman." He traded a glance with Harriman, seeking permission to continue. The CIA nominee drew some more circles on the table before shrugging his approval. "We're confident it will tie everything up."

"It had better, David," Eddy said. "Fargo needs to be gone, and what he knows needs to go with him."

A pause. Harriman and Diamond looked at the speakerphone again.

And again, they got no response, just more breathing.

"The country doesn't need any scandals," Eddy continued, in full statesman mode. "Not in a time of war. It is our job to preserve the security of every single American, even if we have to kill one, as we did with Harry Platte. It's collateral damage, the price of freedom."

Diamond looked at Harriman, whose gaze was fixed on one of the bare off-white walls, and nodded. "I agree."

"Then what're you proposing?"

For the next 10 minutes, David Diamond laid out a plan that Eddy called "pretty audacious" with "not a lot of room for error."

David Diamond said he recognized that.

Eddy worried that it involved the media, brought Anath back into the picture, and required the "recruitment" of a third party that was, to put it charitably, untested.

David Diamond said he recognized that, too.

Then Eddy raised the questions of whether they were moving too fast, whether all the remaining threads—including the blogger's sister and Miles Loki—really were being tied up, and whether there might be a subsequent investigation that could go in a direction not favorable to their goals.

David Diamond said he recognized those concerns, too, all of them.

"Seems kinda risky, like we're going out on a mighty big limb."

"That's where the fruit is, Congressman."

"You mean, as in that fruit Fargo?" Laughing at his own joke, with a cruel edge.

"He means, sir," Vance Harriman said, returning from whatever mental world he'd been visiting, "that in less than 36 hours, Fargo will be dead, and America can rest more easily in the knowledge that it has been rid of an enemy within, a genuine traitor, and that his demise sends a clear and unmistakable signal to the nation and the world that there are consequences, severe consequences, to acting contrary to the national ideal."

"We represent the national ideal," Jasper Eddy said.

"Yes, sir. We are the patriots."

Eddy hesitated. Then: "So are we good to go?"

In the stillness that followed, Diamond and Harriman and Eddy just stared at the speakerphone, almost willing a response from the fourth person in the conversation, the one on the other end of the line, the one who had not uttered a word after coming on, the three of them just staring at it as if watching the unit would somehow set the inevitable into motion.

Which, in a moment, it did.

"Let's do it now," Penn Mallory said without emotion. "But this time, you better get him. One more fuck-up like Florida, and I'll kill all of you myself."

SEVENTY

THAT NIGHT, TOM dreamed again of his father:

Tom pushes his way through the thick black smoke, the Pentagon smoldering and burning, snapshots of the chaos flashing in his mind like a stop-action horror film set in hell—

The jet's mangled, twisted wreckage, jammed through the building's exterior into the corridor, a wheel, the landing gear—

Oak doors, 8 feet high, exploding into splinters—

Golf carts, engines still running, no one in them—

Flames reaching for him, coming from hidden fires, from every direction—

Piles of debris, huge, huge piles, twice his height, blocking his passage—

Wires, pipes, parts of the ventilation system, cables, light fixtures, all dangling from the ceiling—

And the ceiling tiles, melting overhead, reborn as burning hailstones, the size of tennis balls, dropping around him like bombs—

The walls, bowed in and wobbling and trembling, an angel's breath away from collapsing—

And the sounds, inside—

Hissing, popping, screaming—

And outside—

Boom after boom after boom as tanks of propane and aviation fuel ignite—

Suddenly, there is one final, skull-cracking blast that throws him into a huge cloud of fresh white smoke, and then fresh black smoke, Tom almost powerless to do anything but hold his breath and cover his eyes and just go with it, wherever that last concussion delivers him—

When, just like that, everything clears—

And the noise stops—

And he is standing in front of a wall with three large jagged holes in it, each of them big enough to drive a car through—

And Mallory is in front of one, and Diamond another, and Harriman another, and they are all dressed in tuxedos, and they say in unison—

"Door No. 1, Door No. 2, or Door No. 3, which one leads to the final destination, Tom?"—

And he hears cheering, like from a studio audience, competing shouts and cries, "One! Two! Three!"—

Confusion raining down on him like those ceiling-tile air bombs, Tom hesitates, looks at Diamond, who nods, and Harriman, who scowls, before turning to Mallory, who smiles and says, "Son," and steps aside, his open arm inviting Tom to enter Door No. 1, which he does—

Finding himself walking down a tunnel-like corridor that feels longer than the path to eternity—

Nothing ahead of him, no light, no destination, no hope or promise, just—

Wait.

He sees the Old Man, sitting at that crappy little dinette that was in their kitchen, draped in military finery, blues, chest of ribbons and medals, shoes so shiny they reflect the light.

On the table are a cheap plastic clock radio spitting out Benny Goodman, three empty bottles of Busch, and a sweating glass of clear liquid that Tom knows is Beefeater gin.

Tom eyes him for a moment, oddly moved, and sits.

The Old Man smiles. "What now?"

"I'm here to save you."

The Old Man lets loose a kind of cackle that Tom can't quite translate. "Little late for that."

"It can't be."

"Why now, after all this time, all these years?"

Tom is genuinely stupefied by the question. All he can say is, "But I finally found you."

"I'm not the one who's lost."

"I'm not lost."

The Old Man's cackle bursts into a full-on laugh. "Oh, Christ, that is rich."

"I'm not."

"You're as lost as a drop of water in the ocean, boy."

Tom feels his eyes start to swell with tears. "I'm sorry."

"For what?"

"For not understanding. For not trying harder. For hating you."

"Save it. I'm a drunk, and a lousy father—"

"No!"

"And you did what you could to punish me. I get that. Truth is, I probably deserved it." Says it straight-on, no regret, could be reading a news report.

"No. No, you didn't."

The Old Man's smile saddens. "Well, the good news is, you pulled it off."

"Pulled what off?"

"You always said you didn't want to be like me. You wanted to be a good man." He toasts Tom with the glass of Beefeater. "Congratulations."

Tom starts to hear a steady banging in the distance, an insistent hammering. "That's not true."

Life enters the Old Man's eyes, and maybe some mischief. "Which part's not true? You didn't want to be like me, or you wanted to be a good man?" Tom's face goes blank. "Not a trick question, son. You're the thing you hate or the ideal you love." He *pauses, takes another sip of Beefeater. His voice toughens.* "But, by God, you are not the thing you fear. Do you understand me? You are not the thing that you fear."

Tom nods numbly, manages only to say, "Thank you." *Then he asks,* "Can we go now?"

The Old Man stands. "I'm already gone."

The banging, that pounding in his head, gets louder and louder. "No. Please."

The Old Man just shakes his head. "My business is finished, bucko. If yours isn't, figure it out. I hope you find whatever it is you're looking for."

"I'm looking for you." *The Old Man walks past Tom, into the dark corridor, toward the fire.* "But I came to save you."

The Old Man doesn't stop, says, "I'm not the one who needs saving, Tom," *then a couple of steps later, halfway over his shoulder, he adds,* "Because your worst fears, son, they're coming to get you," *and he disappears into the darkness, and in a moment the fire consumes him, and panicked and alone and, yes, lost, Tom turns to see—*

Them:

Mallory and Diamond and Harriman, still in their tuxedos, joined now by Toni Allura, dressed in a black body leotard and a warm, knowing smile, and she says—

"You should listen to your father, Tom"—

And the pounding, the banging, moves from being loud to being unbearable—

And Mallory and Diamond and Harriman nod—

And Toni Allura continues, "Because he's right—"

And Tom claps his hands on his ears, and smashes his eyes shut and grits his teeth, but the pounding has become excruciating, painful, and it feels like his head is going to explode—

"We're coming to get you."

Tom bolted awake, but the noise, the pounding, didn't stop.

He shook his head, trying to separate what was going on in his mind from what was going on in fact, hearing—

"Tom, open the door!"

Re-entering the world, the confusion ebbing with each second, still stretched out on the sofa, still fully clothed—

"Tom! Please!"—

Attaching the voice to a mental image, getting up, turning off the TV set, going to the door and undoing the bolt locks, the alarms, the best security money could buy—

Going on to the patio, doing the same, the door to his privacy fence swinging open—

Revealing Liberty, holding an open laptop, her face the color of a corpse, voice weak and quivering, the words coming at him like dying puffs of smoke:

"You have to see this."

SEVENTY-ONE

TOM STARED AT the screen, at the photo at the center of the Drudge Report home page.

The photo from Munich, him and Anath, and a headline—

"Out of Left Field: Senate Aide Palling Around with Terrorists"—

Recalling how Toni Allura had used those same words in warning him about revealing Hector Rubio's past.

He clicked on the image, and was immediately taken to a blog post from a conservative radio commentator.

"In the days following 9/11, many of us discovered our inner patriot. But there was no more conversion so profound, so baffling—and, let's just say it, so suspect—as the one that took Tom Fargo, left-wing agitator, antiwar activist, from the trenches of liberal America to the hallways of the Senate and the office of terrorist-hunter and Muslim-hater Penn Mallory, a man whose dedication to national security knows no limits.

"The reason for his transformation, the leftist Fargo insisted, was the death of his father at the Pentagon, when Islamic extremists under the direction of the late and unlamented Osama bin Laden hijacked a jet and steered it into the heart of America's defense. And because this was a time of national reflection and unity, we (and I include my humble self among that 'we') gave the leftist Fargo the benefit of the doubt. Because we are, after all, Americans, and as Americans, we believe that all men have good inside them, and that all men have the capacity to change into something better.

"And for more than a decade it appeared that the leftist Fargo had done exactly that. Still, however, there were doubts. One does not oppose the military, oppose the president, oppose the Joint Chiefs, oppose the war plan, and oppose the national interests without inviting some kind of healthy skepticism as to motives. But, once again, we gave the leftist Fargo the benefit of the doubt, and even applauded when he threw his feminazi girlfriend under the bus of national security and sold his made-in-Germany car for an American Jeep.

"But now it appears we were all fooled. It appears that the leftist Fargo has never really shed his liberal clothing, but has instead used it as a shield to fool me, to fool Penn Mallory, to fool his country and the world. Why else would he be palling around with a known terrorist?

"And that disgusts me. Because when I think about the men and women who have given their lives to keep this country free, brave men and women who gave it all to protect the rights of traitors like the leftist Fargo, it just makes me sick that we have this person who has gamed our democracy for his own purposes.

"As tragic as his murder was, the leftist Fargo's father would no doubt prefer death to this kind of dishonor. For at the moment, he is merely spinning in his grave. That is a far better fate than facing the cruel reality that your offspring has turned his back on the country that has never done anything but protect him."

"Is it true?" Liberty asked.

Tom didn't respond immediately. Something was off about the article. The rhetoric was boilerplate, the same things he'd heard years ago in the wake of the "conversion" that *Time* magazine had taken from the personal to the public. But more than that, no one was coming after Mallory, saying he was unfit to lead because he'd been duped by a left-wing fox in his own conservative henhouse.

"Tom? Is it true?"

His gaze didn't leave the screen. They were on his sofa. She was sitting a comfortable distance from him. He recalled the dream, the Old Man's question. "Which part?"

"Is that woman a terrorist?"

He nodded, only halfway paying attention, trying to figure out why the blog commentary felt so off.

"So you were with a terrorist?"

He nodded again, not feeling even the slightest urge to explain himself, or anything else, to her.

Liberty moved an inch or so further away from him. "Are you a terrorist?"

At last, he turned to her, saw the fear and confusion in her eyes. His expression softened. "You know what the biggest threat to freedom is?" Her eyes widened. She shook her head. He smiled sadly. "It's the effort of a small group of zealous people committed to defending it."

Liberty's mouth fell open in puzzlement.

"You probably need to go," he said quietly.

"But what about you?"

Tom started to answer, started to say he'd be all right, but nothing came out, the words unable to find a voice, the only sound in the room coming from inside his head, that dream again, not the Old Man this time, but Toni Allura, dressed in black, a sleek, preying cat, smiling as if she knew secrets that even time would not reveal, hearing her say—

We're coming to get you.

PART FIVE: **CHOICES**

SEVENTY-TWO

HOWARD TRUEMAN LIVED in a smallish, two-bedroom, Cape Cod-style home in Falls Church, Virginia, less than 10 miles from Washington, modest despite its $309,000 market value. He was an ex-Marine who'd gone on to work for the government, a now-retired federal employee who looked the part—balding, jowly, a bit of a gut, and a perpetually blank expression, the kind of eyes that had been dulled by years of pushing paper and robbed of life by monotony.

Type in *images of bureaucrats* on Google, and the first 10 shots would be Howard Trueman.

But, incongruously, Howard Trueman was also something of a rabble-rouser.

It started just after he'd told Uncle Sam to go to hell, saying he was sick and tired of being a wage slave for a "government of the politicians, not the people." He felt overtaxed, hated all the big bailouts, thought running up the federal budget deficit was a criminal act, wanted to break up the unions and jail their leaders, and believed with all his heart and soul and mind that America was on the fast track to socialism, going to hell in a hand basket.

Howard Trueman decided to channel his anger into public service, running for a seat on Falls Church's seven-member City Council. That didn't go too well.

He built his campaign around a promise to abolish the city's Tree Commission and Urban Forestry Division and eliminate the position of city arborist—not a smart strategy in a place that had consistently been named a Tree City USA community for more than three decades. Then there was the whole call-for-secession thing. Howard vowed to end the public service agreements Falls Church had with Arlington and Fairfax, basically gutting essentials like health care, transportation, and fire and rescue.

"We need to declare our independence from the socio-political-humanistic complex," he railed at one campaign stop, "and secede from this union of malfunction."

People who knew the previously mild-mannered Howard Trueman were amazed that he had so much passion. No one, however, was especially surprised when he received fewer than 100 votes on Election Day.

But Howard Trueman didn't care. He had found the experience invigorating. And even though it hadn't been the case in his own campaign, he still believed that one man could make a difference. It just took the strength and courage and dedication—and, yes, the anger—to stand up and say No More.

Howard Trueman saw himself as a modern day Son of Liberty, fighting the "Crown" that had become Washington, throwing off the shackles of imperial authority through his thoughts and words.

And, on this day, his deeds.

Because on this day, Howard Trueman rose shortly after 6, as was his habit, turned on the Mr. Coffee he'd prepared with half-caf the night before, and read *The Washington Times* from front to back while he ate two Eggos with maple syrup.

Then he went into the bedroom and got dressed:

Camo pants, black T-shirt, black boots, black beret.

Strapped on a knife:

A Gerber Mark II, doubled-edged, spear-pointed, which he'd discovered when reading *Hit Man: A Technical Manual for Independent Contractors*, a book that had become something of a

Bible for him, a how-to in the event that America's downward slide required more decisive action than a congressional debate.

Grabbed his sidearm:

An M4A3 service pistol, locked breech, double action, 11 rounds single stacked and one in the chamber, all of them full metal jackets, a Marine's handgun, Semper By God Fi, Second Amendment, Oorah.

Came back to the kitchen, kissed the yellowing photo of his wife, Mamie, still stuck on the front of the ivory-colored Whirlpool, even now, eight years after a brain tumor had taken her.

Fist pump to the wedding picture of his kid, Robbie, pretty successful insurance salesman in Minneapolis, married to a painter who Howard thought had been a space alien in some previous life.

Out the front door, into the Malibu, radio blaring Sinatra, Howard Trueman singing along as he drove, getting on his patriot act face, oblivious to the car that picked him up on Great Falls Street, followed him on I-66 and Virginia 267, then onto 123, heading toward McLean—

Where, in a few hours, if everything went according to plan— one not of his making—the rest of the world would finally see Howard Trueman as he'd seen himself:

A Great American.

SEVENTY-THREE

LIBERTY HAD PUSHED back for about five minutes, but finally caved after Tom made it abundantly clear that he was radioactive.

"I don't know exactly what's going on," he'd said, "but I do know I'm the target of something, and if you're within eight zip codes of me, you'll be in the crossfire, and I have a sense these people don't make too fine a distinction between their intended victim and innocent bystanders."

So he'd all but forced her out the door, shoving $50 in her fist and explaining an off-the-beaten-path route to Prince Street, where she could grab a cab, Liberty asking if that wasn't a little too spy-hokey, Tom grabbing her shoulders with an unintentional ferocity, nearly screaming, "Don't you get it? You're a threat to them! They. Will. Kill. You!"

One look into his eyes, alive with madness, and she got the point.

Alone now, Tom weighed his options.

The logical move was to run, just get the hell out of there. Find a way to Reagan National, buy a ticket on the next flight out, destination anywhere, just go.

Logical, maybe. But not realistic.

Whatever was happening was being orchestrated, and that meant eyes were on him, and they'd find him no matter where he fled, and he'd be damned if he was going to spend the rest of his days wondering who or what was around the next corner.

No, running wasn't an option.

Go to the police? With what? He had what could easily be framed as a half-baked story that could not be confirmed, offered up by Miles Loki, a guy whose currency was deceit and assassination and who very likely may have officially ceased to exist the moment they parted at the Lincoln Memorial. And sure, he had the donor list from Patriot's Blood, but there was little doubt in his mind that the contribution data, while legally confidential, had probably been scrubbed from the computer network.

He hit the remote button, powering up the television, more for white noise than interest, the Fox News Channel full screen—

Showing the photo of him and Anath, a conservative commentator bloviating about turncoats and traitors, Tom watching and listening, still feeling something was off, something didn't make any sense, the same thing he felt when he'd first seen the posting from the Drudge Report.

The landline in his kitchen rang.

"Son, it's Penn."

Tom went rigid. He was unsure whether to feel relieved by Mallory's voice or to brace himself for an angry outburst over the photo, quickly assessing how to explain what he now knew about Unde Malum and Platte's death, not getting so much as a syllable out before his boss knocked him completely off-guard with—

"I know it's all bullshit, this thing with Drudge, this picture deal. It's a setup, and the Cheerleader's behind it, and we're gonna sort it out and then nail her ass to the cross. Nobody, and I mean nobody, fucks with my guy."

Tom just stared at the phone. Now, this *really* made no sense. Mallory should have been bouncing off the walls, pictures of his top aide with a terrorist floating around on the Internet, having God knows what kind of impact on his budding presidential campaign.

But Mallory was stepping up, seeming to put loftier ambitions on the back burner.

"I need you to get some clothes together, enough for a couple of days, and go out in front of your place. I got a car, a leased Lincoln, nobody'll know it's me. I'm on my way. Pick you up in 15 minutes."

Tom said nothing.

"Son, listen to me, and listen good. I am the only friend you got right now, the only person on God's earth who still believes you're a patriot. Do what I say, and we'll make this thing right."

Tom heard himself mumble something in the affirmative, and hung up, and in a trance that felt at once dream-like and adrenaline-fueled, he did as ordered—

Throwing a pair of jeans and some underwear, shoes, socks, shirts into an overnight bag—

Grabbing necessities from the bathroom, stuffing them into a shaving kit—

Taking a hit of Klonopin, then pocketing the bottle—

Fighting with the locks on the door, lot of good they'd do him now, getting madder and madder as he did—

Going to war with the lock on the gate—

Walking quickly down the alley-driveway adjacent to his apartment, starting to sweat slightly under the morning sun and the roaring anxiety—

On the street, looking up and down South Saint Asaph—

Then seeing it approaching, a dark car, tinted windows, maybe Liberty was right, maybe this whole thing was just too spy-hokey—

The car stopping in front of him, Tom's eyes racing in every direction, searching for snipers or black helicopters disgorging men coming to take him away—

Hesitating, then crossing the street, toward the car—

With each step feeling a little bit more secure, like he was approaching a sanctuary—

The rear passenger door swinging open—

The feeling of safety melting away almost instantly when he heard an unexpected voice—

"Tom, get in."

Stopping right there, taking a step back, standing in the middle of the street, cars whizzing by him, horns blaring—

"Tom?"—

Frozen, now looking around for Mallory, his white knight—

The voice from the back seat of the car louder and more insistent—

"Penn Mallory can't be trusted, Tom. You need to know that."

He just stared, confusion-fired anger coming down on him like hot rain. "And why should I trust you?"

"Because I'm going to tell you something that could destroy me."

"What?"

"I killed Arlo Dash," Toni Allura said.

SEVENTY-FOUR

"Don't worry," Toni Allura said as her car sped off. "You're safe."

Tom slid an inch or two farther away from her in the dark-blue leather back seat. "You'll forgive me, Senator, if I greet that guarantee with something less than total confidence."

Toni looked at him—the blue eyes softer than usual—then away, and began massaging her forehead. The famously put-together senator from Fendi appeared less than assembled at the moment, the clinging black V-neck Jil Sander dress notwithstanding. "This has gotten so out of control."

"What has?"

She tossed her hands in the air. Tom noticed they were shaking slightly. "This! All of it!" She hit a button on the door panel, and a divider rose between the front and back seats, separating them from her driver. "I never should have done it."

"Killed Arlo?"

Toni swung her head at him, the blue eyes now full of anger and regret. "I did not kill Arlo Dash. At least, not in the literal sense."

"I'll take figurative, then."

Those eyes, and the face, hardened. "Do not play games with me. You are in no position—"

"Senator, Matt Drudge has accused me of treason, the Internet by now is all abuzz about my terrorist affiliations, and there are probably 10 Montana militiamen who are leaving their aluminum huts in the wilderness right now, guns loaded, looking to track down and shoot a traitor." His voice started to rise. "I've got nothing to lose, which puts me in a better position than you or anyone else. So why don't *you* quit playing games with *me* and explain what is going on!"

She stared at him, and Tom saw the melancholy rise on her face like a black sunrise. "Harry Platte had no business being Defense Secretary. He was reckless, and I believe as surely as I'm sitting here right now that his recklessness would have compromised our national security eventually."

"Were you part of the conspiracy that killed him?"

Toni sighed and shook her head. "No, not that conspiracy."

"There was more than one?"

"Oh, yes. I was part of the conspiracy to keep him alive. The conspiracy that got Arlo Dash killed." She leaned back in the seat, hands folded primly in her lap.

The car slowed to a stop. Tom held his breath, wondering if they'd arrived at the "safe" place. Apparently not. They picked up speed and continued.

"A few weeks before Platte died," she went on, "we received an unconfirmed intelligence report that he might be involved in a questionable relationship with a foreign national, a ballet dancer. Inquiries were made, and the report turned out to be true."

"Platte was sleeping with a spy."

She unfolded her hands, and laid them on her knees. "How did you know?"

"It's not important."

Toni smiled. "Nothing about this is unimportant. Nothing." She refolded her hands in her lap. "The minute certain people learned of Platte's indiscretion, a decision was made to murder him."

"Who made the decision?"

She shook her head, continuing the explanation rather than answering the question. "Miles Loki discovered what was about to happen and decided to do what he could to derail their plans. For reasons that will forever escape me, he respected Platte. Thought he was a great American. Called him an *asset* in the war on terrorism." She laughed. "I, on the other hand, simply called him an ass*hole*."

Tom couldn't have forced a smile at gunpoint.

"Anyway, Miles thought if he could get ahead of the story, as we say, Platte and the dancer, he could save Platte's life because it would just be too, I don't know, *convenient* for Harry to die so soon after the news got out. But he needed a way to leak it, to put it out there first, and he hates the press." She sighed again, and the life began to drain from her voice. "Knowing my feelings about Platte, he approached me with an offer to kill the nomination. That's when I made my first mistake."

"Which was?"

"I listened."

The car screeched to a sudden halt. But this time, Tom had no thoughts about destinations, safe or otherwise. "You gave him Arlo Dash."

She drew a quick, sharp breath and nodded. "I suggested he consider a blogger, someone who has a following, who could stir things up. It would be faster, there would be no tracking down the story, no confirming and reconfirming, which he insisted there was no time for. He needed someone to light the fuse."

"And then the mainstream media would take it from there." She nodded again. "But someone found out." Toni said nothing. "Who?"

They started moving again.

"Was it an Unde Malum operation? Arlo's murder?"

"Technically, I suppose. It sprang from the same poisoned well."

"How much did you know about it? Unde Malum?"

"I knew it existed, that my husband had created it, but was under the impression it had gone away. But when Arlo was murdered, Miles informed me that it was still in the black budget, and that it had a new mission, and that the people behind it were responsible for Arlo's murder."

Tom backtracked the timeline in his head. "That's why you called for the investigation. To expose Unde Malum."

"Or at least send them a message that I knew."

"Then why'd you stop it?"

"I told you. My source dried up."

He cut his eyes left, away from her, trying to piece together the puzzle. It took less than 10 seconds. "Miles Loki was your source."

"Until Munich, anyway, when my investigator photographed you without his authorization. Miles, a man born of suspicion, said I had gone off the reservation, that I could no longer be trusted."

Suddenly, Tom understood why he had been summoned to the Eye Street garage that first night. "So with your investigation dead, mine became his weapon of choice."

Her eyes found and held his. "He wanted Unde Malum and everyone behind it destroyed."

Tom leaned toward her slightly. "Who are they? Who's behind Unde Malum?" Toni bit her lower lip. "David Diamond?"

She rolled her eyes. "David Diamond. He's a pimp."

"Harriman?" She just shook her head. "Jasper Eddy?"

Then she whirled to him, the blue eyes now hard and cold and burning. "Do you really want to know, Tom? Really?"

"Yeah, I do, I'm tired of playing cat and mouse."

"Because if I tell you, your life, everything you believe and think you believe, it will all go inside out."

"It already has, Senator."

"Oh, you haven't seen anything yet. This is just the beginning."

"Goddamnit, Senator, who's behind Unde Malum?"

The metal-on-metal impact arrived like a bomb burst, throwing the car against a concrete safety barricade on the right shoulder of the road—

Toni Allura's head slamming forward into the barrier that sealed off the driver, opening a gash above one eye, Tom pinned against the passenger side, then both of them bouncing around the back seat, a couple of rag dolls, as the car spun around, once, twice, three times, horns honking, Toni wedged into one corner, the cut on her head small but bleeding heavily, the vehicle finally settling to a stop—

Tom frantically reaching for the door handle, trying to get them out, seeing mental images of gas tanks exploding, kicking at the door, hearing tires screeching, Tom thrown against the window when the car was struck again, another crash, this one really loud and jarring, Toni's blond hair spattered in blood—

The world going gray before his eyes, Tom feeling himself slip into something he thought might be death, the gray getting darker and darker, closer and closer to the blackness he had been running from but would now finally be delivered to—

When suddenly a burst of blinding white light pierced the fog of doom, and he thought, *This is it, it's time to cross over*, and he opened his eyes to behold whatever awaited, and then he heard—

"Tom, Jesus Christ, son, we gotta get you outta here"—

And while he knew that death hadn't come for him—

"That goddamned woman didn't get you in Florida"—

At least not yet—

"So she was gonna kill you now."

He was certain there was still an unseen end starting to close in on him, and it was coming fast.

SEVENTY-FIVE

HOWARD TRUEMAN STOPPED the Malibu at the far end of the park, a couple hundred yards away from where the speakers would be. He'd been coming to deals like this, rallies, and had seen his cars dented on more than a few occasions by careless jagoffs who threw open their doors without the first bit of respect for a man's property, chipping the paint and dinging the body.

He got out of the car, made sure the Gerber Mark II was secure in its sheath, the M4A3 locked and loaded.

All good.

He squinted into the late-morning sun, which was bright, a little more intense than usual for this time of the year.

Pulled the black beret a bit tighter on his head, sucked in a gut that made the black T-shirt seem a size or three too small.

Held back for a moment, checking out the crowd.

Young and old, even some toddlers. Not a nonwhite face in sight, which didn't bother Howard Trueman, because he didn't believe in hyphenated Americans, African or otherwise; you either were or you weren't. Professional types, soccer moms, housewives, a few others like him, dressed for combat in whatever form it might come.

Patriots, all.

Taking it in, the people, the atmosphere, the clean air, the green wide-open park, framed on three sides by trees, on the fourth by a six-story brick warehouse that seemed strangely out of place, like it should have been in a more industrial-type setting.

But you know, this was the U. S. of A., and citizens had a God-given right to build whatever they want, wherever they want to build it, government encroachers be damned.

He inhaled deeply. The world at that moment smelled of oranges.

"Mr. Trueman?"

Instinctively, Howard Trueman's right hand found the knife.

He turned to discover two men, dark suits, white shirts, black ties, opaque sunglasses, transmitters in their ears. One taller than the other, but that aside, they could have come from the same government-issue test tube. "Who's asking?"

The shorter one said, "We'd like you to come with us."

"I have a permit to carry this weapon," he said, left hand now resting on the service pistol, "and a Second Amendment right to do so." The two men nodded but said nothing. "And as far as I am aware, the laws of this nation, while eroding many of the personal freedoms that have made our country great, do not deny me the freedom to carry a knife of my choosing."

"No, sir," the shorter man said, "they don't."

A woman with twin girls on each arm, maybe 6 or 7, walked by, the three of them humming "The Battle Hymn of the Republic."

"Then why don't you just let me express myself freely, in the presence of my fellow Americans?"

The taller one's mouth twitched. "You Marine, sir?"

Howard Trueman straightened. "Second Division. Operation Just Cause. Panama."

The taller one nodded. "Camp Fallujah."

"In 2007 and 2008," the other finished.

"Oorah," Howard Trueman said, with feeling.

"Oorah," the shorter one said.

"Oorah," the taller one said. Then he added, "Sir, we would appreciate it if you would come with us."

Howard Trueman's eyes narrowed. "We may be brothers, but I am a free man of free will, and no one tells me what to do."

"Don't make us ask again, sir," the taller one said. "Please."

Howard Trueman's lips curled into a nasty grin. "You threatening me?"

"Not at all sir," the taller one said, just as the shorter one reached into his coat, pulled out a 9mm SIG Sauer P229 fitted with a sound suppressor, and said in a voice so low, calm, and quiet it sounded sedated:

"But if you don't, I will empty all 13 rounds of my weapon into your heart right here, sir, and you will join Mamie in the great hereafter without having had the opportunity to participate in God's greater plan for the Republic."

At the mention of his late wife's name, Howard Trueman slumped, just barely, but enough for the shorter man to grab the Gerber Mark II, for his partner to grab the M4A3, and for both of them to grab the momentarily dazed and confused former Marine and start walking him in the direction of the brick building, where just one window was open, on the sixth floor, overlooking a raised speaker's platform under a huge banner that read, "Freedom Isn't Free! Let's Take Back America!"

And under that, a smaller sign:

"Welcome Senator Penn Mallory!"

SEVENTY-SIX

MALLORY WAS BEHIND the wheel, weaving in and out of traffic with the confidence of a NASCAR driver. His mouth was motoring even faster.

"This whole thing was legit, her deal, the investigation of Harry's death, at least at first. But when that investigator she hired got the picture of you and the terrorist in Munich, all bets were off. She quit caring about who killed Harry Platte, and why."

Tom just stared at him, hoping to find some way to push through the cloud of confusion in his brain, a cloud made even thicker by his sense that he was still missing something essential, that this somehow just didn't track.

Pedal-to-the-metal Mallory turned onto the George Washington Memorial Parkway.

"We going to McLean?" Tom asked.

"Vance knows a place there, like a safe house." He reached over and gripped Tom's shoulder. "It'll give us a chance to sort this out. And sort this out we will, I swear." He smiled.

Tom's sense that everything was sideways deepened. *What is wrong with this picture?* "I know who killed Platte, and I know why." He scanned Mallory's face for a sign of surprise or concern. Nothing. The man looked almost peaceful. "Unde Malum."

Mallory shook his head. "No. Uh-uh. Unde Malum was an operation against terrorists. Pure and simple."

Tom took a deep breath and prepared to cross his personal Rubicon. "Until it stopped targeting terrorists, and started killing businessmen in return for campaign contributions to Patriot's Blood."

The senator swung his head toward Tom. "What?" Tom explained what he knew, Ciudad del Este, the list of names from Miles Loki, the similarities between Platte's death and the crash that killed the executive from Systemos Integrados Avenzados. Mallory slammed his fist on the steering wheel, but when he screamed "That fuckin' David Diamond!" it sounded strangely forced, even for a performer as skilled as his boss.

Tom sat up straighter in the seat, asking himself again what was wrong with all this. Mallory's campaign and, by extension, Mallory himself had just been linked to a series of murders. Staring at the end of the world as he knew it, the senator should have been reeling, his paranoia on steroids. "You didn't know?"

Mallory shot him a pained look. "Hell, I didn't know about any of it until Rubio got iced, and knowin' the Cheerleader's connection to him, I forced her hand. She folded like a bad poker player, told me everything." Tom stared, baffled, like a duck that had forgotten how to paddle. "Her husband created Unde Malum. That was the deal. Rubio got black-budget money, took a cut for himself, spread some out for contributions back to John Allura, and paid the rest to Anath and her crowd to go out and kill bad people."

"Until the mission changed."

"And Rubio found his conscience and took a hike."

"So Toni didn't shut it down. Unde Malum."

Mallory's jaw tightened. He shook his head. "No. I'm guessing she found out, maybe from Rubio, and went to Diamond, and they hatched this little scheme with Patriot's Blood to set me up."

"But why would she set you up? Why not just leak it to the press and let it play out?"

"Leverage, son."

"Leverage for what?"

"She wants a spot on the ticket. My ticket. She wants to be vice president. As long as she's got that hanging out there, I'm over a goddamned barrel."

This had suddenly become one big hall of mirrors, except it seemed that every image contained a reflection of Toni Allura.

"And that photo," Mallory continued, "the one that turned up on Drudge? That came from her. A shot across my bow. She's already negotiating." He reached over and grabbed Tom's shoulder, flashing a smile that was both mean and reassuring. "But don't you worry, son. I'm not lettin' her do this to me or to you. I'm gonna bury that bitch, and her ambitions with her."

With a single firm nod, he put his hand back on the wheel, driving for a moment in silence.

Tom noticed that the senator's grip was loose, easy, like he didn't have a care in the world, a sharp contrast with the Mallory he knew, a man who could melt down faster than a snowman in hell without the slightest bit of provocation.

Something was wrong.

Here was a guy whose presidential dreams could very well be dead because his top aide had been spotted sipping liquor with a known terrorist and a murder-for-contributions conspiracy could be laid at his feet, and he wasn't falling apart, couldn't have been more casual if he was whistling.

It made no sense.

The car slowed to a stop in front of a six-story warehouse that was adjacent to a large park where some kind of rally was going on. Mallory turned off the ignition and looked up. "Hey, good, there's Vance."

Tom saw Harriman gliding toward them. Mallory hopped out, came around, and opened his door. "Let's get you someplace secure."

It made no sense at all.

Ten yards away, Harriman smiled and called out, "Hello, Tom."

And then it did.

"How did you know?" Tom said, swinging a gaze that bordered between hate and betrayal at Mallory. "That Rubio found his conscience and left." Mallory's expression went blank, as if Tom had suddenly become just another face in the crowd, anonymous, someone he'd never see or met. "You just said you didn't know Patriot's Blood mission had changed. Then how could you possibly have known that Rubio saw what it had become, found his conscience, and walked away?"

Harriman stopped at the car and felt the dynamic. "We got a safe room up on the sixth floor," he said, cautiously.

Tom's eyes didn't leave Mallory. "You're behind it all. You leaked the picture. You changed Unde Malum's mission. And when I found out—"

"You became a liability none of us could afford, son." He looked to Harriman. "We're gonna need more than a safe house, Vance."

Harriman nodding—

A syringe appearing out of nowhere—

Tom hearing himself say, "Wait, what?"—

The needle coming at him with the speed of a rattlesnake strike—

Plunging into his neck—

A quick sting—

Mallory saying, "You served your country well and with honor—"

Then a sudden paralysis—

"But sometimes that's just not enough."

Then the darkness that had been stalking Tom Fargo arrived at last and took him in its arms.

SEVENTY-SEVEN

IT WAS BILLED as the Second Coming of an American Revolution, an organized protest against the government and what it does or doesn't do, should or shouldn't do, must or mustn't do.

A thousand people, all ages, from all over the area, milling in the open green space, basking in the warmth of the sun, marshmallow-white clouds hanging overhead, a perfect day for a rally—

Singing angry songs and carrying angry signs, warning of Armageddon, drifting slowly but determinedly toward the speakers' platform at the north end of the park, the huge banner looming over the dais, "Freedom Isn't Free! Let's Take Back America!"

Rage in the air, dense as London fog.

He was among them, angry, but not waving a sign or singing a song or alerting the nation to some unseen peril.

Just carrying a gun, concealed under a loose-fitting suit coat, with a wireless microphone in his ear, playing a part, paying little attention to the picture of Americana coming into focus around him:

A young man, bearded and, were it not for 20 extra pounds, a near-spitting image of Christ, black T-shirt emblazoned with a photo of something that looked like blood and guts, screeching, "Abortion is a greater evil than taxes and slavery and prostitution and Wall Street greed! It is time to repent, to return to God, because 9/11 was not a tragedy, it was a sign that Christians cannot afford to ignore!"

A plumpish 20-something blonde who looked like she'd just relocated from a dairy farm, carrying a sign critical of a leading Democratic candidate for president, shouting, "Boycott Hollywood, McCarthy was right, John Wayne was right, Walt Disney was right, kill all the liberal terrorists in La La Land."

A thin, bespectacled man in his 50s, khaki shorts and white T-shirt, bent nearly in half by the weight of a wooden cross lashed to his back, inviting people in the crowd to write their names on it, "Sign Up For Jesus," more than a few accepting the offer.

A nine-year-old girl, daisies could not have been fresher, angelic smile, singing, "Slavery's a lie, slavery's a lie, hi-ho the derry-o, slavery's a lie."

Chants: "U-S-A, U-S-A!"

But the man with the gun tuned it all out, standing toward the back of the mob, maybe 100 yards from the stage, eyes straight ahead, seeing everything and nothing behind the midnight-black sunglasses, feeling the anger around him get thicker and thicker and thicker.

Ignoring the signs:

Photos of this politician or that one, Hitler-like mustaches scrawled on some of the images, crosshairs over others.

"Rush Limbaugh for President."

"Liberals are a cancer that is slowing killing our country."

"The Holocaust is a hoax."

"End welfare now!"

More chants: "Shame on the press! Shame on the press!"—

Though the chanters were more than willing to give the reviled media an interview, proudly speaking into the microphones, responding to the invitation to explain why they had come out today:

A slender middle-aged white man in a golf visor hat: "To take down this government."

An elementary school librarian: "To stand up for God and our nation, and to preserve our rights and our freedoms and our families."

A pimpled 14-year-old boy in a shirt from a heavy metal concert: "Food stamps, bro, we're spending way too much on food stamps."

A suburban mother in a crimson-colored Polo shirt: "I'm tired of the spending, I'm tired of the lies, and I think it's time we took our country back."

A guy in reflecting wraparound shades, strong jaw, head billiard-ball smooth: "Government should not be supporting these people who lie around all day on the couch, watching television, and having five or six babies."

A gray-haired professional, three days of growth on his face, a look that suggested any sense of hope had been crushed: "Because I'm entitled to a job, and I think there oughtta be such a thing as affirmative action for non-minorities."

More angry chants: "Dem-O-Crats are the Ant-I-Christ!"

So much hatred, the man with the gun thought.

More angry songs: "We shall kill the lib-er-als, We shall kill he lib-er-als."

So much fury.

More angry signs: "Death to all Muslims."

So much madness.

All of it suddenly turning to cheers as a round man in a straw hat, white shirt, and suspenders came to the microphone on the speakers' stand and bellowed, "I don't know about you folks, but I am mad as hell, and I think it's just about time we took back a government that God and the Founding Fathers gave us!"

The cheers getting louder—

"And while I'm not here to endorse anyone or anything, I can tell y'all that there's one fella who can do that, and we need him running this den of thieves we call a political system that's perverting the democratic ideal"—

Cheers really getting louder now, swelling—

"And even though he hasn't officially proclaimed his intentions,

I do believe you can give him a nudge in the right direction, if you get my drift"—

The crowd mad-dog ravenous—

"Ladies and gentlemen, I give you the man who should be president, and if Jesus and the voters are willing, he will be"—

The man with the gun looked around one more time, thinking to himself that the only thing missing from this insanity was a false prophet in sackcloth and ashes, screaming, "The end is near, The end is near."

"The gentleman from the great State of Florida"—

No, that was wrong—

"A true leader of men"—

There was indeed a false prophet here on this gorgeous morning, and his name was—

"Senator! Penn! Mallory!"

The man with the gun began to slowly make his way toward the stage.

SEVENTY-EIGHT

THE DARKNESS FADED gradually, helped along by its own spoken soundtrack:

"Are you sure he's going to come out of it?"

"Yes."

"And you didn't give him too much, so he won't OD, or go into a coma?"

"We do this sort of thing for a living, and we are very good at what we do."

"And will it be traceable, what you shot him up with?"

"You worry too much. As I said, we're professionals."

"Just answer the question."

"No, it will not be traceable. The drug, the solution, is a compound that begins to dissipate within an hour and is undetectable within 12 hours."

"And they won't run any tests for 12 hours?"

"No one will do anything we do not want them to do."

Tom's eyes opened.

Initially, the world he awoke to felt as if it were covered in a thin film, neither fuzzy nor focused, just no sharp edges, blurry without being indistinct, shadows possessing a certain form.

He closed his eyes tightly, opened them wide, his surroundings becoming more defined:

A large room, cool cement floor, low ceiling with spidery stains on the overhead tiles, unpainted walls, stacks of boxes labeled "6," three sawhorses, large sheets of dingy plastic covering doorways and work tables that held an assortment of power tools, the vague odor of cigarettes, a renovation in progress.

A row of windows along one wall, all of them semi-opaque and painted shut except for one, the one farthest to the left, which was open to allow fat bands of sunlight to streak the floor and offered a vista to a brilliant blue sky.

And at the open window, a man in scrubs, assembling a rifle, carefully, methodically.

Tom recognized him instantly as the one who broke into Liberty's apartment.

In that moment, everything became clear, and he began to struggle, tried to get off the floor, unable to stand, to move his arms, his legs, anything, only then fully realizing he was bound at the wrists and feet.

"Well, well, well," David Diamond said, turning to the sound of Tom's frustration. "The cover girl for the New American Patriotism returns."

He was wearing leather gloves. One hand held a pistol, the barrel maybe three inches long, a small grip.

"It's a Kel-Tek P-32," Diamond said, noticing that Tom had seen the gun. "Ideal for ladies, women who shoot." A noxious smirk. "Vance and I thought it would be an appropriate choice for a traitor like you."

Vance Harriman stared at Diamond as if the man were a fungus. "We are still missing one essential element of the strategy, are we not?"

"Not to worry, Director; he's on his way."

Tom's eyes shifted from Diamond to Harriman to the man in scrubs, who was just finishing putting the rifle together. "Who's the target?" he asked.

A piece of plastic that covered one doorway suddenly flew open. Two men, identically dressed in black suits, shoved a third man—decked out in camo and black, a beret, boots, the full weekend warrior look—into the center of the room. The man had an air of defiance about him that seemed to scorch his flesh.

"To start with," David Diamond half-shouted, trying to be heard above the concussive crowd cheers outside, "this gentleman is." He raised the small pistol and shot Howard Trueman once in the chest, the man's eye's going wide in disbelief, dissolving into terror as he clawed at the black T-shirt, slow at first and then furiously, as if there really was a chance to dig the bullet out with his bare hands if he only had the time, ripping at the shirt, tearing at it, the fury and panic abating after a few more seconds as life began its exit, Howard Trueman falling to his knees, then collapsing face down onto the floor, his dark red blood oozing into the concrete.

"Which brings us to you, Fargo," Diamond continued, walking toward Tom, who was so seized at that moment by an electric shock of dread that he barely noticed as the Kel-Tek P-32 was slipped into his hands.

SEVENTY-NINE

PENN MALLORY SMILED the practiced smile of a career politician, one that demonstrated obvious pleasure but that also had a tinge of I'm-not-worthy embarrassment, an expression locked in wonder and disbelief, his apparent awe at the outpouring of love concealing a deep-down belief that he deserved every bit of it.

"Thank you!" he screamed to the adoring crowd. "Thank you very much. And God. Bless. America!"

Sonic applause and cheers. Mallory basked in the glow for a few moments before extending both arms in a tamp-down motion, trying to quiet the masses so he could get to the business at hand.

"Penn for president!" a woman screamed, prompting another teeth-rattling response from the audience that Mallory could only ride out, shaking his head and smiling boyishly, turning to the others seated behind him on the platform—locally elected officials, party chieftains, a 50-ish woman with a tennis tan known for her fundraising prowess—and shrugged, Aw shucks, it's just me.

The round man in the straw hat stood and approached the microphone. "Folks, please, if you could, as they say on TV, hold your applause until the end of the show."

Which, of course, invited more applause.

Mallory said something in his ear, both of them laughing, the senator finally holding up his hands in surrender, What're you gonna do?

The crowd getting louder, but seeming to slip toward restlessness. Some isolated cries:

"This is no time to retreat. It's time to step up to the firing line!"

"I want an America that's armed and dangerous!"

"Us or them! Us or them!"

Mallory continued to smile and wave, pretend-pleading with the crowd to quiet down— "Please, everyone, please, this is too much"—taking a step back from the microphone, his pleasure ebbing just a bit, not wanting their enthusiasm to eclipse this moment, his moment, because he was ready to make a grand entrance, and he was ready now, and like a seasoned actor, he needed to be on the stage rather than waiting in the wings.

The crowd noise lessened slightly. Mallory took the cue.

"I'm only gonna bend your ears for a couple of minutes, because I know that most political speeches are like longhorn steers: a point here, a point there, and a lot of bull in between."

Laughter, cheers.

"But on a more serious note, I want to talk to you about something that's dear to me, close to my heart and, I know, close to all of yours. I want to talk to you about what it means to be an American."

He paused, mostly for effect, and scanned the audience, seeing a stew of hope and hate, dedication and despair, rage and resentment.

What he did not see was the sixth-floor corner window of the brick building next to the park, the tip of a rifle barrel peeking out.

"I don't want to get ahead of myself here, and I think it would be an honor for any man, or any woman, to lead this great nation. But I also think there is a loftier place, a higher office, if you will, that exists somewhere between the gates of the White House and the gates of heaven."

Nor did he see the man, 75 yards away—

"And you know what I would call that higher office, that loftier place?"

The man who was approaching him with slow, deliberate purpose—

"I would call it patriotism!"

The man with the gun—

Miles Loki.

EIGHTY

TOM STARED AT the pistol in his hand while David Diamond explained to him what the next day's papers were going to report.

"It's pretty straightforward. You're a terrorist sympathizer who's been outed. You come to a rally where Mallory is speaking." He gestured to the lifeless but still-bleeding Howard Trueman. "A patriotic American stumbles onto your little sniper's hole. You get one wild shot off at your boss before this place turns into the OK Corral. He dies a hero at your hand; you die a traitor at his. Film at 11."

Tom dropped the pistol as if it were contaminated.

Diamond laughed. "It's as simple as bang, bang, bang." He mimed holding a rifle, aiming it out the window, and pulling the trigger. "Bang." Then formed a pistol with his fingers, aiming at Trueman, pulling that trigger, "Bang," then aiming at Tom and pulling it again. "Bang." He held up Tom's bottle of Klonopin and rattled its contents. "Helps, too, that you're a junkie."

The shorter of the two men in black, both standing by the doorframe as if on guard, snickered.

Sweat streamed down Tom's back and face and neck. "Nobody'll believe you."

"More people believe in space aliens than believe in God," Diamond said. "I don't think it will be a problem."

Tom's fear-fired heart pounded like it was going to launch him into the next century, and he struggled to beat back the malignant nausea curdling in his stomach. Still, he glared at Diamond with a contempt that filled his words with poison. "So you are Unde Malum."

Diamond laughed again. "In a manner of speaking. I ran the show, kind of like the staff director."

"Who'd you answer to? Toni Allura?"

Which cracked David Diamond up. "Jesus, for a smart guy, you are dumber than a lampshade." Tom said nothing, just waited. "It was Mallory. After John Allura croaked, Mallory kept it alive, made sure it still got funded. And he also, shall we say, shifted its emphasis from shooting terrorists to something more consistent with his aspirations."

Tom felt like he should have been surprised, but he was either too tired or two frightened to feel it. "Did Mallory make the call on Harry Platte?"

"Absolutely." Not a second of hesitation.

"Because Platte's affair would have reflected poorly on his presidential ambitions."

"Hey, people have been killed for a lot less in Washington, a whole lot less."

Tom took a moment to try and sort it all out, looking around the room, realizing for the first time that Harriman had vanished. Probably needed plausible deniability, though he was relatively certain that by the time all this played out, the warehouse would bear no evidence of anyone having been here but him and poor Howard Trueman.

His gaze landed on the rifleman, who was in a sniper's crouch, staring through the scope, breathing evenly, lost in a place that existed only in his consciousness.

"Wait a second," Tom said suddenly.

Diamond started to clap. "I was wondering when you were going to pick up on that."

"You said I was only going to get one *wild shot* off."

"Technically, yeah. See, the plan was to leak the photo of you and Anath, which would spoon-feed the press an easy explanation for you going all Lee Harvey Oswald on Mallory. Then the shot at him would create sympathy, and he becomes the victim instead of the fool." Diamond smiled. "At least that was the plan in theory."

"Except you're not going to miss. And he doesn't know it."

"Oops."

"You're not serious, I mean—"

"Come on, Fargo. Christ. You think we can afford a guy in the White House who's directly responsible for the murder of a sitting U.S. senator and likely Secretary of Defense, to say nothing of God knows how many American citizens in South America? What would become of the country, the institution of the presidency, if he was exposed?"

"It's already become that, whatever it is."

"Then let's say we're controlling the damage."

At the corner window, the rifleman said, "I'm good to go."

And just as David Diamond's eyes hardened, and he replied, "Do it"—

The room exploded.

EIGHTY-ONE

AUTOMATIC WEAPON FIRE blew through the plastic doorframe covering, a vertical pattern of red holes opening up and down the stomach, chest, neck, and head of the taller man in black, creating a chunky mist as tissue and blood erupted from his twisting, twitching body—

The shorter man dropping into a crouch at the sound of the first barrage, scrambling toward one stack of boxes—

Tom rolling over on one side, folding himself into a fetal position, feeling the vibrations of the gunfire down to his core, even though it was oddly quiet, muffled, like fast-action staccato whispers, the suppressed sound of madness muted by the rabid, blood-boiled cheering below—

The sniper spinning in the direction of the gunfire, his rifle dropping to the floor, reaching inside the leg of the scrub pants, pulling out a pistol—

The shorter man still scrambling, now firing back from behind, blindly and madly—

Bullets tracing a line along the wall, bits of plaster sprinkling down on Tom—

David Diamond just standing there, frozen—

The sniper aiming at the doorframe—

The shorter man getting to the boxes, turning to shoot back, taking a half-dozen rounds in his legs, screaming—

Ceiling tiles shattering—

Tom looking up, toward the doorframe, seeing nothing but short, rapid bursts of light penetrating the smoking chaos—

The sniper getting off a single shot, a defensive move, before flying backward into the corner, convulsing, arms flapping, legs jumping, head slamming forward and back and right and left, a shower of bullets leaving him in a blood-soaked heap—

Then silence.

The only things Tom heard were the sound of his own breathing, labored and gasping, and the cheers below in the park.

Then cries, the shorter man moaning, his shot-up legs revealing bone.

Then a single shot, the man's throat bursting, the whimpers and sobs replaced by a gurgling sound, and then nothing at all.

Then David Diamond, saying, "You will pay for this."

Then another single shot, Diamond's forehead opening into a yawning red pit, brains and bone blowing out the back of his skull onto the floor, his body collapsing.

In that moment, Tom knew he was going to die, and with that knowledge came a strange peace, a sense that he would at last be free of the things that had terrorized him all these years.

The fear of what might happen.

The fear of not being prepared.

The fear of not being able to prevent it.

The fear of what he couldn't see, which blinded him.

The fear of what he could see, which blinded him as well.

For the first time since his father died, since he had assumed a role he'd neither sought nor worn comfortably, the role of patriot, Tom Fargo was no longer afraid of what awaited him, certain he was ready for whatever lay ahead.

But when he looked up to see a slender figuring cutting through the cloud of putrid gunfire smoke—

Weapon pointed not at him but at the floor—

And heard a chillingly familiar voice say, "You have a choice"—

Tom Fargo knew he wasn't going to die—

But it was not fear he felt now, it was anger, a drug-like rage so pure and hot it felt shot into his veins, coursing through his body, taking him someplace he'd never been—

And by the time Anath added, "But you do not have long to make it," and cut off the binding at his hands and feet, Tom knew what she was going to say, and had already made up his mind.

EIGHTY-TWO

TOM SAT AT the corner window, looking out onto the park below as Penn Mallory spoke about what it meant to be an American, a patriot—

"Patriotism is the willingness to defend one's country against the government!"—

Paying no attention to the death that had arrived so unexpectedly in the room, the bodies and blood, the consequences, just getting angrier and angrier as he watched the man who in many ways had saved him, and in all ways had believed in him, protected him, given him security when the rest of the political class—left and right, Sarah, all of them—had wanted to exile him, set him adrift on a sea of oblivion, simply because he refused to believe that in an uncertain world, you sometimes had to bend, even break, because that was the price of navigating the danger that lurked everywhere.

No, Penn Mallory had taken him in, like a son.

And now this:

"Do I believe you should support your country all the time? You bet I do. And I believe you should support your government, too, but only when your government deserves it. And I fear, ladies and gentlemen, I truly do, that if we change course right now, if we turn our backs on the policies of the past eight years, we will find ourselves with a government worthy of neither our support nor our respect!"

"Why is it," Tom said distantly, feeling exhausted, beaten down, watching the carnivorous crowd below chew on every one of Mallory's words, "that people who hate government want to lead it?"

He turned to Anath. She appeared almost featureless, lifeless, a killing-machine mannequin in jeans and a tunic-like shirt that was less white now than it had been a few minutes earlier. "I don't care."

"Yeah. Well, I do."

"Then shoot him, if that is your choice."

He looked down at the sniper rifle that now rested in his lap and smiled with the sadness of inevitability. "Political power grows out of the barrel of a gun, huh?"

"I wouldn't know," Anath replied. "I am not a follower of Mao."

"Then what do you follow?"

Something cracked in her face, making Tom think it was the first time she'd actually ever been asked, or considered, the question. "Nothing," she replied after a brief silence. "It's easier that way."

Outside, in the park, Mallory:

"Let us never forget that we are heirs to the American Revolution! Let us never forget how much blood it cost to gain our independence! And most of all, let us never forget that the American Revolution was the beginning of a journey and not a destination, and the enduring path to freedom must be built and rebuilt, every day, with the paving stones of true patriotism!"

Tom raised the rifle and aimed.

"As I told you, if we leave now, I can provide you safe passage from your country," Anath said.

"Love it or leave it, right?"

"You have enemies. I can assure that you will be well hidden from them."

"I'm an American. I was born here."

"We can protect you."

"No, you can't." Looking through the scope, not at her. "No one can."

"Gandhi said that an eye for an eye makes the whole word blind."

The nausea that had been raging in Tom's gut suddenly exploded. His saliva turned bitter, his throat and mouth began to burn, his stomach muscles contracted, and he expelled the venom from deep within his system. But he never put the gun down.

He spit out the acrid taste that remained. "That man down there talking about patriotism, about American values, that man who I was devoted to, would have done anything for, that man was going to have me murdered." Tom took a deep breath and tried to expel his rage. It didn't work. He turned to her. "The world is already blind."

Anath nodded. "Mine is, yes. I was hoping that yours perhaps was not."

Tom held her eyes. "So was I." He looked back through the scope.

"In that case, I shall leave you in the arms of your vengeance."

He heard her start to walk away. "Tell me something," he said, still staring through the scope, searching for Penn Mallory. "It was you, wasn't it, who saved me in Florida." Silence. "Why? And why here, today?"

This time, there was no pause, no hesitation.

"Because you are a man of conviction, Mr. Fargo. And you are alone in a world populated by men and women of vast ambition. And while yes, that world may seem blind, without people such as yourself, there would never be the promise of sight."

Tom stayed glued to the scope. "What if this *man of conviction* hadn't seen your warning, the message to get off the boat?"

"You would be dead." No hesitation this time, either, no remorse, voice empty as a robbed grave.

Tom blinked, finally turning to look at her once more—

But Anath had vanished.

He stared for a moment at the doorframe, then at the bodies—Howard Trueman, the men in black, scrub sniper, David Diamond—then at the destruction, human and otherwise, that had settled into the room, and was struck by the fact that he felt nothing. It was as if his heart and soul and conscience had been amputated, as if he were someone who was and wasn't a living being, but just a remnant of what once had been.

Someone just like Anath, he thought.

No feeling, no regret, no compassion.

Recalling that line, from the old cartoon strip, *We have met the enemy, and he is us.*

Tom Fargo looked back through the rifle's scope—

First getting Penn Mallory in the crosshairs—

"I want to sleep soundly at night, cradled in the big strong hands of a secure America"—

Thinking, *So do I*—

Then a fat man in overalls and a trucker's hat, singing, "My heart beats true for the red, white, and blue"—

So does mine—

Then a girl in cutoffs and a sorority jersey, shouting, "I believe in America"—

I do, too—

Shaking his head, like he was trying to wake up, snap out of it, the scope's crosshairs scanning the crowd, landing next on a tall man, 50 or so yards from where Mallory was speaking—

Who was reaching into his coat—

Tom knowing what he was reaching for, what was about to happen—

Clarity arriving with the speed and suddenness and force of a tornado—

Dropping the rifle, grabbing the handgun that had killed Howard Trueman—

Racing past the death and deceit that was seemingly

everywhere—

Barely hearing Penn Mallory say, "We should choose neither a path of surrender nor one of submission"—

And I won't, Tom thought as he flew through the doorframe and down the stairs.

I won't.

EIGHTY-THREE

TOM KNIFED THROUGH the crowd, no attempt at being graceful or polite, jostling and caroming off whoever and whatever got in his way, lots of protests—

"Hey, what's your problem?"—

"Damn, man, slow down!"—

"You better watch yourself, buddy!"—

Not caring, not listening, not worrying about whether the protest would turn to anger, and the anger to violence—

Not concerned about his own safety, because it didn't matter, not in this world, a world that protected only powerful men with powerful motivations, where security was less a pursuit than a weapon to be used by those willing to exploit the fear that danger could never outrun—

Just keeping one hand on the pistol, jammed in his front coat pocket, the other hand stiff-arming human hurdles—

"Where's the fire?"—

"I'm gonna kick your ass!"—

"Don't tread on me!"—

Eyes focused ahead, 20 yards, the distance shrinking, trying not to lose sight of—

Miles Loki, his back to Tom, looking every bit like Secret Service, people respectfully getting out of his path, some smiling, patting him on the shoulder, saying, "Thank you for your courage, Thank you for your dedication, Honored you could join us," not reacting to any of them, gaze fixed in front of him, watching the platform, Mallory—

"America is not a piece of land. It is not cities and farms and rivers and mountains. America is a principle, and the value that guides that principle, the value that informs and animates it, is patriotism"—

Tom felt the sweat starting to really build, shirt sticking to him like cellophane wrap, chest rising and falling, ignoring the slaps, the comments, the threats, the pushes as he advanced, tuning everything out, like he was on fast-forward autopilot, using Miles Loki's sun-glistened shaved head as a reference point, closing in, trying to see the next minute or so in his mind, wondering if there was any way to change what was about to happen, wondering how and why it had come to this, and then not thinking anymore because the hows and whys and whats were irrelevant, secondary to—

Miles Loki slowed to get a personal situation report, looking around, quickly assessing the potential for collateral damage, which he wanted to keep to a minimum, and the opportunities for escape, which he was less concerned about, seeing a kids' baseball team at his right, uniforms with Nationals on the front and the name of a local hardware store on the back, turning away from them, to his left, finding a crease open in the crowd, moving easily into it, past a young couple holding hands, high school kids he guessed, the guy with a sticker on the back of his shirt, Stop the Lies, past a bearded man ringing a cowbell like it was a call to arms, past a little kid, maybe 10, hat with earflaps, pounding on a dime-store drum, in cadence with Mallory—

•

"And if being a true American patriot means being an enemy to all else, then I say, So! Be! It!"—

"Omigod! He's got a gun!"

At the woman's terrified scream, Tom's world went suddenly silent, and everything stopped moving in its normal flow, becoming a series of freeze frames in his mind—

A mother, dropping to both knees, wrapping angel-wing arms around her two small sons—

Two young men in their 20s, seeing Tom, and the gun, and shoving an elderly couple out of the way as they retreated—

A teenaged girl wearing an American flag baseball hat and matching sleeveless blouse, dissolving into tears—

A clot of middle-aged men, baggy jeans and T-shirts, one with a gray ponytail and wearing a motorcycle club wifebeater, pushing anyone within reach to the ground—

A sign dropping, picture of a baby, big letters, Stop Spending My Future—

A vendor's cart toppling over in the crowd's panicked crush, Statue of Liberty trinkets and Uncle Sam shot glasses and automatic-rifle key chains scattering everywhere—

Yellow balloons floating into the sky, black-markered with unhappy, non-smiley faces and "Ephesians 6:12," from the New Testament, "For our struggle is not against flesh and blood, but against the rulers"—

Those freeze frames starting to thaw, speeding up, going into hyperdrive as—

Miles Loki glanced around when he heard the cries, confused, because he hadn't reached for his weapon yet, couldn't understand what they were screaming about, *Who's got a gun?*—

Then turning to see Tom Fargo, the mass of people parting as if he were Moses—

Tom Fargo holding something at his side—

The confusion burning off, Miles Loki knowing instinctively what it was, because this was how it had to end—

Looking quickly back toward the speaker's platform, where the chaos had yet to travel, to Mallory—

"I believe in my country, right or wrong. When it's right, we must do whatever is necessary to keep it that way, and when it's wrong, we must do whatever is necessary to make it right!"—

Tom Fargo and Miles Loki, ten yards separating them, eyes digging into one another like nails, finding a strange communion, as if no one else existed—

Screams and terror all around—

Tom hesitating—

But not Loki, aiming, jostled by someone, still firing once—

Tom knocked around and down by the force of impact—

More shrieks—

"Oh God oh God oh God!"—

Loki spinning away from Tom, back toward the platform, and Mallory—

"The best way to look out for America is to look out for yourself!"—

The rage rising in Loki, because that was a lie, he knew it, a complete lie, the only interest being the American interest, and self-interest was its worst enemy—

More cries, "Get down get down get down!"—

More screams, "Kill him kill him kill him!"—

Miles Loki thinking, *And I shall,* looking at Mallory—

Who had gone mute, suddenly aware of what was unfolding, taking a step back from the microphone, mouth moving but no sound coming out, his face a portrait of horror, the others on the stage leaping to the side, out of the way, to safety—

Miles Loki raising the gun, savoring the moment, wanting Mallory to see his expression, disrespect and utter disdain, wanting that to be the image he took with him to the afterlife or whatever awaited men of such total corruption, and who corrupted everything they touched—

Hearing a shot—

Staggering forward to the platform, reeling, unsteady, like a firecracker had gone off in his back—

Turning, hearing a second shot—

A missile through his chest wall, the bullet ricocheting around inside, breaking his ribs, flying into his spinal column, an odd tingling sensation over his body, legs starting to give way, unable to hold the gun up, falling backward—

Lungs tightening, breaths getting shorter and shorter and more agonizing—

Vision clouding, everything going to white—

But not before looking up to see, with the strangest clarity—

Tom Fargo lurching forward like a zombie, body a mishmash of strange angles, gun in hand, ragged hole the size of a silver dollar between his neck and shoulder, deep crimson stain on his dirty white shirt, blood bubbling from his mouth as he rasped—

"I chose to love it"—

Firing a third shot that tore away the right side of Miles Loki's skull, the body sprawling onto the edge of the speaker's platform, then collapsing in a heap on the soft grass in front of it—

Tom Fargo falling to the ground, too, "Get him get him get him" ringing in his ears, the white-hot pain in his shoulder becoming more excruciating as more people piled on top of him, "Get the gun get the gun get the gun," crushed by their weight but feeling oddly light, as if the burdens he'd borne for all these years were gone, and he was at long last free.

EIGHTY-FOUR

TOM SAT ALONE on a bench, watching as a small, long-haired dog the size of a mutant rat tortured the Great Pyrenees he'd rescued 10 months earlier. The big dog's name was Barry, after Barry White, which Tom thought was appropriate given that Barry was huge and white, roughly the size of a teacup polar bear, and, well, Barry White was huge and black.

On the other side of the dog park, Liberty Dash filled a stainless steel bowl with water from a fountain. Barry lapped it up with all the finesse of a longshoreman.

Other than a playful Great Dane puppy that raced around in circles, already big enough to pull a wagon, all legs and not a bit of gracefulness, they were alone in the fenced-in, tree-shaded area.

"I see you have a new friend."

Tom glanced up, first noticing a flock of black Chevrolet Suburbans taking up space in an adjacent library parking lot, then the Secret Service agents in their trademark suits, wired and wary, no doubt sweltering in the August sun—

And then Penn Mallory, tan and fit, looking like he'd dropped some weight, appearing very, very presidential.

Tom stared at him briefly, without expression. "You know what they say about Washington. If you want a friend, get a dog." He returned his attention to Barry and Liberty.

"I hear they're great therapy dogs. Old people, kids with autism, that kind of thing." Tom said nothing. "Ah, the quiet hero."

"You better hope so," Tom replied evenly, careful not to let what he was feeling show, unsure as to what the feeling was anyway.

"Can I sit?"

"It's a public park." Mallory sat. "Congratulations on the nomination."

"You know what they say about presidential campaigns. Survive an assassination attempt, and the political world is your oyster." He chuckled easily.

"Is that what they say?" Eyes straight ahead, barely acknowledging Mallory's presence.

"Tom, I feel I owe you—"

"You don't owe me anything, Senator. Not an explanation, not an apology, not a drink. Nothing."

"I owe you my life."

"Especially not that."

Mallory considered him closely and coughed falsely. "We probably need to talk about this, just to, uh, you know, to be clear, put it to rest for good."

"Seems to me it's already been put to rest." He closed his eyes, as if a headline were tattooed inside the lids. "Aide thwarts Mallory's would-be killer. Senator calls wounded hero a great American and a true patriot."

"How is the shoulder, by the way?"

Tom's rage nearly ignited. "Don't."

Liberty approached them, a panting Barry at her side.

"Hello, Miss Dash," Mallory said, watching her, looking for any evidence that she knew what had happened.

"Hi, Senator. Nice to see you again." She reached out to shake his hand, which Mallory took without hesitation.

Barry dropped to the wood-chip-covered ground in a big white lump. Tom reached down and stroked his ear. "We probably ought to be going. I have an appointment at 3."

"Job interview?" Mallory asked, trying to sound playful and

interested. "Don't tell me you're leaving the Senate payroll."

Tom shook his head. "Shrink." He turned to Mallory. "I believe today's session is about my yearning for the lost object."

Mallory blinked. "The lost object?"

Tom nodded. "Yeah. As I understand it, you lose something—they call it a traumatic act of separation—and that loss defines you the rest of your life." He smiled. "Apparently, I am destined to keep trying to find something that's irretrievably lost."

Mallory's eyes went wide with alarm, the fear that unspoken secrets had been given form in Tom's sessions with the therapist. "You, uh, mean your father?"

Tom's gaze hit him like a slap. "Among other things."

Sensing the tension, Liberty latched a red nylon collar around Barry's neck and hooked it up to a matching 6-foot leash. "Good luck in the fall," she said to Mallory, who nodded in thanks. With a semi-exhausted Barry in tow, she headed back toward Tom's Jeep Cherokee.

"Sweet girl," Mallory said, watching her go.

"She has no idea about any of it. Arlo. You. Diamond. Harriman. None of it." His eyes found Mallory's. "Anything happens to her, she so much as breaks a fingernail, stubs her toe, fucking sneezes, it's over for you." He exhaled deeply, leaned back on both hands. Mallory was silent. "Speaking of Harriman . . . " His voice trailed off.

"Vance is a big boy. He understood that when your No. 2 turns out to be an assassin-in-waiting, right under your nose, it's kinda tough to play the whole I-can-keep-the-world-safe card, y'know? But I'll take care of him. Somehow."

"Payback for cleaning up that little mess in the warehouse?" Mallory's face was as blank as an empty page, neither admitting nor denying anything. "Well, Jasper Eddy seems to be doing okay at Defense. I keep hearing you're going to pick him for vice president."

"Don't believe everything you hear." He laughed. "I mean, did you hear the one about the Senate staffer, looked like he was having a drink with a radical terrorist, turned out the whole thing was Photoshopped by that very same radical terrorist because she wanted to kill the presidential ambitions of his tough-on-terrorism boss?"

Tom had. Everyone had. It was now part of Mallory's presidential campaign narrative, fueled by the dependable complicity of a media machine that was blissfully unaware of its role as an unintended co-conspirator in the cover-up. But he sometimes wondered what Anath thought about being held responsible for that, whether she cared, whether she even knew. Her silence spoke for itself, though, and the lack of a counter story combined with Mallory's survival in McLean only served to burnish the senator's standing as one tough sonofabitch, the candidate the terrorists most feared and, therefore, the candidate who was most qualified to occupy the Oval Office.

"You know, there's a place for you in a Mallory White House." Laughter spewed from Tom like lava. "I'm serious. It's a dangerous world. You know that better than anyone. You understand the imperatives of security, I know you do, and I know you share my belief that the only way for America to be truly free is to be truly secure. That's why—"

"Stop, stop, stop," Tom interrupted, hands up, palms out, as if pushing Mallory away. "You're a thug, Senator. You're all thugs. You embrace poll-tested, warm-feeling words and phrases to exploit our fears. But you're not interested in making the country any safer. Not really. You just want more power. And then you get it, and you use it against us. It's a racket, a security racket, except we're paying with our votes instead of our money."

"I think given a choice, the American people—"

"You don't know the first thing about *the American people*, what we want or need. We're just bit players in a game that's fixed. You manufacture hope, and then you feed it, and then you do whatever it takes to build obstacles that keep us from achieving it. Then at some point we just get exhausted trying to overcome all those obstacles. We get tired of the fight. We give up. And that's when you've got us. That's when you've won." He torched Mallory with a searing stare. "You're merchants of manipulation, nothing more." Tom looked away, shook his head, and summoned a smile that bitterness quickly chased off. "*The American people.* Christ, every time I hear one of you say that, I want to hide the silver."

Mallory let him simmer for a moment. "I'm just saying that the American"—catching himself—"that, uh, most people, given their choice, would choose security over liberty."

"Yeah, but that's their choice, *our* choice, not yours."

"And you don't think I'm capable of making it on their behalf?"

"Not at all, Senator. You ordered the execution of Harry Platte because he was a speed bump along your road to the White House. I think you're capable of anything." He stood. "That's why you'll make a hell of a president."

A look of confusion seized Mallory's face, as if he couldn't decide whether Tom had just endorsed him or threatened him. It evaporated quickly, morphing into a campaign poster-perfect smile. "I'm gonna win, you know."

Tom didn't reply, just started walking toward the Jeep.

"And when I do, this country will never have anything to fear again."

He stopped, but didn't turn. "You guys. Jesus. You think the absence of fear is the same thing as the existence of security."

"You don't?"

"I think my father was pretty damned unafraid the morning of September 11th, Senator. That's what I think about security." He started walking again.

"You can run, Tom, run from me all you like. But you can't hide. Ever."

Tom stopped again, paused for a second and turned, and in a voice that blew out of him as hot and lifeless as a blast from a convection oven, said—

"Neither can you, Senator. Neither can you"—

Turning back around—

Not waiting for Mallory's reaction—
Not caring—
Not anymore.

EIGHTY-FIVE

IT WAS TWO weeks later, and, unlike the rest of the world—or what the politicians perceived to be the world—Tom Fargo didn't much care who Mallory picked as his running mate. MSNBC was on, sure, but it was muted, and Tom sat on the sofa reading the put-off-for-too-long bio of Steve Jobs and listening to Creedence Clearwater Revival on his iPod, John Fogerty wondering who'll stop the rain.

Barry was on the sofa next to him, racked out on his back, all four legs up in the air.

On the television, images of Mallory at a news conference packed with media and friends and supporters, about to make the announcement, Fogerty now vocalizing about singers singing and audiences cheering for more—

Tom glanced up occasionally, but not paying attention, not really—

Fogerty singing about how the rain kept falling—

And then the announcement came, and Tom saw, bounding onto the stage, incandescent smile, grabbing Mallory's hand, thrusting it into the air victoriously—

Toni Allura.

He hit the pause button on the iPod and unmuted the TV, hearing Mallory say, "Yes, we have had our differences, but we share the belief that those who can rise above their sometimes-selfish disagreements for the betterment of this great land are the truest of patriots, and that's what Toni Allura is, a true patriot who will make a terrific vice president!"

Muting the television, the sound of cheers ending abruptly, Tom stared at the set, disbelieving but still understanding—almost marveling at—the warped logic of it all, knowing that Toni Allura had probably played her "leverage" card and won.

Which left Tom as the only remaining time bomb, the final threat.

He got up and went to the Santa Fe table, where his laptop sat. Barry started yipping, massive feet jerking in a dream of chasing and maybe capturing something that could only be chased and captured in dreams.

Tom sat down at the computer, looked at the screen—

Veracitaurus Redux looking back at him, accompanied by the words—

A blog about keeping the truth alive—

And these—

In memory of Arlo Dash.

Tom considered what to write, whether to write—

Suddenly hearing a noise, outside, on the back patio, like a shuffling, maybe a rattling, the gate, someone trying to get in.

He got up. Walked to the door. Checked the locks. Looked out. Listened.

Nothing.

Thinking maybe it was all in his head, going back toward the laptop—

But it returned, the sound, Tom's body tensing, rigid as a dagger, edgy, nerves knotting up—

Then his eyes shot back to the TV, to Mallory and Toni Allura, and there was a moment when the camera went in for a close-up on the two of them, and he felt like they were looking straight at him, and for an instant their beaming personas seemed to waver, ever so slightly, becoming momentarily severe, bordering on menacing, as if sending a warning that they were more than willing to take away something he held dear—

And just like that, the anxiety, the uncertainty, the oppressive feeling of dread, just like that it stopped, all of it, he stopped it, saying—

"No," because they already had taken something dear from him, and from the country—

Feeling the window start to close on fears real and imagined, the nerves unknotting, the edge easing but not disappearing—

"Never again."

Tom walked to the tiny bathroom, pulled the bottle of Klonopin from the medicine cabinet and flushed its contents into the Alexandria sewage system, then went into the kitchen and found a screwdriver, then to the front door, where he began to remove all the protection, the flush bolts and the double-cylinder deadbolt locks and the vertical deadbolt lock and the chain locks, letting each of them fall noisily to the floor, and then he deactivated the keyless entry lock to put the elaborate security system out of commission at last, leaving his life once again vulnerable to whatever risks awaited, whatever dangers lay on the other side of the privacy fence, whatever terror lurked in the shadows of his consciousness—

Looking out into the darkness, defying it—

"Come on"—

Taunting it—

"Come and get me"—

Facing it down—

"I dare you"—

No longer thinking about his unprotected front door, and who might come through it, and for what reason, just challenging the night and its secrets before returning to the laptop, sitting down, and starting to write.

ACKNOWLEDGMENTS

Thanks to Larry Beinhart for his honesty and guidance; Bill Martin and Chris Keane for contributions they had no idea they were making; and Dr. Daniela White for helping me understand anxieties that were not my own and to channel them into a character.

To B.K. Gunter, the best eyes a writer could ask for.

To Patrick Creed and Rick Newman, whose riveting book *Firefight: Inside the Battle to Save the Pentagon on 9/11* was the source material for Tom Fargo's dream sequences.

To the Federal Elections Commission, which corrected my assumptions about political action committees.

To Nikki Winn for setting me straight on how I should attack the book from the opening.

To Tom Mullikin for the stayover in Ushuaia en route to Antarctica.

To Ron Starbuck, who had a major role in the production of what you're now holding.

And to Elise DeSilva and Linda Limb for their creative help, support, and design brilliance.

Any errors of fact are purely the responsibility of the author.

ABOUT THE AUTHOR

Doug Williams is a former journalist and U.S. Senate press secretary, and is currently a partner in a public relations, public affairs, corporate training, and marketing firm. He is also an award-winning screenwriter, a playwright with four New York credits, and a co-founder of Ransom Note Films, an independent production company based in Houston.

CPSIA information can be obtained at www.ICGtesting.com
Printed in the USA
LVOW11*0328140614

390026LV00001B/1/P